Amazon Stories

Volume 2: Pedro & Lourenço

By Arthur O. Friel

Off-Trail Publications

Elkhorn, California

AMAZON STORIES: VOLUME 2: PEDRO & LOURENÇO
Copyright © 2009, Off-Trail Publications
ISBN-10: 1-935031-06-6
ISBN-13: 978-1-935031-06-2

OFF-TRAIL PUBLICATIONS
2036 Elkhorn Road
Castroville, CA 95012
offtrail@redshift.com

Printed in the United States of America
First printing: January 2009

CONTENTS

All stories and excerpts from *Adventure* magazine

Expanding Horizons *by John Locke*. 1
    Bibliography 10

THE ARMADILHO. 11
    August 18, 1920

THE TAPIR 31
    Excerpt from The Camp-Fire 53
    October 3, 1920

THE FIREFLY 55
    November 3, 1920

THE TUCANDEIRA 75
    Excerpt from The Camp-Fire 105
    December 3, 1920

THE VULTURE. 107
    Excerpt from The Camp-Fire 133
    January 3, 1921

THE TAILED MEN 135
    Excerpt from The Camp-Fire 157
    February 18, 1921

WILD WOMEN. 161
    March 18, 1921

THE TRUMPETER 185
    May 3, 1921

THE BARRIGUDO 211
    June 3, 1921

    Excerpt from The Camp-Fire 247
    July 3, 1921

CONTENTS (cont.)

THE BOUTO 249

    Excerpt from The Camp-Fire 273
    July 18, 1921

Glossary 275

Expanding Horizons
By John Locke

Here, in our second volume of Arthur O. Friel's tales of the Amazon, we present the next ten stories of Pedro and Lourenço, scattered through *Adventure* magazine on a near-monthly basis from the issues of August 18, 1920 to July 18, 1921.

In Volume 1, we discussed Friel's background and the basis for his Amazon stories. To briefly summarize, Friel, a New Hampshire resident, graduated from Yale in 1909, most likely in English. After college, he worked for the Associated Press, at times their South American editor. He was an avid outdoorsman, as well as a reader of magazine fiction. His Amazon stories first appeared in *Adventure* in 1919 and were an immediate success due, in part, no doubt, to his convincing depiction of the harsh conditions of Amazonia. However, he was extremely circumspect about his own experiences, despite the fact that *Adventure*, through the column The Camp-Fire, afforded ample opportunity for self-revelation. It turns out that Friel had never actually been to the Amazon, and that the bulk of his research was derived from a travel book, *In the Amazon Jungle*, published in 1912 by an American explorer, Algot Lange. Friel eventually took his own explorer's journey down Venezuela's Orinoco River in 1922, writing of his experiences in the 1924 book, *The River of Seven Stars*.

We can add little to the biographical details included in Volume 1; however, a rare nonfiction piece by Friel has surfaced, "Going It Alone" in the December 1919 issue of *Outing* magazine. In the article, Friel describes his experiences camping in the New Hampshire mountains. The magazine included a brief profile of the author:

> When Mr. Friel was twelve years old he had his first dog and gun, and from that time forward was an uncrowned king. As a Yale freshman he was a member of the Varsity cross-country team; also the N.Y.A.C. team which won the A.A.U. championship of the United States in 1905. During recent years he has shot very little game except with the camera, which he always carries as a sidearm. When he works, Mr. Friel is an editor; when he doesn't, well—he's just a camper.

No other nonfiction magazine pieces by Friel are known. Since it came out at the same time as his early stories for *Adventure*, we might suppose that his early success as a fictioneer determined his course as a freelance writer.

Over the nearly two year period in which these stories were published, his fiction grew in several respects. First, the stories crept up in length. They range in length from his first story, "The Snake," at just over 3,000 words, to "The Barrigudo," the nineteenth entry, which comes in at just under 17,000. The first ten stories average 9,000 words; the second ten, 12,000.

With increased length came increased narrative complexity; the added length wasn't achieved through padding. Not only do Friel's plots grow more involved over time, but he uses the Amazon's seasonal flooding, which was only hinted at in the first ten stories, as a device to unify a number of sequential stories into an episodic narrative. When the snow in the Andes melts, draining to the east, the Amazon and its many tributaries rise to flood the adjacent lowlands. The flooding starts around December, peaks around April/May, maintains the peak for several months, then subsides until about October, leaving time for a short dry season.

The first mention of the floods comes in the sixth story, "Clay John" (February 3, 1920):

> . . . it was only a little creek now because it was the dry season, but we could see that when the flood came it would be a powerful torrent.

Thereafter, every story is situated with regard to the flood conditions, but usually only with incidental comments, e.g.:

> As I say, it was the season of the great floods, and all of us men who gathered rubber on the *seringal* of Coronel Nunes had been driven out of the Javary forests until the waters should go down again. [ninth story, "The Mother of the Moon"]

> One day in the flood season I was paddling down a swollen little river among wild hills in the Javary region. [twelfth story, "The Tapir"]

Friel uses the flood as an excuse to free Pedro and Lourenço from their work duties, and get them out exploring. In the fifteenth story, "The Vulture," Friel finally integrates the flooding into the plot in a meaningful way. Pedro and Lourenço visit Remate de Males, a river-town first mentioned in "The Vampire" (and lifted from Lange's account). It is a "flooded town": "The *barracão*, you understand, was built high on poles, just as all houses there must be built to stand above the flood waters." Door-to-door navigation must be conducted by canoe: "we hitched our dugout to one of the posts before the door of a trader named Joaquim." In the water underneath one house dwells a "huge alligator," which plays an important part in the story.

In the eighteenth story, "The Trumpeter," Pedro remarks on the urgency of their return to the *seringal*:

> "Lourenço, we had best paddle a little harder tomorrow. The *enchente* has ended and the *vasante* has set in."
>
> As he said, the great rise had reached its height. On the trees around us were wet stains showing that it was beginning to ebb. From now on the waters would drop steadily until they were fifty feet or more below their present level. We had never traveled on this *furo* before, knew nothing of its depth ahead of us, and were not even sure that it ran all the way to the Javary region. So, though we did not worry, we knew it would be well to waste no time and take no chance of finding ourselves stranded in unknown country.

The sense of urgency persists through the final two stories. In the twentieth, "The Bouto," the pair's freelancing adventures come to a close:

> The great annual flood, which turns nearly one-third of our Brazil into a vast tree-choked sea, was nearly at its end. Indeed, the flood itself was long past, and in many places the wet land had risen once more above the water. To me and my comrade Pedro, urging our canoe northwestward through the jungle toward the river Tecuahy, this reappearance of the muddy earth was both welcome and unwelcome. Welcome, because it meant that the time was near when we could return to our rubber-work in the forests of old Coronel Nunes and earn more money. Unwelcome, because we had not yet reached the river we sought, and the rising of the thick bush from under the flood had made our travel slower and harder.

Friel is incorrect about the extent of the flooding, but accurate information wouldn't have been available in his day. Approximately 2% of the Amazon watershed is submerged during the flood season, but that still constitutes a lot of area. However, as someone who hadn't visited the Amazon, the one-third figure distorted Friel's perceptions. The later stories give the impression that the flooding creates wholesale opportunities for cross-country travel by canoe which are available until the water subsides. This is certainly an exaggeration. Today, the phenomenon can be easily studied through aerial and satellite photography.

Another respect in which Friel grew through his first twenty stories is the breadth of the research he drew upon, including Algot Lange. Lange's second book, *The Lower Amazon* (1914), included an appendix, "Vocabulary of the Ararandeüaras of the Moju River," which gives an introduction to the

Tupi language. The Tupian language family represents the similar dialects spoken by Indians in Brazil. It was standardized by Jesuit missionaries into the *lingoa geral*, which Friel refers to in "The Tucandeira" and "The Tailed Men." Lange's appendix lists a vocabulary, a guide to pronunciation, and a list of common phrases. Selections from these start to appear in Friel's stories, starting with "Wild Women." For example, in that story, Lourenço says to a native woman:

> "*Jahŷ ahûh, apotáre hahóh heiruhm*? New Moon, do you want to go away with me?"

Friel supplies the Tupi—and the English translation for the reader's sake—but the expressions are straight out of Lange's appendix.

At some point, Friel must have felt he'd tapped out the story potential in Lange's books; and other inspirations, not available from Lange, start appearing in the stories. For example, in his Camp-Fire missive regarding "The Tailed Men" (reprinted herein), Friel reveals his source for the anthropological oddity as Lt. William Lewis Herndon, USN. Herndon was sent to the Amazon by the Navy Department in 1850 to evaluate the commercial and agricultural capabilities of the region. His 1854 book, *Exploration of the Valley of the Amazon*, chronicled his journeys and discoveries. Herndon quoted three sources for the existence of a tribe of tailed men, the Uginas, a cross between humans and monkeys. Friel repeats all three sources in his missive, then excuses the reader for snickering. As a matter of anthropology, the snickers would be justified. Herndon's account wasn't taken seriously when the book was published. In the March 1854 *Putnam's Monthly*, the reviewer of *Exploration* wrote: "Mr. Herndon himself does not confirm [the existence of tailed men], which we suspect the Count [Herndon's main source] borrowed from Voltaire's *Candide*." Still, "The Tailed Men" is written to Friel's customary high standards, but its dubious factual basis nudges it into the realm of fantasy.

Incidentally, all of Friel's stories up to "The Tailed Men" were named for Amazonian animals and featured characters who took on their physical and behavioral characteristics. "The Tailed Men," and the following story, "Wild Women," break that pattern.

There were many other resources available to Friel, books written by naturalists or explorers, including: *Travels on the Amazon and Rio Negro* (1853), Alfred Russel Wallace; *The Highlands of the Brazil* (1869), by Captain Richard F. Burton; *The Amazon and Madeira Rivers* (1874), Franz Keller; *The Amazon and its Wonders* (1879); *Exploring and Travelling Three Thousand Miles Through Brazil* (1886), James W. Wells; and even Theodore Roosevelt's *Through the Brazilian Wilderness* (1914).

One work, *The Naturalist on the River Amazons* (1863) by Henry Walter Bates, seems to have been of particular value to Friel. There are many odd terms in Bates, not easily unearthed elsewhere, which turn up in Friel. For example, in "Wild Women" we learn of *terras cahidas* (falling riverbanks), *isca* (a tough substance made by ants), *zarabatana* (blow gun), *pira-purasséya* (the fish-dance). In "The Trumpeter," we learn of exotic birds by their Indian names, like the *uirá-mimbéu* (fife-bird). In "The Barrigudo," the *barrigudo* itself (bag-bellied monkey) is described, as well as *pajémarióba* (a bitter medicinal herb), and the Indian musical instruments, the *gambá* (log drum) and the *caracashá* (notched tube used as a rattle). In "The Bouto," we learn the Indian names for various alligators, *jacaré uassú* (large caiman, 18-20 feet), *jacaré tinga* (small, five feet), and *jacaré curúa* (small, two feet, found in creeks). There are many other examples.

The twenty stories in Volumes 1 and 2 of *Amazon Stories* complete, in essence, the first phase of Friel's work. Friel was clearly ready to expand the scope of his work. After a two-and-half month absence from *Adventure* following "The Bouto," he reemerged with his first serial, a four-parter called *The Pathless Trail* (October 10 - November 10, 1921). It featured Pedro and Lourenço, and some new characters, and ran about 100,000 words. Thereafter the vast majority of his contributions to *Adventure* would be either serials, or lengthy novelettes in the 30-50,000-word range.

A theme that emerges through the twenty stories is Friel's cavalier attitude toward the more primitive tribes of Amazonia. Particularly in "The Armadilho" and "The Tailed Men," Pedro and Lourenço participate in near genocide. It makes for action-filled adventure, with plenty of danger and daring, but such tales would be harder to tell today.

In both stories, violent behavior by the tribes results in an even more violent response. The "justification" allows Pedro and Lourenço to retain their status as morally upstanding men; which would have been surrendered if they simply shot the tribal people for sport. The attitude of the stories bears a striking resemblance to the treatment of American Indians typically found in westerns: primitive people are hostile and threatening and must be eliminated for the good of civilization. Civilization, of course, loves peace while seeking to absorb all the world into its orbit.

Friel gave a hint of his views in a *New York Times* "Books and Authors" item (August 27, 1922) that followed the book publication of *The Pathless Trail*:

> "Darwin is right," is the verdict of Arthur O. Friel. . . . He bases
> his opinion upon observations of the aborigines of Africa, some of

whom he says are but little higher than animals. He finds that the lowest forms of human life are found in the thickest jungles, which he thinks have a stifling effect on the intellect.

Friel was a hunter and, as such, defining people as virtual animals makes killing them much easier to swallow. Finger-wagging does not serve much purpose at this date, however; it would be fair simply to call Friel a man of his times, and not a man ahead of his time.

A few additional remarks on Algot Lange. . . . The unmistakable connections between the lore in Lange's Amazon books and Friel's Amazon stories are more than sufficient to establish Lange's influence. A separate question is how Friel might have discovered Lange. In Volume 1, we surmised that Friel, as the AP South American editor, would have known about Lange's expeditions, which were covered in the press. Additionally, Lange's books were prominently reviewed and, in fact, his first, *In the Amazon Jungle* (1912), stirred some controversy over its accuracy. Since examining the question for Volume 1, we've discovered Lange's prominent presence in *Adventure*, which gives Friel, a probable reader of the magazine during the era of Lange's fame, another opportunity to discover him.

Lange's sole article in *Adventure* came several months after *In the Amazon Jungle* was published. In the June 1912 issue, "My Friends, the Cannibal Mangeromas" summarized the most sensational aspect of *In the Amazon Jungle*: his rescue by cannibals and how he survived it. In the August 1912 Camp-Fire, *Adventure's* editor, Arthur Sullivant Hoffman, recounted a meeting he had with Lange. Lange was planning a second expedition to the Amazon, under the sponsorship of the Museum of the University of Pennsylvania, with the object of studying the indigenous tribes of the Amazon Valley. Lange hoped to recruit a few of *Adventure's* readers to join him. In the November issue, Hoffman followed up on the recruitment drive:

> As to Algot Lange's three-year expedition to the unknown territory of the upper Amazon and its tributaries. In the August number we stated that he wanted men. At this writing something over a hundred and ten applications have been forwarded to Mr. Lange from this office. Others have gone direct to his headquarters at the University Museum, University of Pennsylvania. "I have had to hire a secretary to handle the mail that comes in from you. It simply pours," he writes me.
>
> Who said that the spirit of adventure is dead?
>
> And all of these applicants are members of the Camp-Fire. I am proud of that. I have, of course, nothing whatever to do with selecting

the men, but from what Mr. Lange writes me, it is likely there will be at least one or two Camp-Fire men among the tiny handful he takes with him. Whoever goes will go through sheer love of adventure, for I do not think Mr. Lange promises any financial profit, and the three years will be three years not of amusement and easy living, but of untold hardship and danger.

When Mr. Lange brings his little steamer to New York I can give you more of the details, though they will be well on their way by the time you read this. Three cheers for them, and here's hoping they all come back safe from the many dangers that will assail them.

This must have stirred *Adventure's* readers. How could they not have viewed the magazine as a portal to the great wide world? In the February 1913 issue, Lange wrote that he had selected two men out of the 387 inquiries and applications that had come through *Adventure*. Friel was not among them. For the record, the lucky pair was Dr. Franklin Church of Boonville, New York, and Sandy McNab, former police chief of an Arizona town. Lange added: "I am glad to see that there are so many good men in the U.S.A. The day *may* come when I need several hundreds of men to go down with me to the Amazon and 'do things.' " Newspaper reports indicate that Lange took five companions with him on the second expedition.

The July 1913 Camp-Fire reprinted a letter from Lange, written from Rio de Janeiro, updating the circumstances. Some disagreement with the museum had prompted Lange to switch sponsorship to the Brazilian Government. The mission had changed as well:

> The purpose of this Government expedition is the pacification of the Parintintin Indians, a wild and hostile and very powerful tribe, who up to the present time have repelled all attempts of domestication or even approach. They are considered by this department the only remaining great tribal body that still remains in absolute savagery in Brazilian territory. They are much dreaded even by the Mundurucu head-hunters.

It sounds like the time to "do things" had arrived sooner than expected. Additionally:

> The Brazilian Government has purchased a quantity of special flexible mail shirts, in order to invulneralize the men whose work it is to place themselves in friendly communication with the Parintintins, thereby producing a desirable moral effect upon these Indians.

Echoes of this are found in the first entry in this collection, "The Armadilho," the tale of an armored man in the jungle. Lange concluded: "I would appreciate to receive a word from you, and would certainly enjoy the sight of a few copies of my old friend the *Adventure* to cheer me up in the 'Jungles of the Amazon.'"

In the September Camp-Fire, Lange wrote from Pará, Brazil: "provided it does not get me first, I will bring the snake that has caused my friends home so many sleepless nights." He was referring to one of the charges of inaccuracy leveled against *In the Amazon Jungle*, his claim to have seen anacondas exceeding fifty feet in length, a zoological whopper.

Lange returned to the U.S. in the middle of 1914, far short of the projected three-year duration of the trip. He brought back a collection of 5,000 pieces of prehistoric pottery taken from a sunken island at the mouth of the Amazon. He had trouble selling the pottery to a museum, and threatened to dump it all into the East River. Lange's second book, *The Lower Amazon* (1914), chronicled the expedition.

Our last known Lange appearance in the Camp-Fire comes in the December 1915 *Adventure*. Lange was departing for yet another expedition to the Amazon—his third. His letter, dated August 6, 1915, alludes to another recruiting drive facilitated by *Adventure*:

> Your cooperation through the medium of your magazine and its Camp-Fire department has proven of inestimable value to me in getting in touch with the kind of men that come under the category of real men.
>
> You are well acquainted with the facts concerning my Amazon Expedition, its scope, object and character, and you have realized as well as I do that the men who may prove of sufficient physical and mental resistance to withstand the effects of the Amazonian climate are few and far between.
>
> I have received a total of 381 letters and inquiries from your readers. I am sincerely flattered by this attention from men who so sincerely desire to join my exploring outfit, because it proves to me that there are a great many red-corpuscled lads who are willing to go with me till the Amazon freezes over and then skate with me on the ice.

He concluded: "The *Adventure* magazine remains as the only recreative literature on my expedition."

One wonders whether Friel didn't weigh his fascination with Amazonia against the craziness of actually going there. In "The Barrigudo," an American explains his presence in the jungle:

> "Drifted into Brazil as 'doctor' of a crowd of wealthy bums who

came up the Amazon on a steam-yacht, calling themselves 'explorers.' Lots of money and fool ideas, but no brains. Only thing they explored was every known variety of Brazilian booze."

In "The Trumpeter," a group of destitute World War veterans are enticed by a strange man in New York's Union Square:

> "He wanted trusty and fearless men to go with him into South America and help him seek something of which he would tell them later on. They would be handsomely paid, and if he found what he sought they would all be made quite rich."

The recruiter eventually rounds up five companions. But after journeying up strange rivers, the man continually refuses to divulge the nature of the mission. Echoes of Lange. When the man eventually turns crazy, he and the recruits fight it out with firearms.

Friel's stories often feature foreigners who come to bad ends in the jungle, and it may be that Lange's recruiting inspired some of that sentiment.

Finally, in Volume 1 we reprinted the July 3, 1920 Camp-Fire which listed results of reader favorites for 1919, and showed Friel's immediate popularity with *Adventure's* readers. We do the same for this volume, reprinting the July 3, 1921 listing of 1920 reader favorites. But, as regarding Friel, the results are ambiguous. "The Armadilho," from the August 18, 1920 issue ranked seventeenth among stories of any length, and fifth among stories under 20,000 words. No other Friel stories made the two top-twenty lists. On the surface, this would seem to indicate a drop in popularity from 1919 when all three of Friel's stories ranked in the top six of the under-20,000 list. But this doesn't seem likely. A plausible explanation is that because Friel's ten 1920 stories were of such uniform high quality, he split his support into too many slices. A poll based on author, rather than story, probably would have shown Friel near the top of *Adventure's* favorites. The poll for 1921 will show Friel back among the leaders, but more of that in a later volume.

Bibliography

Bates, Henry Walter. *The Naturalist on the River Amazons: A Record of Adventures, Habits of Animals, Sketches of Brazilian and Indian Life, and Aspects of Nature Under the Equator, During Eleven Years of Travel.* John Murray, London, 1973, Third Edition.

"Explorer Lange Backs Roosevelt." *New York Times*, June 25, 1914.

"Explorer Lange Returns." *New York Times*, July 2, 1914.

Friel, Arthur O. *The River of Seven Stars*. Harper & Brothers, New York, 1924.

Goulding, Michael. *Amazon: The Flooded Forest*. Sterling Publishing Company, New York, 1990.

Lange, Algot. *In the Amazon Jungle: Adventures in Remote Parts of the Upper Amazon River, Including a Sojourn Among Cannibal Indians*. G.P. Putnam's Sons, New York, 1912.

——. *The Lower Amazon: A Narrative of Explorations in the Little Known Regions of the State of Pará, on the Lower Amazon, with a Record of Archæological Excavations on Marajô Island at the Mouth of the Amazon River, and Observations on the General Resources of the Country*. G.P. Putnam's Sons, New York, 1914.

"Threatens to Dump Antiques in River." *New York Times*, April 7, 1915.

The Armadilho

Once, *senhores*, I met a fighting *armadilho*.

I do not wonder that you smile. You were just saying that the *armadilho*—or, as you call him, "armadillo"—has survived for thousands of years only because he is protected by his bony armor, and because he can run fast and dig a hole with surprizing speed.

You said too that even though he has big claws he does not fight with them, but defends himself only by digging them into the sides of his burrow to keep from being dragged out. Those are true words, *senhores*. The poor timid *tatu* of our Brazilian jungle will not fight even when you have caught him.

Yet what I tell you, droll as it may seem, is also true. Once I met a great *armadilho* more than six feet high, walking on his hind legs and seeking the blood of men. And how I met him, and what happened after, I will tell to you two American explorers tonight while we float on down the Amazon.

Pedro and I, two rubber-workers employed on the great *seringal* of old Coronel Nunes near the Javary river, had taken a canoe when the yearly floods stopped all work in the low-lying rubber forests, and in it we had gone on a carefree cruise into a land of low hills to the southwest. There, paddling up a river which gradually grew more narrow and swift, we had finally met a roaring rapid up which we could not go. So we had gone ashore to rest and smoke, intending then to turn back.

But then we had met a queer fellow who ate ants, and who lived there with a little monkey while he got gold from a small creek; and we had stayed with him until he took his fortune and paddled away homeward with it. And now, after sleeping through a wet night under a little shelter which we built at the foot of the rapids, we prepared to tramp up along the banks and learn how far the bad water extended.

"This *cachoeira* is a bad one, Lourenço," said Pedro, studying the white water raging down between steep rocky banks, "and if we were wise men we should turn back here. Yet if we were wise men perhaps we should not be here at all, but back in the dull safety of the *coronel's* headquarters."

"That may be true," I said. "But since we are only a pair of fools, let us keep on being foolish and see what our folly brings us. Often it is more interesting to be foolish than wise."

Laughing, we made up our packs, hid our canoe and tramped away into the rough hills beside the stream. The ground rose steadily, so that we were climbing all the time. But the bush was not so thick as that to which we were accustomed in the lowlands, and our march was not hard.

Often we stopped to look down into the rapids, hoping to find that we could bring up our canoe by poles and ropes; but this, we soon found, would be impossible. Yet we kept on going, for no reason at all except that we had started in that direction; and at length we reached the head of the rapid.

There the stream swung sharply westward and the water became more quiet. Though it was now well past noon we kept on tramping for three or four hours more. Then the little river made another sharp turn to the right. At that place we stopped.

"A foolish sort of stream, comrade," grumbled Pedro, looking up it. "First it ran northward, then it came out of the west, and now it flows from the northwest. It runs all around itself before it really starts for the Amazon."

"I have known men who worked in the same way," I replied. "They could not do anything in a straightforward fashion, but made a great deal of work out of the simplest matter. And you can not expect a river to have more sense than men."

"All the same it is a foolish stream," he repeated. "And, as you said when we started, we are a pair of fools to be following it. The wisest thing we can do now is to keep on beside it and then cut back eastward through the bush, so that we can reach the canoe again without going back over the same ground.

"And yet," he added thoughtfully, "somehow I felt that if we came along this river we should find something that would interest us. And though we have met nothing I still feel that way."

Before I could answer there came to us a sound. From somewhere up that stream floated such a noise as we never had heard before in all our years in the jungle—a weird, wailing, droning sound that rose and fell and that might be near or far away.

We stared at each other. The sound stopped.

"*Por Deus!*" whispered Pedro. "That is something new. Have you ever heard such a thing as that?"

I shook my head. We listened, but heard nothing. And after a time I said:

"It grows late, comrade, and I have hunger. We can not find the strange thing this day, for night will soon be on us. Let us make camp."

He nodded slowly.

"That is sense," he agreed. "The thing may be miles away, for the wind is from the northwest and may have brought the sound from far off."

So we quickly built a *tambo*, slung our hammocks, made a fire and ate. Night fell, wet and black. Under the palm-leaf roof of our *tambo* we sat in our hammocks and smoked and argued about this strange thing. And suddenly

Pedro broke off in the middle of a sentence and cried—

"Listen!"

Through the darkness the sound came again. And this time it did not stop. It rose and fell as before, wailing away in the gloom, with that droning undertone too.

"It is music!" whispered Pedro. "Indians?"

"No," said I. "It makes one think of Indians, but no Indians make that sound. There are no drums."

We sat silent, forgetting even to smoke. The music kept on, strange and sad, and savage too. It made us sorrowful, *senhores*, as we sat there in the blackness, and yet it also made us think of fighting, though we had no enemies here nor any reason to fight. Finally it died away, and we heard only the usual night sounds of the jungle.

"I do not think we shall go back to our canoe tomorrow," said Pedro. "There must be other wanderers here besides ourselves, and I would see what they are."

Then we slept, and knew no more until morning.

For much of the next day we tramped on up the stream, traveling quietly, talking little and listening much. Yet with all our bushcraft we could neither see nor hear anything to indicate that any man but ourselves was in this country; and we began to feel that we should find nothing that day, and to hope only that we should hear the weird music again, at night. But at last our stealthy hunting brought us something for which we were not looking but which we eagerly took—fresh meat.

Pedro was ahead. At the top of a little hill he halted. Below him sounded several sudden grunts, followed by splashing. He threw up his rifle and shot. Heavier splashes sounded. Then all was quiet.

"Ha!" he laughed in a satisfied way, and down the hill he ran, with me close behind.

At the edge of the water lay a fine young capybara, shot behind the shoulder.

"Four of them," he said, pointing at the river, which was full of ripples. "The others went in there."

We made sure that the big web-footed water-hog was dead, and then we made camp on the hillside. With a fine feast like this before us we had no thought of going farther that day.

When the meat was cooked we attacked it with the relish of men who for days had had only *farinha* and dried *pirarucu*. We thought of nothing else but our feast until we were so full that we could eat no more. Then we looked at all the meat that was left and wished we had bigger bellies.

"It was well that we put up our hammocks before we ate, comrade," laughed Pedro. "I do not believe I could do it now. I want a drink of water too, but I am so stuffed that I do not know whether I can go after it— Huh!"

His startled grunt made me look up. And there I saw a thing that made my jaw hang loose.

"*Nossa Senhora!*" muttered Pedro. "What is this? A great *tatu* with plates on his belly as well as on his back? Do you see the thing that I see?"

I did, and I had never seen anything like it. *Senhores*, it was a great man of iron which stood quietly there in the bush and seemed to be watching us. As Pedro had said, it had plates around its belly, and also around its arms and legs and head. It did not even have a face—only slits in the steel where a face ought to be.

The only human thing about it that I saw was its hands—big strong hands curled around the handle of the greatest *machete* I ever looked upon. It was a huge two-edged weapon, that *machete*, with cross-pieces slanting outward and downward below the hilt; so big and heavy that a man would have to use both hands to swing it. Later on I learned that its name was "claymore."

The iron man made no move, and I saw that his weapon was not held in a threatening way, but rested with its point on the ground. And then as my first astonishment passed off there came to me the feeling that something was behind me. Looking swiftly around, I found that this was true. At my back stood a big Indian, painted for war.

Beyond him were other Indians, almost hidden in the bush. And as I glanced about us I saw more of them, standing as still as the iron man. We were surrounded.

Pedro saw them too. We did not make the mistake of snatching at our rides or jumping up. We sat very still and studied them. They looked hard and grim, but still they did not seem hostile.

And though I did not know why they were here, or what the nature of that silent iron-plated *tatu* might be, I do know something of Indians; and when an Indian has not decided whether to be your friend or your enemy the first step toward making him your friend is to give him something good to eat. So, taking care to make no sudden movement, I cut off a chunk of our meat, grinned up at the savage and offered it to him.

With a grunt he took it. We beckoned to his mates, pointing to the capybara and telling them to come and eat. They came, and we found that they numbered more than a dozen.

Without further words we cut more flesh from our water-hog and cooked it—that is, we tried to cook it, but each chunk was grabbed and eaten by a hungry savage before it was more than warm.

When we stopped work for a minute we heard a dry voice over our shoulders.

"Ye might e'en gie me some o' that too, lads," it said.

The iron *armadilho* had come up to us, and now we saw what he was. The slits in the metal had been shoved up on top of his head; and out from under it looked a strong, sad, gray-bearded face with a long nose and deep eyes colored like steel—the face of a white man. His voice sounded tired, and he looked tired, and his eyes held no smile. Yet they were kindly eyes, and we knew that he and all his wild gang were now our friends.

"Welcome, friend *tatu*," said Pedro. "We did not know whether you were a living man or not. Your men have left little meat, but there is enough for a taste."

He made no answer, but stood silent until the flesh we cut for him was well cooked. Then he ate it slowly. When it was gone he asked—

"Wha are ye, and what will ye be doin' here?"

"We are Pedro and Lourenço, of the *seringal* of Coronel Nunes, east of the Javary," my comrade told him. "And we are here because we are a pair of wandering fools who have heard strange music in the night and would know what makes it. Have you too heard that music, father?"

The steely eyes seemed to soften a little as they looked into the handsome, boyish face of my partner.

"Feyther?" he repeated. "I am not your feyther, laddie. Yet, gin ye had gray een instead o' brown, and brown hair instead o' black, ye might be ma ain braw Jamie."

He sighed, as if at a memory.

"So the skirl o' the pipes brought ye here—as the crack o' your goon brought me here. Gin ye would be seein' the thing that will be makin' the strange music, come wi' me. Aiblins it will be soundin' tonight for the last time; for we are on the trail o' a pack o' murderin' hounds, and hope soon to close wi' them."

He turned away and went into the bush. The big savage who had stood behind me, and who seemed to be a chief, grunted something to the others and followed him.

All but one of the Indians went with their leader. That one stood waiting while we took down our hammocks and prepared to go. When we were ready he too faded into the jungle, and we trailed after him grunting under the weight of our packs and wishing we had not eaten so much.

The iron *armadilho* and the warriors with him had disappeared. The light was very dim, and there was no path. But the wild man ahead of us slipped on through the bush as only a wild man can, never hesitating or looking around, and walking at a rate that made us pant.

After a time, though we saw no fire, we smelled smoke creeping along in the heavy air. Soon after that we passed two silent Indians who seemed to have been waiting for us and who now followed us.

And before long we came out into a clear space under a great *matamata* tree, where we found a tent with a small, smoky fire before it. Our guide grunted, pointed, then turned aside and was gone.

We knew of course that the tent was that of the iron *tatu*. We dropped our packs and stood where we were, waiting for that strange man to come out.

The two wild men who had followed us also stopped, standing beside us watchfully, each gripping in his right fist the handle of a big war-club. We saw that they had not been among those who ate of our meat, but were men who had stayed here and were wary of us.

Wondering how large this band of fighters was, and who were the "murderin' hounds" they hunted, we leaned on our rifles and watched that little cloth house under the tree.

So suddenly that we jumped, out from that tent came a deep drone and queer high-pitched squeaky sounds. Quickly they grew louder and became music—the music we had heard down the river.

And then in the doorway we saw the white man. He wore no iron plates around him now, and though he was big-boned and broad-shouldered he seemed too old a man to be leading a savage tribe on a jungle trail of death. But this thought quickly faded out of our minds as we watched what he was doing and listened to the barbaric sounds he made.

Under one arm he held a leather bag, and into this he blew through a sort of pipe. Three other pipes stuck out from the bag, two of them pointing upward over his shoulder while the third was in his hands.

On this third pipe his fingers moved, and with their movement the shrill tones changed from one note to another. The deep drone, though, did not change. Hoarse and menacing, it sounded steadily on while the other tones rose and fell.

And as we listened there crept over us again that feeling of sadness which the music of these pipes had brought to us before; and we saw that the face of the piper too was sad, and that he was looking at something far away. The music seemed a wail of sorrow for some one who was dead; and somehow my thoughts went back to a time when I lost one who was very dear to me, and my sight became blurred.

Then this passed off, and instead came a feeling that this death must be avenged. It grew stronger, this thirst for vengeance, until I saw myself trailing an enemy through the jungle, driven by a power that told me I must find him and kill, kill, kill!

And then I came up with my foe, and we fought a bitter fight, and I slew him. And I stood on his body and yelled in victory—

With a dying drone the wild music stopped. I blinked, and realized where I was.

Beside me the Indian with the war-club was breathing hard, and the one at the side of Pedro had a glare in his eyes. And all about us were warriors who had come in from the bush and now ringed around the clear space— more men than we had seen, and all bearing in their faces that fierce desire to kill.

"A bit mair, lads, and ye would be flyin' at one another's throats," said the piper soberly. "The pipes are wild, and they will be rousin' wild thoughts in the hearts of fightin' men. Aweel, an auld man must console himsel'. Come noo and sit by me, where ye will be safe."

He stepped back into the tent and came out again without his music-bag. We lifted our packs and carried them to the fire, where we dropped them. Then we got out our rubber-covered tobacco-bags and offered him tobacco. He took it, packed it into a pipe and waited until we had rolled our cigarets. And then as the day died we squatted beside the fire and smoked and talked.

At first we did the talking, telling him of ourselves, our work and our wanderings which had brought us into his camp. Then, feeling that now we had the right to ask, we inquired what he did here with his wild men and his iron clothes. And slowly, stopping at times to stare into the fire, he told us.

He was of an island of mountains, far away across the ocean, called Scotland, where the people were like the English but yet were not English. He had left this island many years ago and come in to South America to trade with Indians.

Then he had married a lady of Peru and settled in Iquitos, where a son was born to them. This son was his only child, for when the boy was born the mother died. And as the boy grew he taught him all he could, and then he sailed back across the seas with him to Scotland, where he put him in school and tried to content himself with the life of a city man.

But this, he found, he could not do. Though he had hungered for years to return to his own mountains, now that he was there he soon grew restless and dissatisfied. It seemed a cold country where life was slow, and he felt the call of the wild jungle and of the Peruvian town where his wife lay buried.

He learned too that he could make little money in his own land; and though he had enough to keep himself and his boy in comfort he was neither rich enough nor lazy enough to remain idle. So at length he left his son in the care of relatives and came sailing back to the headwaters of the Amazon, where he became again a trader with Indians.

The boy, Jamie, grew into a strong man. War came—the great war in Europe—and he joined the soldiers of Scotland and fought the Germans. Then one night while he and his mates slept in a hole down in the ground the enemy sent deadly gas creeping across from their trenches, and it hurt his lungs so that he nearly died.

He was sent back to the mountains of Scotland, and there he grew strong again. But before he was well enough to go back to the battle-fields the war ended.

And then, though he had grown up in Scotland, he felt the same call that had come to his father—the call to go back to the Amazon. So he went.

As I have said, he was a fighting man. The blood in his veins was fighting blood. For hundreds of years before him his family had been big fighting men of the highlands.

And there had been a time, the old man told us, when guns and cannon were not much used in war, and the fighting was mostly with arrows and axes and swords. In those days, he said, the richer men wore great suits of steel to protect themselves while they killed their enemies.

And in the family of Jamie, handed down through the years and kept in good condition by one generation after another, was one of these suits of steel armor and a great sword with which some long-dead ancestor had fought. And now the young soldier Jamie brought this armor across the ocean with him, and when he reached Iquitos he used to put it on sometimes and show his father how well it fitted him, and how he could swing the huge two-handed sword.

Of course the sword and the armor were kept only as family treasures in the home of these two in Iquitos, for they never thought of making any real use of them. When the father and son went on trading-trips they wore only the clothing of white men in the jungle, relying for safety on their guns and the friendly feeling of the wild men toward the old man, who had dealt with them for years.

They had no trouble with any of the Indians, for the trader knew well who were his friends and who were not, and he kept away from those who were hostile toward white men. So all went well until Jamie became too daring.

Now you may have heard, *senhores*, that around the river Maranon, which flows for many miles northward in Peru and then swings eastward, forming one of the important heads of the Amazon, there is a fierce tribe of brutal savages who cut off the heads of men and shrink them to a size much smaller. They hate every one; they are always fighting with the other tribes around them and taking their heads; and their hatred of white men is especially strong, so that no white man can go into their country and come out alive.

But in this country there is said to be much gold; and I have noticed that where gold is there are always white men daring enough to try to get it. And Jamie, who had been through the hell of the Great War and feared nothing, heard of this and determined to go after some of the gold.

He had been told of these murderous savages by his father of course, and warned to keep away from that country of death. He had even seen some of those shrunken heads, which sometimes are captured by other tribes fighting the head-hunters and then are traded by them, so that finally they reach Iquitos.

But he had also met in Iquitos two young men who had more bravery than sense, and who believed they could get gold in the land of the head-shrinkers and escape with it. So, being restless and eager for adventure, Jamie secretly prepared to go with them. And he did go, leaving behind a note telling his father only that he had gone on a "little trading-trip" of his own.

Never suspecting where his boy had gone, the father did not worry about him. He himself went out among his Indian friends.

At length as he was returning to Iquitos he met a band of wild men whom he knew and who now were on their way back to their own village after a raid into the country of the head-hunters. It had only been a small raid, and the invaders had had to retreat quickly because they had found themselves near a big war-party.

But before retreating they had killed several of their enemies and looted a small camp; and in this camp they had found the shrunken heads of three white men. Knowing how highly their foes prized these heads, they brought them back as trophies. And now the leader of the band showed them to the old man of Scotland.

They were the heads of Jamie and his comrades.

The father went back to his empty home in Iquitos. He buried the head of his boy beside the grave of his wife. Then, taking the great sword and the armor which his son had brought him, he returned to the jungle and appealed to the wild men to join him in a war of vengeance against those murderous brutes.

They needed little urging, for every man of them was a bitter enemy of the shrinkers of heads. From chief to chief the trader went, and each in turn took his fighters and went out on the war-trails.

The iron man did not try to make a great army of all these warriors, knowing that they would be hard to manage and would probably fight better under their own chiefs. After learning the plan of each leader he told this plan to the next chief who went out, so that each would know where the others were and could shape his own campaign.

And he himself, though he burned to fight the slayers of his boy, delayed his own attack upon them until he could finish his work of arousing his savage friends to war; for the tribe of the head-hunters was big and powerful, and as many men as possible must be sent against them. When this was done he would go himself and slay as many as he could.

Then when this work was almost complete he learned that a big war-party of those head-hunters had gone far south of the Maranon—too far south for their own safety, for some of the Indians friendly to the Iron *Tatu* had crept in between them and their own land, and had killed a number of them by trailing along and striking them down with arrows whenever the chance came.

Also these trailing Indians had caught a wounded head-hunter and forced from him the information that this was the same gang which had killed the three white men; that they had come southward to find those heads again and to take also the heads of the raiders who had stolen them. But now, finding the country of their enemies more dangerous than they had expected, they had swung off to the east and were trying to return to their own country.

Hearing this, the father at once took the trail. More than a hundred wild men were with him now, he told us, and farther north others were trying to cut in ahead of the retreating head-hunters. The end of the trail, he said, was near at hand, for the *bárbaros* would soon be attacked in front and behind.

" 'Twas weel for ye that ye came frae the south," he added. "Had ye been comin' frae the east ye would ha' been meetin' them, and your own heids would noo be danglin' by the hair.

"I counsel ye to gang awa the morn, for the fechtin' wi' yon murderers will be sair, and it isna your affair. Gang back doon the reever, lads, and ye will be reachin' your hame a' richt."

"Do you take us for children to be sent home to our mothers?" demanded Pedro. "We go with you, *Senhor Tatu*, to fight those beasts."

The sad-faced man almost smiled.

"Juist like ma Jamie!" he said. "Hot-heided and fearless—puir bairn! Gin ye will be fechtin' for the auld man, ye will, and there's an end o't. Ye should be braw fechters, wi' your bush experience and rifles and ammuneetion; and twa sic riflemen should pit mony a savage doon."

"Yes," I said; "and why have you not brought your own rifle and many bullets instead of that *armadilho* suit and sword? You could kill many more men with a gun."

But he shook his head.

"Ye're wrang, Lourenço," he disputed.

But why I was wrong he did not say. I did not argue the point, but asked him another question—why, when he was near his enemies, he played that strange music at night instead of keeping quiet.

He had three reasons for this, he explained. First, as he had said before, "an auld man must console himsel' "; and I remembered how the pipes had mourned the dead and then followed the enemy to his doom and exulted over the vengeance. Besides this it had great effect on his Indian allies, and kept alive in their hearts the fires of war and hate, and confidence that they would destroy all their foes.

And if those foes heard it, as he hoped they did, it would worry them;

for they would not know what made it, and the weird music would carry to them the message that they were being relentlessly tracked through a hostile country by something that would kill them in the end. So they would not rest well at night, and because of this they would not fight so well when overtaken.

Then he rose, knocked out his pipe and looked around him. We arose also, surprized to find that night had come upon us without our realizing it.

We three seemed to be alone. The tiny fire gave little light, and around us was dense blackness, with nothing to show that more than a hundred fighting men were all about us in the bush.

"Aweel, 'tis time we sleepit," said the iron *tatu*. "I am verra sorry I canna be invitin' ye to share ma tent—it isna big enough, ye ken. But aiblins ye can make shift. Sleep weel the nicht and hae no fear—ye will be far safer here wi' ma rough freends aroond ye than ye would be in your ain camp."

It was on my tongue to tell him that we were not in the habit of having fear, but I left it unsaid; for I saw that he did not think us to be afraid, but that it pleased him to speak in fatherly fashion, as if we were sons of his. We freshened the fire to give more light, cut some stakes, planted them near the tent and slung our hammocks from them. And there with the smoke of the fire creeping around us and keeping insects away, we curled up to sleep.

"Good night, father," smiled Pedro.

"Guid nicht, lads," said the old man softly.

Then we slept.

At dawn we were up. We got out our extra cartridges, put our hammocks on our packs, took down the tent of the old man of Scotland and breakfasted with him. Then he got into his armor.

When this was done the chief of the fighting men came and talked briefly with him, and he explained that we would fight with them against the head-hunters. The chief nodded as if he had known we would do so, and said something to us which we did not understand. I turned to the man in iron.

"If we fight with you we fight under your directions alone," I told him. "We take no orders from an Indian, *senhor*—I have not heard your name."

"Ye may be callin' me Mac," he answered. "And dinna fash yersel'. The chief isna tryin' to give ye orders. He is but tellin' ye what ye juist said—that ye will be stayin' wi' me."

As the chief turned to go, up came four more savages. Two were clubmen. The others carried no weapons, were painted differently and were covered with sweat and breathing hard. They grunted rapidly to the chief, pointing northward. He nodded and spoke to the clubmen, who took the other two away. The chief followed.

"Runners frae anither tribe to the north," explained Mac. "They ha' traveled through the nicht to tell us the heid-hunters are cut off frae their ain land. 'Twill no' be lang noo before we are on them. I doot ye will hae leetle ammuneetion left, lads, when this day is ower."

We filed out into the bush, heading north. Behind us came the chief and his men. As I have told you, the country was fully and rough, but the jungle was not so thick as that of our own low river-country, and so we passed on easily enough.

The old *armadilho* too, a veteran bush-traveler, stalked along without much effort. I heard him pant, though, when we met stiff climbing. And, thinking it was rather foolish for him to tire himself wearing that heavy weight all the time, I asked him why he did not have it carried for him until he came near the enemy.

He showed me that I was the one who was foolish. For, he said, he had worn that armor day after day so that he might become accustomed to its weight and able to handle himself easily in it. If he waited until he met his foes and then loaded himself down with steel, he asked, what sort of fight would he be able to make?

I felt rather simple then. He said too that it made the Indians with him feel that he was more than an ordinary man and so would surely lead them to victory. After that I asked no more questions.

For hours we tramped on at a steady rate which ate up the distance but did not tire us. At length we halted to eat. But before we tasted the first mouthful we dropped it and sprang up.

The fight had begun.

Out of the north came a low, confused sound that quickly grew louder. It swelled into a dull roar—the deep yells of fighting savages, with now and then the report of some old-fashioned rifle.

"Hear yon goons!" cried Mac. "The rifles o' the wild laddies to the north! The heid-hunters hae no rifles—they will be fechtin' wi' bows and arrows. Ma braw freends are on them!"

And he yelled, *senhores*—a wild, fierce yell of war that must have echoed more than once in past years among the mountains of his own Scotland, a yell as savage as ever came from any Indian throat. And from the warriors around us came a hoarse "Hough!" of joy, and their faces flamed with the lust for killing.

Then came men tearing through the bush—scouts who had been far out ahead. They gasped their news to the chief.

Some of the wild men, listening, surged northward as if about to start a rush. But the chief barked sharply at them and they stopped. Then he gave other commands, and his warriors shifted about as he ordered.

Several men carrying old Winchesters came up and stood with us—all the riflemen in the company. Bowmen took places behind us. Other men did as they were told, but they were farther back in the bush and I could see little of them.

"We advance in a body and then spread oot," the *armadilho* told us. "Noo come awa, laddies a'—yon is the fechtin'!"

And in a body, as he said, we trotted forward in the wake of the scouts.

We ran silently, making no sound except that caused by our feet and the rustle of our bodies through the leaves. Yet we could have shouted to one another and done no harm; for ahead of us, as we crossed the low hills, the howling, screeching, roaring noise of fight rose ever louder—such a hellish sound of savage hate as I hope never to hear again. We knew the head-shrinkers and their foes were at close grips, and we ran all the faster to come up before the murderers of white men could break through and win.

At length the steel *armadilho* stopped and barked over his shoulder—

"Spread oot!"

With the words he reached upward and pulled the slitted mask down over his face. I stepped to his right, Pedro to his left.

The Indian riflemen went to right and left in turn. Then we slipped forward in a thin line to the place where rose that snarling chorus of battle, which now seemed to be almost under us.

We were on the rim of a valley, not very deep but quite wide, in which the bush seemed scattered and thin. In this valley and on its slopes the battle raged.

Down below, behind such cover as they could get, *bárbaros* with great bows shot arrows upward at the thicker bush along the heights. Long blow-guns flicked out from unexpected places, hung an instant, sent their poisoned darts into the air and sank again.

Here and there on the rising ground I caught glimpses of men struggling in death-grapples and rolling down the slope like close-locked fighting jungle beasts. From the top of the hillsides arrows flashed down into the valley-floor where the bowmen of the head-hunters hid. No rifle-shots cracked out now, and I knew the few cartridges of the attacking Indians were gone.

All this I saw in far less time than it takes to tell it; and even as I slipped toward a tree and cocked my rifle I thought the head-hunters were fools to let themselves be caught in such a trap.

Then I stumbled over a dead man. A long arrow stuck out from his ribs, and he lay huddled as he had fallen. I kicked him over on his back, and one glance at his brutal face showed me he was one of the shrinkers of heads.

And in a flash I saw how the attacking Indians had herded their enemies into the valley—by harrying their retreating line as the old man had told me, killing their scouts and then slipping away, making them think only a few men were trailing them and at the same time preventing them from learning of the ambush ahead. This dead man under me, shot from the side, was a sample of that sort of work.

A rifle barked nearby. I jumped behind my tree, picked a bowman down below and fired. Other shots smashed out and became a ragged chorus of gunfire. A new burst of arrows whizzed out from the jungle around me, shot by the followers of the iron *tatu*.

For an instant the fighting seemed to halt as both the head-hunters and the northern Indians turned toward the sound of our guns. Then a mighty battle-yell broke from our men. Back came an answering yell of welcome from the Indians who had been holding the *bárbaros* in that trap. And at once the fighting grew hotter than before.

Then for a time I was too busy pumping lead into those accursed shrinkers of heads to see anything else. I picked them swiftly but carefully, and I did not often have to shoot twice at the same man.

Arrows thudded into my tree and stuck there, quivering, until I dropped to all fours and worked rapidly to another tree which was not so good a mark. I found a dead man there, too—one of our own bowmen, killed by an arrow which had struck one eye and gone through the brain.

But it gave me protection enough, that tree, for I did not have to expose myself so much as the dead man had been forced to do with his big bow. And there I shot again until the rifle-barrel burned my hands.

As I stopped a moment to let the gun cool, I realized that only one other rifle was shooting—that of Pedro. He and I were the only riflemen who had any cartridges left.

The arrows too were falling thinly now. Spearmen and clubmen had leaped out and were charging down the slopes to meet their enemies at close quarters. And those enemies, snarling with rage, sprang to meet them.

They arose from places where bullets had not found them and, swinging great clubs or dodging the spear-points and closing with the spearmen, they battled like the human animals they were. They bit and clawed, they choked and stabbed, they struck the foulest blows known to men. If they killed their opponents they came on upward until others struck them down.

One huge, horrible savage came bounding up the slope directly under me, and I snapped a bullet into him barely in time. It was the last shot in my gun, and the last one I ever fired from that rifle; for before I could reload it I lost it.

A scrambling rush and a snarl sounded at my right, and another of those head-shrinkers came leaping at me with a war-club. So sudden was his attack that only chance saved me from death. He tripped over a low, tough vine and fell against a tree.

It halted him only an instant, but that was enough for me. As he shoved himself upright I jumped for him and swung my rifle down on his head with all my power. The blow killed him. Also, it broke my gun.

It broke in two that rifle at the narrow place where the metal joined the wooden stock. The barrel tumbled aside into the bush, leaving me with numbed hands holding the useless butt.

Dropping it, I yanked my *machete* from my belt and peered around for any other assailant. None came. So I whirled back to the edge and looked down.

Roaring up the valley toward us came a knot of *bárbaros* clustered around a hideous brute who seemed a chief. Arrows dropped among them, and three of them fell. Clubbers and spearmen dashed at them and killed or were killed. Still they came on in a grim rush.

Swiftly I wondered whether I had better wait until they came to me or jump down to meet them with my *machete*—it meant death either way. And while I hung there undecided I found that I need not do either.

They stopped.

They halted all at once, staring at a place beyond me, to my left. They ceased their yelling, too, and stood like men struck breathless. Then out from the bush, slow and terrible, a great steely figure with a dripping red sword came to meet them—the iron *tatu*.

He made no sound, showed no haste. His sure, silent, steady advance spoke doom. It seemed to say:

"I am Death!

"I am red with the blood of your brothers!

"I come to destroy you also!

"Ye are all dead men!

"I am Death!"

And as he walked on toward that chief whose men had slain his son, a silence came down on that death-stained valley. White men and brown, we all stood watching.

The chief and his guard were as still as if turned to stone. Not until the steel *armadilho* was almost upon them did they move. And that move, *senhores*, was backward.

Several of the chief's men shrank back. Though they stood with weapons lifted their arms seemed paralyzed. They crowded back upon their mates behind.

Then a hoarse snarl broke from the chief himself. Knocking aside the fear-stricken savages before him, he sprang with upraised club at the man of steel.

With that huge club he struck a mighty blow. But as he struck the old man of Scotland took one long step to the side and whirled up his great claymore.

It flashed redly sidewise and down. And the chief, *senhores*, dropped apart.

His head and one shoulder and arm all fell off him in one piece. The rest of his body flopped forward and down.

And as the other *bárbaros* stood paralyzed, staring at the thing that had been their leader, the iron man swung his sword once around his head and struck again—a long, sweeping, sidewise blow. The heavy blade sliced off the head of another savage and killed also the man beyond him, cutting his spine at the back of the neck.

Then he yelled—the wild yell of his own Scotland. Yells burst from the head-hunters, too—yells of rage and fear. Some attacked him. Others turned and ran.

One of these, with terror stamped on his face, came scrambling up straight at me. I sprang down on him and killed him with my *machete*. When I looked again toward the iron man I could not see him.

I could see his red claymore though, rising and falling in a knot of struggling savages. And when it fell a man fell with it.

Suddenly the rest gave way and scrambled aside from him. He leaped at them with another sweeping swing and one more body flopped headless on the ground. The others bolted.

Pedro's rifle cracked twice, and two more head-shrinkers dropped.

Arrows and blow-gun darts, fired by *bárbaros* hidden beyond the chief's fleeing men, struck the iron *tatu*. But they only splintered on his armor, and he heeded them no more than buzzing insects.

"Came awa, laddies a'—cut them doon!" he roared.

We obeyed. From every side we came bounding down the slopes and threw ourselves on our enemies wherever we found them.

It was close work, and I was too busy keeping myself alive, with only my *machete* for a weapon, to know much about the other fights around me. I knew, though, that the victory now was ours, and this killing was what I have heard you *senhores* call "mopping up"; for most of the head-hunters now were dead, and the rest were dying as fast as they could be found.

Soon a long shout arose down the valley and came upward, growing as it came. I leaned against a tree, feeling suddenly tired. That shout told me that the murderous band from beyond the Maranon was wiped out.

For a little time I rested. Men of our own Indian force came past, hunting for any enemy who still might live.

They halted and asked by signs whether I was wounded. It was not strange that they thought so, for I had just had a hard struggle with one savage and was splashed with his blood and my own. But I showed them that I was not much hurt, and they nodded and went on.

Before they left though they pointed behind them, and one said something which I did not understand. While I was puzzling about this there came a long call—

"Lourenço-o-o-o!"

It was Pedro's voice, and it came from the place to which the Indians had pointed. I jumped out and ran toward him, fearing he was hurt. He was not, for I met him coming for me; and though he carried marks of battle he showed no weakness nor signs of a real wound. His face though was very sober.

"What is it, comrade?" I asked.

"It is death," he answered. "The iron *tatu* dies."

The reply struck me speechless. That big steel-armored fighter dying? It could not be so!

But I quickly found that it was true. Grasping my arm, Pedro hurried me back with him, and as we went he explained.

"His old armor must be thin," he said. "Some head-hunter shot him in the back with one of those big war-arrows. It struck a weak place and went through. He will go soon, and he is asking for you."

Ahead of us, beside a low clump of bush, I saw the chief standing with a score of his men. And under that bush I found the old man of Scotland. One look showed me that, as Pedro had said, he was dying.

He lay on one side, and out from his back stuck the shaft of a big war-arrow. The slitted mask of steel had been raised from his face, and that face was very pale.

Yet though the sign of death was on it, it was no longer sad. Peace and contentment were there, and as I squatted beside him he smiled.

"I'll be leavin' ye, Lourenço," he said. "I would be thankin' ye before I go. I was fearin' ye micht not come in time. Ye hae been twa guid freends to me. Ye are guid lads to tak' up an auld man's quarrel wi' no hope o' reward."

He coughed and gasped. Then as I bent over the arrow he said quickly—

"No, no; dinna tak' it oot—'twill only mak' it worse."

And I saw that this was so, and did not touch it.

"Braw fechters ye are," he went on after another coughing fit. "Aye, I saw ye pit the heid-shrinkers doon, as I knew ye would be doin'.

" 'Twas half o' the battle won, the sudden belch o' your goons behind they murderers. It pit fear in them—and fear, lads, is a michty weapon. And did ye see the dogs blench when they spied a man o' iron walkin' at them?"

"I did, comrade," I told him. "And I can see now that you were wise in making yourself a man of iron. You knew that the sight of you and the fact that they could not kill you would strike them with fear. And if they had not feared they might have won."

"Aye," he agreed—and coughed again.

Life was going from him fast. He lay very quiet, and for a time he spoke no more. A gray shadow grew on his face.

"I canna see," he whispered at last.

"The nicht comes. Jamie! Jamie, lad—are ye there?"

Weakly he reached a hand upward. And then Pedro did a very kindly thing. He dropped on one knee and grasped that hand and spoke in the words he had heard the old man use.

"Aye, feyther," he said softly. "Here am I. Hold fast, and we will gang oot into the dark together."

Again a smile spread over the old face—a wan, gray smile.

"We gang togither, laddie—but we willna gang into the dark. Ower yon, lad, your mither waits—"

A little quiver ran through him.

Slowly we got up. Gently Pedro loosened the clasp of the old man's hand. After a moment he bent again and drew the steel mask down over the dead face.

"The iron *tatu* shall be buried in his shell of steel," he said huskily. "It shall be his coffin. He and his claymore and his strange bag of music shall lie in the same grave. Where are those pipes of his?"

I did not answer at once, for something seemed to choke me. After a time I said:

"I think they must be back where we were about to eat. We left everything there except our weapons."

So we turned to the chief, around whom most of the warriors now had gathered in silence, and made him understand that we would bury the iron man here, and that we wanted all his belongings brought up, as well as our own. He nodded and gave orders to his men.

Four of them turned and went away. Four more came forward and lifted the dead man. And back across the quiet battle-ground we went with him, and up the hillside to the place where he had first stood and looked down on the fight below him.

There in a high dry spot where no flooding stream would ever disturb his resting-place we dug a deep grave. Before this was finished the four Indians returned with his tent and bagpipes, bringing with them also our packs; and other Indians, after moving about over the valley-floor and slopes, quietly brought back certain things which at first we did not notice.

We clasped the hands of the old fighter around the hilt of his great sword and laid the bagpipes under the arm which had pressed them in life. And then around him, his armor, his claymore and his pipes, we wrapped the little tent which had sheltered him from the night rains. When this was done we lowered him into the ground.

Then after the grave was filled and covered with creeping vines which would soon form a tough network of protection the Indians came forward with the things which they had brought.

Senhores, those things were the heads of the head-shrinkers. Heads which the steel *armadilho* himself had slashed from fighting *bárbaros*, heads which these followers of his had chopped from the bodies of their dead foes—they brought these and piled them in a heap above him as a terrible memorial of an old man's vengeance for the murder of his son.

This was their wild idea of natural justice—that the *bárbaros* of the north through taking a white man's head should lose their own to mark a white man's grave. And in truth I do not know that a more fitting tribute than this could have been laid on the last bed of the old fighter who had trailed those murderers by day, piped them to doom at night, and brought death to them in the end.

We turned away. We looked at the battle-ground, at the silent Indians, at each other. And Pedro said:

"Comrade, let us go eastward, back to the river where our canoe waits. We have time to leave this valley of death behind us before dark, and in another day or two we should find our dugout. And then it would be well for us to go back home, for we now have only one rifle, few cartridges and not much food."

"You are right," I told him. "I have rambled enough, and we had best return to headquarters."

We lifted our packs, nodded farewell to the Indians, and tramped away eastward.

No, *senhores*, I can tell you nothing of the fighting north of the Maranon when those other tribes roused by the iron *tatu* swept into the country of the shrinkers of heads. Bitter and bloody it must have been but no word of it ever has come to us. I know that the head-shrinkers still live there, however, and that shrunken heads of white and Indian men still come out from their land.

But the band that took the head of Jamie of Scotland will never take another, for I do not believe that one of them escaped. And up on the hillside, with their skulls heaped above him and his hands clasped around the hilt of his claymore, the father of Jamie must sleep well.

October 3, 1920

The Tapir

That is a queer thing, *senhores*. You say that the tapir, so common here in South America, is found in no other continent except Asia, and there only in a section which you call Malaysia; and that place is thousands of miles from our Brazil and across a vast ocean. How could our tapir have gotten there? He never could swim so far!

Oh, I see. Pardon my foolish question. Long ago there were tapirs all over the world, but now they have died out almost everywhere? Yes, I can believe that, for the tapir has no defense except his thick hide and his habit of jumping into water when attacked; and both animals and men must be able to defend themselves, or they will be wiped out by others which are more fierce and better armed. So perhaps the odd part of it is not that there are so few tapirs on earth now, but rather that there are any at all.

He is a shy fellow, the tapir. He needs to be, for he is hunted both by beasts and by men. Among the wild Indians of our jungle, as you perhaps know, the greatest hunter is he who can find and kill that big thick-skinned animal with funny nose. The prowling jaguar, too, is always eager to make a meal from him. Possibly you two North Americans also, during your explorations here at the Amazon headwaters, have slain a tapir or two for the sake of fresh meat. Yes? Then I need not tell you any more about that animal, for you probably know as much about him as I.

Still, I can tell you a tale of a tapir tonight, while this steamer slides along down the Amazon, which probably will amuse you. You have seen the tapir, observed his ways and tasted his flesh. But did you ever find one up in a tree, moaning and weeping from love?

Yes, it sounds ridiculous. But let me tell you, *senhores*, if ever I meet another love-sick tapir I shall go straight away and leave him, unless I am willing to get myself into trouble. And this is why:

One day in the flood season I was paddling down a swollen little river among wild hills in the Javary region—whether it was in Brazil or in Peru I do not know, for I had been on a long rambling trip into unknown country and neither knew nor cared where the boundary might be. With me was a fearless young comrade named Pedro, who, like myself, was a rubber-worker on the great *seringal* of the Coronel Nunes. The floods having stopped our work in the swampy lowlands, we had taken a canoe and gone out to seek adventures—and had found them. And now, having used up nearly all our cartridges in a battle with head-hunting savages, we were on our way back to the headquarters of the *coronel*, paddling with our regular long distance stroke and expecting nothing at all to happen. But suddenly from the jungle near us came a mournful sound.

We held our paddles and looked. Only a few feet away was the hilly western shore of the stream, thick with bush. The sound had come from there, seeming to be a little distance away from the water and quite high up in the trees. We could not see anything in the tangle overhead, nor hear anything moving there. So after a minute I said softly to Pedro—

"Only a sick monkey grunting to himself."

He nodded slowly, as if in doubt, and continued squinting upward. I stroked again with my paddle, intending to go on. But before I put any power into the push the noise came again. I halted my arms.

"O-ho-o-o!" wailed a voice. "Ohoo-oo! Boo-hoo-hoo!"

We looked and listened. There was no sign of any man being in this place, but the voice was that of a man crying. It was a heavy voice, which ought to belong to a strong man; yet it was snuffling and sobbing there in the bush like that of a woman. To me, and I think also to Pedro, that sound was more dreadful than a cry of pain or a scream of fear; for it seemed that the man must be in a terrible condition to break down in that way. We turned the canoe, which had been drifting down the current, and silently paddled back.

Pedro, in the bow, jerked his head toward the shore. Looking closely, I saw what I had not noticed before—a quiet creek almost hidden by big drooping palm-leaves. We slipped the canoe through these leaves and stopped short. A few feet ahead of us was another canoe.

Then the voice came again. It was up over our heads.

"Oho-oo! What shall I do? I can not live!" it sobbed.

More than twenty feet above the ground we spied a sort of house built in the branches of a big tree—a hut made from split palm logs and palm leaves. Up the trunk of the tree ran a stout notched pole making a ladder, such as we rubber-workers use in high tapping.

"The man must be dying alone up there, poor fellow," said Pedro.

I nodded. We stepped out on shore and went to the pole.

"What is the matter, friend?" Pedro called.

No answer came. There was a dead silence. Then we heard a slight movement up there, and out from a doorway at the top of the ladder came a head. We saw a dark face, with black hair and eyes. It peered down at us, and we started back. Then, without replying, the man swung himself out of the hut and came down the pole.

"*Por Deus!*" muttered Pedro. "He is not dying, nor even sick. He is as big and healthy as—as a tapir."

It was so. The fellow was so broad and heavy that it seemed as if the pole, stout though it was, ought to snap under him. Yet he was not clumsy; he came down so easily that we knew his muscles were strong and worked smoothly. I began to believe that there must be some one else up in that house, for it did not seem likely that this big man would have been moaning and blubbering so. But when he stood on the ground I saw that his eyes were wet and his face streaked, and the corners of his mouth turned down as if he were ready to start crying again.

As I looked at him I could not help grinning—partly because I was relieved, partly because his doleful face looked funny to me, and partly because Pedro's chance remark about a tapir was so near the truth. Above his heavy body and thick neck was the face of a tapir: for it was much narrower at the jaws than above the eyes, and the nose was so long and curving that it seemed to be not a nose but a snout. And, as I have said, the face was very dark, as the face of a tapir would be. He was a *caboclo*, with some white blood in him. Still, he looked like a good-natured young fellow, and he was not enough of an Indian to keep from showing his grief.

"What is the matter with you?" Pedro repeated. "We thought you were dying."

The other's mouth worked, and he sniffled.

"Maybe I am," he said in a choked tone. "I think I shall die. Oh, my poor little Bellie! Ah-hoo-wow!" He began to bawl.

"Your poor little belly?" demanded Pedro. "What ails your belly? It looks very healthy to me. Have you swallowed a live turtle?"

I snickered, and the tapir-man himself laughed. In the middle of a wail he changed his noise to a snort, and that in turn became heavy laughter. But then his mouth turned down again.

"You do not understand," he said. "I have lost my so-beautiful Bellie. It is a great misfortune, and not a thing to laugh about."

"Lost your appetite, do you mean?" asked my comrade. "That is nothing to make so much noise over. And I do not think your belly is so beautiful. It sticks out too much."

"No, no, you have it wrong!" the Tapir protested. "It is true I have no appetite—I have eaten nothing today, except some *chibeh* and a few handfuls of *pirarucu*-fish and some monkey-meat and a few other things. But that is because they have shut up my little Bellie for so long and will not let me have her. Even when they let her out I can not have her—ah-hoo!"

"Stop that noise!" I ordered. "And stop your weeping also—it is wet enough here from the rains. Now tell us, what is this Bellie that gives you so much trouble? The matter must be serious if, as you say, you can not eat more than two men need."

He nodded as quickly as his thick neck would let him, and told us:

"Indeed it is serious. My Bellie is a girl who has come to womanhood and should be given in marriage, but her father has not made ready for the feast, and so she is shut up. And the father does not favor me, but will give her to Gastoa. So you see it is a terrible misfortune."

"So I see," I said, "although I do not yet know just what you are talking about. Why is your girl shut up, and what has the feast to do with it? Tell us all about this matter. We are Pedro and Lourenço, *seringueiros* of Coronel Nunes. Perhaps we can help you."

He looked at us as if a little doubtful.

"I do not think you can help me," he said. "What I, Deodoro Maia, can not do for myself is something no strangers can do for me. And perhaps even if we could free my Bellie I still should lose her. She likes men who are tall and handsome."

He looked at Pedro as he spoke. Pedro made a very low bow.

"Thank you, friend Deodoro," he laughed. "But have no fear. Girls do not interest me much. And if they did, I think perhaps I could get one without stealing her from another man."

Deodoro thought this over and nodded again.

"I think that is true," he admitted. After looking at both of us a while longer, he said: "Yes, I will tell you all about it. Will you come up into my house? I have some *cachaça*, but no tobacco."

"And we have tobacco but no *cachaça*," I replied. "It is a fair exchange— a smoke for a drink."

So I climbed the ladder and entered his house. He and Pedro followed.

It was dark inside the place, for it had only one small window-hole, its doorway was hardly big enough to let the tapir-man in, and the daylight outside was dull. Yet the hut was comfortable enough, and it was dry. When we were all inside Deodoro lifted a jug from a dim corner and passed it to us. After a good pull at the *cachaça* which it contained we sat down on the floor, with our backs to the wall, and tossed him the makings of a smoke. He could hardly wait to roll the cigaret before he lit it.

"Ah, that is good!" he grunted, sucking a huge drag of smoke down into his lungs and blowing it slowly out. "I have not had a smoke for days."

"That may be one reason why you have felt so badly," I told him. "It is a mistake to be without tobacco when you are in trouble. A drink and a smoke will go far toward easing any kind of pain."

"That is so," he agreed. "But I have been so miserable that I did not think of it. Besides, there is only one place where I can get tobacco—that is at the town; and Gastoa and his brothers and Bernardo, the father of my Bellie, drive me away from there."

We said nothing, but waited. Sitting in his big hammock, he puffed at the cigaret until it burned his fingers. The tobacco soothed him, as we knew it would; and with the smoke, another drink, and somebody to talk to, he became quite cheerful. Then he told us of his trouble.

He, Deodoro Maia, was a native of a small *caboclo* village some miles to the west, on another little river. The people of this town were jealous of their women and watched them closely. The young girls, who were only children, had nearly as much freedom as the boys; but from the time when a girl reached womanhood until she was married she was watched continually— and after marriage too, for that matter. And it was the custom among these people, when a girl was old enough to take a man, for her parents to make a feast, and a celebration was held and every one was told that the girl now could marry.

Now this custom, like many others, had both a good and a bad side. Whenever a girl grew up the whole village could have a merry time at the celebration. But the rule of having a feast at that time was so strong that unless the girls' parents were able to give that feast she could not be declared marriageable. In that case she was in a bad position; for she was no longer a child, with the child's freedom, nor yet a woman in the eyes of her people— she was nothing at all. Because of this, and also to keep her always guarded, her father would shut her up until he could give the usual feast.

This did not mean that she only had to stay in the house. A cage would be built—a tight, strong cage of woven cane inside the house—and she would be put into that cage and kept there like a beast. She might have to stay in that thing for many days; there was no escape for her until the feast was ready. Deodoro told us that sometimes a girl would be shut up so long that when she came out her copper-colored skin had faded almost to white.

Now Bernardo, father of the girl whom Deodoro wanted, was lazy and drunken, and meant to use his pretty daughter for his own benefit. So he intended to give her to a fellow named Gastoa, who was considered rich in his own village and had brothers who might help support the old drunkard in idleness; at least that was the father's plan. The man Gastoa was known to be cruel, and the girl feared and hated him; but that made no difference to old Bernardo, who thought only of an easy life for himself. He was so worthless, though, that when his girl-child turned into a woman he had nothing with which he could give the feast. Worse yet, he would not do enough hunting to get the monkey-meat usually dried and kept for the celebration. He only shut the girl into a cage and kept on drinking and sleeping.

So the moons came and went, and poor Bella—or Bellie, as the Tapir called her—was still a caged woman with no prospect of release.

The girl's mother did all she could for her. She worked hard to grow enough green foods for the feasting, and she tried to get Gastoa and his brothers to kill monkeys and salt away fish. But Gastoa was so sure he would have Bella in the end that he could not see any use in doing so much work for her, and so he and his family only laughed and sneered and did nothing.

And then a misfortune came to the crops. A herd of peccaries got into them and tore up almost everything, so that Bella's family had hardly enough left to live on, and all hope of the celebration was destroyed until new crops could grow.

When this happened Bernardo flew into a drunken rage. As might be expected, he vented his spleen on those who were not to blame. He beat his wife, and then he dragged his daughter out of her cage and beat her too because she was causing so much trouble to him. While he was still ugly, Deodoro came in. A fight followed.

Deodoro, hoping to win the girl for himself, had done the thing which both Bernardo and Gastoa refused to do—he had hunted monkeys, birds, and fish, and dried or salted their meat. He had been very quiet about this, doing his work here at this house which he had built up in the tree, where nobody would be likely to find him. Now, with some of the best pieces of meat, he had gone back to the village to tell Bernardo he would give all he had toward the feast if he could have Bella for his own. But he came at a bad time, for, as I have said, Bernardo was ugly.

When he heard the young man's proposition he called him a vile name and kicked the meat into the dirt, where some dogs snatched it and ran off with it. Then he ordered Deodoro out; and when Deodoro hesitated he struck him. This was too much for even the slow, good-humored tapir-man to stand. He hit back and then started in to give the old fool the best thrashing of his life.

If he had been let alone he might have beaten some sense into Bernardo. But Bernardo, getting the worst of it, yelled for Gastoa to help him. Gastoa came, and his brothers with him, and jumped on Deodoro. They gave him such a beating that he was lucky to escape alive. Then they threw him out of the village, warning him not to come back.

In spite of this, Deodoro went back—though he took care not to go openly. Several times he went by moonlight, late at night when he knew the village was asleep. He even succeeded in talking a little with the girl through the thin cane wall of the house, and offered to cut a hole there and take her away with him. But, though she hated to be shut up so, still she wanted to be made a woman with the usual ceremony, and she would not consent to running off to some unknown place where she could not see the people whom she had always known. Besides, she did not think very seriously of Deodoro. Nobody did, he said.

When we asked him why this was, he said it was partly because of his white blood. He was neither a full-blooded *caboclo* nor a white man. His mother's father, he said, had been a white Brazilian trader who stayed for a time on that river while buying sarsaparilla for the market. Before his mother was born this man sailed away, and he never came back. So the girl was laughed at by the others because she had no father, and when she grew up she was sneered at because she was half white. In the same way her son Deodoro was laughed at in his turn, though his own father was a *caboclo*. The only one who did not jeer at him, he said, was the girl Bella, who sympathized with him when the rest mocked him.

This story made us sorry and angry—sorry for the young fellow and angry at those who had treated him so. We saw that he was not by nature a fighter, and that, with the whole town against him and the girl unwilling, he felt that there was nothing he could do but stay in his tree and be miserable. He was much in need of help.

"The big question is, does the girl care for you?" said Pedro. "Does she want you more than another?"

Deodoro stared out of the door awhile before he answered.

"I do not know just what she wants," he said then. "I do not think she knows either. She has not seemed to think much about men. I know she likes me as well as any one, and much better than she likes Gastoa. She does not like him at all."

"She likes you but she does not admire you," said Pedro. "Then you have two things to do—to free her and to make her respect you. Women admire men who are strong and bold. Be strong and bold, friend, and she will realize that you are a man. Now she thinks of you as a boy. Am I right?"

The Tapir thought again and agreed.

"You have it right," he said. "But what can I do? I can not go into the town and shoot everybody that tries to stop me from taking her away. My bullets are all gone."

We laughed.

"Of course you can not," said Pedro. "That would be a blundering way. Even if you shot down the whole town you would not win what you want most—the girl herself. She would then fear you more than she fears Gastoa. You want her to admire you, not to be afraid of you. Now let us try to make a plan."

So we talked about different ideas that came to us, but none of them got us anywhere. At length I said:

"We are wasting time. You and I, Pedro, have never been at this place where Deodoro lived, and all we know about it is what he tells us. We might sit here and talk for a week, and then go there and have our great idea smashed by some little thing none of us had thought of. The one thing we are sure about is that first the girl must be gotten out of her cage. The best way to get that done is to go ahead and do it."

Deodoro nodded seriously, as if I had said a very wise thing. Pedro laughed, but he agreed.

"That is the best plan of all," he said. "Let us go with God and trust to luck."

We arose and turned toward the door. But Deodoro halted us.

"Wait," he said. "I am feeling much better, and I think I can eat something before we start. I have all the meat I saved for the feast—except the few pieces I lost at Bernardo's house—and now I shall not give any of it to those who have not treated me well, but will keep it for myself and Bellie and my friends Pedro and Lourenço. I think we had better have some of it now."

"You have spoken most wisely, friend," Pedro answered with a grin. "My comrade and I have not been eating much for the last few days. We have been on a long trip and our supplies are nearly gone. So we shall not throw your meat to the dogs as Bernardo did. But where do you keep it?"

"Since you are my friends, I will show you," he replied with a sly look.

Lifting a couple of the split palms that made his floor, he brought out meat.

"See, my floor is double," he explained. "The big branches of this tree hold up my house, and between the branches I have made boxes, and then covered branches and all with my floor. It is a good way to hide things."

"Deodoro, you are one of the cleverest fellows I ever met," said Pedro. "Few men would have thought of such a thing!"

Deodoro's face beamed. Probably it was the first time anybody had ever praised him; and somehow he seemed to grow bigger as he thought about it. Pedro gave me a slight wink, and I saw what he was trying to do—to make this shy, downcast fellow think well of himself. And indeed, *senhores*, that is a thing that has much power to help or harm a man; for if he does not feel himself to be the equal of other men, who else will believe him to be so? Seeing Pedro's thought and realizing its value, I changed my own manner toward the young tapir-man and no longer treated him as a boy.

We went down the pole, built a little fire and ate. Pedro and I were hungry, and we did not spare the meat; but I do not believe that both of us together ate as much as Deodoro put away alone. When the food was gone he was still hungry, and he climbed the ladder and brought down more. This time he brought down his jug also. We found that it held more *cachaça* than we had thought, but we emptied it. Then, feeling quite merry, we got into our canoes and pushed out into the river.

With our new comrade leading, we paddled downstream until he swerved to the left. Up another quiet creek we followed him. The stream widened into a long swampy lake which seemed to have no end, for it wound along among the low hills so that whenever we thought we had reached the end we found that there was more of it. At length, when we had about concluded that it was no lake but a flooded arm of the river ahead, Deodoro led us into another narrow stream. Down this we went, and soon we came out into another river.

"It is not far now," said Deodoro in a low tone. "It is only a short paddle upstream."

"Very good," Pedro replied. "But why do you speak so quietly? You are not afraid if the whole world hears you."

Again Deodoro seemed to swell.

"No!" he agreed, and his heavy voice boomed like a gun. "I do not fear any man!"

He began paddling again with a bold stroke.

As he said, it was not far to the town. We heard it before we saw it. Shouts and laughter came to us, and then some one began to beat a drum in Indian time. Deodoro suddenly stopped paddling.

"There is a celebration," he said. "I wonder—it can not be—it is not possible that Bernardo has made the feast!"

"If there is a feast, so much the better," I said. "Every one will get drunk. Is it not so?"

He nodded.

"Then it will be easier for us to do what we came for," I explained. "When all are drunk, who shall stop us?"

He made no answer. We saw that he was worried, thinking the noise might mean that his girl was given to the man Gastoa.

"Come, comrade," said Pedro. "We are stopping here as if we were afraid."

The hint was enough. Deodoro's head came up, and he swung into his stroke as if he owned the river. Pedro let out a yell, and we joined in. Shouting and paddling hard, we surged up to the town like men sure of a welcome.

Like all towns in that region, it was on a hill above the reach of any floods. In the dry time it probably was some distance from the stream, but now the high water made it easy for boatmen to land beside it. As we stepped out on shore the drum-beating stopped. Several men came to meet us, and some barking dogs rushed at us.

Pedro knocked the dogs aside with his rifle. I had no gun, for I had broken mine and lost it in that fight with the head-hunters of which I have told you. But I had two good feet in heavy boots, and I used them. One of the dogs, an ugly brute, snarled as if about to spring at me, but I kicked him again so hard that he yelped and retreated. At this, one of the men scowled at me in evil fashion.

"Kick my dog again and you will get yourself into trouble," he growled.

"I am used to trouble," I retorted. "And I kick an ugly dog wherever I meet him—whether he stands on four legs or on two."

He glared and took a step toward me. Then he halted as if not quite sure of himself. After glowering at me for a minute he shifted his gaze to Deodoro.

"You Deodoro!" he snarled. "Did I not tell you not to come back here?"

"You did, Gastoa," answered the tapir-man. "But you see I am back. I think I shall stay, too." His voice was strong and steady.

Three other men scowled when they heard this. I judged that they were the brothers of Gastoa, who had helped to beat Deodoro and drive him out. More *caboclos* had gathered around us now, and among them I noticed a short, piggish-looking man of middle age who seemed quite drunk. Pointing at Deodoro, this man yelled:

"Throw that one into the river! Throw the others in! Drown them all! What business have they here?"

Gastoa and his brothers growled again, but they did not quite dare to rush us. We stood shoulder to shoulder, and they could easily see that we did not intend to be driven away without a fight. Before they could decide just what to do Pedro spoke.

"Is your name Bernardo?" he asked.

The drunken man blinked at him.

"Yes, I am Bernardo."

"I thought so," said Pedro. "I had heard that in this town lived a man named Bernardo who was a know-nothing and a drunkard. I knew you must be the one, because nobody but a drunken fool would try to drown strangers who came to trade and make his town rich."

Bernardo became furious. He screeched that Pedro lied. But the other men looked at us with a new expression in their faces. Then one of them roughly told Bernardo to be quiet; and when he kept on yelling two others shoved him away. By this time every one in the place was there at the shore. They all stood staring, and I saw some whispering to one another.

"Is that the truth?" demanded Gastoa. "Have you come to trade?"

"You do not think we came to look at your handsome face, do you?" sneered Pedro. "Who is the head man here? I will do my business with him."

The crowd opened, and out stepped a man who was rather old but looked strong and shrewd.

"I am chief," he said. "I, Araujo."

His sharp eyes went to our canoe, which now held only the few supplies that remained after our long trip.

"If you come to trade, where are your trade goods?" he asked.

"Greetings to you, *compadre*," said Pedro, as if the head man were no better than the rest. "Surely you do not think we would bring our goods in that little canoe. It will take a big *batelão* to carry the things we have for you—that is, if we decide to trade with you. This is not a small matter of wax and salt fish."

His insolent manner made Araujo frown, but I could see that he and all the rest were impressed by it and by his big talk. I had no idea of what tale Pedro intended to tell, but I saw he had made a good beginning; so I tried to look like an important trader, instead of what I was—a bush-tramp with hardly enough food and cartridges to get home on. The thought came to me that Deodoro might show surprize and betray us. But a glance at him showed me he had more sense than that. His face was like wood, and he was looking straight ahead.

"What do you want for this *batelão* full of riches?" asked the head man.

"We will talk alone with you about that," Pedro told him. "We do not do our business on the river-bank. And before we do any business at all we want food for ourselves and this guide of ours, Deodoro."

Araujo looked us all over again, staring hard at Deodoro, who stared back at him. Then he nodded and turned away. We followed him, and I noticed that the crowd now was looking in friendly fashion at our Tapir companion and sourly at Gastoa. The reason was easy to see; they believed Deodoro had brought us there to make them rich, and that Gastoa had angered us and might have lost them their chance to trade. I had hard work to keep from grinning.

"You have come in time to eat at the feast," said Araujo. "This is a feast-day here. A girl has come to womanhood."

"What girl?" asked the Tapir.

"Not the one you are thinking of," the old man answered. "It is the youngest daughter of Fontoura."

"Oho! So you have a girl here, Deodoro!" teased Pedro, as if he had not heard of it. "You sly fellow, why did you not tell us?"

Deodoro looked queerly at him, but made no answer. The head man chuckled.

"There are several men between him and his girl," he explained. "And the girl has not yet been made a woman. So I would not say that he has any."

We had gotten away from the crowd by this time, and he stopped.

"Now you can tell me your business," he said.

"*Amanhã*—tomorrow," Pedro answered. "I never do business on a feast-day; and since we have been lucky enough to come at a time of merry-making, we will join you in it. Tomorrow, when I have rested, we can talk of this matter."

Araujo scowled again. So Pedro added—

"Today it is enough to ask you whether you can get sarsaparilla roots, and perhaps Peruvian bark, for us from the forest near here."

The face of the chief brightened.

"Yes, yes! There is much in the hills above here."

"Then our guide has not lied to us," said Pedro, as if well pleased. "Perhaps you have heard of the big new company of Englishmen who now are working out of Tabatinga and preparing to buy these medical things for the markets in Europe?"

Araujo had not. Neither had I, and neither had Pedro. But the chief now thought he understood.

"And you are the scouts of this company," he guessed. "You are very welcome. We can make much trade for you. What do you give for those roots?"

But Pedro shook his head.

"*Amanhã,*" he said again.

So, seeing that he would talk no more of business that day, Araujo told us the town was ours.

The drum started up again, and others joined in. Men came to us with liquor and meat, and we ate and drank well—for we had paddled several miles since eating at Deodoro's tree-hut, and our appetites again were strong. Every one made us welcome—that is, all but Bernardo and Gastoa and his gang. They stayed by themselves, talking angrily and drinking much.

I was glad to see that they drank, for I felt that they were the ones whom we needed to watch most, and hoped that in the end they would make themselves senseless. If we waited until night, I thought, it should be quite easy to get the girl out of her prison and escape with her. But Deodoro spoiled that plan.

Before long the *caboclos* formed for a dance around the drummers. It was not much of a dance. They only trotted around and around, yelling and laughing, and dropping out one by one for a drink now and then. Araujo, the chief, trotted with the rest, tooting solemnly on a little tin whistle he had gotten somewhere. Some of the men shouted to us to join in, and I saw several young women making eyes at Pedro; but we said we were tired and squatted by ourselves, smoking and watching. Then Pedro said to Deodoro:

"Now is a good time for you, comrade, to slip away and talk to your girl. She must feel very badly at hearing all this merriment, knowing that it is for another girl, while she remains cooped up. She ought to be ready to run away with you now. If she is, tell her that at the right time we will take her where she can be happy."

The young fellow started to rise. Pedro grabbed him and pulled him down.

"Not like that!" he cautioned. "Do not get up and walk away in plain sight. Creep around behind us and then crawl behind this house at our backs. After that you can walk."

The big fellow grunted and obeyed. Like the tapir he resembled, he was not very good at creeping. He made some noise as he went. But nobody seemed to notice his going. Between the liquor and the dancing, the *caboclos* now were getting quite drunk and thinking of nothing but their own fun. So our companion got away without being seen.

We sat for a while longer watching the circling crowd. Then Pedro said:

"They are a worthless lot, Lourenço. Even if we were the traders they think us to be I doubt if I should want to do business with them. They look lazy, mean and treacherous. They have no welcome to a stranger unless they hope to make something from him, and their laughter now is only the kind born of drink and drums. I shall be glad when we are out of this place. This is the first time I ever took a hand in a woman-stealing."

"That is the way I feel too," I agreed. "I am not afraid of them, but I dislike them all. And unless Deodoro's girl is better than the women I have seen here she is hardly worth our time and trouble."

"He thinks she is," he laughed. "And every man must be his own judge in such matters. But I wish he would come back. I want to get up and walk around—those drums make me restless. If we do that, though, the *caboclos* will notice that he is gone."

It did seem that Deodoro had been gone for some time, and as the throbbing of the drums went on I too wished I could move around. A few minutes later I was moving around more than I had expected to.

A yell broke out. The dancers stopped. We hopped up. Then, before a house near the water, we saw men fighting and a girl running toward the stream.

"The fool!" snorted Pedro. "He has let her out too soon!"

We ran toward the struggle. So did every one else. One of the fighting men broke away and dashed after the girl. Another fell backward and lay still. But there were four of them left, and three of them were attacking Deodoro. They were Gastoa and two of his brothers. The man on the ground was the third brother.

As we reached them, Gastoa himself went down. The Tapir was fighting only with his hands, but those hands were terrible enough.

He got a clumsy swing into Gastoa's face, and it cracked like flat wood hitting water. Gastoa fell like a dead man. After he was down I caught a glimpse of his face. It looked as if a real tapir had jumped on it—mashed flat.

Pedro and I knocked down the other two men and yelled to Deodoro to run. All three of us jumped for our canoes. We ran into the girl and the man who had seized her. She was screaming and trying to escape. The man was her father, and he was striking her brutally in the face and body.

Pedro, the quickest of us three, reached them first. He jolted Bernardo in the head with his rifle-butt, and the drunkard fell sprawling. Without a pause Pedro snatched the girl off the ground and kept on running. But the crowd was almost on us, and as we slowed at the water's edge they caught us.

"Go!" I grunted to Pedro. Then I yanked his gun from his fist, whirled and struck around me. Men fell, but others swarmed in. I heard grunts and blows beside me and knew somebody was helping me to fight, but I had no time to see who it was. I thought it must be Pedro. Later I was surprised to find that it was Deodoro.

Pedro had hastily pushed the girl into our canoe and then turned back. But Deodoro, thinking only of getting the girl away, shoved Pedro backward so that he tumbled into the canoe, and then he heaved the boat out into the river. In falling, Pedro hit his head hard against the bottom of the canoe, and the blow stunned him so that he lay there a few minutes while he and the girl drifted away downstream. Then the fighting Tapir wheeled back to help me hold off the furious crowd.

Between us we did some rough work. But we were outnumbered; and to tell truth, *senhores*, I never got such a beating in my life. I have fought hard before and since that time, and have had far more serious wounds than I received then; but those *caboclos* knew how to hit where it would hurt. If they had had their weapons they would have cut me to pieces. But none of them had stopped to pick up a knife, and now they could fight only with hands, feet and teeth. Those were enough.

Somehow I did not think of shooting. I could not have shot well if I had tried, for they were too close. They wrenched at the gun while they beat me, and how I kept it I do not know. But I did keep it, and slugged around me with muzzle and butt. Finally, though, they knocked my legs out from under me. I fell hard, and they jumped all over me.

I kicked and squirmed and bit, but they had me. Then suddenly I felt a tremendous tug at one foot. I went sliding and bumping down the bank with two men hanging to me. Blows sounded and the men fell away. Somebody tumbled me head-first into a canoe. The canoe slid outward.

A raging yell sounded behind me. Sitting up, I found myself afloat. With me was the Tapir. His face was battered and his big snout was gushing red, but he was as strong as ever. He had grabbed a paddle and was shoving the boat downstream with strokes so powerful that the dugout seemed to leap from the water. As I looked at him he grinned through split lips.

"I had to pull hard to get you out of that tangle," he said. "You seemed stuck to the ground."

I tried to answer, but all I could do was to make a wheezing sound. The wind was beaten out of me. So I sat still while my breath came back and my head grew clear. I saw that the *caboclos* were jumping into boats and coming after us. Then we caught up with my own canoe, where the girl was crouching and Pedro was getting up and reaching for a paddle.

Pedro had a surprized look, as if wondering how he had come there, but he wasted no time in talk. Scooping up a handful of water, he threw it on his head and then began to paddle hard.

I looked for a paddle too, but there was none. Deodoro was using the only one in this canoe. I still had the rifle, though; and, seeing that the maddened men behind were gaining on us, I began shooting. I did not shoot to kill, for I do not like to kill men if it can be avoided. At the same time, I shot close enough to make them think I meant death.

Aiming carefully, I sent several bullets thumping along the sides of their dugouts. They slowed up at once. Some yelled to stop, others shouted to go on, and they paddled both ways at once—some trying to keep after us and others backing water. While this was going on we drew away fast.

The Tapir swerved into the bank and up the same stream we had traveled before. Pedro followed. For some time we kept on at the same rate of speed, and then we came out into the long crooked lake. There we stopped, listened—and heard nothing.

"They have given up," panted Pedro.

The Tapir shook his head.

"They have gone back for guns, and they follow," he said. "But we can dodge them. There is more than one way out of this lake."

Looking around as if to get his bearings, he pushed on again. Down around a bushy point we went, and there turned sharp to the right. A short arm of water ran that way, and we traveled down this until we seemed about to bump the shore. Then he swung to the left, and we were in a quiet, winding stream. There we stopped.

I got up with grunts and groans, for I had been sitting still and my bruised muscles had stiffened so that each one had a pain of its own. Deodoro grinned again. The grin annoyed me.

"Now," I demanded, "tell me why you got us into all this trouble. Why did you not come back to us and wait until we were ready?"

"You said yourself that the first thing to do was to free Bellie, and that the quickest way to free her was to go ahead and do it," he answered. "So I went and did it. And your comrade Pedro told me to be strong and bold. Have I not been strong and bold?"

His face and voice were so serious that Pedro and I laughed.

"More bold than we wanted you to be," I told him.

"I am sorry you got hurt," he said. "But I went and talked to Bellie and found her mad to get out at once. So I thought I had better take her before she changed her mind, and I cut a hole and pulled her through. If Gastoa and his brothers had not sneaked up just then we should have gotten away without trouble. And nobody would have thought you two traders had anything to do with it, because you were sitting in plain sight all the time."

"I see," I said. "And now that we are all here I think you had better take your girl and let me get into my own canoe."

We had been holding to bushes while we talked, and now Pedro drew our canoe up beside me. For the first time I had a good look at the girl, and after that look I did not blame Deodoro for wanting her. She was very pretty. True, she looked thin and weak, and her skin seemed pale; but I remembered that she had been caged for a long time, and knew that a healthy life outdoors and plenty to eat would quickly make her plump and strong. Her eyes and mouth were beautiful, and she looked no more like the other women we had seen than a butterfly looks like a mud-worm. Remembering the evil face of Gastoa and the brutality of her father, I was glad I had gone to help her, even though I now was full of aches and pains.

Then I noticed something that was not so pleasing. She did not want to leave Pedro and come to Deodoro. She looked long at Pedro, then glanced at the tapir-man and wrinkled her nose. I too looked at both the men, and saw what a difference there was. Pedro was a graceful fellow, with merry brown eyes and curly hair; and he had not been hit during the fight, so his face was not marked at all. Deodoro, with his clumsy-looking body and lank hair and big nose, was not a beauty at any time; and now his eyes were swollen so that they peered through slits, and his whole face was bruised and bloody.

It came to me, too, that though Deodoro had given the girl her chance to escape from the house, it was Pedro who had attacked Bernardo when she was being beaten and had run with her in his arms to the water; so that she might easily feel that it was the handsome stranger who had saved her. Besides, she had not seen Deodoro's fine fight at the house, because then she was running for the river. And she probably did not know much about his battle on the bank, for then she was floating away and we were all tangled up in a fighting knot. Poor Deodoro! Everything seemed to be against him.

Whether he saw all this I did not know, but I hoped not. When the girl made no move to change canoes I spoke gruffly to her, telling her to make room for me. She rose then, though slowly, and took my place without a word.

As I settled down and picked up my paddle I heard voices out on the lake. We slipped the canoes silently downstream and looked. The Tapir was right—two boatloads of armed *caboclos* were passing, the men working hard and looking ahead. Others came behind them. We kept very quiet until they were gone.

"They will go down the lake to the end hunting us," said the Tapir. "Then they will work back and search all the coves. We shall be at my house long before they have finished here. Are you not glad to be free, Bellie?"

The girl made no answer. Her eyes came again to Pedro's face, and then she looked down into the water. Deodoro looked long at her, then at Pedro, then at me. His face grew sad. With a deep sigh he pushed his canoe against the slow current, and we passed silently up the creek.

After a time we came into a network of winding water courses without any current that I could see. Deodoro hesitated several times, but seemed always to pick the right one. At length we found ourselves again in flowing water, and now we went downstream instead of up. At length we entered the river on which Pedro and I had been traveling that morning.

There our leader turned downward, and we saw that he had brought us out above his house. Keeping near the left shore and watching sharply for *caboclos*, we soon reached the little inlet masked by the palms.

"Now you are safe, Bella," I said when we stepped out on shore. "See the fine house Deodoro has built for you up here in the tree, where you can always be dry and comfortable. It is much better than any house in your town, and you will never have to live in a cage again. He has much meat too, and you and he will have plenty to eat. You will be very happy here."

"Do you two stay here also?" she asked.

"No," I said. "This is Deodoro's place. We must go on, for we live far from here."

She glanced once more at the house in the tree. Then she cried:

"I do not want to stay here. I will not stay here! Take me away!"

We all stood silent, staring at her. I wanted to scold her, but knew that would do no good. So I said the first thing that seemed best.

"We can not take you away today, Bella—it will soon be night. And we two are not going until tomorrow. We shall rest and eat here. Tomorrow we shall see what is best to be done. Now go up and see what a fine house that is."

She stood still, stubbornly, until Pedro also told her to mount the ladder. Then she obeyed, climbing as if afraid she would fall, but going upward until she got into the hut.

"*Nossa Senhora!*" muttered Pedro. "Now this is a pretty mess! After all our trouble she wants to go back home."

Slowly the Tapir shook his head. His face was full of pain.

"No, it is not that," he said. "It is as I told you before we went. She likes tall handsome men, and I am not tall nor handsome."

He swallowed hard, as if trying to keep from crying. And then, through his teeth, he added:

"She wants to—to go with you, Pedro. If she will—be happier with you, comrade, then—then you had better take her with you."

He choked and turned away.

For an instant Pedro stared. Then he sprang and caught him by the shoulder.

"*Por Deus*, you are a man!" he said. "Why, comrade, I do not want your girl! I do not want any girl at all. And you are wrong—she does not want me either. She may be interested in me because I am a new man whom she has not seen before, but after I am gone she will quickly forget me."

But Deodoro shook his head again, and so did I. I had seen women fall swiftly in love with Pedro before this—women who knew more about men than this little girl-woman knew; and I felt that Bella would not forget him so quickly as he said, and that neither she nor Deodoro would be happy because of this. When Pedro asked me if I did not agree with him, I said no.

"There is some truth in what Deodoro says," I told him. "If she had not seen you she might have been happy with him. I think our work is only half-done. We have freed her, but how are we to make her satisfied?"

He scowled and stood thinking. Then his eyes began to twinkle, and he threw up his head and laughed.

"Deodoro, let me talk to you," he said. "Lourenço, climb up and talk with her so that she will not overhear us. Ask her if she would like to go away with me—but try to show her that she would be foolish to do such a thing."

I did as he said. Up the pole I went, and in the hammock I found the girl, looking very small and sad and dissatisfied. When I came in she brightened up and glanced beyond me as if expecting some one else. Seeing that nobody followed, she seemed disappointed.

"The others will be up soon," I informed her.

Then I sat down against the wall, grunting from the pain of my stiff muscles.

"I am very lame," I went on. "Still, I am glad I am alive to feel lame. If it had not been for the splendid fighting of Deodoro I should probably be dead—and you would be back in your cage, to be beaten by your father and given to Gastoa."

She turned more pale at that thought, but looked surprized too. And she asked what Deodoro had done that was so brave. So I saw that I was right—she did not realize what a fight he had made. Taking care not to praise him over-much, I told her how he had fought off the gang of Gastoa and then battled beside me so that she could get away, and how he had pulled me out when I was down. Her big dark eyes grew larger as I talked.

Then, when her mind was full of this new fighting Deodoro, I suddenly asked her whether she would like to go away with us.

"My friend Pedro likes you," I said, "and if you want to go with him we can fool Deodoro in some way. You might not be happy with Pedro, but—"

"Why not?" she cut in.

"Well, of course he is a handsome man," I pointed out, "and other girls like him very well, and you could not expect him to give all his time to you.

He would not stay with you as this simple Deodoro would do. And he likes his fun with men too, and so he would drink and gamble with them. And he is restless and will not stay long in one place—and you know he would not want you trailing after him everywhere. If you expected him to be as faithful to you as Deodoro would be, you might not be happy. But if you are willing to be reasonable about those things we can take you away when we go. He is keeping Deodoro down below while I ask you about this."

Senhores, that gave her a good deal to think about. At first she looked as if she wanted to cry, and I felt sorry for her—but I did not let her see that. Then she asked the question I expected.

"If he wants me, why does he not talk to me himself instead of sending you?"

I laughed as if that were a foolish question.

"Because Deodoro would probably fight to keep you, and Pedro knows how hard he would fight. Pedro probably would get his handsome face hurt. And besides, what is the sense of fighting over a woman? Deodoro thinks you are the only pretty woman in the world, but Pedro and I know you are not."

She looked at me then as if beginning to dislike me. Before we could talk more we heard Pedro's voice down below, and it was loud and ugly.

"Then if you have more *cachaça*, why did you not say so?" he demanded. "I want a drink and I want it now! After we have gone to that dirty town of yours and brought back that female for you, I call it shabby treatment to try to hide your liquor!"

"You can have a drink if you want it," came the voice of the Tapir. "But do not speak so of my girl. She is not the kind of girl that a man like you ought to talk about."

"Bah! The world is full of girls, and not one of them is worth anything. I want that drink!"

"Then come up and you shall have it."

I stuck my head out of the door beside me and looked down. Deodoro, I noticed, had washed his face and looked much better. As he came upward and saw me he grinned. Pedro, behind him, winked at me. But when they came into the house their expressions had changed. Deodoro looked very serious, and Pedro scowled.

The Tapir lifted part of his floor again, and this time he pulled up a jar which he handed Pedro. My partner seemed to take a huge drink. When he passed the jar to me, however, I found that very little of the liquor was gone. I took as much as I wanted, and then held it out toward Deodoro. But Pedro snatched it and appeared to swallow about half of what was left, making a guzzling noise and letting some of the *cachaça* drip off his chin. The girl watched all this, and a look of disgust crept across her face. The thought came to me that my comrade's actions must remind her of her drunken, worthless father.

Then Pedro slumped down beside me and rolled a cigaret. Usually he was very deft at making a smoke, but now his fingers seemed clumsy. He spilled most of his tobacco, and then he snarled. He tried again, and made a worse mess than before. Finally he ordered me to make his cigaret for him. I did so, but I took my time about it. Then he abused me because I was so slow, and growled once more at Deodoro because he had not been more free with his liquor. After the cigaret was lit and going well, though, he quieted somewhat.

None of us spoke while he smoked. Deodoro watched us solemnly, and I saw the girl studying him and Pedro in turn. Pedro's face grew more heavy, as if the *cachaça* were working on him. Presently he began to leer at Bella.

"Think I will take you down-river with me, girl," he said roughly. "You do not want to stay here and you do not want to go back to your cage. You have to go somewhere, so come with me."

She looked him straight in the eyes. Then she said—

"I do not think I want to go with you."

"What!" snapped Pedro. "Do not be a little fool!" He looked at Deodoro and grinned in a nasty way, as if the liquor had given him courage which he had lacked before. "You, Deodoro, you can stay here with your *cachaça*. I am going away with this woman of yours. I am going now!"

He lurched up and staggered toward the girl.

Then the Tapir moved. He swooped at the rifle Pedro had left leaning against the wall. He jammed the muzzle into my comrade's stomach, and I heard the hammer click back.

"Stop where you are!" he ordered. "You shall not take her away. She is too good for you."

Pedro stood very still, staring down at the gun as if stricken with fear. I got up as quickly as I could, drawing my *machete*, for I did not like the sound of that hammer going back. But before I could get within arm's length of Deodoro the girl jumped at me.

She came so suddenly and swiftly that before I realized it she had knocked my bush-knife from my hands. With another lightning move she threw it out of the door, and I heard it thump on the ground below. Then, her face full of fury, she warned me—

"Keep back or I will tear your eyes out!"

I kept back. Her nails were very long, and I had seen how quick she was. Her sudden action had taken us all by surprize, and we stood staring at her. Then Deodoro spoke again to Pedro.

"If she wished to go with you and if you would be kind to her I would let her go. But I know you have other women. You boasted about it when you first came here and drank my *cachaça*. You said you only played with women, and that when you tired of one you left her and got another. You will not do so with Bellie."

Pedro made no answer. He looked at Bella. She looked back at him as if now she hated him. To Deodoro she said:

"You are the only honest man I know, Deodoro. I will stay with you and be your good girl. Drive these two into the river! This one is no better than the other." She pointed at me. "He wanted me to fool you and run away with them. Drive them out!"

"Get down the pole!" grunted the Tapir savagely. "Bellie, stay here!"

Pedro glanced at me and jerked his head toward the door. We went down the pole, Deodoro still covering us.

"Do not touch that *machete*!" he warned, as I stepped toward my knife. "Go to your canoe."

"Come, Lourenço," whispered Pedro. "He will follow."

So we got into our canoe. Deodoro came down, picked up my weapon and stepped into his own boat.

"Out into the river!" he commanded.

Pedro, looking much afraid, splashed his paddle quickly into the water and we moved outward. Behind us came the Tapir.

As we went downstream I felt the canoe shaking. I could not understand this until I looked at Pedro. The drunken look was gone from his face, and, though he made no sound, he was laughing so hard that he could scarcely use his paddle.

"Over to the right, where you see that *massaranduba* tree," came the voice of the Tapir.

We turned to the place. Below the tree we found a little cove which twisted around like a hook. At its end, where it could not be seen from the river, was a small hut.

There we got out. Pedro leaned on his paddle and laughed again. The Tapir, grinning, handed us our weapons.

"You can sleep dry here, comrades," he said. "I built this place while I was hunting monkey-meat. I do not think the men from the town will come to this river until tomorrow—the darknesses coming. If they should come, they will not find you here."

"Be careful that they do not find you either, friend," Pedro answered.

"They will not find us. If they do they will be sorry."

He spoke with a calm strength that made me think what a difference a few hours had made in him. That morning he had been a blubbering boy. Now, with the knowledge that Bella was his own and that he could thrash any two of those *caboclos* who had made his life and hers so wretched, he was a man. Rather slow of thought, perhaps, but able to take care of himself from this time on—that was the new Deodoro who now talked so surely and called us "comrades." His eye was steady and his head was up, and he feared no man.

"I am sorry that I had to drive you out in such a way," he went on. "You are the first men who ever did anything for me, and you have done the greatest thing any man could do for me. So I do not like to seem ungrateful, even though you understand and know that I am not. If ever I can do anything for you, Pedro and Lourenço, call on me and I will do it, no matter what it is."

He grinned again.

"That was a very wise plan of yours, Pedro—you know women better than I do. But Bellie nearly spoiled it all when she jumped at Lourenço. I almost forgot everything you had told me to say and do."

"So did I," admitted my partner. "After she did that it was not really necessary to talk about the women I had abandoned—ha ha ha! I nearly laughed in your face. But she is all yours now, friend. Treat her well—but be strong and bold, strong and bold!"

"I will," the Tapir promised earnestly. "*Adeos!*"

He stepped back into his canoe and left us.

Pedro took cartridges from a pocket and reloaded his rifle.

Excerpt from The Camp-Fire

In Arthur O. Friel's story in this issue there recurs a pun on a proper name. The pun is really dependent upon the English translation of a common noun—a darned common one, not upon the Portuguese for that word. Hence a problem which we put up to Mr. Friel. Here's his letter. As you'll see, we decided to let it run as it stands.

> I'll admit that this time I've used "literary license" in order to make a laugh. The Portuguese word is *barriga*. It's a pretty safe bet, however, that 99% of our readers won't know this, and that the others won't give a rip. I've noticed that most folks, given a choice between meticulous precision and a chance to snicker, will reach for the snicker and let precision go hang.
>
> However, if you think it's really essential, I'll fix it up somehow. I haven't yet had time to figure on it, though, and right now it looks as if I'd have to use an ax—chop out the humor at that point. To me it seems that the story would lose more than it would gain by this operation. . . .
>
> The custom of confining a girl when she reaches womanhood is quite wide-spread among the Amazonian Indians, particularly at the head-waters; and it is nothing uncommon for a girl to be kept in her cage until she bleaches out and becomes sickly—in fact, some of them die from it.
>
> —Arthur O. Friel.

While we have more stories by Mr. Friel in our safe, there are not likely to be any more for some time, I'm sorry to say, as he has temporarily given up writing for other work. Later, however, I'm hoping he will take up the pen again and, if he does, I think he'll be writing for our magazine.

November 3, 1920

The Firefly

Beautiful but false, *senhores*, is the firefly. Beautiful as a flashing jewel floating in the darkness of the jungle night; false as flame without heat, which will neither comfort your body nor cheer your mind.

When the cold southwest winds blow and the *tempo da friagem* sweeps across this upper Amazon, you may cover yourself with those brilliant insects until you blaze with light, but does the chill leave your bones? No. And if the gleam of the firefly in the gloom moves you to follow after and reach for it—beware! You may sink suddenly in sucking mud whence there is no escape. False fires they are, *senhores*—false and cold.

In your own North America, you tell me, the firefly is a weak and tiny thing compared to the big beetle which glows so bright in our Brazilian jungle. That does not surprise me, for the United States is a colder country— is it not?—and so the little light-bugs can not grow so big and strong.

But I am much astonished to hear you say that the fireflies flash their lanterns so that they can recognize comrades and friends, just as men use lights to see one another in the dark. You tell me, too, that the reason why other beetles which have no lights make noises in the night is because they know one another's voices, as we do; and in this way they find their friends whom they can not see.

It may be so. I have noticed that you two explorers know many odd things about living creatures—things which even we rubber-workers who live among those creatures do not know. We are too busy keeping ourselves alive among the dangers of the deadly Javary region to study deeply into the lives of beasts and birds and bugs.

Yet as the months pass by we too see strange things, *senhores*. And I sometimes think that the most strange and wonderful thing in all the world is life itself—that unseen power and impulse within a creature which makes it move and act in different ways under different conditions.

Why are we what we are? Why do we do what we do? Why do some men hate each other at sight? Why can some women be trusted and others not? I do not know. I know only that we are wrong as often as right, and I think perhaps we are little better than those lightless beetles of which you spoke, straggling along in life, making a noise as we go, and doing the best we can.

What is that, *senhor*? You say I am a philosopher? I do not know what sort of thing a "philosopher" may be, for I am only an humble *seringueiro* of the Amazon headwaters, and those big words mean nothing to me.

You will pardon me if my talk is tiresome. But perhaps now I can speak of something more interesting as we float on down the great river and those fireflies flash over yonder on the black shore. Listen, and you shall hear of a firefly far more beautiful than they.

In the time of the great floods, when all work in the swampy rubber-forests of old Coronel Nunes was stopped by the high water, I had gone out on an adventurous canoe-trip with another *seringueiro*—a handsome, happy-go-lucky young comrade of mine named Pedro. We had paddled far into hilly country on the frontier of Brazil and Peru, and, after using up most of our food and cartridges, had started back to headquarters.

On this return trip I had gotten into a bad fight with some *caboclos* while helping a young fellow to rescue the girl he loved from a cage where she was shut up by her drunken father; and in this fight I had been pounded so severely that every muscle in me was lame. So now, paddling on down the river the next day, I found myself so stiff and full of aches that it was hard for me to keep at work.

I shut my teeth and said nothing, hoping that the pain would work out as my muscles loosened up. In this I was disappointed. True, my arms did not hurt so much after a while, but the ache in my legs grew worse, as they were cramped by the canoe. Besides, I had wrenched my back, and the swing of paddling seemed to give me a sharp stab every time I stroked.

So, though I choked back the grunts and groans boiling up inside me and tried to do my share of the work, Pedro soon felt the difference from my usual power. He stopped paddling and looked back.

"Let us go ashore, Lourenço, and rest today," he suggested. "You are too lame to keep on. I will give you a good rubbing now and another tonight, and tomorrow you will be yourself again."

He spoke sense. But I was feeling sour, both from pain and from vexation at myself, and I would not quit.

"I am not an old woman," I growled. "And you know very well that we can not waste time in resting now—we have hardly any food left, and very few cartridges. I will not go ashore at all today, even to eat. I will push this canoe until dark."

He laughed.

"If you are not an old woman, do not talk like one," he advised me. "You speak like a cross old grandmother. What if we have only a little food? The time to worry is when we have none at all. But if you enjoy torturing yourself do not let me interfere with your pleasure. Let me see you do this."

And he twirled his paddle over his head and around behind him in a way that would have made me yelp with pain if I had tried it.

"Let me see you do this," I retorted, shoving with my paddle so hard that the canoe jumped and he nearly fell overboard.

It hurt my aching back, but it showed him that I was in earnest. He laughed again, then settled down to his regular long-distance stroke. And all that day we swung on down the river, covering considerable distance with the aid of the current.

At last, when night was nearly on us, he moved his head toward a cove at our left.

"Unless you wish to paddle all night, *senhora*, perhaps we had better go ashore there," he said. "We must make camp soon if we are to make it at all, and we are not likely to find a better place."

I knew that as well as he did, and I was more than ready to stop. I was rather ashamed of myself, too, for having answered him so sharply that morning. But now he had spoken as if to an unreasonable old woman and even called me "*senhora*," with a mocking grin that made me cross again. So I only grunted as I turned the dugout up the cove, and after we went ashore and made camp I kept my mouth shut. He was in a teasing mood, and I was not in the humor to be plagued.

We slung our hammocks, ate and smoked. Night came before our cigarets were burned down. I intended, after finishing my smoke, to curl up in my hammock and sleep. But that intention, like some others I have had, was not to be carried out.

Lights came into the darkness—spots of light twinkling above us and all around us there in the bush. They floated out over the black water too, looking very beautiful as they rose and dipped and drifted in the gloom. Watching them, I forgot my aches and pains.

"We have come into a bay of *cucujus*," I said. "They will swing their little lanterns over us while we sleep."

"I hope they will not show us to some hungry jaguar," laughed Pedro. "I am tired tonight, and I expect to sleep soundly. It would be unpleasant to wake up in the morning and find myself trotting around in the belly of the big cat."

Before I could answer there came a sound. It made us sit motionless, breathless, staring in wonder at each other. It was not a noise of the jungle, nor even the voices of men. There in the darkness, somewhere out beyond the gliding fireflies, a woman was singing!

Soft, sweet, low but clear, the music of her voice floated to us along the water. In that wild and savage place, far from where any woman should be, it seemed a voice from another world—an impossible dream, which presently would flit away like wind-blown smoke. Yet, dream or not, it held us still as men of wood while it sang on. After a time it died out of the air.

"*Nossa Senhora!*" whispered Pedro. "Are we awake, comrade, and in our right minds? A woman, singing in this black hole where only fireflies live! A white woman, too—for no Indian could sing so sweetly, or would even try to. We have not seen any human thing in all this day, and the last persons we did see were only *caboclos*. Did you too hear that voice?"

I made no answer for a time, and we both strained our ears for some further sound of human life. None came. At length I said:

"Pedro, I do not know what this thing may be, but I shall not sleep well tonight unless I find out. A sound drifting along the surface of the water is hard to place, but this singing seemed to come from the right, at the end of this *enseada*. We have not been down there, and it must be that some one lives there. Let us go and see."

We had some trouble in starting, for the night was so black that we could hardly find the canoe, though we knew just where it was. We had been sitting beside our little fire, you understand, and at first our eyes would not see in the dark. But after we left the shore behind us we began to make out the things near us, though faintly. Very slowly and carefully we felt our way along the murky water toward the head of the flooded bay.

Though the distance was not great, we took some time in covering it. The darkness seemed to grow even more dense as we moved, and the fireflies which before had looked so beautiful now confused us—for in thick gloom a man's gaze will follow a moving spot of light in spite of himself, and where his eyes turn his body is likely to turn also.

Yet they helped us too, those tiny lanterns, for we knew most of them were on the land, and so by keeping away from them we avoided running aground. Finally, however, the canoe bumped softly into the shore and stopped.

"We are at the end," said Pedro, up in the bow. "I do not see anything new. Do you?"

I saw nothing at all but the flaming insects. We stayed there for a time listening. No sound came, except a few of the usual night noises of the bush.

"We had best go back—" I started to say, when I was struck dumb. Near us, ahead of us in the unseen bush, the voice broke out again in song.

> "Glitter, glitter, pretty firefly!
> Born but to dance and flash and die!
> Blaze ye the way through the dark night's span;
> Leading me back to the love of my man!
> Back to the lights on a far-off shore,
> Back to the laughter I hear no more—
> Floating along like a star above,
> Show me the road back to life and love!"

For long minutes after the song ended we crouched there, motionless and wordless. Somehow I felt chilly, and the skin of my back prickled. The thing was so weird that I wished I were back beside my fire, where I could see Pedro's face and my hammock and the other things to which I was accustomed. And while I was thinking of this, a thing occurred that made me doubt my senses.

Some of the fireflies drifting about in the bush before us suddenly disappeared. They vanished as if seized by a swift, silent hand. Then they blazed out again, but now they were not floating along as before, but resting on something—something that moved. It was too small to be a man, but still it acted like a man. It snatched at the flies and put them on itself. Yet, though the cluster of insects grew larger and their combined light increased, we could not see the thing that did this.

Before us grew the outline of a small head and shoulders, and at times I thought I could catch the glimmer of little eyes, but that was all. It made no sound. It seemed alive yet not alive, human but not human, an uncanny creature made of the darkness itself.

Then we found that this thing was real. It coughed. The noise told us instantly what it was.

"A monkey!" marveled Pedro. "A monkey as big as a child, lighting himself with fireflies like a village belle! Did you ever see such a thing?"

At the sound of his voice the creature stood very still. We knew it was looking at us. Then instead of jumping away and hiding, it moved straight toward us.

It came rather slowly, stopping now and then, but advancing each time. We kept very quiet. Finally it halted at the bow of our dugout and stood watching us. Some of the light-bugs had jumped off it and others had been brushed away by the leaves as it came, but enough remained to let us see its head quite plainly.

As my partner had said, it was as big as a child. It seemed as unafraid as a child, too. Soon it swung itself up into the boat, and I saw a shadowy arm reach out toward Pedro.

"Welcome, *compadre!*" chuckled Pedro. "You are a friendly fellow. I am glad to find that you are flesh and blood—I almost thought you were a demon. Now sing again for us."

Senhores, I should not have been greatly surprized if that monkey had done so. He had already amazed me much, and he seemed to be the only living thing there besides ourselves and the bugs. But he made no sound at all. I could not see him well, because Pedro was between him and me, but it seemed that he was pulling at my comrade. Soon I found that this was so.

"He is trying to take me ashore, Lourenço," said Pedro. "He wants me to go somewhere with him. And I am going."

Stepping out on land, he added to the monkey:

"Take my finger, *compadre*, and lead me where you want to go. 'Show me the road to light and love.' "

I got out, pulled the canoe farther up on shore so that it would not drift off, and followed. It was quite easy to see the little animal and my partner stooping to give him a good hold on his hand, but I could not see much else.

As I trailed behind the pair I marveled. I have been guided through the bush in odd ways, following sights and sounds and even smells, but never before nor since have I followed an illuminated monkey through blackness, seeking a voice. Yet I could not ask for a better guide than that wordless beast proved to be. Perhaps he did not know where we wanted to go, but he knew exactly where he wished us to go, and it came to the same thing.

The ground under foot was firm and fairly clear of bush, feeling like an old path nearly grown over. We followed our queer guide with no difficulty and with little noise. Presently Pedro halted.

"A house!" he whispered.

Peering around him, I saw close beside him a section of mud wall showing in the light from the monkey's fireflies. It looked old; it was cracked, and vines grew on it. Somehow I felt that the house was empty. This proved to be true.

The monkey tugged at Pedro, and we went on. I passed my hand along the wall until it struck a window. There I looked in and sniffed. The place was black and had an odor of decay. Nobody lived there.

Beyond this house the monkey pulled Pedro to the right. My comrade made a soft noise in his throat. I looked again. A few strides ahead of us a faint light came out through the window of another house.

Under this window the monkey stopped. Strong wooden bars ran across the opening, but they were meant only for safety, and it was easy to see between them. We peered in, and stood amazed by what we saw.

The room beyond those bars was well lit, but the light was not made by fire or oil. It came from two large hanging cages, out of which shone the lights of many fireflies. This use of the insects was not new to us, for we had sometimes seen little cages of them in other parts of our river country, so that we were not much surprised now. It was the woman under them that held us silent and still.

She too was ablaze with fireflies. They were fastened in her black hair, on the dark-red gown that flowed down around her, and even on her bare arms and her throat. She was slender and shapely, with big dark eyes, a pouting scarlet mouth and a skin as clear and white as the waters of a brook falling over a cliff.

Facing us, she was looking at something near the window where we stood, smiling a little as if she saw something that pleased her and holding her head to one side in an alluring way. With the silent lights of the caged night insects shining softly down on her and the other beetles flashing from her hair to her knees, she was so beautiful that she seemed more than human.

She moved toward us a little, still looking at the same spot, and slowly moved her round bare arms out to the side and overhead. I saw how she kept the fireflies on her smooth skin—they were fastened into narrow bracelets and a necklace made from small vines. Gradually her arms came down until her hands rested on her shoulders, then sank to her sides. Her lips opened in song.

> "Come through the night, O heart of my heart!
> Speed o'er the leagues that hold us apart!
> Clasped in your arms I will—"

We lost the rest. A black hairy thing rose into our faces, startling us so that we jumped back and poised to strike at it. Then, seeing what it was, we withheld the blow. It was the monkey, which we had forgotten and which now had swung himself up to the opening. Grasping the bars, he chattered through them to the woman. She broke off her song.

"You—you little beast!" she scolded. "You frightened me. Stop shaking those bars. Go to the door, and you may come in."

She passed to one side, and at her movement the monkey dropped to the ground. We followed close behind him. A bar dropped and a door opened, letting out a vague path of light. The monkey swung himself inside. We stepped into the light and halted.

"Good evening, *senhorita*," Pedro greeted her, sweeping off his hat and bowing. "Do not fear. We are friends."

With a startled gasp she sprang back. One hand leaped to her breast, rose a little, and stopped. Below, her fingers we caught the glint of a half-drawn dagger.

"If we frightened you, *senhorita*, pardon us—we shall go away at once," my comrade added. "We are here only because we heard a wonderful voice singing in the night and could not rest until we found the singer. Our camp is down the *enseada*.

"But before we go, will you not sing once more for us? It is not often that travelers in the wilderness hear the voice of an angel."

Though I did not glance at him, I knew he was smiling at her. I knew too what a winning smile this handsome young partner of mine could give a woman if he would. An answering smile came into her face, and in her eyes dawned the look of admiration I had seen in the eyes of other women when they gazed at him. The knife slipped out of sight.

"Perhaps I may," she said. "First tell me who you are."

"Pedro, *senhorita*—Pedro Andrada. I have with me a cross old lady named Senhora Lourenço Moraes. She is very lame, and really ought not to be out at night, but I dared not leave her behind for fear she would fall into the fire."

The Firefly Lady laughed at that, looking much more lovely than before. I grinned, though I did not like to be made fun of before her.

"Your old lady needs to shave," she answered. "Her beard is terribly black. You must have traveled far; is it not so?"

Now I saw my chance to repay Pedro. At the place where we had recently fought the *caboclos* he had led the people to think we were scouts of a big company which dealt in medicinal herbs and bark. So now, to plague him, I spoke up and told her the same tale, intending then to enjoy his efforts to carry out his part.

"We have traveled far, indeed, *senhorita*," I told her. "We have been seeking sarsaparilla and Peruvian bark and such things among the Indian towns above here for the markets in Europe. A big new company of Englishmen at Tabatinga, on the Solimões, has sent us out as scouts to find where good trade is, before beginning to send in boats for these medical things. We are now on our way back."

She smiled again, very graciously this time, and said she could see we were honest men. Would we not come in? We would, and we did.

As we stepped inside I glanced at the place near the window where she had been looking when we first saw her. I expected to find some one sitting or lying there. But there was nobody at all. Wondering what she had been looking at, I kept my eye on that spot as I advanced. Then I saw. The thing she had been smiling at and flirting with was her own face.

On the wall hung a round mirror half as large as my head, with a handle that looked like silver. It must have cost considerable money somewhere, and it looked out of place there against that old dingy mud. Yet as I looked back at the Firefly Lady it did not seem so strange, and I did not blame her for wanting to see her own pretty face; for the rest of the room was very ugly, and there was nothing at all worth looking at. I wondered, though, that she should deck herself with fireflies and pose and sing when there was nobody to see her except that black monkey. Still, women do queer things.

In the farther wall I noticed a door standing partly open. Beyond it was darkness and silence. Nowhere was any sign of another person. She seemed all alone.

"Have you hunger, *senhores*?" she asked. "I have not much food, but you are welcome."

"Do not trouble yourself, *senhorita*," Pedro declined. "We have eaten. It is not food we hunger for, but the sound of your voice—and the charm of your companionship."

She laughed lightly again, and her eyes spoke very kindly to my comrade.

"Tell me more of your company of Englishmen," she said. "They are at Tabatinga? They have not been long in this country! They are rather old men?"

Pedro gave me a queer look. I bit my tongue to keep from laughing and spoke no word. After an instant of hesitation he answered easily:

"You have it partly right. They have not been here long, but they are young men, not old. They are very rich too, *senhorita*—three young men, handsome and wealthy."

"So? And married?"

"No. At least I do not think so. I have not seen nor heard of any wives."

She glanced at the mirror. Then she lifted her arms and floated around for a few steps, her face alight with some pleasant thought. But as she again faced the open door through which we had entered she started and fear flashed into her eyes. We whirled.

Nothing was there. Only the blackness of the night met our gaze.

"What is it?" I asked.

"There!" she whispered, pointing. "By the door! Has he—has he come back?"

We jumped through the doorway, seeking whatever might be lurking outside. We found nothing.

"Is this a joke, *senhorita*?" demanded Pedro, as we came in again. "There is no danger."

"No, no!" She still looked frightened. "I thought—I thought I saw the terrible face of—of Carlos Guimaraes. If he should find you here he would kill us all."

"Why?"

"Why? Because you are men and here with me. He—he keeps me here as his prisoner."

"Oh! So that is why you are here alone! Let him come," Pedro said grimly. "Killing is a game which more than one man can play. I should much like to meet this Carlos. But he is not there now. Who is this man, and who are you, and how came you here?"

Still seeming nervous, she asked him to shut the door. He closed and barred it. Then, glancing at the other door, he asked where it led. She said it was only the door to her sleeping-room, and so there was no danger from that direction. Then she smiled again.

"It is very comforting to have two strong men here to protect me," she said. "Now come, let us sit by the table, and I will tell you all."

She sank into a rough chair beside a small bare table, directly under the light-cages. There was one other chair, and we looked at each other but remained standing. She rose and sat on the table itself.

"Now there is a chair for each of you," she said. "See the table holds me easily—I am so much lighter than you big men. Sit, *senhores*."

"We are not '*senhores*,'" said Pedro bluntly. "We are but plain men. Call us 'friends' or by our names, *senhorita*—"

He paused and looked a question.

"My name is Francisca."

He bowed, glanced swiftly around him and sat down in the chair she had used. I lifted the other and set it against the wall where I could watch her face, the window, or the door to her room, all with a mere turn of the eyes. As I sat down I thought I heard a small sound from that other room.

"Is there a window in that room?" I asked.

She looked quickly at me, her eyes narrowing.

"Yes, surely. Why do you ask?"

"I heard something."

"It is nothing," was her swift answer. "There is a—a sick monkey in there—a poor little baby monkey which seems hurt. I found it yesterday and have made a little bed for it, where I can feed it and no snake or other evil thing can harm it."

"That is truly kind of you, *senhorita*," I told her, and said no more.

For a little time none of us spoke. No further noise came from the other room, and the only sound was the continual clicking of the *cucujus* in their cages as they tried to leap up and fly. We men watched the big black monkey which had guided us there, and which now had climbed up on the table and squatted beside her. A few of the fireflies still remained on him, and he picked them off one by one and put them on her.

Knowing how a pet monkey will imitate people around him, I could easily see how he had learned this trick—he had seen his mistress fasten fireflies on herself, and had caught the habit of doing the same thing and then bringing the insects to her. She laughed now as she took them from him, and I thought that she did indeed feel safe with us there.

Soon, though, she grew very serious and began to tell her story.

She was not a Brazilian girl, she said, but the daughter of a wealthy Italian. This surprised me a little; for, though I had noticed that she did not speak Portuguese in our own way, she did not seem much like the few Italian people I had seen. Still, different kinds of people may come from the same country, and the Italians I had met were rather poor, while it was easy to see that she was accustomed to the things of wealth. My eye went to that expensive mirror as I thought this, and I was all the more curious to know how she had ever come there. She soon told us.

Her father, she said, had become interested in reports of immense wealth waiting in the Amazon Valley for men who would develop it—lumber, rubber, medicinal herbs and other things—and had decided to come to Brazil and see for himself whether these stories were true. As she was his only child and anxious to see something of South America, he took her with him to Rio, where he intended to leave her with friends to enjoy the society and fashion of the capital while he made his long trip. But after staying for a time in Rio she felt that she would be lonely there during the long weeks when her father was gone; and so she coaxed him into taking her with him.

All the way up the great river, even to the headwaters, these two journeyed together. They stopped at towns along the river, saw what there was to see, and talked with men who were in business of various kinds. Then, as they were nearing the upper reaches and thinking that soon they would turn about and travel back seaward, they became acquainted with a man who had recently come onboard—a Senhor Azevedo, who was developing a large rubber estate for some rich men living in Rio. This man invited them to visit his headquarters for a time and see how the work was done. They accepted.

Leaving the steamer, they traveled up into the Javary region in the private boat of Senhor Azevedo. He was a courteous host, and all his men took much interest in showing her father about.

One of these men—Guimaraes, a sort of foreman—showed much interest in Francisca also. Indeed, he was so attentive that she had to complain of it to her father, who told Senhor Azevedo. This resulted in a sharp rebuke for the man Guimaraes, and for a time after that he did not trouble her.

Then death struck her father. A snake bit him, and in an hour he was dead. And that very night Guimaraes managed to get into her room, struck her senseless before she could cry out, carried her silently to the river, put her into a canoe, and fled up the river in the moonlight.

He paddled hard until dawn, and for several days after that he kept on, until at last they came to this place. What place it was she did not know—it was a town without a name; a few old mud houses, totally deserted except by bats and snakes.

Since coming here she had seen nobody but the man who had stolen her; and even he deserted her at times, going away somewhere for days and leaving her with only the black monkey for a companion. He was away now, and she was alone in this wild jungle with no way of escape.

I heard this with wrath growing hot within me. I wished this Guimaraes would come back now and give me a chance at him. Pedro perhaps was thinking the same thing, for, with a hard note in his voice, he asked—

"Do you think he will return tonight?"

"I do not think so," she said, looking at the door as if frightened by the thought. "He went only yesterday, and he usually stays away for days. Yet I never know when he will come."

"I wonder, *senhorita*, that you can sing when you are alone and a prisoner," said Pedro.

"If I did not I should go mad!" she cried. "When the night comes—the blackness and the loneliness and the cries of animals killing in the jungle—oh, you do not know!"

Jumping from the table, she held out her arms to him.

"Oh, take me away!" she pleaded. "Take me out of this awful place—to Tabatinga, to any place where I can find people who will be kind and help me to get home. Your employers, the Englishmen—surely they will help a girl in distress."

Then, *senhores*, I felt meaner than ever before in my life. I had lied to her—there were no Englishmen, nor were we going within many miles of Tabatinga. But the thought came to me that this did not matter so much after all; for we could take her to the headquarters of our kindly *coronel*, who has a daughter of his own in Rio and would surely do everything possible for the poor little Firefly Lady.

Pedro spoke.

"Truly, *senhorita*, we shall do our best for you. We go on down the river in the morning, and you shall go with us. We will take you to some one who will gladly help you."

"Oh!" she cried joyously.

With a swift movement she threw her arms around his neck and kissed him. Then, glowing, she turned toward me. I got up rather hastily.

"Will you not sing for us now, *senhorita*?" I asked.

She laughed, a clear, ringing laugh.

"Are you afraid to be kissed?" she teased.

"Remember that I am a cross old lady with a terrible black beard," I grinned. "Wait until I am shaved. Pedro has had his kiss, but I can look forward to mine. Now sing—sing something in your own tongue."

Again her eyes seemed to grow narrow.

"Do you know Italian?" she asked.

"No," I said truthfully, "I do not. But I should like to hear a song of your own land, even though I do not understand the words."

"And so you shall," she promised.

Breathing deep, she began to sing in a foreign tongue.

As she sang she seemed to forget us, and into her eyes came a far-away look as if she were gazing across the jungle and the ocean at her home-land, to which she would soon return. What she sang I do not know; but it was gay and lively, showing the joy she felt over her coming escape from this dreary cage. Soon she began to dance also—swift, whirling steps in time to the measure of her songs, which carried her around the dingy room in a flashing swirl of fireflies until she was breathless. Then she stopped, panting, her white skin flushed.

Glancing at Pedro, I was puzzled to find on his face a thoughtful frown. But as she turned to him this disappeared, and he gave her many compliments on her voice. Then he suggested:

"We start at dawn, *senhorita*, and it would be well for all of us to get some sleep. We will lie down on the floor beside that outer door, if you wish, and see that nothing disturbs you."

"But no, that is not necessary. You will be more comfortable at your own camp, and I shall be safe enough—Carlos will not come so late as this, and I shall bar the door. I—I would rather be alone, my friends, this last night here."

"As you will," my partner bowed. "We shall come for you at daybreak."

We turned toward the door. She slipped in front of us.

"You will not forget? You will not go and leave me?"

"There is no danger of that," we assured her. "Sleep well, and have no fear."

She gave us each a little white hand, and we passed out.

"*Por Deos!*" grumbled Pedro. "How black it is! We shall have to feel our way back to the canoe."

I said nothing. We crept back the way we had come, guiding ourselves along the wall with our finger-tips. As we went we heard the door close and the bar go into place.

We found the next house, felt our way along that, and reached the corner where we should turn. There Pedro stopped. I bumped into him.

"What is it?" I whispered, thinking he must have made out something in front of him.

"I am thinking," he whispered back.

"Then think fast. I want to sleep."

Softly he turned around and spoke in my ear.

"Lourenço, I think there is more here than we have seen. It might be well for us not to hasten away. Did you hear that thing move in the back room of her house?"

"Yes. The baby monkey."

"If it was a baby monkey it was the biggest baby I ever heard. It moved only a little, but it was heavier than even a full-grown monkey would be. And here is another thing: She said she feared that this Carlos would come and kill us, and so she had us bar the door. Then she sat down under those light-cages and had us sit beside her. All of us were in plain sight from the window. If any one had come, could he not have shot us through the window?

Certainly."

"I thought of that too, and sat where I could watch it," I reminded him.

"I know you did. I saw how you placed your chair. But I doubt if she really fears this Carlos. Perhaps there is no Carlos at all. And do you remember her story of Azevedo, a developer of a big rubber estate in this Javary region? We are rubber-workers, and I never have heard of any big estate run by a man named Azevedo. And here is one thing more: She did not sing in Italian."

"Are you sure?"

"I am sure. Some years ago I knew a man of Italy and learned enough of his language to recognize it when I hear it. What tongue she used in those songs I do not know, but it was not Italian nor English nor Portuguese. She said she would sing in her own language, and I believe she did so. If she deceived us about one thing, why not about others?"

"But surely she stays here only because she must," I objected. "A woman like her would never pick this forsaken place to live in, or even find it. And she is mad to get away."

"True. But—Lourenço, I want to know what is in that back room. Let us go back softly and look and listen."

Very carefully we stole back to the barred window where the light showed. Even before we reached it I knew Pedro's suspicion was well founded, for we heard a voice—not the voice of Francisca, but that of a man.

It was a low voice and seemed weak. We could not make out the words until we stopped at the window and put our eyes and ears at the openings. The room which we had just left was empty now, and the voice came from beyond the door in the farther wall.

"But you will not leave me to die!" it pleaded. "To starve and die here alone like a sick rat in a hole! You would not do such a thing to a man who has ruined his life for you!"

Then came the voice of the woman. It was so cold and cruel that we hardly knew it.

"If you die I can not help it. I did not give you the fever, and neither can I cure it. If you think I intend to throw away this chance to escape from this place you are much mistaken. These men are traveling fast and hard—they are gaunt and unshaven—and they will not wait. I shall go with them, and there is an end of it."

"An end of me, you mean," said the man hoarsely. "An end of the idiot who sacrificed everything to go with you to the end of the earth—who stole for you and even killed for you. I saved you by knifing that police agent who trailed us all the way up the Amazon—and this is your reward! This is the love you promised me! To leave me dying, starving, screaming at the empty blackness—"

"What else can I do?" she cut in. "You yourself say you are dying. You are as good as dead already. You can not go out. Even if you were well you could not go out. The police—"

"Yes, the police!" he cried. "I would rather die in the hands of the police than here alone. They would at least be human toward a dying man. And what do you think the police will do to you? You, the enemy of their country— you, the Austrian singer who spied during the war—you, the woman who married a Brazilian for the protection of his name and then poisoned him and fled with his money and the jewels he gave you? Your record is far blacker than mine. What do you think will happen to you?"

"I do not care!" she cried wildly. "Anything is better than staying here in this place where only snakes and monkeys live, and where the only jewels I have are fireflies! Fool! You do well to speak of jewels! You made that blunder in Rio that set the police on us and destroyed our chance of escaping to Europe.

"When that servant of my husband found you taking the jewels, you only tied and gagged him instead of making him silent forever, and so he was able to talk when he was found and freed. That made the police seek both us and Azul, and they found him too—dead. And when we had fled up the Amazon you let yourself be robbed—robbed, fool, of all our fortune!"

"That is true," he admitted. "But I could not murder that poor old servant. I was never a criminal until love for you made me one, and I am no cutthroat."

"The old story!" she jeered. " 'The woman beguiled me.' No, oh no, you are no criminal—you are not clever enough! But your stabbing of that man who trailed us makes your record black enough, Manoel *meo*, to send you to death."

"I killed him for your sake," he insisted. "And I killed him in fight— he was drawing a revolver. An instant more and we would both have been prisoners. I never poisoned a fond old man as you did—I did not even know you had killed him until you told me. And I am glad I did not slit the servant's throat. A killer I may be, but not a cold-blooded murderer."

"Bah! It makes no difference. You must die if you go out. You will soon die here. Death here or outside—what does it matter? You deserve to die alone after the blunders you have made, and so you shall. And I shall find a way to escape your Brazilian police. You Brazilians are all alike—stupid fools!"

Pedro drew in his breath softly, and I heard him mutter—

"I think you are mistaken, my lady."

The sick voice came again, stronger with wrath.

"Yes, I know your way—a way of falsehood. False to your husband—false to me—you will be false to these men and to the Englishmen, also. You are a good actress, with your pretended fear of an imaginary Carlos Guimaraes. You are a fine liar, with your wild tale of abduction and an Azevedo who never existed and a wealthy Italian father—Italian! Ha!

"You have made these strangers swallow your story, and you are trying to lure them also—yes, I heard you kiss one of them! But you will forsake them as soon as they have served your purpose.

"Then you will play on the hearts of those young Englishmen as you have played on mine. You will try to set them against one another, to rob and ruin them as you have done to other men. Or you will tell them you are French, perhaps, and persuade them to help you reach Europe.

"If you are caught, you will swear that I was the one who poisoned your husband and that I forced you to come with me. Otherwise you will think no more of me whom you leave to perish."

"Since you are so wise," she replied, her voice harder than ever, "I will tell you that you are nearly right. I shall make the Englishmen send me to Europe, and there I shall go home to Austria and find again the one man I love—Karl, my Karl, captain of hussars.

"And you are right, too, when you say I shall forget you and your whines, and the fat old fool I married in Rio, and all the rest of your accursed country. And I shall be happy—"

"Ha-ha-ha!" The man burst into a terrible laugh. "Happy! Yes, you will be happy! You will be happy in a Brazilian prison! I am not dead yet, and we shall see!"

"What do you mean?"

He laughed again in a crazed way.

"I am not the only fool! You are one also! Those men return at dawn for you. I shall see to it that they hear me and come into this room, and I will tell them who you are and what you have done. Then you will charm the Englishmen—oh yes—ha-ha-ha!"

For a moment she made no reply. When she did speak her voice sounded like the hiss of a snake.

"So! You will do that! Then you must become silent before they return!"

"*Deos meo!* Put away that dagger! Will you stab me?"

"Hold!" shouted Pedro.

Seizing the wooden bars, he tugged at them. They bent, but stayed in place. I grabbed them with both hands and we heaved together. The whole frame flew outward and I tumbled on my back. As I jumped up I saw Pedro go squirming through the opening.

The instant he got through I followed him, landing on hands and knees inside. As I rose I saw the Firefly Woman leap into the doorway beyond. Fear and anger both showed in her face. In her right hand glimmered her dagger.

Seeing Pedro bounding toward her, she realized instantly that her scheme had failed. With a scream of fury she sprang at him like a jungle-cat. She stabbed at his stomach. He slipped aside and the thrust missed him. His rifle-barrel smacked against her wrist. The knife flew from her hand to the floor.

Swiftly she stooped to recover it. But he blocked her, grabbed her, swung her up off the ground. She fought, kicked, tore at him with both hands; but he twisted his face downward, shielding his eyes from her nails. I was beside him now, and I caught up the dagger.

"I have it," I told him. "You can drop her."

But before he put her down he strode into that other room. There he caught her hands and held them, and as he let her down he commanded:

"Be still! You will only get yourself hurt. You can not harm us nor get away, and you had best stop trying."

She twisted and tugged, but could not free herself. So, though her eyes still blazed, she ceased struggling and stood breathing hard.

"Welcome back, friends!" cried the man's voice from a dim corner. "You come just in time to save me from being butchered."

We made out the gleam of teeth, the glint of eyes and the pallor of a sick white face. I turned back into the outer room, cut the hangings of one of the light-cages and brought it in with me. By the new light we saw a tall, fever-thinned young fellow lying on a rough bed. We saw, too, that he had not long to live.

"You came back and listened, is it not so?" he asked.

We nodded.

"Then you know us, and it is useless to try to deceive you further. A little while ago I dreaded to have you find me. Now I do not care. I am Manoel de Mello, of Rio, and this gentle companion of mine is Frances Andravery—or Senhora Francisca Azul, widow by her own deed. You know, of course, of the murder of her husband, Affonso Azul."

We nodded again. The truth was that we never had heard of this Azul or his murder; for Rio was many hundreds of miles from us, and the news of that city is not likely to reach the ears of jungle-workers at the head of the Amazon. Yet we knew he spoke truth, for we had heard him accuse her of the crime while we listened at the window, and even now she did not deny it. So, as I say, we let him think we knew all about it.

"And now what will you do with us?" he asked.

We looked at him thoughtfully. A few months ago he must have been a strong, active, handsome fellow. Now he was a wreck, too far gone to have a chance for life. We had no medicines, and we knew he would die before we could reach the headquarters of the *coronel* with him. More than this, our canoe was a light two-man craft, and it never would carry all four of us.

"Where is your canoe?" I asked.

He laughed as if the question were a ghastly joke.

"Canoe? Gone, weeks ago! We stole it when we were hard pressed on the Amazon, traveled in it until we found this dead town, and stopped here to hide and rest. Then one night when the water rose it floated away. We never found it. We have no canoe. I ask you again, what will you do with us?"

"I do not know," said Pedro slowly. "If we take you out it will be only to death. We are not police, and it is not for us to punish you. We are not doctors, and we can not cure you. We are not priests, and we can not save you. And I am much afraid, friend Manoel, that you will see few more dawns."

"You have it right," agreed Manoel. "There is little hope for me. And I am not afraid to die—I am glad to die, now that I know how cruel and false this woman is. But I do not want to die alone and deserted."

The woman spoke.

"It is as I said. It is useless to take you out. But these men will take me out, if only to punishment. Even that will be better than staying here."

Looking keenly at her, I guessed her thought: that in some way she would yet succeed in saving herself—perhaps by charming the young Englishmen, who we had said were our employers, and convincing them that we were liars and that she was a much wronged girl. So I decided to kill that idea.

"Perhaps we will take you out, *senhorita*—I mean *senhora*. But not to Tabatinga. We stay here until we have done all we can do for Manoel. Then you go with us to the headquarters of Coronel Nunes, our employer.

"The tale I told you was a joke. There are no young Englishmen at Tabatinga—at least none that I know—and we are not scouts but rubber-workers of the *coronel*. And the *coronel* is no young fool. He is old and shrewd, and you could neither beguile him nor deceive him."

My guess had been right. Her face writhed. With a sudden wrench she twisted her hands from Pedro's grip and sprang at me. I slipped her dagger into my belt at the back, where she could not reach it, and held her off. After fighting me a minute she stood still and began to curse me.

I had heard rough talk from women sometimes in the past, for the women of the frontier are not always choice in their language, especially when angered; but never, *senhores*, have I listened to such words from a woman's mouth as I heard then. No man could have called me such names and lived. But, since she was not a man, I could only stand and let her rave.

At length she choked with rage and could say no more. In keeping her away from me I had moved about so that my back was toward the sick man. Now I heard his voice again, and to my astonishment it was almost at my ear. Turning, I found that he had managed to drag himself up and stood supporting himself against the wall. His sunken eyes glittered.

"A sweet, dainty, lovable woman for men to throw away life and honor for, is she not?" he said. "Yet I have loved her—God, how I have loved her! Now I have nearly reached my end, and there is no escape for me. But for you, Francisca, there is still a way to avoid the prison and the shame awaiting you down the river. It is very simple."

His voice grew weak, and he swayed.

"Since this is the last thing I can do for you, Francisca, I will tell you—"

We could hardly hear him now. He seemed about to drop. But he moved his head, beckoning her closer.

"You will tell me what? Speak quickly."

Eagerly she stepped close to him. He straightened. His teeth flashed again. Something else flashed too—cold steel.

A scream broke from her. She staggered back, reeled, and fell.

Swiftly on the breast of her red gown spread a deeper red. Her white face grew whiter. She lay utterly still.

We whirled on Manoel. As we did so, he too dropped. Whether he stabbed himself before falling or collapsed from weakness and fell on the knife I do not know. But he struck on his face, and when we turned him over we found the dagger in his breast, driven in to the hilt.

It looked like Francisca's own dagger. I threw a hand to my belt. Her weapon was gone. Then I realized what he had done. While my back was toward him and both Pedro and I were looking at the furious woman, he had drawn on his last strength to rise, slip the knife from me and stand against the wall until he could lure her within reach. The dagger with which she had intended to silence him forever had done its work—but had found her own heart first.

"The simplest way," Manoel gasped. "No prison. No lonely death. We lived together—we die together. I go out with her blood on my hands. Yet I have been through hell for her. Perhaps the good God will have mercy on me."

"Perhaps he will, Manoel," Pedro echoed. "Truly, there is no hell like the one into which a woman can drag a man."

Manoel twisted once and was still.

We rose and gazed down at both of them. In Francisca's black hair, on her red gown and her white arms and throat the fireflies still gleamed bright and cold. From Manoel's haggard face the lines of pain and weakness were gone. Both slept the long sleep, freed forever from the fear and struggle and disgrace which were the only things left them in life.

"As he said, it was the simplest way," mused Pedro. "It is best for them and best for us. They themselves have finished what they began. Now there is only one thing we can do for them."

Stooping, he lifted her. I straightened Manoel and laid him back on his bed. Pedro lowered the girl beside him.

Then, taking with us the firefly cage, we went to the door, pulled it shut behind us, crossed the outer room, and crawled out through the window. Back down the path we went, found our canoe, and silently paddled back to our hammocks.

At dawn we returned. As she had said, there was a small window in that room where she and Manoel lay. Across it ran wooden bars like those at the front of the house. With our *machetes* we cut vines and creepers, wove them into the openings until they were tight, and plastered the whole frame thickly with clay.

Then we repaired the broken frame we had torn from the front window, put that also in place, and clayed it like the other. With its outer door still barred and its windows sealed, the last refuge of the Firefly and her lover had become their tomb.

One long look we gave at the dreary, silent town half-buried in the bush. Then we went down the path for the last time. As we stopped at our canoe Pedro whirled, his rifle up. Then he lowered it. Behind us was the black monkey.

"*Adeos, compadre,*" Pedro said soberly. "I am glad you did not get walled into that house, for we had forgotten you. Now we go. This is your town. We leave you here to live your own life, as we go out to live ours. Farewell."

We pushed off and paddled away, leaving the queer fellow watching us.

He may be there tonight, that monkey, snatching at fireflies in the gloom at the head of the cove and putting them on himself as he once saw his mistress do. But neither he nor I nor any of us will ever again hear that voice singing in the night:

> "Glitter, glitter, pretty firefly!
> Born but to dance and flash and die."

Nor will any of us ever again see that woman, driven from the lights of a far-off shore by her crime, decking herself with the only jewels left to her—the natural jewels of the jungle. And it is as well. For all fireflies, beautiful though they may be, are false, *senhores*—false and cold.

The Tucandeira

Take care, *senhor!*

Lift your hand from the rail! Quick!

Now you are safe. You did not see that big black ant crawling toward you, but you would soon have felt him. You would not have slept at all tonight, for your whole arm would have been full of keen, throbbing pain. Let me knock him to the deck and step on him. There, now he can do no harm.

He is a *tucandeira*—the biggest, fiercest and most terrible ant to be found in all our Brazilian jungle. My foot has smeared him, but he must be an inch and a half long, and you can guess how powerful his jaws were. Yet his bite, bad as it is, is not so much to be dreaded as the torment that comes afterward—a maddening pain caused by the poison he throws into your flesh.

What this poison may be I do not know; but I do know it is so strong that some of the wild Indians use *tucandeiras*, along with certain roots and bark, to make the tips of darts and arrows deadly. I know too that many people say the bites of four of these ants will kill a man

Yet I believed that it would take more than four of them to destroy the life of a strong man. You know how it is—one man may die from a thing that would only hurt another. And—well, let me tell you of something I once saw with my own eyes.

I was afloat in the flood-time, as I am now. But I was not sitting on the deck of a fine steamer like this, nor was I on my way down this great Amazon, with nothing to do but smoke and talk. Instead I was in a canoe, among the wild hills of the upper Javary region, speeding back toward the headquarters of old Coronel Nunes, my employer.

With me was a young comrade named Pedro, a rubber-worker like myself, who had been out with me on a long roving trip. We had met rough experiences, and now we had little food, few cartridges, and only one rifle; so that we did not wish to lose any time in reaching the end of our journey.

But we were not to end our trip as soon as we hoped to. Delay was not only waiting for us—it was coming to meet us.

Ahead of us was a rather nasty bend in the little flooded river we were following—a place where the water swirled against a steep cliff and was turned sharply away in a new direction. The stream had been washing against this cliff for so many years that it had eaten the stone inward, and the upper part now hung out over the current.

Under it the water sucked and boiled and whirled, making a place where it would be easy to capsize and hard to get out. We remembered it well, having had some difficulty there when we came up, and decided to go around it as fast as we could.

Just as we were making the turn, Pedro, up in the bow, yelled sharply. Another yell blended with his. Something struck us a thumping, glancing blow. We heeled over so suddenly that I almost went overboard. But the canoe stopped tilting, and I saved myself by a grab at its higher edge. Then we went whirling and bumping along the face of the cliff until an eddy swept us clear.

We were afoul of another canoe. It had struck us slantwise, slid along our side, and nearly tipped itself over as well as us. Both Pedro and the other man had done the same thing—seized the other's gunwale to save his own craft; and now, while their grip held, we were locked together as if by steel hooks. That was all that saved either boat.

Luckily our dugout was a stout one with solid sides, and the grinding against the rock did no real harm. As soon as we found we were not wrecked we did the usual thing—blamed the other man. I asked him if he was blind, and Pedro wanted to know if he thought this was his own private river. He promptly told us both to go to the devil.

He said it, though, with a little twitch of the lips, as if the whole thing were a joke. Then he added:

"Before we start expressing opinions as to each other's ancestry and so on, let's get ashore and pump ship. Then we can bawl each other out at our leisure."

That was sense, for both of us had taken in much water when we tipped. So we headed for the other shore, ran into a small hollow between hills, got out, and turned the water out of our boats. This was easy enough for us two, but harder for the stranger; for he was alone and had a good deal of stuff stowed away which had to be taken out first.

He asked no help, and at first we offered none. Then, knowing the collision was an accident, we grew ashamed of ourselves, and I stepped toward him to give him a hand at his work.

He straightened and looked me in the eye, and I stopped as suddenly as if he had drawn a gun. He had made no threatening move—though his right thumb was hooked over his belt, and below that hand hung a long revolver—nor had he said anything. It was his look that halted me; a cool, piercing look that warned me not to come too close.

He was a big man, as tall and straight as Pedro, and even wider across the chest. His hair, his pointed beard, and his straight eyebrows were so black that they seemed to shine, and his dark eyes also appeared to gleam as he watched me. His skin, though, was not swarthy. Without his healthy tan he would have been very fair.

I saw all this in a glance, and saw also why he held me off. We were strangers, who had come upon him suddenly, nearly thrown him overboard, and spoken in ugly fashion. More than that, we had recently been in fights, and bore some marks of them in plain sight. We were unshaven and ragged, and probably looked hard and rough.

He was not at all afraid, but he was wary, and I could not blame him. I recalled now that since he landed he had not once turned his back to us. He was no fool.

"If we can help you, *senhor*, we will gladly do so," I told him. "We are not so bad as we look, and we do not want anything of yours. We are *seringueiros* of Coronel Nunes, who have been out on a foolish cruise and are now returning as fast as we can. Probably you have heard of the *coronel*."

His eyes seemed to bore holes in me while I talked. Now he nodded.

"Are you Lourenço or Pedro?" he asked.

"Lourenço, *senhor*," I told him, much astonished. "My comrade is Pedro. How did you know us?"

"What is your last name?"

"Moraes," said I.

He nodded again, smiled, and unhooked the thumb from his belt.

"The *coronel* told me about you," he explained. "I've just spent a few days at his place. He said you fellows were out here somewhere, though he had no idea where you might be. You sure are a hard-looking pair of brigands, I'll say. But I might have expected that, after what the *coronel* said."

"What did he say, *senhor*?" I grinned.

"He said you were a couple of rambling scamps who were quite likely to go poking into —— if you thought you would find it interesting. And he said if you did go there the devil would have to step lively or get his tail twisted."

We all laughed.

"I am afraid the *coronel* made you think us to be eaters of fire," said Pedro. "We are really peaceable men. Are you American, *senhor*, or English?"

"Half and half. My name's Locke. First name, Douglas. Ancestry, English and Scotch. Born in England, raised in the States. Been hopping all around the world for the last ten years, and got so used to moving that I couldn't stop now if I wanted to. I don't know where I'm going, and I'm here because I'm here. Now if you gents want to lend a hand with this bally tub I'll let you."

So we helped him remove his equipment and drain the boat. It was a big craft, and almost too heavy for one man to handle—indeed, a smaller man than he could not have managed it at all in swift water. We found, too, that it was quite heavily loaded, and that he seemed to have much more food and other things than he needed. This appeared to be poor judgment; but after we finished the work, squatted and smoked, and told each other more of ourselves, we found that he had good reason for a large boat and many supplies.

He had come from the Ucayali, and intended to go in this craft all the way down the Amazon, paddling up any tributary stream where he thought he might find anything strange and new. Before leaving the Ucayali country he had been scouting about between that river and the Huallaga for a big company which intended to apply for a great oil concession there. This he had done until he tired of that region, when he outfitted this boat, hired Indian paddlers, and started on his long journey of more than two thousand miles.

As the Indians would go only a certain distance from their homes, he had changed crews several times, and the last change had been a bad one. At Loreto* he had been able to get only two—"bad actors," as he called them, who carried knives. When he decided to turn southward and explore this region the Loreto men became surly, and the farther they went the uglier they grew. Finally, two days before he met us, they tried to kill him. So after that he had to paddle alone.

He did not say what had become of those two cutthroats, and we did not ask. He saw us glance at his revolver, and he laughed, showing a double row of big white teeth.

"Say, I like you jiggers!" he said. "You know when not to ask questions. You've knocked around some yourselves."

We nodded. Then we told of what we had seen and done here on this wild river. We spoke of caves of vampires where we had been in danger of death; of a crazed Indian woman who lived in a hollow tree and poisoned all who came near it by thorns set in the ground; of a human ant-eater who lived with a monkey, dug gold, and killed three men who had shot that monkey and would have taken the gold. We told of savages who shrank men's heads, and of an old Scotchman in armor who had led us into battle against them.

We described how we had fought a whole village of drunken *caboclos* in order to free a girl from a cage where she was kept by her brutal father. Last, we spoke of a wonderful voice we had heard singing in the night beside a bay full of fireflies, and how we had found the singer to be a murderess.

"I'll say you gents have had some trip," said Senhor Locke, "or else you have the finest imaginations I've met up with."

"Do you mean, *senhor*, that we are liars?" Pedro asked softly.

"Ho ho! Not at all, *hombre*. Loosen up your grip on that rifle. Don't go on the prod until somebody says something. And let me give you a friendly tip: Start anything with me and I may bite your face plumb off. I'm hasty that way."

---

* Region of Peru encompassing the northernmost third.

"It would take strong jaws to do that."

"Which same I have."

He grinned again, and a devil danced in his dark eyes. "Always pleased to demonstrate."

And he reached his left hand to a bush beside him, put a branch as thick as a finger into his mouth, and bit. Then he spat out a piece of wood.

I picked it up. It was cut through as if by a knife.

"Easy!" he laughed. "Try it yourself."

Pedro tried. He stepped over to the same bush and bit the same branch. He bit so hard that I could see the veins in his temples swell. Then he ground his teeth. Finally, angered, he yanked at the bush.

"Don't tear it up by the roots," the black-bearded man snickered. "Don't chew it, either. Just bite."

Pedro let go, spat out shreds of bush, and rubbed a bleeding lip. The branch was deeply dented, but not bitten off.

"Your jaws are better than mine," he admitted.

"Quite so. Let's see you try this one."

Rising, he stepped over to a tree with low limbs, picked one at the height of his mouth, clipped off some leaves with a knife, and set his teeth into the clear space. Then he lifted his feet from the ground and hung there, held up by the grip of his jaws.

For a minute or two he stayed in that position before dropping his feet. As he let go he said easily:

"It's really harder than the other. It gets your neck muscles too, you see."

"I see," said Pedro. "And I am not foolish enough to try it. I may want to eat again after a while, and how could I do it with a broken jaw and no teeth? *Por Deos, senhor*, you can bite like a *tucandeira!*"

"I happen to be good at it," he said, as we turned back toward the canoes. "Probably you have some stunt of your own that would make me look foolish. But it isn't gun-play, old-timer, so don't—*chkk!*"

He choked and stumbled sidewise. I caught a glimpse of something around his neck. Then something flicked down past my eyes and yanked at my stomach so hard that I fell backward.

I turned as I fell, trying to put one hand to the ground and draw my *machete* with the other. But my arms were fastened to my body. I fell flat. Shrill yells sounded. Living bodies jumped on me. Something warm and heavy struck my head, forced my face into the dirt, and held it there.

Shots cracked out—six fast shots, followed by clicks of an empty gun. The weight on my head rolled off and thumped down beside me. I tried to heave myself up, but could not. So I twisted my face upward and looked.

Beside me was a naked Indian, lying very quiet. He had been the weight on my head—had sat on it until shot off. I tried to squirm over farther, but the other men holding me forced me down. All I could see was a mass of bush and a big bare foot that stepped within an inch of my nose, then lifted and disappeared. I could hear other feet swishing around me and sounds of a struggle—gasps and blows. Then everything was quiet except for grunting voices.

Strong hands forced my own hands up behind my back and tied my wrists. I felt my *machete* drawn from my belt. The men on me got off. I scrambled to my knees and then to my feet.

Pedro and Senhor Locke were on the ground, both tied. The American's face was red and bloated from choking, but he was still trying to fight. One booted foot shot up and caught a savage in the groin, and the man yelped and fell backward. But others jumped on his legs again and pinned them down, and he could only wrench his shoulders uselessly.

I started toward him, but stopped short, held by the rope around my stomach. Then I looked around at the men who had caught us.

They numbered about a dozen, and, for *bárbaros*, they were fine-looking men. They were of medium height, well muscled, beardless, very smooth-skinned, and naked except for belts and mats of woven fibers and bark. Their faces were grim, but not so brutal as those of many wild men I had seen.

This cheered me, for I thought they probably were not cannibals. So, having been in the hands of *bárbaros* before without suffering any serious harm—though that was mostly because I was lucky enough to escape in time—I decided to put on a cheerful face and make the best of it.

"You had better stop fighting, Senhor Tucandeira," I said.

Why I called him Tucandeira instead of Locke I do not know—the name came naturally from my tongue.

"We are helpless, and we may get better treatment by not resisting further now. Later on we may have a chance to fight again."

He coughed and made a hoarse noise, trying to talk. Soon he managed to make his throat work as it should.

"Roped!" he snorted. "Roped and hogtied! We're a bunch of bally short-horns, I'll say! But I salivated a couple of 'em anyhow. Didn't hit you too, did I?"

I told him no. Glancing around, I saw two of our captors dead on the ground and a third holding a bleeding shoulder.

"Glad of it. They had a hangman's hold on my neck and I had to shoot blind. Hullo, I winged another in the shoulder! Not so bad—three hits out of six shots, and me being lynched at the moment. Now it's their turn, and I reckon they'll make us prance around some, what?"

"If you mean that they will torture us, I do not think so," I assured him.

"Our Indians usually do not torture, but kill quickly."

Then I grinned, though I did not feel very funny, and added:

"You came here to see things, *senhor*. Now you are seeing them."

Whether he answered I do not know. One of the *bárbaros*, who seemed to be the leader, stepped in front of me and looked me in the face. He had big staring eyes, and in them was a queer expression which I could not read.

For what seemed a very long time he stood there looking at me without once blinking. I stared straight back. At length I smiled and spoke to him, asking him what he meant to do with us.

He did not understand. I tried again and again, speaking slowly in Portuguese and Spanish, then in the Tupi *lingoa geral*, and finally using bits of other Indian dialect I had picked up at different times. The first two meant nothing to him, and he scowled as if he did not like their sound. The Indian words made his face brighten, but I saw that he did not understand these either.

As my hands were tied, I could not make signs with them, and thus I had no way at all of talking with him. So I turned to Pedro.

"I have tried everything I know," I said. "Can you speak any tongue I have not used?"

Pedro, who was sitting quietly and watching, began to grunt and click his tongue in some sort of strange language. The big-eyed leader left me and went to him. Soon he made several noises as if trying to answer. Pedro grunted away more rapidly, but the wild man was silent, Finally he turned away.

"I thought he understood, but he does not," said my comrade. "I did not understand him."

The leader said something to his men. One of them, holding the noose of twisted fibers around my body, pulled on it and moved his head toward the American. We stepped over beside Senhor Locke. Pedro and another wild man came also, and we three prisoners stood there in a row, each held in a tight noose. The other *bárbaros* picked up everything belonging to us, and four of them also lifted the two dead men by shoulders and feet. The ropes tugged at us again, and we filed away into the bush.

Noticing that they were carrying their dead, I guessed that we would not go far. I was partly right. We went only a short distance between the hills before we stopped and all the burdens were laid on the ground. But we had not reached any place where we were to stay.

Several of the men picked up the two bodies and went away. The rest of us waited. After a time the absent *bárbaros* returned without the dead men. We fell into line once more, and now the real march began.

All the rest of that day we trudged on through the jungle. Nobody spoke. There was little use in talk, since we had no idea of what lay ahead and could not learn anything from our captors.

I noticed that the wild men did not seem very hostile toward Pedro and me, but that they treated Senhor Locke more roughly. If we stumbled, nothing came of it. If he stumbled, the wild man holding his rope yanked savagely at it; and every time the others looked at him they scowled. This, I thought, was because he had killed two of their mates and crippled a third. But I was to learn that there was another reason for it—a reason much older and born in them.

At last we stopped for the night. Then Senhor Locke spoke.

"What do you think of these people?"

We told him we did not know what to think; that they were not like any wild people we had ever met, and we could not guess why we were led on instead of being killed.

"I can answer that last part of it," he said. "They're taking us to their chief, I'll bet. Old Googoo-Eyes yonder is the head of the party, but he doesn't act like a heap big Injun chief and they don't treat him like one. I notice they seem to have it in for me in particular. Any idea why?"

We had no idea.

"Well, I'm getting a hunch. Guess I'll play it and see how it works."

The one he called Googoo was standing near, listening and looking at him unpleasantly. Senhor Locke spoke to him slowly in a tongue I never had heard. An astonished expression came into the leader's face. After staring a minute he answered.

The face of the Tucandeira wrinkled as if he did not quite understand, but he spoke again. Again Googoo replied. Others of the *bárbaros* came closer and stood looking much interested.

I saw that the American had hit on a language that meant something to them. He grinned, squatted, and moved his head for Googoo to do likewise. Then he talked more in the same slow, careful way.

The talk went on for some time. I could not get any hint of what they said, or even of what tongue they spoke—it meant nothing at all to me. I could perceive, though, that they were having no easy time of it, and that each often had to repeat what he had said. Finally the Indian shook his head, said something more, arose and left us.

"Blessed is he who playeth a hunch," mused the Tucandeira. "Fellow-pilgrims, I have broken through the wall between them and us. They speak a sort of Quichua."

We stared and said nothing.

"You no savvy Quichua? It's the language that was spoken in Peru in the days of the Incas, before the Spaniards came. For that matter, it's still used—there are oodles of Quichuans scattered around the country. Some of them are quite civilized and some are not. These jiggers are emphatically not.

"There were all kinds of them even in Inca times, including a lot of independent chaps over here in the woods who wouldn't let the Incas themselves boss them. Maybe our chums here are some of that bunch, or perhaps they are descendants of the Incas who lit out for the timber after the conquest and sort of backslid.

"Anyhow, the language they speak is either very good or very bad Quichua—I don't know which, because all the Quichua I know is some I picked up over in the *montaña*, and it may be rotten. I couldn't get very close to them, but I learned two pertinent things—that they hate Spaniards, and that I'm out of luck."

"In what way do you lack luck, *senhor*?" I asked.

"They think I'm a Spaniard. My hair, eyes, and beard are so black they won't believe I'm anything else. Can't blame them for that—I've known Spaniards themselves to make the same mistake.

"These jaspers have been hating Spaniards for nearly four hundred years, and now they've caught a goat. Weather for tomorrow—unsettled, probably squalls."

"But can you not tell them you are American?" suggested Pedro.

"Sure. I did. They don't even know what North America is! They're bally boobs from away back. I'm a Spaniard to them, and that's all there is to it. But cheer up! You fellows are not in the same boat with me. They seem to realize that you're different—probably they know a Brazilian when they see him. You'll probably get a better deal."

"You have it wrong, Senhor Locke," Pedro said stiffly. "We are in your boat. We shall stay in it until we all get out or all go down. Am I right, Lourenço?"

I said, rather warmly, that he was. And the Tucandeira at once told us that we were a pair of fools.

"If you get a chance, beat it," he urged. "You don't owe me anything. I got you into this, anyhow. If I hadn't bumped you and brought you ashore you'd be away down the river now. Take care of yourselves, and don't bother about me."

"Fools we may be, but not cowards," retorted Pedro. "We three are partners until this thing ends. Now say no more about that. Where are they taking us?"

"As I said before, I like you jiggers," laughed Locke. "I don't know where we're going, but we get there tomorrow. I asked Googoo to untie our hands, but he refused. Suppose we may as well try to sleep a while, what?"

We did sleep as well as we could. To me it seemed that the night would never end, for my wrists were so firmly tied that I did not rest comfortably. When day came again I saw that my companions also were hollow-eyed, and we all were stiff when we got up.

"I hate to ask any favors of that goggle-eyed billiken," grumbled Senhor Locke, "but I'm mortally tired of these bush handcuffs."

"Bite them off," smiled Pedro.

"Believe me, I would if I could get at 'em—and then I'd spit 'em into his face. But it takes some contortionist to get his teeth around to the small of his back, and I'm no boneless wonder. I say, Googoo old chappie, come here a minute. I want to kiss you good morning."

Googoo did not know what he said, of course, but he saw us looking at him and came closer. The American spoke again in the Quichua language. The Indian scowled, but slowly nodded. After searching us and taking everything from our pockets, he called another wild man, who came with my *machete* and cut the cords on our wrists.

Our hands dropped to our sides like lumps of wood. We moved our arms, bent our wrists, and worked our fingers to make the blood run more freely. While we did this Googoo spoke in a warning tone.

"He says we shall soon reach the end of this hike," said the Tucandeira, "and that if we try to fight or run we shall be killed. Let's not start anything. I'm agog to see what sort of dump we're headed for."

He and the leader talked again, and his black brows lifted.

"The plot thickens. Somewhere ahead of us is a female woman, and she's going to have something to say about us. Dog-gone the bally luck! Rudyard was right."

"Who is Rudyard?" I asked him.

"Rudyard Kipling, a fellow who sometimes writes poems. When he does he says a mouthful. A while ago he said that 'the female of the species is more deadly than the male.' He said two mouthfuls that time. A squaw is worse than a buck eight days in the week. I told you I was out of luck."

Googoo made another set of noises. Locke frowned and made him repeat. When the Indian had spoken three times the American shook his head.

"I don't get you at all, old kid. Sorry I didn't study my Quichua more."

Patiently the Indian talked with his hands. He pointed to the hair and eyes of us in turn, then shook his head. After that he pointed to his own hair and eyes, and again shook his head.

"Something about the woman and hair and eyes. Guess he means she hasn't any. Old as the hills and blind as a bat."

Then he laughed.

"Say, can you fellows cough like a jaguar?"

For answer Pedro made a noise so much like a jaguar that we all jumped.

"Fine! Say, we'll fix the old she-devil before she can think up any dirty work to put on to us. If she's blind she can't see us, of course. You fellows make a racket like jaguars, I'll hiss like a snake—and she'll drop dead. Very simple, what?"

We laughed. Googoo scowled.

"He knows we're laughing about the woman, and it makes him sore," said the *senhor*. "Better wipe off our grins, maybe. I don't want my hands tied again, and I'd rather not get rough until I've had a look at what's ahead. As I said before, I'm all agog."

We ate and resumed our tramp. Each of us still was held by the noose around his body, and *bárbaros* with clubs watched us closely as we traveled on. The way led through the same broken country, but the trees were big and the undergrowth thin, so that we walked easily. At last we heard dogs barking, and our captors pushed on a little faster toward the noise.

Soon after this we came into a cleared place where houses stood. I had expected to see a big *maloca*, or tribal house, where all slept together; but there was none. Instead there were small houses of mud all around the clearing with a larger one in the middle. Men, women, children and dogs came to look at us as we passed, but none of them crowded us except the dogs, and a few kicks taught them to keep away.

We went straight on toward the big house in the center. A few feet from its low door we stopped.

Our guard laid all our property except our weapons in a heap on the ground. Googoo swung up to the doorway, halted outside, and spoke. A man's voice answered.

Googoo stepped back and gave an order to the men holding our ropes. The nooses were taken away and we stood unbound. Then we all waited.

A figure appeared in the opening, stooped, came through and straightened up. We saw at once that this was the chief. He was a man of middle age, taller than any of the others, straight as a blow-gun, steady-eyed and calm of manner.

Like his men, he wore only belt and mat, but these were broader and woven of finer material than theirs, and decorated with small bright feathers. His face was ornamented with two big blue feathers set into his nose, slanting upward and outward like a strange mustache.

He stood quietly, with arms folded, looking at each of us in turn while Googoo talked. His gaze rested longest on the Tucandeira, and his eyes grew narrow. He, too, believed our companion to be a Spaniard. Yet he said nothing until Googoo finished his report about us. Then, slowly and gravely, he spoke to Senhor Locke.

In the same solemn tone the American answered him. He talked for some time, partly with his tongue and partly with his hands. Once he made a slow movement of both arms as if speaking of something very large and wide. Once he pointed to us and shook his head. Before he finished his face grew ugly, as if he talked of something hateful. Then he moved as if trampling on something and spat on the ground. When he was through he folded his arms like the chief and stood looking steadily into his eyes.

The chief seemed thoughtful and a little doubtful. He said nothing. I thought he was decided what to do with us; and though I held my head high and stood as if unafraid, I was a little nervous, for I felt that he was unfriendly. But before he spoke again another thing happened.

Voices came to us—merry young voices somewhere behind the house. We heard quick footfalls too, and calls and laughter, as if girls were playing with one another. Then around a corner dashed several young women. As they saw us they stopped short.

"*Nossa Senhora!*" gulped Pedro.

"I'll be ——!" muttered the Tucandeira.

I said nothing. I was too much surprized for words.

The girl in the lead, *senhores*, was white!

Not only was she white, but she was strikingly beautiful. Her hair was wonderful—a rich, glossy red, and so long and thick that it seemed like a mantle of flame, rippling down almost to her knees. Her deep gray eyes were still full of laughter, and her little red mouth kept its smile as she looked us over. She was breathing fast from her running, her face was flushed, and her whole body glowed pink through the light tan on her smooth skin.

Unlike the Indian girls with her, she wore a little clothing; for she had a skirt of feathers reaching to her knees, and around her breasts was a wide girdle of some bright blue material. Her throat, too, was encircled by a necklace of small, irregular globes of gold.

This, I felt, must be the woman of whom Googoo had spoken. Instead of telling us she was bald and blind he had been trying to show us that her hair was not black like ours and that her eyes were neither black nor brown. The memory of what the American had said came to me and made me grin.

"I do not hear you hissing like a snake, *senhor*," I said. "And Pedro has forgotten to make his noise of a jaguar."

Senhor Locke told me I was a "boob" and asked me to shut up. But Pedro, still looking at her, laughed. She did not like it. Her face and throat flushed still more, her eyes snapped, and she stamped a little foot on the ground. Then she spoke to the chief, and her tone was angry. At once the men around us seemed to become hostile.

Before the chief could answer, though, the Tucandeira bowed gracefully to her and talked again. She looked surprised at the sound of her own language coming from his mouth. Then she glanced at us and laughed.

Lifting her hands, she covered her head as if to show us how she would look with no hair, then put her hands before her eyes. Our companion had explained our mistake in expecting to find her an old hag, and she thought it very funny.

The *bárbaros* guarding us grinned too, and I saw a slight smile at the corners of the mouth of the chief himself. I felt, though, that they were pleased only because she was, and that if she had remained angry it might have gone hard with us.

"I'd advise you jiggers to go slow on the wit and humor," Senhor Locke said. "This little lady seems to be the whole works, and she was sore as a boil when she thought you were laughing at her. Be meek and mild, like me."

Then the chief said something to the girl, and she looked at us again more seriously. Her eyes rested only a moment on me, longer on my good-looking comrade Pedro, longest on the black-bearded man who spoke her tongue.

At length she replied in a rather doubtful tone, as if not able to decide something just then. The tall Indian nodded slightly, gave directions to Googoo, turned his back on us and went inside. After another long look at us, the red-haired girl followed him.

Now that she was gone, I glanced around at the others. All were maidens except one older woman who had come up behind them, and all were Indians. Their hair was damp, and I judged that the party had been bathing in some private pool.

As we looked at them they giggled and went away toward the smaller houses. Googoo touched my arm, motioned with his head, and led us to a mud house where, he told us, we were to stay.

Everything we owned, except our weapons, was brought there also and left on the floor. Pedro's rifle, the rifle and revolver of Senhor Locke, and our *machetes* had been put into the house of the chief. Two men were left as guards at our door, one armed with a big club and the other with a bow. Googoo said something, then went away with the others.

"He says food will be brought," explained Locke. "Nothing for us to do now but sit around and wait for the chow. Say, stand in the doorway a minute and let me run through this pile of junk. I think they overlooked my pocket-knife."

We did as he said, filling up the doorway, talking, and pointing across the clearing. The guards looked that way to see what drew our attention. Soon the Tucandeira spoke again.

"All right, I got it. These jiggers didn't understand it because it's closed. It has a four-inch blade that might come in handy. Here, Lourenço, put your hand behind you."

I did so, and felt the knife come into my palm.

"Slip it into your pocket. Oh, don't worry about me—I'm heeled. I've got a sweet little automatic inside my shirt, under my left arm, where they never thought to look. Now let's get outside and smoke and look innocent."

The guards scowled and lifted their weapons as we stepped out. But we showed them that we only wanted to rest our backs against the wall, and they made no trouble. Squatting and smoking, we talked things over.

First, the Tucandeira told us what he had said to the chief. He had explained that he was not of Peru, but of a great country far to the north, and that he had come across a wide water to reach this place. Then, knowing that the chief felt unfriendly toward him because of the idea that he was a Spaniard, he had tried to help us by saying we were not countrymen of his but men of Brazil, and that we were not even his companions, but that we had met on the river just before our capture.

"You fellows think you're in my boat," he went on, "but I've got something to say about who rides with me when I'm heading into the rapids, and don't you forget it. If I'm due to hit the rocks that's no reason why you should drown, too. Get me?"

We made no protest. The thing was done now, and it was useless to wrangle over it.

"What were you trampling and spitting on?" I asked.

"Spaniards," he laughed. "I played that card clear across the boards. I told him my country fought the Spaniards twenty years ago and mopped up the earth with them. That's true.

"But I made it stronger by telling him my people still hated all Spaniards, and that whenever we met one there was a holy riot; that we kicked their pants off and stamped their faces into the mud. That's not true at all, of course. But it's up to me to convince him I'm no Spaniard myself, and the best way to put that over is to let him think I hate 'em as much as he does.

"I don't know whether he fell for it or not. But what interests me more is the mystery of little Red-Bird. How the Sam Hill did she ever get here? She's as white as I am, and if she isn't American or English by blood I'll eat crow. Yet she speaks only Quichua, apparently, and she seems as thoroughly a native as the copper-colored girls. What do you fellows make of it?"

We made nothing of it, although we argued until women came with food for us. The food was good and there was plenty of it—a big clay pot of thick meat stew, broiled fish wrapped in large leaves, bananas, and nuts. We ate so much that we were sluggish afterward, but we were not too sleepy to talk. We asked the American what had been said between the chief and the girl when she looked at us so thoughtfully.

"I didn't quite get that," he admitted. "The old boy seemed to be asking her whether one of us would do, and she didn't know. We've been roped and dragged here for some purpose, but I can't dope out what it is. There's Googoo now. I say, old squirt, come here a minute."

The big-eyed Indian, seeing him beckon, came to us. The two talked for some time. Googoo smiled a little, but his answers did not seem to be very satisfactory. After a while a man came out of the chief's house and called to him, and he went at once to the doorway and disappeared inside.

"He says the girl is the Golden One," the Tucandeira told us. "She came to the chief years ago when she was very small. The chief was then a young man and had just become chief through the death of his father. It was the time when turtles lay their eggs, and all this tribe had gone to a big sandy *praia*, on a river west of here, to get these eggs.

"The chief went away alone to bathe, and while he was doing this a great turtle covered with gold arose in the water before him with the Golden One sitting in its back. It came straight to him, and the little girl jumped off and up into the chief's arms. Then the golden turtle sank and was not seen again. So the chief brought the Golden One home with him, and she has grown up as his daughter and bosses everybody, including the chief himself.

"That's Googoo's yarn. Of course that golden turtle stuff is all bunk invented by the chief, but Googoo believes it, and no doubt everybody else does. But I think the rest of it is partly true—the chief found the little girl at that time and place, and she sure does seem to be the big noise around here. And she is to decide what happens to us.

"Googoo sidestepped when I tried to pump him on that point. All he would do was to grin and say that what is to be will be. Here he comes again."

Googoo approached and spoke. The Tucandeira rose.

"Come on, you chaps. We're invited to attend another powwow."

We walked into the house of the chief, finding him sitting in a hammock. The Golden One was beside him, gazing steadily at us and unsmiling. When we stood in a row before him the chief spoke to me.

I showed him I did not understand. Then he addressed Pedro, with the same result. He sat then for a moment watching Senhor Locke. The American turned to us.

"He wants to know just where you come from. I know you work for Coronel Nunes, but where are your homes?"

We told him, and he repeated this in Quichua. Then he kept on talking, and as I could not tell what he was saying I glanced around the place. It had a palm partition with a doorway leading into another room, and against that palm wall I saw something that worried me.

Behind the chief, leaning in a row near one corner, were our guns—and several others. All except ours were very rusty. Counting these, I found that there were six: four repeating rifles of the kind commonly used in our jungle, and two "trade" guns of large bore. On the floor beside them lay our *machetes* and the American's revolver.

Six men with guns had been here before us. The guns still were here. What had become of the men?

While I was thinking of this, Senhor Locke stopped speaking. The chief gazed at each of us again. Then he moved his head toward me and spoke to the Golden One.

For a moment she and I looked into each other's eyes. I thought of what a wonderfully beautiful girl she was, and perhaps my face showed this; for she laughed very prettily and made a little teasing mouth at me. But then she shook her head, and I could see that she was saying, "No." The chief made a sign with one hand, and Googoo stepped out of the house.

Pedro's turn was next. She smiled at him too, but again said, "No." Then she and Senhor Locke stood looking at each other for a much longer time. And I was much surprized to see that the Golden One became confused.

A slow blush came into her cheeks, and her gaze dropped. She breathed quickly, her breast quivering as it rose and fell. She half-turned as if to go away, then faced us again and raised her eyes to his as timidly as any shy young Indian maid. When she spoke she hesitated, and her voice was so low we could hardly hear it.

The chief looked astonished and annoyed. He granted a few words and moved a thumb toward Pedro. At once she recovered herself. Her eyes snapped, and she told the chief something in a decided tone.

The Indian's eyes went back and forth between Pedro and Senhor Locke. Though I did not know just what this was all about, I could see that a choice was to be made between my two companions; that the chief favored Pedro, while the Golden One wanted the American; and that I was out of it.

The light sound of bare feet at the door made us turn and look. Googoo had come back, and six other men with him. All were armed, all looked grim, and all watched the chief as if expecting orders. I slipped a hand into the pocket where that big clasp-knife lay.

"Looks like a squall," said the Tucandeira softly. "If they start anything I'll plug the chief. You chaps hurdle his hammock and grab your guns."

Glancing at him, I saw that his shirt was unbuttoned and the tips of his right fingers were inside it.

The chief sat still and argued with the girl. She stamped a foot and answered sharply. He sighed. An instant later my arms were clutched from behind. Too late I saw that the chief, without raising his hands from his knees, had lifted two fingers to show that Pedro and I were to be seized.

I kicked backward, wrenched myself out of the hands holding me and jumped for the corner where the guns stood. But I collided with the chief, who had risen and now swept his wiry arms around me. I trampled on his bare feet, tried to throw him and get past; but I might as well have tried to push away the crushing loop of a boa.

Hands clamped my wrists again from behind, and though I plunged and strained I could neither break free nor draw the knife. Then some man at my back got an arm around my throat and choked me until I fell.

When my head cleared again I was lying back against the wall, and two wild men were squatting on my hands with all their weight. Pedro, exhausted, was sprawling on the floor with three badly mauled *bárbaros* holding him down. The sixth Indian stood between us with a club raised as if only waiting for a word to crush our skulls. Googoo stood between Senhor Locke and the chief, protecting the tribal ruler with his own body, and the Golden One had twined herself around the American and was trying to hold down his gun hand, in which he gripped a flat pistol.

Later I learned that only my jump toward the chief saved his life. I had leaped between him and the American, who had drawn his pistol and barely escaped shooting me in the back. Instantly the girl had thrown herself on him to protect the man who was a father to her, and after that there was such a whirling tangle of struggling men that he could not fire without danger of hitting me or Pedro.

Not one of the *bárbaros* had attacked him. Now he snapped out a question and a command. The girl answered in a pleading way. He jerked his head toward us and repeated his order, adding something else in a milder tone. She took her arms from him and stepped back, watching him. He slipped his pistol into a pocket and stood with hands empty. Then she turned and gave an order to the wild men holding us. They looked at her as if they thought her crazed, then turned their eyes to the chief, who seemed as calm as ever. He and the Golden One talked, the chief quietly and the girl excitedly, and he nodded to the men. Slowly they arose and left us free.

"Take it easy, fellows," Senhor Locke advised us. "I think we'll come through without anymore rough stuff. I'm getting the hang of this thing now."

We arose, set our backs to the wall, and breathed. Our American comrade began talking to the chief, pointing at us and shaking his head. After a time the chief spoke curtly to Googoo and his men. Looking surprized, they went outdoors.

The chief quietly sat down and listened to further things said by Senhor Locke. A long talk between them followed. The Golden One became shy again, standing with her gaze on the floor, glancing up quickly now and then and blushing as she met the eye of the black-bearded man.

Suddenly, at something the chief said, she paled, stared at the Tucandeira, opened her lips, then changed her mind and said nothing. Soon after that Senhor Locke nodded and turned to us.

"Come on, let's go," he said.

"Where?" I asked.

"Back to our shack. Everything's fixed up until tomorrow. Googoo and his gang will ride herd on us, but outside of that we're as free as if we were in jail."

Before we left, though, he put out his right hand to the Golden One. She took it, and they stood silent, looking deep into each other's eyes. They made the most striking pair I have ever seen, *senhores*—the man, white of skin and black of hair, square-jawed and strong and clean-limbed, and the princess of the tribe with her flaming hair and wide eyes, her dainty figure, and her clear skin glowing pink above and below her brilliant feather-dress and girdle. He smiled and spoke softly to her, and as he released her hand she looked both happy and afraid.

At the door of our own house the two guards were waiting for us. They had been among those whom we fought in the house of the chief, and they showed marks of the struggle; but their faces now were like wood, and they gave no sign of either friendliness or enmity as we passed between them.

"Well, gents, a merry time has been had by all, and now I reckon you want to know what it's all about," said the Tucandeira. "So I'll give you an earful. Boiled down, this is the situation:

"Our little friend, the Golden One, has reached the age when, according to the ideas of these people, she should take a man. In fact, she's well past that age, for I understand that the Amazon Indians mate at fourteen or even younger, while she must be at least seventeen. Up in my country that would be considered pretty young, but of course a girl matures quicker down here. Anyhow, the chief has felt—and perhaps she herself has—that it's about time she made some chap happy or miserable, according to the luck of the game.

"But the trouble was to find the man. She has flatly refused to hook up with any of the young sprigs in this social set. Can't blame her for that, either. She realizes she's white and far superior to any of them, even though she's known only their kind of life since she was a kiddie, and she refuses to become the squaw of any copper-skin.

"The chief is a wise old skate, and he understands. So he's ordered his men to rope in every white or near-white man they run across, bring him here with as little damage as possible, and let the little lady give him the once-over.

"Up till now they've drawn blanks. Several men have come and gone—and I've got a fat hunch that they didn't go far after they left here. They left their guns behind, as you probably noticed. Besides, you fellows say you never heard of these people, and if any of the chaps who were here got out again they sure would have talked, and the yarn would have gone around for hundreds of miles. They didn't suit the Golden One, and so they were just taken out and disposed of, or else my guess is wrong.

"I don't suppose it ever entered her pretty head that she was sending those fellows to death, but that's about what it came to. We'd be on our way to the same port right now, only she seems to be—er—slightly interested."

"She is more than interested, *senhor*," said Pedro. "You are the man she has been waiting for. I am not a woman's man myself, but I have met a few and I can read the signs. And I thank you, *senhor*, for saving us. I can see now that the one you call Googoo, and his men, were about to drag us away and crush our heads."

"Well, since you mention it, that's about the size of it. But forget that gratitude stuff—we're all in the same boat after all. The next move in the game is this: I'm elected to do a little stunt tomorrow just to prove that I'm worthy to be the Golden One's man. The chief can't get that Spaniard idea out of his head, and if the choice were left with him he'd pick you, Pedro, for the girl's partner. But she can't see it that way, so he figures to make me prove I'm a man before the wedding bells ring out. I don't know just what the stunt is, but he calls it the test of the *tucandeira*."

We glanced swiftly at each other and back at him. My skin began to prickle and crawl.

"Judging from your squirmy expressions, I reckon the test is rather unpleasant, what? I noticed the Golden One looked sort of upset about it too. I know bally well what a *tucandeira* is, of course. Do I have to let one of them bite me?"

"Not only one of them, *senhor*, but many," I told him. "I have never seen this test, but I have heard of it, for it is used by some of the Indian tribes of our river country. When a young man would take a wife he must put his arms into a cylinder in which many of those ants have been kept without food until they are even more savage than usual. If he can endure the torment he is considered fit to live with a woman."

"Ouch!" he muttered.

Slowly he made a cigaret, and slowly he smoked it.

"But that seems impossible," he objected when the cigaret was dead. "I have been bitten once by one *tucandeira*, and it put me in agony. I have heard that four *tucandeiras* can kill a man. How can any man be bitten many times and live?"

I could not answer this, nor could Pedro. We all squatted there for some time without speaking. Finally the American said:

"It may be possible after all. Perhaps the ants used are not all *tucandeiras*—they may be mostly other ants with a few of those bad fellows mixed in. Otherwise there are only two ways I can figure it.

"In the first place, the bite of friend *tucandeira* hurts like the devil. Death can be caused by too much pain, even without poison. The *tucandeira* gives you pain and poison too.

"Now this matter of pain depends altogether on your nerves. An Indian's nerves are nowhere near as sensitive as those of highly civilized folks, and maybe that gives him greater endurance, simply because he doesn't feel the same amount of pain a white man would.

"And as for the poison—well, these Indians have been living among these ants for hundreds of years. At one time or another they or their ancestors have been bitten a good many times, and no doubt they've acquired some immunity to the poison. The upshot of all this is that your jungle Indian can live through this *tucandeira* test when it would knock a white man dead. I bet that's the answer. Sounds reasonable, what?"

"You may have it right," I agreed. "But that only makes it worse for you. You are a white man, and your fathers have not been bitten by these horrible things. And to speak plainly, *senhor*, I do not believe you will be given any false *tucandeiras* in your test. They will all be real ones."

"Which means that they will kill me," he nodded, "unless I can dope out some way to beat the game. Cheerful old joker, that chief. Do you jiggers know any antidote to that ant-juice?"

We thought, and after a time an idea came to me.

"I know of nothing except this," I said. "Most of the wild men of our jungle use the blow-gun and poisoned darts in hunting. The poison they use will quickly paralyze and kill anything after it enters the blood, but still it does not make the animal or bird unfit for food. Different tribes make this poison in different ways, but I know that at least one tribe makes it from certain roots and *tucandeiras*.

"Now it sometimes happens that a wild man wants to strike down an animal but not to kill it—he wants to keep it alive. He weakens his poison with water, so that the animal falls and lies still but does not die. When he has secured it he puts a little salt in its mouth, and this makes the beast lively again. It may be, *senhor*, that salt would weaken the effect of the *tucandeira* bites."

He slapped his thigh.

"Good dope!" he said. "It's worth trying anyhow. Yep, I'll give it a whirl just to see if it works."

Pedro and I, however, had the same idea, and we told it to him—that the best thing to do was to try to escape in the night. There were only two guards, and he still had his pistol, while I had his knife. But he shook his head.

"There are several little things against that plan," he said. "Unless they're bigger fools than I think, they'll put more guards here at night. We couldn't kill them all without a racket, and then the whole outfit would be on us. Besides that, I promised the Golden One I wouldn't use my gun if she'd protect you fellows. She and the chief took my word for it, and I have a bad habit of keeping my promises.

"And that isn't all. I'm going to take that test and win the little lady if I can. She's decidedly worth it."

There was nothing more for us to say, so we said nothing.

"You see, there are two sides to this thing—my side and hers," he went on after a pause. "As you say, Pedro, she seems to have found her man. Like you, I've known a few women and can read the signs. She's in a tough position here, marooned among these copperheads, and now that she's met the one man she wants I'd be all kinds of a bally skunk to duck and leave her in the hole. Life would never be the same to her again.

"For that matter, the chief might get sore at her for her part in saving us, and if he did he'd make it —— for her. Nope, I can't cut and run, fellows. It just isn't done, that's all.

"And as for my side of it—well, this isn't the first time folks have tried to rope me into marriage, but it's the first time I ever wanted to be roped. Up in my own country I've had considerable money at times, and I shouldn't wonder if there might be a few dollars of mine left in one or two banks right now; and besides that, my folks are rather prominent in a way. That means that I've had to step lively a few times to stay unmarried.

"I've nothing against women, but until now I haven't met up with any that I wanted to travel with. Mostly they're insincere, artificial, and worshipers of money and social position. But the Golden One is a real honest-to-God *girl*, uncontaminated by mercenary ideas, and a whizzer of a beauty besides.

"Run away and leave her? You couldn't drive me out of here with a machine gun until she's ready to go out with me.

"Tell you what I'll do, though. If you jiggers are set on making a break tonight I'll help you all I can, short of shooting up the place. No? All right. Then I'll start dolling myself up for this ant-fest."

He began rummaging among his goods, whistling away as if the coming ordeal were something pleasant. Out from a big rubber-covered bag he took smaller bags full of salt. Leaving these hidden behind other things, he went to the door and argued with the guards until one of them yelled to some one. Soon women came with four big jars of water.

"Strip and take a bath," he told us. "I convinced these chaps that we needed water for bathing and drinking, so we'll have to make good."

Each taking a jar, we bathed, while the guards watched us from the doorway. After a while they turned away and went back to their places. Then Senhor Locke slopped most of the water from his jar, and into it he swiftly emptied the bags of salt.

"That ought to make brine that would pickle a horse," he said, beginning to dress.

"It will make you sick if you drink much of it," said Pedro.

"Drink it? Lord, I'm not going to drink it, but pickle my arms in it. If the salt is an antidote to the ant-juice, the chances are that they don't like it and won't chew me up so bad. Savvy?"

I was doubtful about that value of this, but I said nothing. It was worth trying, and I knew of nothing else. When he was clothed again he stirred the salty water with his hands and then rubbed it into his arms up to the shoulders.

After that we lay in our hammocks and talked. The time dragged. At length the Tucandeira arose and dug out from another bundle a bunch of cards. As he did so, a small rubber bag rolled out on the dirt floor. He picked this up, and suddenly he laughed as if a bright idea had struck him. Glancing out at the *bárbaros*, he slipped the bag inside his shirt. Then he brought the cards over and began showing them to us.

They were colored pictures of many things—tall buildings, men and horses, steamboats, mountains, and so on. They had been printed from photographs taken in his country, he said, and he had brought them from America to give to Indians who might do little jobs for him. We were so much interested in them that we did not know any one else was there until a soft voice spoke at the door.

The Golden One stood there smiling at us. She had come to look again at her man. Pedro and I arose and offered her our hammocks. Then we went outside and squatted against the wall.

The guards were uneasy. They grunted to each other, moved several times, and finally stood where they could look inside and watch us too.

We heard the man and the girl behind us talking and laughing for a time, and then they seemed to speak more seriously. After that we paid no more attention to their voices, for we began to pass the time by talking about the *bárbaros* whom we could see passing about the village. None of them gave much attention to us, except a few girls who gathered at a distance and giggled.

At last we noticed that the pair in the hut behind us were not talking. Then came a little noise that sounded much like a kiss.

We winked at each other, and the grins were still on our faces when the Golden One came out laughing and blushing and looking very lovely. She saw our smiles, blushed still more, and ran swiftly away to the house of the chief.

"Well, *amigos*, I win," said the Tucandeira, coming out.

"We knew that, *senhor*," laughed Pedro.

"Oh slush; I don't mean what you think I mean. I bet you jiggers that the Golden One was American or English, and I win that bet. She's American!

"See these post-cards? I showed them to her too, and she recognized some things right away and called them by their right names.

"See this one of the cow-puncher and his horse? She knew the horse right off the bat—called it 'horsie,' as a little kid would do. She's never seen a horse since she came here, because there aren't any in this jungly river country; so she must remember those she saw before she left the States. And she's never seen a steamer here, of course; yet she recognized that too, and called it a ' 'teamboat.'

"Besides that, she knows part of her name—says she is 'Baby Mary.' And she remembers a man she calls 'daddy' lying dead in a canoe with a stick in him—an arrow, of course—and awful black birds following overhead for a long distance, and then the canoe grounding on sand where she got out and a tall Indian finally found her. Poor little kid, she must have had a devil of a time! Good thing a jaguar didn't find her before the chief did."

"Did she tell you anything about the test?" I asked.

"Yes, some. It's just what you fellows predicted. One thing in my favor is that they haven't any starved ants on hand, so they've got to use some that have eaten recently. Men are out catching them now. Not that it will make much difference, but every little bit helps. Ho-hum. 'Most time for the chuck-wagon to roll around again."

It was nearly time to eat, as he said. Soon women brought us food, and he showed that nothing ailed his appetite. When we finished we found that his guess had been correct—the guards were to be increased at night. Six of them, heavily armed and led by Googoo himself, relieved the two who had watched us through the afternoon.

Darkness came; a cloudy night with a watery moon. We got into our hammocks and slept.

Twice in the night I awoke to hear a soft slopping sound and found the Tucandeira soaking his arms again. I said nothing, knowing that the sound of my voice would bring the *bárbaros* in at once.

How many times he got up I do not know, for I heard him only twice. When day came, though, I noticed that he seemed sleepy and his arms were caked white with dried salt.

After our morning meal he yawned several times, and a smoke only seemed to make him sleepier than before. Snapping away the cigaret, he growled disgustedly, stretched himself, and muttered:

"Might as well start it now. Stand in the doorway a second, gents."

We blocked up the entrance, lounging there lazily a minute until he said, "All right." When we looked back he was chewing on something, and as he came out I saw that one cheek was swollen.

Thinking he had taken a mouthful of tobacco, I did not puzzle over it, except to wonder in a lazy way why he had hidden from the guards.

I noticed, though, that his sleepiness was leaving him and his eyes were growing brighter.

Squatting against the wall, we waited for something to happen. We waited for some time. The *bárbaros* went about the village as usual; but all looked often at us, and we knew they too were waiting for the test to begin. Once the Golden One came to the door of the chief's house and waved a hand, but she did not come near us. Pedro and I dozed a little and the Tucandeira sat silent, chewing all the time.

After a while two men approached the house of the chief, squatted, and began to beat drums. At that the village woke up. Men came from all the huts, followed by the women and children.

"There goes the overture," said Senhor Locke, rising. "Curtain goes up in three minutes. Being the star performer, I'll slide into my dressing-room and prink a bit. Let me know when the bally audience is ready."

The bally audience was ready quite soon. The chief, the Golden One, and an old man carefully holding something round stood at the chief's door. The two drummers squatted in a clear space before them, and beyond this open space all the other Indians stood close together, all looking toward us.

Then the chief raised a hand toward Googoo, who was still on duty with all five of his men. Googoo started toward us.

"They come, *senhor*," I called.

He came out, nodded easily at Googoo, and strode away toward the chief. We walked behind him, and the guards behind us. I noticed that his arms no longer glistened with the dry salt, and wondered if he had washed it off.

Later on, I learned that he had soaked them again, then partly dried them with cloth, so that the salt was all there but was damp and did not show. Also, he still carried that big chew in his mouth.

Straight up to the Golden One he went, spoke to her as if telling her not to worry, and smiled. She smiled in answer, but the smile quickly died and she looked very sober. The chief said something and moved his head toward the old man, who seemed to be the *pajé*, or medicine-man, of the tribe.

The American put out his hands. The old man pulled open a sort of cloth at the end of a woven fiber tube, slipped the tube quickly up the white man's arms, pulled the cloth tight and tied it firmly. This cloth made a sort of sleeve, preventing the ants from running beyond the place where it was tied. When this was fastened the *pajé* stepped back. At once the drummers stopped beating.

With the end of the drumming it seemed very quiet. We could hear the breathing of the *bárbaros* around us, but nothing else. Nobody spoke or moved. Every eye was on the face of Senhor Locke, every ear waiting to hear him whimper with pain.

He stood silent, moving no muscle except those of his jaws, which chewed away steadily. As the minutes dragged by he still made no sound, but his face changed a little. His eyes became set.

His lips twitched slightly.

Then his jaws stopped and their muscles stood out before his ears. Under his tan his skin grew gray. I knew the salt was not keeping off all the ants. Somehow I felt sick.

But he did not flinch. He neither groaned nor writhed. Rigid as a rifle he stood. The only sound he made was his hoarse breathing, which was deep and slow, with a sort of quiver in it.

A low murmur went around the circle of watching Indians. They were whispering and speaking among themselves. Yet nobody moved, nobody talked aloud.

More time dragged past—how long I do not know. I feared to see him stagger and fall, overcome by poison and pain. But he did not waver, and it was another who was first to move.

That other was the *pajé*. At last he came forward, peering into the eyes of Senhor Locke, which stared straight past him. Then he loosened the cords which held the sleeve, drew the cloth down carefully to keep the *tucandeiras* inside the cylinder, flipped the tube suddenly away and swiftly closed it.

Slowly the *senhor* turned toward our hut. The Golden One sprang to his side, laughing and joyous. But he made no answer to her eager talk, nor even looked at her. He stalked to the house, went inside, and dropped on his knees beside a water-jar.

We trailed close behind him, and after us came the crowd, talking loudly now and anxious to watch him longer. But we turned in the doorway and blocked it, ordering them all away. We would not let even the Golden One come in. We knew our comrade was going to be sick.

And sick he was, *senhores*. We heard him splashing water and retching. Yet even now he did not groan. I told Pedro to go to him while I held the door, which I could easily do because the opening was narrow and I am broad; and besides I was now in an ugly temper, for I knew from experience how the *tucandeira* bite hurts, and I would gladly have kicked some of those Indians in the stomach if they had crowded me.

But they kept back. The American had endured the test and would be the Golden One's man, and we were his companions, and not even the armed guards thought it best to go too far. I had some trouble, though, with the Golden One herself.

She was furious because I would not let her pass. She tried to push me aside, and when she could not do that she cried out at me in anger, stamping her foot and looking at me with eyes blazing. I tried to tell her she could see the *senhor* when he was ready, but since she did not understand my language this meant little to her. I half-expected her to order Googoo and his men to throw me out of the way, but she was too sensible to do that—probably knowing that a serious fight would follow.

Finding me stubborn, she grew quiet and listened to the sounds from inside. Then she spoke sharply to the others, and they went away, looking back often. After that she called to the *pajé*, who now was talking to the chief. He, too, went somewhere, returning soon with two small clay jars, one of which held liquid and the other a sort of paste. Knowing this must be medicine, I let him pass. Before I could stop her the Golden One slipped in after him.

Senhor Locke now was in his hammock, looking weak but able to smile a little at the girl. The old man gave him a drink from one jar, then smeared his arms with the paste.

Soon the white man appeared to feel better. The grayish look left his face, and some of the hard lines around his mouth smoothed out. He spoke to the Golden One. She swiftly bent and kissed him.

"I think, Lourenço," said Pedro, "that we are not needed here. Senhor Locke, we are going to walk."

"Go as far as you like," he answered. We did.

We walked all about the village. The guards made no attempt to stop us—indeed, Googoo alone came with us, acting more friendly now. Every one else seemed friendly too, and some of the *bárbaros* gave us *jabutí-púhe* and *cumá* and other fruits to eat. Though we could not talk to them, we managed to exchange ideas by making signs and wrinkling our faces, and the time passed pleasantly until we decided to return to our own hut.

There we found the Tucandeira sitting up in his hammock and talking with the Golden One, who was in the same hammock and very close to him. Except that his arms looked swollen he showed hardly any effects of the ant-bites. I was astonished, even though I had had some experience myself with Indian remedies.

"Has the pain left you, *senhor*?" I asked.

"Mostly. The flesh is tender and my bones ache some—sort of a rheumatic feeling—but it isn't half-bad now," he said cheerfully. "That old medicine-man is a ring-tailed whizzer, I'll say. I think the salt helped a good deal too—kept off some of the bugs. But the dose I got was plenty, thanks. If it hadn't been for the coca I might have squirmed some."

"The what?"

"Coca. Coca and a little lime. You saw me hide it in my shirt and chew it. I learned that little trick from Indians over in the Andes. It gives 'em tremendous endurance; I've seen them go forty-eight hours without sleep by chewing it.

"Me, I don't like the stuff, but I brought some away with me for emergencies. It's no painkiller, but it sure helps a chap to hold out."

Then he laughed and glanced at the Golden One.

"This little lady and I both put one over on each other," he said. "I've owned up to her about the salt and the coca, and she's admitted that she could have saved me all the pain. She says there is a bitter vegetable oil that all ants hate, and she thought of smuggling me some to smear on myself so that they wouldn't bite. Then she changed her mind because she wanted to find out whether I was a sure enough he-man. She never realized that the ants might kill me.

"But now everybody's satisfied, and the next thing is a huge wedding. You jiggers can get howling drunk and stay that way for the next three days. Everybody else will."

"That will be very sad," grinned Pedro. "But what will you do after that, *senhor*? I do not believe the chief will let her go out with you."

"Won't he?"

The other's eyes narrowed.

"He'd better! If he cuts up rough all bets are off, and he'll find some lead pills in his gizzard. I reckon I've got something to say about where my own wife lives. What's more, she's keen to go out, and now that I've won her I'm betting the chief will come through like a man."

He seemed to be right. At least, the chief made no objection to the marriage celebration. For the next three days, as the *senhor* had said, there was much feasting and drinking, dancing and games. We did not become "howling drunk," for we knew better than to take too much of the strong liquor brought out by the *bárbaros*—it is easy to start a deadly fight between different races when all are drinking. Yet none of the Indians became quarrelsome from their liquor. It made them like happy children.

Some put on huge masks of cloth made from the inner bark of trees, painted red and yellow and black and shaped like heads of beasts or birds. The chief himself donned a great headdress of bright parrot and toucan feathers, painted his face and chest, and changed the two blue feathers in his nose for flaming red ones. These slipped out of place after he had taken a number of drinks and made him look very funny, one pointing at his left eye and the other drooping toward his mouth.

Googoo became very drunk indeed, so that his big eyes bulged like those of a tipsy owl, and he reeled around with Pedro and me all the time, hiccoughing and blabbing many things which we did not understand at all. The men masked as animals pranced around on all fours and tripped other men so that they flopped on their faces.

The joke which every one enjoyed most, however, was Pedro's idea. Through Senhor Locke, who did not know why he wanted it, he obtained the fiber rope which had been looped around the American's body while we were prisoners. Then, catching the *senhor* and the Golden One standing, side by side, he threw the noose over both of them, yanked it tight, and gave the end of the rope to Googoo.

At once the rest of the gang which had brought us there came staggering forward and grabbed the rope also. Then, yelping like a flock of crazy toucans and falling over one another's feet, they drove the pair around the village while every one screeched with laughter.

The Golden One and her black-bearded mate enjoyed this as much as we. When the loop was loosened Senhor Locke laughed:

"I'm going to keep this rope. It's a queer wedding ring, but it's the only one we'll have until we get out to where I can buy one of gold and have our knot tied according to white man's law."

And he did keep it. When we all went out together he wore it coiled over one shoulder and across his chest.

Yes, *senhores*, we all went out. After the *festa* ended and every one at last was sober, the Tucandeira and the Golden One talked long with the chief. Finding that she was eager to go out into the great world with her man, the ruler of the tribe slowly nodded and gave orders to Googoo. And the next day at dawn we left the town.

The chief himself led the long file of men who went with us. Every man in the village, except the *pajé* and a few others who were old or not strong, swung away through the bush to the place where they were to say farewell to their Golden One. Some carried the few things Pedro and I had had when caught; others bore the larger packages belonging to Senhor Locke; and still others conveyed much food for us to eat after we should leave them. It seemed that every one in the band carried something except the chief, the girl, and we three men. We traveled at a steady jog through the cool jungle shade, and it was not late in the day when we reached the spot where our canoes had been left.

There our weapons were given back to us and the boats were loaded again. When all was ready Pedro and I pushed out and hung to an overhanging limb.

The Golden One took a place in the middle of her man's big canoe. He stepped aboard, lifted his paddle, and nodded to the men holding it to the bank. But the chief spoke, and they kept their grip on the boat.

Then the chief took from a man beside him a bundle, which he gave to the girl. He spoke again, slowly and gravely, pointing once to the thing he had given her. Then the men holding the boat shoved it away. We sunk our paddles in the water and moved out into the river.

Silent, motionless, with arms folded and head high, the chief watched us go. The men around him all stood still as the trees. Only when the Golden

One called to them and waved a hand in farewell did they move. Then their hands rose together, a shrill yell broke from them, and the swift current swept us around a bend and we saw them no more.

It was not until we reached the headquarters of our old *coronel*, several days later, that we learned what was in that package given by the chief in parting. The *coronel* gave us all a warm welcome, made Senhor Locke and his bride at home in his house, and hastily presented the Golden One with some civilized clothing left there by his daughter Flora, who was at school far away in Rio. Then, as we all sat talking by the lamp-light, Senhor Locke opened the bundle and looked over several things it contained.

"The chief said," he told us, "that he found these things at the time when the Golden One came to him on the back of the golden turtle. That means, of course, that he found her daddy's body—or what was left of it—and took this stuff from it. Seems to be mostly junk. Guess this black note-book will give us the best tip."

He ran through it while we talked of other things. Suddenly he whistled.

"Ye gods and little horned-toads! Mary girl, your father was 'Red Jim' McMurray!

"He was a big mining man—I've heard of him. When he was away past forty he married a young doll who had roped him in for his money. She made life miserable for him. Finally he disappeared, taking his little daughter and leaving a note saying he was going to a place where he'd never see another white woman as long as he lived. And he sure did!

"He fixed his will, too, as I remember it, so that if he should be declared legally dead his wife wouldn't get his money, and she fought like a wildcat to bust that will. Before the case could be settled she got killed in an automobile smash. And you're little Mary McMurray— Oh rats! You don't understand a word I'm saying!"

But she did know a few words, *senhores*. She smiled brightly and said:

"Baby Mary! Mary wants horsie."

"I reckon you can have several horsies," laughed the Tucandeira. "And you're going to live out in the big country where the horsies grow, too. You'd perish in a city, surrounded by a lot of jealous, supercilious cats."

"Then you are not going to poke into the other rivers along the Amazon and seek trouble there, *senhor*?" asked Pedro.

"Nope. Not now. I fancy I've found trouble enough to keep me busy for a while. I've got to teach my Mary girl how to talk and eat with a fork and wear clothes and ride horsies and—and everything. Yep, your old pal the Tucandeira has bitten off a man-sized mouthful, I'll say. *Coronel*, how soon can we catch the bally boat for the States?"

December 3, 1920

Excerpt from The Camp-Fire

Concerning his story in this issue a word from Arthur O. Friel:

Brooklyn.

The test of the tucandeira which the American hero of this tale has to undergo is quite widespread among the tribes of the southern rivers tributary to the Amazon. Its details differ with different tribes, but its essentials are the same—the proving of manhood by enduring the torments of these huge ants, which have been kept for a time in fiber cylinders or hollow palm-logs, through which the victim has to pass his arms. Sometimes he also has to go to each hut and do a sort of clog-dance while being bitten, but I have dispensed with that in this instance as being unnecessary and also detracting somewhat from the dignity of the white man.

—ARTHUR O. FRIEL.

January 3, 1921

The Vulture

I believe that story of yours, *senhor*. You tell me that while you two North Americans were far out on the great ocean, steaming southward on your way to explore our Amazon headwaters, a vulture came speeding from nowhere and settled in the rigging of another boat near you; and that soon afterward a terrible storm swept that vessel to her doom.

Yes, I believe it. For I know, as all Brazilians know, the fiendish power those ugly birds have of scenting death even before death strikes. And we rubber-workers of the wild Javary region, who see much of death, see much also of those vile things which live on death.

Sometimes, *senhores*, we see vultures without wings, which walk about in the shape of men. Yes, human vultures, who scent human weakness as do their foul brothers of the air, and come from afar to prey on that weakness until they have stripped their victims to the bare bones. And now, while we stream on down the Amazon, I can tell you the tale of one of those creatures—a tale of the bush but yet not of the bush; for these things came about not in the depths of the unknown jungle but in a jungle town on the banks of the Javary.

That town is Remate de Males. In your language Remate de Males means "culmination of evils." Yet it is not a bad town, as these upper Amazon towns go. It got its name, I have heard, from the sufferings of the first people who settled there—fever and famine and other misfortunes which attacked them until out of twenty settlers only four survived. Even now it is no real town like Manaos and other places on this great river.

But to us *seringueiros*, who toil for months among the dangers and diseases of the swamp-lands, it is a place where we can go and amuse ourselves when the floods drive us from our work. And when men have labored long in the wilderness with Death always lurking at their backs, any town where they can play is not a bad town at all.

At the time of high water I came into Remate de Males with a young comrade, Pedro Andrada, who, like myself, worked on the big *seringal* of Coronel Nunes. We were more than fellow workers; we were comrades. Recently we had been out on a long roving trip along the Brazilian-Peruvian frontier, and had come back so gaunt and tired that we were glad to rest for a time at the headquarters of the *coronel*.

But after a few days of ease we found this very dull, since most of the other men had gone out to spend their time and money at their homes, or, if their homes were too far away, at Remate de Males. So, after drawing some money from the *coronel*, we paddled down the river for several days until we reached the town.

There we hitched our dugout to one of the posts before the door of a trader named Joaquim, whom we knew well, and went inside. Several friends of ours were loafing there, and for a time they kept us busy telling of our adventures on that rambling trip. Then we asked what we could do to enjoy ourselves. They grinned.

"If you have a pocketful of money you can do anything you like at the house of Urubu," answered one.

"The house of the Vulture? I do not understand," I said.

"You are behind the times, Lourenço," another man laughed. "You have not been here since the last flood; is it not so? We now have a real *urubu*, and he will give you any game you like and pick you clean."

"This sounds interesting," said my comrade Pedro, his brown eyes twinkling. "Remate de Males is becoming quite a city. What sort of thing is this Urubu of which you speak?"

Then spoke Joaquim the trader, and his tone was sour:

"He is a *remate de males* in himself. If there is anything worse than he I have not yet seen it. He takes the life from honest men and devours their bodies afterward."

The men looked at one another. Then one said:

"That is a hard thing to say, Joaquim. I think you are jealous because we spend money there instead of here. Urubu is no cannibal."

"Where are Ricardo Bautista and Alberto Alencar?" demanded Joaquim. "Each was drunk at his place, and the next morning each was gone. Gone where? No man has seen them since."

Nobody spoke. Joaquim went on.

"I would not say that he actually ate them. But there is a *jacaré-assu*—a huge alligator—living under his house, and perhaps that reptile could tell things if he would. *A jacaré* does not live where it finds no food."

Again there was silence. Then Helio Alves said slowly:

"I have been wondering what became of that girl Januaria. You remember her, friends—the big girl with the very red mouth. I liked her. The last time I saw her she said she was going to quit him. That was nearly a week ago. Has any one seen her lately?"

The others shook their heads. A fellow named Miguel said:

"There has been no boat this week. She must be here still. Perhaps she is sick."

"Ask that *jacaré* under the house where she is," sneered Joaquim.

"I will ask Urubu to his face where she is," growled Helio.

"And I will ask Maria, my own sweetheart, what has become of her," added Miguel.

. . .

I broke in then and told them we were still waiting to learn who and what this Urubu might be. Miguel told me:

"His name is Aracu. But some man who was half-drunk in his place, so that his tongue got twisted, called him Urubu, and the name fitted him so well that he has been Urubu here ever since. He looks like a king vulture.

"He came first, they tell me, to Nazareth, across the river there in Peru. He wanted a house here in Remate de Males, where more people come; but he could not find one empty and he would not build one. Instead he got Domicio Malagueita to drinking and gambling in his place in Nazareth. Domicio owned the finest house here, except the hotel. Before long that house and everything in it belonged to Urubu.

"Domicio and his family had to go and live in a mean little *barracão*, where he and his wife died of fever. The place that used to be Domicio's home is now a house of entertainment run by Urubu. Perhaps you remember Domicio."

I did remember Domicio. He had been quite a prosperous trader, and a steady sort of man, though fond of his drink. I was sorry to hear of his miserable end. As I thought of it I remembered something else.

"Domicio had a pretty young daughter," I said. "What has become of her?"

"She is in the house of Urubu. She had no money, and a girl must live. She is not so pretty now."

At this we scowled. The daughter of Domicio was nothing to us, but this thing displeased us. Miguel went on:

"There are other girls. Where they come from I do not know, but they come here with Domengos Peixoto. Domengos is a great friend of Urubu, and he seems quite prosperous now. He wears a gold watch and chain, travels up and down the big river, and does not drink so hard as he did."

This was surprising news to us. When we had last been here this Domengos Peixoto had been a low, ragged drunkard whom nobody liked and nobody would trust—a hanger-on at places where card games were played, and always thirsting for a drink. It was hard to imagine him sober, well-dressed and traveling about like a gentleman.

"I see," said Pedro, his voice hard. "Domengos travels on the river—and brings girls here. I see. I think I will go and look at Domengos. I am curious to know how he looks with his face washed."

"He is not here now," said someone. "He has been away for a time."

"Then I will look at this Urubu who owns Domengos. I suppose I shall not offend you by offering to buy you all a drink?"

Every one sat up as if he had suddenly heard a voice calling him.

"To show you how much offended I am," Miguel laughed, "I will allow you to buy me two drinks."

We trooped out, leaving Joaquim looking after us sourly, but wistfully, too. After what he had said, he could not well go to the house of Urubu and drink. Perhaps he consoled himself with some of his own *cachaça* when we were gone.

In our dugouts and *montarias* we paddled up the street, where the water was several feet deep, to the house of Urubu. Pedro and I had never been in it before, for Domicio Malagueita had not invited *seringueiros* to be his guests. Now we found it fitted with the furnishings of a comfortable home, but with some partitions taken out to make a long room across the front.

In this room, around several small tables, sat a few men and girls quietly playing cards. Another girl, lolling in a richly colored hammock at one end, was picking idly at a wire guitar. A sort of bar ran halfway across the room beside the farther wall, and on it were a liquor jar and a few cups.

"Wake up!" shouted Miguel. "Here are Lourenço Moraes and Pedro Andrada, with a six-months' thirst and pockets full of money. Where is that Urubu? We want drinks!"

They woke up. The men, most of whom knew us, shouted greetings. The women swiftly looked us over and then smiled and called to us. The one in the hammock sat up, and I saw that she was the Malagueita girl. She had been rather proud and shy, but now she was as bold as any of them. She made eyes at my handsome partner and asked if he would buy her a drink, too.

"I buy for all, little one," said Pedro, as if he did not remember her. "My thirst is long and my pocket strong. Boys and girls, let us see who can empty his cup quickest. Who fills the cups?"

"I," said a deep voice behind the bar. A door had opened there, and beside the jar and cups stood Urubu.

As Miguel had said, the man looked like a king vulture—that bird which drives the common buzzards from their feasts to gorge himself. Bulky and squat, with humped shoulders, he had also the vulture's head and face. His head, blunt as a bullet, was red and bare except for a little short black hair. His nose was a hooked beak. His eyes were cold as those of the bird of death. His mouth was a hard slit. His hands, curled around cups on the bar, looked like claws. Looking at him and remembering what I had just been told, I felt that the drunken man who named him Urubu had been only drunk enough to speak truth.

He watched us with a cold stare. His mouth stretched into a smirk.

"What is your pleasure, *senhores*?" he asked.

"What have you?" Pedro wanted to know.

"Anything you like. *Cachaça*, of course"—and he pointed a thumb at the jar—"or *aguardente, cauim*—all those things. There is also fine liquor from

Europe and North America—cognac, whisky, gin, cordials—whatever you wish, *senhores*."

"I have drunk no liquor but *cachaça* for months," said Pedro. "I want something fancy. Make me a tail of the cock."

Urubu stared. So did the rest of us.

"A what?" demanded Urubu.

"A tail of the cock. An American whom I knew in Santarem used to make them for himself, and they are very fine. They are made by mixing several things together. Can you make one?"

"Certainly I can make you a cocktail, *senhor*. I did not quite understand you."

He reached under the bar, produced several bottles, mixed up the liquors, and asked—

"What will your broad-shouldered friend have?"

I said I would have a cocktail, also. The others ordered their drinks, and we quickly emptied our cups.

Pedro and I burst out coughing. That drink was the worst I had ever swallowed. Every one laughed at us except Urubu, whose face was like wood.

"What do you call that?" demanded Pedro angrily. "That is no tail of the cock."

"Perhaps you have forgotten the taste of a real cocktail," answered Urubu, a slight sneer in his tone. "Or perhaps you are accustomed to such drinks as are made for girls."

"Perhaps you are accustomed to mixing drinks only for ignorant Indians—the kind of Indians who eat rotten turtle," retorted Pedro. "And if you think me a girl, step out here and I will show you how girlish I am."

For a moment it was very quiet. Unwinking, expressionless, the vulture eyes of Urubu stared into the hot brown eyes of my comrade. Then his slit of a mouth stretched again and he shrugged his humpy shoulders.

"Do not be so hasty, *senhor*," he said. "That was only my little joke. Perhaps the American *senhor* made his cocktails differently—there are several ways of mixing those drinks. Will you have some of the North American whisky?"

"I will drink anything to take this taste out of my mouth."

"Then here is something very fine."

The beak-nosed man set a bottle on the bar.

"You see it is a new bottle, and the cork has not been drawn."

"Yes, and I see that I do not want it," refused Pedro. "I have seen that label before. The American *senhor* had a bottle like that one. He said that the stuff in it looked like whisky and tasted like whisky, but it was really Old Crow. I do not want anything made from old crows. Give me some *cachaça*."

Urubu said nothing more. I had some *cachaça* also, and the familiar taste soothed my tongue. The vulture-man glanced at the Malagueita girl, who stood beside Pedro and drank with him. At once she invited Pedro to sit in her hammock and let her play to him.

"Gladly, my lady," he accepted. "I have not heard a guitar for a long time." And they turned away.

I too turned and took a few steps toward one of the card tables. Then I whirled on my heel. As I expected, the eyes of Urubu were on my partner's back, and there was a threat in them—a threat of evil that put me on my guard. I strode to the bar.

"More meat for the *jacaré*," I said in a low tone. "Was that what you were thinking?"

For the first time his eyelids flickered. His unpleasant gaze centered on my face. After a minute he answered—

"I do not get your meaning, *senhor*."

"I think you do," I shot back. "And make no mistake. We are men of the bush, he and I, and we are accustomed to *jacarés*—and to *urubus*, also."

With another shrug he said he did not quite grasp my little joke. I said no more, for no more was necessary. But Helio, who had been standing near, now spoke up.

"I do not see Januaria here," he said. "Where is she?"

"She has fever," Urubu answered promptly. "I sent her down to the Solimões, where the air is better."

"When? How? To what place on the Solimões?"

"When? When she was taken sick. The fever came on her late at night, and I saw it would be bad, so I sent her out at once to Tabatinga."

"How?" insisted Helio. "Who took her?"

"By canoe. Ricardo Bautista and Alberto Alencar were here, and they paddled away with her."

"Ricardo and Alberto! They disappeared weeks ago."

"I know. They had no money left, so they went downriver to earn some. They came back together late that night, and I coaxed them to take her away until she should be well. Ricardo was a friend of Januaria, you remember."

Helio nodded slowly as if that were true, but he could not believe the rest of it. Without saying anything further he took another drink and then sat down at a table. The rest of us also drifted to the tables, and I sat for a time smoking, drinking, and talking to a couple of men who, like myself, were not in the mood for cards. One of the women bothered me at first with her attentions, but after I succeeded in discouraging her I was left in peace.

The Malagueita girl, I noticed, was softly singing love songs to Pedro, but he did not seem much interested. After a time he looked at me, moved his head toward the door, and arose. Urubu, who had been standing quiet and waiting, looked sharply at our rolls of *milréis* as we paid for all the drinks. Then he asked why we left so soon.

We told him the truth—that we must find a place to live in. He urged us to stay there, saying he could make room for us and would make us very comfortable. The girls, of course, said the same. But we refused and went out.

"A cold rascal," said my partner as we paddled away. "He spoiled my thirst, and I dislike him much. But I intend to see more of him. He interests me."

Back to the store of Joaquim we went, and there we tied our canoe as before.

"We have seen your Urubu and we do not like him," I told him. He grinned in a satisfied way.

"I knew you would not," he answered. "You two are not blind spendthrifts, and you have heads on your shoulders. Yet if you would buy supplies here you had best buy them now, for Urubu will get your money as he gets that of others."

"How?"

"By drink, gambling, women—or in other ways. I know you are not easily made drunk and are not passionate gamblers or lovers of women, but he will get you in some way. I am surprised that he did not ask you to stay there until your money was gone."

We answered that Urubu had done so, but that we preferred to live elsewhere and had come to ask if he knew of a place. We added that if we could find a house where we could live by ourselves we should want to buy a number of things in his store. It did not take him long to think of the place we wanted, and soon we were settled in a small *barracão* facing the river Tecuahy.

Before long a *montaria* came up to our door, and in it was Helio, looking both doubtful and grim.

"I do not believe Urubu's story of Januaria," he growled. "She showed no sign of sickness when I last saw her. And the part about Ricardo and Alberto sounds queer to me. They did not disappear at the same time, and they were not comrades as you two are, so why should they work together and return together? And they were rough, hard men who thought only of themselves, and if they came back with money they would not let a girl's sickness interfere with their staying here and drinking.

"What is more, they have had plenty of time to return from Tabatinga, but they have not come back. The tale does not sound good to me at all. And what Joaquim said about the *jacaré* disturbs me. It is true that a *jacaré-assu* lives under the house of Urubu—I have seen the beast myself."

"Miguel was to talk to his sweetheart," I reminded him. "Perhaps he will learn something."

"He has talked to her and has learned nothing," Helio replied. "I have just seen Miguel. Maria said she knew nothing about Januaria's sickness or her going away. She would not talk about it, and she seemed afraid Urubu might overhear what Miguel said."

"That does not look very good either," said Pedro. "The story of Urubu may be true, and we can not prove it is not. But there is one thing you can do, Helio, if you are really interested in this matter. Say nothing to any one, but start at dawn tomorrow and go to Tabatinga. It is only about thirty miles, and you can soon learn whether your girl is there."

"I will do it!" vowed Helio. "I will go before any one else is awake. When I come back I will tell you what I find out."

He left us, putting a vicious punch into his strokes as he pulled away.

"I think," said Pedro, watching him, "that before long Helio and Urubu are going to have trouble."

"And I think," I added, "that if any one else here disappears I should like to kill that *jacaré* and see what is inside him."

"I had the same thought," he nodded. "But I hardly believe there will be anything new before Helio returns."

He was not quite right. Before Helio came back to us something new did come about, and as the result of it my comrade forced himself into the affairs of the Vulture.

In the next two or three days we went several times to the house of Urubu. We lost a little money at cards, but not enough to hurt us much. We drank as much as we liked, but that was only enough to make us merry. And though the girls did their best to charm us we paid no more attention to them than to the men—joking with them, playing cards with them and buying drinks, but not allowing any foolishness.

We knew that this was not at all what Urubu wanted, but he gave no sign of impatience. The flood waters were high, we could do no work, and he had no reason to suppose we should go elsewhere before the dry season. So he watched and waited, as a true vulture watches and waits for its victim to fall into its power.

Then came a boat. On the boat came Domengos Peixoto. With Domengos came a girl. And then Pedro woke up.

The boat was one of these fine English steamers of the Amazon, which call at Remate de Males to leave passengers and mail. We were loafing in Joaquim's place when she came in, and for a minute we thought a fight had started down the street, for we heard yells and the explosions of rifles. But then came the hoarse roar of the whistle, and we knew the shouting and shooting were only the celebration that always welcomes the steamer.

Like the other men in the store, we started for our canoe. But in the confusion some man got our craft and paddled off in it before we could reach it. We promptly grabbed the next boat—a good-sized *montaria*—and in that we pulled away to the river.

Only four people left the steamer: two traveling traders, Domengos, and the girl. We gave no attention to the traders, but we were interested in the other two. Domengos, standing with his stomach stuck out importantly, looked for a boat to take him to the house of Urubu, but found none. Then he saw us and the roomy *montaria* we had borrowed.

"Here!" he called. "Come here to me. Take us to Urubu's place and I will give you a drink."

At his offensive tone we growled.

"We can buy our own drinks," retorted Pedro. "We are not boatmen for such as you. You can swim ashore. Unless you bathe more often than you used to it will do you good."

Domengos scowled and his face seemed to swell. But then he swallowed his rage and changed his manner.

"Oh, you are my old friends Pedro and Lourenço! I have not seen you for months, and I did not know you. Will you not take me and my niece to the house, old friends?"

"That tone sounds more familiar," said Pedro contemptuously. "It is the same one you used when you begged drinks from us last year. You can go—"

He stopped with a queer sort of gulp. His eyes had shifted to the girl, and sudden surprise had shot into his face.

I had only glanced at her, but now I looked at her more closely. She was rather small, but she appeared healthy and strong of body and pretty of face. These things were to be expected of a girl going to the house of the Vulture, but it was something else that interested me—she seemed shy, and she was looking at Domengos as if Pedro's scorn had stirred up doubt of her companion. Then Pedro spoke again, and like Domengos he had changed his manner.

"You can come with us. We have room for you."

Puzzled, I helped him move the *montaria* into position. Domengos started to get in, but Pedro blocked him.

"Hand the lady in first," he told him. "Have you no politeness?"

Domengos showed his teeth, but handed the girl down into the *montaria*. Pedro helped her to seat herself. Then, before Domengos could get in, he shoved the boat away.

Domengos teetered on his toes and narrowly escaped stepping off into the river. Other men in boats around us laughed.

"What is this?" demanded Domengos. "One of your jokes? Come back and take me in."

"I have changed my mind," grinned Pedro. "You can swim. Lourenço, paddle hard! Straight to our *barracão!*"

Much astonished, I heaved on my paddle and we surged away. Pedro also stroked hard a few times. Then he turned, faced the girl, and asked sharply—

"Angela, what are you doing here?"

A little cry of surprise came from her.

"Pedro! Pedro Andrada! I did not know you. How big you have grown!"

"Three years makes a difference in a man in this Javary country," he said. "Here a man must either be strong or die. But how come you here? Do you know that man Peixoto?"

Before she could answer, yells from Domengos broke in.

"Stop them!" he bellowed. "They are stealing her! *Capitão*, they steal my niece! They are kidnappers of the bush! They will hold her for ransom or worse! Will you let a woman passenger be stolen under your nose? Stop them!"

"Halt there!" barked an English voice behind us.

Pedro only shoved his paddle in deep. We almost lifted the boat with our strokes.

"Halt!" roared the voice again. A moment later a bullet smacked on the water beside us, followed instantly by the crack of a rifle.

Pedro tossed his paddle in the air and held it there. I lifted mine, too. The *montaria* kept on going of itself, but as we took no more strokes no more bullets came. The same voice barked orders on the steamer, and a ship's boat of men took the water and spurted after us.

While they came Pedro turned again to the girl.

"Angela," he said, "when I knew you in Santarem you were a good girl."

"And I am now!" she cried, her head high.

"I believe you. That is why I am doing what I do. Peixoto is not your uncle. You must not go with him. He is a lying dog, and he takes you to a place where no girl can go and remain good."

Then up swept the ship's boat, backed oars, and stopped. A gray-mustached, grim-faced officer with rifle in hand snapped:

"Hand over the lady, and be quick! What do you mean by this?"

"I mean to see that she is protected," Pedro explained with dignity. "You do not understand the matter. That Peixoto is a liar and worse—much worse. He brings an innocent girl here to put her in the house of the Vulture. Perhaps you can judge what sort of house that is by the name of it.

"I know this girl—we grew up in the same town, Santarem. She can tell you whether I am a woman-stealer or an honest man."

The keen eyes of the officer went to her. And though she was much disturbed she nodded quickly.

"It is true," she said. "I know Pedro, and he is to be trusted. And I—I do not know that other man well. He told me he would get me a fine place to work in the house of an English gentleman, where I could care for the children and live very well. He told me to say I was his niece so that we could travel without questions. I—I— Oh, what shall I do now?"

"Do not trouble yourself about that, Angela *mea*," Pedro soothed her. "You shall be well cared for until you can go home. You see, *senhor*, it is as I said."

The officer gazed shrewdly at him, at me, at Angela, and at other men in the boats around us. Snapping down a finger at one of those men and holding it like a revolver, he barked—

"You! What sort of a man is Peixoto?"

The man laughed harshly and told him just what sort of man Peixoto was. The officer nodded.

"I have wondered about him before this," he said. "He will not travel on our ship again. Give way!"

The oars dipped. The boat moved, turned, went back to the steamer. We saw Domengos being taken off, and not very gently.

"I think, Pedro," I said as we watched this, "that you have pushed Domengos off his perch. The officer said he would travel no more on the English boats. If he can not bring women here he will be useless to Urubu. He will soon be ragged and dirty again and whining for drinks as he used to. Are you not ashamed to have ruined so worthy a citizen?"

Pedro grinned and made some answer, but I lost it because the other men around us laughed and drowned his words. And the thing I had predicted came true, *senhores*—Domengos did become once more a hanger-on and beggar. But it was not because Urubu dismissed him. The big boats do not call often at that town, and before the next one came several things had happened which stopped any attempt he might have made to travel again.

Now we pushed on toward our *barracão*, and there we heard more of the story of Angela. Domengos had found her, she said, not at Santarem but at Ega, a town much nearer to us and on the river Teffe. In the years since Pedro had left Santarem her mother had died and her father had moved to Ega, taking Angela with him. Then he too died, and she had to work in the house of an Italian settler whose wife was ill-tempered and treated her badly. This was very disagreeable for the girl, but she could not leave because she had no other home and never was given any money.

Then Domengos came, looking important and telling the people of Ega he was an upriver trader. He visited the white people of the town, who were glad to learn from him the latest news of affairs along the big river, and in this way he came into the house where she lived.

Soon after that he managed to talk with her alone and ask her questions, and she told him her whole story. Then he told her his lie about the English gentleman he knew, whose wife wanted a girl to help her with the children and would give her money and pretty things to wear. So, believing all he said and thinking him very kind, she took her few belongings and ran away from her bad-tempered mistress.

On the way up the river he treated her well, she said, and it was not until she heard Pedro's contemptuous answers that she began to suspect he was not the respectable trader he claimed to be. Even now she found it hard to realize that he was so bad, and asked if we were sure it was true. We left no doubt in her mind about that. We pointed out that he would not dare treat her ill on the steamer because there she could appeal to the captain and make trouble for him; but after he got her into the house of Urubu she would have found him a low dog.

We told her little about the Vulture, and nothing at all about the disappearance of a girl and two men at his house. But she had heard enough to know it was far from being the sort of place she had expected, and now she looked very forlorn.

A poor little girl, homeless and penniless and deceived, with only us two hardened bushmen for friends and her dream of a happy life with kind people broken, she found it hard to hold back the tears. And when she stepped to the doorway and looked at the flooded town she could keep them back no longer.

"Even the town is dirty and dismal!" she cried. "Santarem and Ega are clean, green towns with fine sandy beaches, but this is nothing but a drowned mud-hole. And the air—the air is so damp it chokes me."

"Have courage, Angela," Pedro said. "You shall leave it on the next boat that goes down. We would put you on that steamer which brought you, but it is up-bound and must go many miles westward before turning down again. This is a dreary place, as you say, but no harm shall come to you here."

"But where can I go from here? I have no money, and one can not travel free on the steamer. I have nothing at all—that Peixoto must have my bundle with my other dress and my beads and all."

"Do not trouble about the money," he urged her. "We will see to that. And if Domengos has anything of yours he will not keep it long. I will go and get it now."

Taking his rifle, he stepped toward the door. I too picked up my gun, but he told me to stay there and see that nobody bothered Angela. I hesitated, and then suggested that we take her with us and leave her for a time with Joaquim and his wife. This little *barracão*, I said, was no fit place for her, though it was good enough for him and me; and she would be more comfortable and fully as safe at Joaquim's place. He agreed that this was so.

"Come, Angela," he said. "You will like Paula, the wife of Joaquim, for she has a very good heart. And it will be better for you to stay there than here, for one never knows what may happen, and later on in your life some spiteful person might say you lived with two men here, and it might do you much harm."

So we took her to Joaquim's home. As we expected, he had already heard of the matter from other men, and after one look into Angela's innocent face he consented to her staying with his family. Paula, a motherly woman, also was glad to have her there, and the girl herself seemed to feel better for their hearty welcome.

"Now she will be safe," Pedro said as we paddled away.

"If she does not get fever," I added.

He nodded grudgingly, and I knew he thought of her words about the air choking her. The air of the Javary is heavy, and it is loaded with disease, as you *senhores* know well. And it is an odd thing but true that people accustomed to the air of the Amazon often sicken and die soon after leaving it for one of the branch rivers, even though they go only a few miles from the main stream. I wished now that I had not said that. But it was said, and I could not call it back. Neither of us spoke again until we reached the house of the Vulture.

Domengos had arrived there before us, but neither he nor Urubu was in the big room. The men and girls loitering there sat up with a jerk as we strode in with our guns. We saw that they had heard the news. Nobody spoke, and all watched us in tense silence.

"Where is that *cachorro*?" growled Pedro, looking about him.

"That dog? What dog?" someone replied.

"That dog Peixoto. He has a bundle which is not his."

"He is inside talking with Urubu," a man answered. "The bundle he brought is there on the bar."

In six strides Pedro was at the bar and had seized a small package. I stood back and watched every one. As my partner turned away the door behind the bar opened, and through it came Domengos and Urubu.

"Behind you, Pedro," I said.

He whirled and faced them. But they made no threatening move. I do not think they had known we were there, for we had spoken quietly, and Urubu looked slightly surprised. Domengos seemed much distressed; his face glistened with sweat, and he cringed like a kicked cur. Urubu, I judged, had been saying unpleasant things to him.

"I thank you, Domengos, for leaving this bundle where I could get it so easily," Pedro mocked. "It will go straight back to its owner. If either or both of you wish to do anything about this matter, now is the time."

"You will pay me the passage money spent on your woman," sputtered Domengos.

"Are you sure? Come here to me and collect it."

Domengos opened his mouth and let it stay open, but no words came. He looked sidewise at Urubu, whose harsh face remained expressionless. We knew well that the money spent on bringing Angela here had come from the pocket of the Vulture, not from that of Domengos. But he said no word.

Then Pedro cursed them both. He cursed them thoroughly and well. He called them such names as no real man would have swallowed. Yet he said nothing of the *jacaré* under the house, or of the two men and the girl who had disappeared. He used fighting talk, meant to goad them into fight then and there.

But he had forgotten the nature of vultures. A vulture does not attack anything dangerous, nor did Urubu show fight now. And Domengos, looking at our faces and our guns, not only cringed still more—he cowered behind the bar.

When Pedro stopped, Urubu spoke coldly.

"Your talk is for Domengos, not for me. If he deceived any girl that is his mistake; I want no girl here who does not come of her own wish. When you have grown cooler you will realize that this is not such a place as you say. Our girls are well treated, as they will tell you, and no girl need stay here unless she wants to. And if Domengos has brought you a friend who does not know men that is your good fortune—if you care for green fruit. Every man to his taste."

"Bah!" snorted Pedro. "I will waste no more words on you except to tell you again that you are a foul liar."

He spat and turned to the door. I backed out, keeping my eyes on the pair behind the bar. We paddled away.

As we cruised down the street an odd thing happened. Up in the air two birds got to fighting, and one of them came tumbling down into the water, stunned and bleeding from a beak-blow on the head. We swung toward it, but before we reached it the water around it seethed and it was dragged under. Several fish showed for an instant on the surface. We knew them for *piranhas*, those strong-jawed fish which, maddened by blood, will chop to fragments any wounded creature they find.

"*Piranhas!*" muttered Pedro. "Here in the street! Perhaps they, and not the *jacaré-assu*, could tell us what became of Ricardo and Alberto."

"If so, we shall know when the waters go down," I said. "There will be bones. The *jacaré* would leave no bones, but would swallow all."

"Weeks must pass before this street will be dry," he answered. "Unless I am mistaken, we shall learn more before that time." And we did.

Back at Joaquim's place we gave the bundle to Angela. She had become more cheerful now, and with the return of her little treasures she smiled again. The smile and the warm look of gratitude she gave Pedro made me realize for the first time how pretty and appealing she was. I thought, too, that this strong but gentle-hearted comrade of mine was just such a man as she should have to protect her through life, and I saw Paula glance at Joaquim as if the same thought came to her.

But the young couple themselves seemed to have no such idea. Angela only asked whether he had had any trouble in getting the bundle, and he said no; he had simply picked it up and walked out with it.

Then we settled down to await the return of Helio. We did our waiting at Joaquim's, and there other men joined us—the quieter and steadier who did not care for the attractions of the Vulture's house, but who liked a drink and a card game when in the mood. Joaquim, of course, was a trader, and his store was not built for a place of entertainment; but Pedro suggested that it would be good business to make room for some gaming tables, sell us our drinks, and take some payment for the use of his store. When we pointed out that this would draw some trade away from Urubu he consented at once, and it was done.

Soon there were three sets of men in the town: those who would not go to the house of the Vulture, those who did go there for the women, and those who went to either Joaquim's or Urubu's as the whim took them. Through these men who went back and forth we kept well informed as to what went on at the Urubu house.

There was little news at first—a fight or two caused by drink and jealousy over the girls, but nothing of personal interest to us two. Then Miguel told us that both his girl Maria and the Malagueita girl were asking about us.

"I think, friends, that Urubu has been expecting you to tire of staying away and come back to have a lively time there," he said. "But now he is trying to learn through the girls whether you intend to keep on drawing away business to this store. And Anna Malagueita, your little friend of the hammock and guitar, seems eager to have you come and see her again, Pedro."

"Tell Maria that Urubu will be in a hotter place than this before we spend any more money in that house," said Pedro. "And I hope Anna will find a friend who will amuse her in my place. I stay here."

When we saw Miguel again he grinned and told us the Malagueita girl had asked him many questions about Angela, and whether she and Pedro were living together. He had said no, that Angela lived at Joaquim's, and Pedro saw no more of her than any one else there. Then she had told him to warn Pedro to be careful lest some unexpected misfortune come to him.

"She would not say what sort of misfortune," he went on. "Perhaps she does not know. But she was very anxious that I tell you, and she was nervous lest Urubu know that she sent the message. There is something behind it, I am sure."

"Thank her for me," said my partner, "and tell her I will keep my eyes open. And tell her if there is anything I can do to help her in return she has only to send word to me."

The truth was that Miguel was wrong when he said Pedro saw little of Angela. He was with her quite often, going into the family quarters behind the store and talking with her and Paula while I sat outside and told stories with other men. But Miguel spent more time at Urubu's place than with us, and he did not know this.

The warning did not bother us, but it did make us keep our eyes open. And that same night, when we entered our *barracão* rather late after a game at Joaquim's, we nearly stepped on a big snake.

It was a *surucucú*. As you know, the bite of that snake means death, swift and sure. Even a small one will kill a strong man, and this one was more than six feet long. If we had not been a little more careful than usual one of us would have died that night.

It was our habit, on returning late, to find our hammocks and sleep without making any light. But this time, with the warning fresh in our minds, we thought it well to light a candle and look about us. And there on the floor not far from us was that deadly thing.

It had not yet coiled to strike, but lay as if about to do so. I yelled, jumped away, and threw my *machete* at it. The knife struck edge downward, cutting the reptile so that it was easily killed with a rifle butt.

"As Miguel said, there seems to be something behind that warning," said Pedro. "This *barracão* is surrounded by water. So is the whole town. How did this beast come here?"

"Snakes sometimes come floating down on drifting trees," I reminded him. "It is possible that some small driftwood lodged against our door for a while and the *surucucú* crawled off it. But it is not at all likely."

"No. It will do no harm to look further and see whether we have any other guests."

After throwing the snake outside we made a thorough search, but found nothing. Then, still suspicious, we inspected our rifles, which had been left in the house while we were away. No harm had been done to them, nor to anything else in the place. There was no sign that any one had been there. So we said no more and went to sleep.

The next night a more violent thing came about. A heavy, solid blow struck the *barracão*, and we sprang from our hammocks to find the place shaking dangerously. A grinding, crushing sound was passing slowly along one side, and when we got a light we found the wall on that side caved in. We peered out in time to see a big tree go drifting suddenly away downstream.

We had been unpleasantly close to death. The *barracão*, you understand, was built high on poles, just as all houses there must be built to stand above the flood waters.

The floating tree had come very near knocking it off its posts and crumpling it into a wreck from which we would have little chance of escape. Held in that sunken cage, carried away down the black waters among alligators and *piranhas* and other evil things—no, we should not have had much chance. It was our luck that the house happened to be firm and that the heavy tree had not hit it squarely.

The night was dull, but not black. We could see a short distance out across the Tecuahy, but nothing strange was in sight. We listened, but heard nothing. As on the night when we found the snake, there was no sign that it was not mere chance. Yet we were quite sure it was not chance at all, for this reason: there was little current around our house, and the drifting things that came down usually passed by at quite a distance, out where the flow was stronger. It seemed almost impossible for such a thing to happen unless a boat somewhere above us had drawn that tree aside and guided it to strike us. And, as I say, the night was not so dark but that men could do this.

"It seems to me, Lourenço," said Pedro, "that before that thing hit us I heard voices and paddles. Perhaps I was dreaming. Perhaps I was not dreaming but was partly awake and really heard it. I am not sure. But things are becoming interesting in this house."

"Quite so," I agreed. "So interesting that I am going to sit up a while and see if anything else may come."

And I did sit up, with my rifle across my lap, while my partner dozed with his own gun close at hand. But nothing at all happened before morning.

Then, after eating and loafing a while and talking over the two narrow escapes we had just had, we decided to go to Joaquim's place and ask someone in a casual way about the movements of Urubu last night. Before we started, though, I suggested that we finish up a small jug of *cachaça* which we had bought from Joaquim some days before, and which now needed refilling. He laughingly agreed that this was a happy thought, and with a mock bow to me, he lifted the vessel to his mouth.

An inch from his lips he stopped it. For an instant he held it there, peering at it. Then he lowered it, stepped to the door, and again looked sharply at the clay.

"Have you been using white powder for anything?" he asked.

"No. I have not had anything of that sort."

"Neither have I. Yet there is white powder on this jug."

It was so. On the clay was a tiny smear of white dust. We scowled at it and at each other.

"I would not drink that *cachaça*," I advised.

"I do not intend to. When did you drink last from it?"

"Yesterday afternoon. We both drank, you remember. It was good then."

"Yes, it was good then. But this is another day."

He drew back his arm to throw the jug into the water. But then he changed his mind and held it.

"On our way to Joaquim's place let us stop and see Meldo Salles," he said.

And when we got into our canoe he still held the jug. Also, we took our rifles with us.

Meldo's house was nearby, and when we stopped there we found him lazily smoking at the door.

"Meldo, you said yesterday that you had a pet monkey which was growing old and ugly and must be killed," Pedro reminded him. "You also said he was a thief and drank your *cachaça*. Have you killed him yet?"

"Ho-hum!" he yawned. "No, not yet. I thought I would do it today."

"Then let me see him drink some *cachaça* first. We have a little left here. Bring him out."

Meldo yawned again, got up sluggishly, went inside, and brought out a heavy black *barrigudo* monkey which showed its teeth and seemed sullen. When my partner lifted the jug, though, the animal chattered and reached toward it. Pedro handed it to him, and he drank greedily.

"Drink deep, you thieving *bicho*," Meldo said grimly. "It is the last drink you will get. Before night I shall knock you in the head."

"Perhaps you need not do that," said Pedro.

Then he began talking about something else, glancing now and then at the monkey, which still clutched the jug as if determined to keep it. After a time he broke off in the middle of a sentence. Following his eye, Meldo and I looked at the black *barrigudo*.

The animal was swaying on his haunches and seemed dazed. Soon he lost his hold on the jug and slumped down on the floor. After lying there a minute he kicked a couple of times and was still.

"Ha, ha, ha!" laughed Meldo. "He is dead drunk. That rum of yours must be strong."

Without answering, Pedro pulled the monkey to him and felt for its heart. Presently he took away his hand and replied:

"You are partly right. He is not drunk, but he is dead."

Then he told Meldo of the snake and the tree. Meldo, one of the quiet men who often joined us at Joaquim's stopped yawning and became wide awake.

"A little thing like a snake on my floor does not disturb me much—I see plenty of snakes when I am in the bush," added Pedro. "And if people wish to amuse themselves by bumping trees against my *barracão* they can have their little joke. But any one who would spoil good liquor is a vile brute and should be shot."

Meldo grinned at his way of putting it, but quickly became serious again.

"Here is another thing," he said. "Helio Alves has not been seen for days. He disappeared overnight. And he had been saying ugly things about Urubu because the girl Januaria was gone."

"Do not worry about Helio," I said. "I think he is safe and will be back soon. He should have been here before now. After we see him we shall know more about what to do."

Meldo asked questions, of course, but we told him no more then, and got his promise to say nothing until we were ready. He sank the poisoned jug where it would do no harm, threw the dead monkey out into the current, and went on to Joaquim's place.

Meldo came with us, and, with a couple of other men, we got up a game at one of the tables. Our careless questions about Urubu got us no information, so we said nothing further and gave our attention to the cards. We were still playing when Helio arrived.

He came striding heavily in, looking gaunt and gloomy. One glance at his face told me what to expect. Briefly and bitterly he spoke out.

"Januaria is not at Tabatinga and has never been there. Ricardo and Alberto have not been there either. What is more, they never went down this river as Urubu said. I have spent days on my way back from Tabatinga, stopping and questioning every one between there and here. Not one person has seen or heard of them. They never left here, and that —— —— Urubu is their murderer. I am going now to cut out his foul heart."

"Wait!" called Pedro.

Then he told him what had happened since he left. To all except Meldo and me the story of the snake, the tree, and the poison was news, and they listened with faces hardening. While he talked two other men came in, and one of these was Miguel.

"But even yet we have no proof," Pedro concluded. "Urubu will say those three must have been drowned and devoured on their way to Tabatinga, and no man can prove otherwise. There is nothing at all against him except suspicion."

"Then here is another suspicion for you," Miguel broke in. "Your little friend Anna Malagueita is 'sick,' as Januaria was.

"She was not to be seen yesterday or last night. Urubu said she was sick, and at first I thought nothing of it. But late last night I grew suspicious, and this is why: Each of the girls there has a little room to herself, as you perhaps know, and the room of Anna is next to that of my girl Maria. I was with Maria last night for a while, and on my way out I went into Anna's room to ask how she felt and see whether she wished to send any further word to you. The room was empty.

"Maria had not come out yet, and I stepped back and asked her where Anna was. Maria is a jealous girl, and she asked what I cared about Anna. To tease her I said I was much interested in Anna, and a few other things of the sort. She was angered, and cried out—

" 'You are too late, Miguel *meo*—you will not see her again!'

"Then she seemed suddenly scared because she had said this, and I could not get another word from her. When we came out into the big room and found that Urubu was busy gambling she seemed much relieved. That is all."

"That is enough," growled Pedro, his face black.

Seizing his rifle, he started for the door.

"What will you do, Pedro?" Joaquim called.

"Search that whole house and find Anna. If I do not find her, Urubu will tell me where she is—and I will make him tell truth."

"Bah! Who could make that creature tell truth?" snorted Joaquim. "If you want truth, do as I told you before—ask that *jacaré* under the house."

Pedro swung on his heel and stared at him.

"Joaquim, you speak sense," he said. "I will talk first to the *jacaré* and then to the Vulture."

We talked and agreed what we should do. Helio, Pedro and I stayed with Joaquim. The others went and got guns and long poles. When all had returned Pedro said grimly:

"Helio, do not kill him until we know. Curse him as much as you like. Keep him busy."

"I will keep him busy," Helio promised, his voice harsh with hate.

We got into our boats, and he paddled straight to the house of Urubu. The rest of us went there, too; but by roundabout ways. Soon we had closed in around the place on all sides.

The posts holding up the house were stout and high, and the water was not up to its floor. A careful look along the surface under that floor showed that no alligator was floating there. Inside the place we could hear Helio cursing Urubu as a liar and other things far more vile, and demanding to know just what had become of Januaria. We had no time to listen for the low-spoken replies, for we now began prodding the mud with the poles we had brought.

At first we got no results, and after a time we began to think the alligator was not there now. But then Miguel's pole moved in his hand, and he passed the word that he had struck something alive. More jabbing followed. Then suddenly a rifle cracked.

It was Joaquim who slew the beast. The thing had risen near him, swimming sluggishly, and the trader had put a bullet squarely into one eye. With a rolling surge it turned belly upward.

Men got their poles under it and held it there. Pedro and I worked up beside it and slashed open its bloated belly. Then we all looked at one another with sick faces.

We knew what had become of Anna Malagueita.

Through the silence around us came the voice of Helio yelling another blast of oaths at the Vulture. Sudden fury seized us. Hoarse curses broke from us. We drove our paddles into the water and threw our canoes and ourselves around to the front of the house.

In a snarling, panting, struggling knot we leaped out on the platform and plunged through the doorway. Of the people in that big room we saw only two—Helio and the Vulture. They stood at the bar, and that bar was between them. Helio, leaning across it, had his face almost in that of Urubu, and he still spat burning curses. The Vulture's eyes were half-shut, with an evil gleam in them, and both his hands were out of sight below the wood.

Even as we charged into the place Helio lost control of himself and seized Urubu by the throat. The Vulture heaved himself backward and sidewise, trying to escape. But Helio's hold was like an iron clamp, and he throttled him and shook him as a dog would shake a rat.

Then came a swift flash of steel. Helio grunted and lost his hold. Urubu had stabbed him in the shoulder.

With the knife still in his hand the Vulture turned to leap away from us into his room. But he never reached that room. We threw ourselves headlong over the bar and fell on him. Some man cried out as the knife of Urubu bit into him, but after that thrust the Vulture stabbed no more. The weapon was knocked or wrested from him, and savage blows battered him to his knees.

Some of those blows fell on us also. Every man of us was like a maddened jaguar, thinking only of destroying him; and we struck in blind rage, so that in our struggles to get at him we got in the way of our own attack. Someone's rifle barrel or butt hit me hard on the head, dazing me so that I staggered and had to grab the bar to keep from falling.

While I leaned there I saw Joaquim too go stumbling back, clutching an arm cut by a jabbing *machete*. Miguel also was out of the fight, for he was the man who had been stabbed after Helio, and now he was limping away, bending over with pain.

Then I saw the Vulture rise in the air. Pedro had dragged him up, and now he threw him over the bar into the clear space beyond. There Helio kicked him hard and then fell on him, his good hand pounding him furiously. Pedro hurled himself across the bar and jumped on him, too. The rest of us stayed where we were for a few minutes, for our first hot rage was partly satisfied and we were willing to let Pedro and Helio settle their score.

Pedro had dropped his rifle in the struggle, and some other man had pulled his *machete* from his belt to kill Urubu with, so that also was gone. Helio carried a knife, but he did not draw it now; he wanted to wring the Vulture's neck in his hands.

Urubu, fighting for his vicious life, showed desperate strength, and the three of them went rolling and tumbling about the floor, battering and clawing and tearing like fighting jungle cats. And then came one of those freaks of fight by which a loser sometimes wins.

In a twisting, plunging scramble Pedro and Helio struck their heads together so violently that the blow partly stunned them. They did not lose their senses, but for a few seconds they lay without moving, waiting for the numbness to pass. And in that time the Vulture wrenched himself out of their clutch and reeled up to his feet.

He was a frightful-looking thing now. His clothes hung in bloody tatters. Red streams trickled from broken nose, smashed mouth, and gashes on head and body. One hand hung as if broken, and he breathed in wheezing gasps as if ribs were crushed. For an instant he stood there rocking on his heels. Then, as the men on the floor scrambled up and at him, he sprang for the door.

"Shoot him!" yelled someone, and a man beside me snatched a fallen rifle up off the floor and twitched back the hammer.

But he could not fire, for Pedro and Helio were bounding after Urubu, and a bullet would have hit them. We leaped over the bar. As we struck the floor we heard a heavy splash outside.

We reached the door before the fugitive came to the surface. Pedro and Helio were poised to leap in after him, but they waited until he reappeared so that he could not trick them by turning underwater and swimming away to one side.

But when he did break water again they did not follow him. Instead they hung there on their toes an instant, then settled back. Helio laughed harshly.

The Vulture could not swim.

He came up splashing and fighting the water with both hands. His mouth opened wide in a gulp for air. Before he got it he strangled, coughed, and went down with a bubbling gasp. Around him grew a red stain as the water washed his open wounds.

Again he came up. His face now was clay-white. From his choked throat burst a groaning cry. As one hand came out of water a gleaming thing fell from it. Other things glinted around him on the surface. The water boiled.

"*Por Deos!*" shouted Pedro. "*Piranhas!*"

Yes, *senhores*, the *piranhas* had found the Vulture. Just as they had seized on that hurt parrot a few days before, they now attacked the man who had thrown himself among them. Before our eyes they chopped him to death. And no man moved until the red waters had closed over his writhing face for the last time and smothered his cries forever.

Then Pedro and Helio looked at each other. And Helio said—"Let us have a drink."

I think we all felt the need of a drink. From the wreckage behind the bar we pulled out bottles not broken in the struggle there, and from these we gulped stiff drinks. While we did so the room filled with men who had seen or heard of the death of the Vulture and now came to learn all about it. We told them all we knew. And soon we learned other things.

"Who is in that room?" demanded a man, pointing at the door from which Urubu used to come.

I was nearest that door, and for the first time I noticed that since the fight it had been pushed almost shut. Kicking it open, I found Domengos Peixoto beyond it. He was just hiding something inside his shirt.

Jumping at him, I forced his hand out and saw he held a huge roll of *milréis*. I wrenched this from him and shoved him out to face the crowd.

"Old friends," he whined, cowering back, "do not be harsh with me. I have done you no harm, and I am only taking what is mine. That cursed Urubu owes me much money."

"That is our money," yelled a man. "The money he got by cheating us with cards and liquor."

"No, it is our money," cried a woman. "He robbed and cheated us girls and made us slaves."

"Hold that money, Lourenço," called Pedro, and he shouldered his way to me. Then he told the rest:

"Before any one gets this money we want the truth about Ricardo, Alberto, and Januaria. We want to know how these things were done. Domengos, and you girls too, speak out. You will profit by it."

So they spoke out. And though no one of them seemed to know all, yet each knew something, and by putting these things together and searching the room of the Vulture afterward we got the whole truth.

All those who disappeared had died by poison. The poison was that same whitish powder which we had found on our *cachaça* jug. It killed quickly, but with so little pain that the victim seemed only to fall into sudden sleep. Thus there were no cries or struggles from those who took it in their liquor, and nobody would be alarmed by any noise. Before morning Urubu could quietly carry the body to his own room, where a part of his floor could be lifted out and the murdered man or woman dropped through to the big *jacaré* waiting below.

Ricardo and Alberto, though slain at different times, had both been killed for the same reason—their money. Each was a shrewd gambler and a dangerous fighter; and the Vulture, finding them hard to cheat and knowing he could not rob them alive, had robbed them dead.

The girl Januaria had been put out of the way because she knew far too much about Urubu and was likely to prove dangerous to him—indeed, she had openly threatened to tell certain things she knew. And Anna Malagueita must have died because the Vulture knew she had warned us to be on our guard.

Urubu had been behind all the attempts to kill us also, but had not himself taken a hand with the snake and the tree. He had worked through two worthless men of the town who would do anything if well paid, and who became scared and went away after the second attempt failed—we could not find them when we went looking for them, and we never saw them again. But the poisoning of our *cachaça* must have been done by Urubu himself while we were passing the evening at Joaquim's place.

If the floating tree should destroy us, you see, no trace would be left of the poisoned jug. If the tree spared us and the poison killed us there would still be no proof that he had been concerned in it, for men would know we bought our *cachaça* from Joaquim, and suspicion would be most likely to fall on the man who had sold it to us. To ruin his enemy Joaquim as well as to kill us would be much to the taste of the Vulture.

With these things settled in our minds, we settled the matter of the money. Pedro pointed out that no man could prove how much he had lost here; that the losers had had some pleasure in spending it; that we all could earn more money if we needed it, and that any attempt to divide it among us would probably lead to trouble. So he suggested that we give it all in equal shares to the girls of the house, who had been pleasant companions and who now had nothing. The men agreed. And it was done.

When the girls had come up and taken their money Pedro still held one share.

"This," he explained, "goes to the little girl who nearly came to this house but is now at the house of Joaquim. She must have money to take her home, and I intend to see that she has plenty."

After a minute of silence a whining voice asked:

"And do I get nothing at all? You promised me—"

"Be still, Domengos!" I cut in. "If we gave you what you deserve you would get only a good kicking. Yet since you have told the truth, we will give you something worth your while. It would do no good to give you money. You would only drink it up. But there is much liquor left here behind the bar, and you may have as much of it as you can carry away at one load.

Now bend your back and sweat."

He did sweat. He got bags and crammed them with the strongest liquors in the place, working fast for fear we might change our minds. He loaded himself down so that he could scarcely walk, and when he carried his burden to the door he puffed and staggered and splashed sweat on the floor.

Outside he got into a *montaria* and went away. And it was a long time before any one again saw him sober.

Then, after looking at Miguel and finding that his wound was painful but not mortal, and that his girl Maria was taking good care of him, Pedro and Joaquim and I left the house which no longer was that of the Vulture and paddled back to Angela.

Into her hands Pedro put the money, telling her that now she could return to Ega or to Santarem as she pleased. But after holding it and staring at it—more money than she had seen in all her life—she passed it back to him.

"Keep it for me," she said. "I do not—I do not know that I want to go. I—I like this place better than I did."

We stared at her. She dropped her eyes and looked at the floor. Glancing at Paula, I saw a wise smile grow on her face.

"But you must go, Angela," Pedro told her. "This place is unhealthful in more ways than one. You have been here only a short time, but even now you do not look so strong as when you came. You will be much more healthy and far more happy at one of those towns on the great river."

Still she gazed at the floor. Then she looked shyly up at him and glanced quickly aside.

"Santarem and Ega are far from here," she said in a small voice. "I do not want to travel so far—alone."

He put a hand under her chin and lifted her face to his. A hot blush flamed in her cheeks, but she met his eyes steadily. When he spoke again his voice was very gentle.

"I would go down the river with you, Angela, but I am not yet ready to leave the Javary. I intend to work one more season on the *seringal* of the *coronel*, and then to go out and stay out.

"Go back to Santarem and find Vincente Honorio, my godfather. Say to him that when the next great flood rises I come back home, and that in the meantime he is to take very good care of you. Tell him that I, Pedro Andrada, have said this. Now be a good girl and do as I say, and all will be well."

She did as he said. On the next down boat she sailed away, taking with her the money he had brought her from the Vulture, the memory of all he had done for her, and his promise that in another year he would come home. And with her going Remate de Males settled back into his usual habit—waiting.

Our friends, the rubber workers, waited for the time when they could go back to work in the swampy forests. The townsmen waited for the flood waters to ebb until they could walk about on dry land and kick the bones of the Vulture out of the street. And Pedro and I, with a new jug of *cachaça* which we knew would not be poisoned, yawned and waited for whatever might happen next.

January 3, 1921

Excerpt from The Camp-Fire

Concerning his story in this issue a word from Arthur O. Friel. His letter enclosing it was dated April 23, 1920.

> This story gives Lourenço and Pedro further adventures after their return to the headquarters of the Coronel. The town of Remate de Males, where these experiences take place, is a real town on the Javary, about thirty miles up from the Solimões (Amazon), where the rubber-workers of the region gather during the high floods.
>
> —ARTHUR O. FRIEL.

The Tailed Men

Those are true words, *senhor*, though spoken in jest. You say that if men were shaped to fit their natures some would find it hard to wear hat and trousers, because they would have horns and tails.

I have met men who should have been so marked, and who ought also to have had claws instead of hands and split hoofs instead of feet; for, though their bodies were human, they were fiends at heart. True, in time their malice became known, and at last their own evil deeds caused their deaths, but not until they had brought much misery to others. How much blood and tears could be saved if only *Deos Padre* would make men—and women too—so that their natures could be seen at once.

Yes, that is a useless wish. But your remark, *senhor*, brings to my mind a memory of the strangest creatures I ever saw—creatures so queer that perhaps you will not believe me when I tell of them. Yet the tale will pass the time while we lounge here on the steamer's deck, and anything which kills the tedium of this long journey down the Amazon is worthwhile.

Now you two North American explorers, if I am not mistaken, have been adventuring in the country along the river Javary and westward in Peru toward the Ucayali. Then you have not visited the river Juruá, east of the Javary? It is well. If ever you return to Brazil and go far up that river, be prepared for trouble.

I have been there—and I am not going back. If the floods had not been very heavy that year I should never have gone there at all. With my comrade, Pedro Andrada, I had recently been out on a long rambling trip through the wild jungle along the border of Brazil and Peru, and there we had met with hardships which made us satisfied to stay in idleness at Remate de Males, a Javary town where we rubber-workers gathered in the rainy season. But now, loafing one day at the store of a trader with nothing to do but smoke and watch the dirty waters swirling past, we grew restless again.

"Lourenço, too much idleness is worse than too much work," said Pedro, yawning and stretching his powerful arms. "I feel stupid, and you are getting fat. If the flood does not go down soon you will get such a big belly that you will grunt like a sloth every time you tap a tree."

This was only a joke, for, though I am broad and had grown heavy from inaction, I had not swollen up along the belt-line. But I felt sluggish, as he did, and so weary of lounging that I wished someone would start a fight, or anything else that would quicken my blood. Lazily I tried to think of something we could do, but the only ideas that came to me were old ones and not worth trying. So I only grunted and sat still, looking up the river.

Something was floating down toward us and I watched it because there was nothing else to look at—drifting trees were so common that I hardly ever noticed them. As this thing came nearer, though, I saw that it was not a tree but a small canoe. It swung slowly around on the current, seeming empty and useless.

"There is something we can do," I said, nodding toward it. "A short paddle will stretch our muscles and give us another boat."

He yawned again and untied our own canoe, fastened to a post of the store. I got up and splashed toward it—the water was so high that, in spite of the tall poles on which the store stood, it flowed over the platform—and we were about to step in when Pedro started.

"*Por amor de Deos!*" he cried. "Look!"

The drifting boat was quite near us now. Above its edge something had risen and was moving weakly in little jerks; a thing like a skinny claw, or the hand of a man almost dead from starvation or fever, trying to attract attention and bring help. As we stared it dropped out of sight.

Without a word we leaped into our canoe and drove our paddles in deep. We were both old in the ways of the bush, and we knew what to expect. Yet the man we found out there on the river was in such a condition that even we, who had looked on many hard sights, turned cold as we stared down at him.

He seemed dead. His eyes were fixed and glassy, his mouth open, his chest motionless, his body shrunken to a skeleton. This did not disturb us, for we who work in the jungle of Javary see much of death. He was totally naked, and scabbed from head to foot by the bites of thousands of *piums* or *carrapatos*. Yet this did not shock us either, for any man who travels the Brazilian bush will be badly bitten at times by insects, and if he loses his clothing he will suffer much. The things that chilled us were two—the fear stamped deep in his ghastly face, and the marks of torture.

The scars were not new, but they were plain. They were the marks of fire and knife. And the worst of all was that he had been not only burned and cut, but mutilated.

Gripping the edge of his canoe, we went drifting down the current, looking at him and at each other. It seemed useless to take him ashore, for there was nothing to show who he was or whence he came, and the water was so high that we should have some trouble in finding a good place to bury him. Yet we nodded to each other, and were preparing to tow him in, when we jumped as if a snake had struck at us. He moved!

We had fully decided that he was dead, and that the fluttering movement of the hand we had seen was his last struggle. And when you see a dead man move, *senhores*, you are likely to recoil from him. We twitched our hands away from his boat. Before it could float off, though, we grabbed it again and hung on. His movement had been slight, only a quivering of the arms and a rise of the chest, with a low moaning sound as he breathed. Now, seeing that he still lived, we swiftly fastened his craft to ours and bent our paddles in hard strokes back to town.

Other men loafing at the doors facing the river had been watching us, and some of them were coming in their *montarias* and dugouts to see what we had found. Warning them out of the way, we drove ahead at full speed straight to the small *barracão* where we lived. There we put him into a hammock and poured brandy into his mouth.

He strangled, shivered a little, and coughed. We rubbed his cold hands and feet, raised and lowered his arms and legs, and gave him more brandy. Soon he began to breathe more deeply, and his eyes moved and stared at us. But no light showed in those eyes; they were as blank as those of a fish.

"You are safe now, friend," said Pedro. "Lie still and rest, and you will soon be strong again." Then he turned to the men who had crowded into our house after us.

"Do not stand idle!" he commanded. "Do you not see that he is naked and starving? Meldo, your woman is a good cook—go at once and have her make some broth. You others, go to Joaquim's store and get more brandy—this is gone. And bring clothes."

They went, all except Domengos Peixoto, a surly sot whom nobody liked. I asked him what he waited for, and he answered that there was no sense in rushing about for a man who would soon be dead. This angered us both. Pedro roughly grabbed him and shoved him toward the door, and I kicked him out into the water. He scrambled out, got into his *montaria*, and went away cursing.

After he was gone, though, we had to admit that he probably was right when he said this man would not live. Not only was he at the point of death from sickness and suffering and starvation, but he was crazed. Staring straight ahead, he was whispering and muttering, and his look of fear was even stronger than before.

We bent over him, listening. His talk was broken and confused. The terrible mud was dragging him down, he said. The jungle was black, black, and a jaguar was snarling under his tree. A huge snake was coiled beside his canoe, and if he could kill it he would eat it, but he had no weapon. The *piums* were a torment as bad as fire. Something with a long black tail was grinning at him. Oh for a *machete* or a rifle! These things, and many more, he mumbled.

"Poor fellow, he raves of the terrors of the unknown jungle where he has been," said Pedro. I nodded, for I too had seen men whose brains were twisted by hardship. But before I could answer, the man screamed out:

"The tailed men! The tailed men! Devils of hell, they—ah! Drop that knife! I will do it; I will do it; yes, yes, but put away that knife!"

He cringed and shivered miserably as he screeched.

"Have courage, comrade!" Pedro soothed. "We will protect you. There are no knives or—or tailed *demônios* here."

But the human wreck lay whimpering and moaning, and we could make nothing of his words. Then Meldo came hastening in with a bowl of hot broth, and the other men arrived with clothes and more brandy, followed by still more men who had come to see what was going on. We raised the sufferer in his hammock and began to feed him the soup.

The smell of that food seemed to give him strength, and he sucked it up so greedily that we had to restrain him from seizing it and burning himself. When it was gone we pulled shirt and trousers on him and laid him back. He grew stupid, like an animal which has starved and then gorged itself. Our hopes rose a little, for we thought he might sleep and gain power to live. So we drove every one out, and, though some would not go away but stayed outside in their boats, the house became quiet. We sat in the other hammock, silently waiting.

All that afternoon we waited. The sick man seemed not to sleep but to doze with eyes partly open. It was nearly night when he breathed deep and the eyes opened wide. As we rose and stood beside him we saw two things: that the gray shade of death was on him, but that he had become sane.

Under his matted black hair his eyes gleamed hollowly first at me, then at Pedro. A light came into his scarred face, and a weak smile grew on his bearded mouth.

"Pedro!" he whispered.

My partner stared down at him.

"Yes, I am Pedro, friend," he said. "But I do not know you."

"Luis Pitta," breathed the other.

"Luis Pitta! *Deos meo!* Are you Luis?"

The dying man nodded slightly.

"Luis. I die."

He lay breathing a moment, then went on:

"I am glad—to die and be at peace. Keep away—Juruá."

"Luis Pitta!" repeated Pedro in a shocked tone. "Luis—Luis, old comrade, who has treated you so? You were a strong man, and now—"

Luis shivered. Fear shot back into his face. As he answered his voice rose to a scream.

"The tailed men! The black men with tails! The demons of the Juruá! O God, save me from—"

He went limp. His jaw dropped. He was dead.

Again I felt cold. From the door, where other men heard that awful cry, came a low mumble of whispers and exclamations. Over the dead man Pedro made the sign of the cross. Then he began making a cigaret, and his hands shook. When it was lighted he began pacing up and down. His face grew hard and his eyes burned. Stopping suddenly, he demanded—

"Who remembers Luis Pitta?"

Nobody answered. The men outside had left their boats and edged in at the door, where they stared at the dead man as if trying to remember him, but none seemed to know him. The name of Luis Pitta meant nothing to me either, so I kept silence.

"We were boys together in Santarem, long before we came into this cursed Javary country," said Pedro. "Luis went to work as a *seringueiro* at the rubber estate of Senhor da Costa on the Branco, while I worked for Coronel Nunes. I have not heard anything of him since two years ago, when a man of the da Costa *seringal* told me Luis had grown restless and homesick for the open *campos* and clean sandy beaches of Santarem, and, in the time of high-water, had left for the East. He intended to paddle through flooded lakes and channels until he reached the Juruá, go down that river to Fonteboa on the Solimões, and there get an Amazon boat which would carry him home.

"He was a strong, merry-hearted, fearless man, was Luis. Now look at him! A broken, tortured, fear-ridden wreck who raved of demons on the Juruá. *Por Deos!* Demons they are, the things which have done such work on my old comrade. But, demons or not, they shall pay!"

He choked with rage and struck one fist hard into the other hand.

"Who will go with me?" he roared. "Who will go to the Juruá and fight these fiends? Luis was a *seringueiro* like ourselves. Who goes to avenge him?"

Still no one spoke. The men glanced at one another, stared at the dead Luis, shuffled their feet, but made no answer.

"Pah! You sicken me!" Pedro growled. "You are not men of the bush, but potbellied town loafers. Get out! The air around you stinks!"

Then up spoke a man shamed by my partner's scorn.

"Pedro, you are mad. From the mouth of the Javary to the mouth of the Juruá is more than four hundred miles, and from there to the upper reaches of that river is at least six hundred. Shall we go a thousand miles to avenge a man we did not know? No. And this man Luis said the ones who broke him were devils—*demônios* with tails! Any of us will fight men, but we will not go far away to attack things spawned in hell. So long as they stay where they are we will let them alone."

The others grunted their approval of this. After glaring at them a moment, Pedro slowly nodded.

"You have it right," he admitted. "This is not your business. What is more, I do not want any of you now. If you would travel a thousand miles to get to a place that can be reached by paddling a hundred miles in another direction, you have not brains enough to be worth taking with me. I will go alone."

He motioned for them to leave the house. They went, shaking their heads and saying he was crazed. Then he turned to me, and found me squinting down the barrel of my rifle.

"I am not asking you to go either," he told me.

"You do not need to," I said. "Where is the oil? This barrel is rusty again."

He laughed out suddenly.

"Good old Lourenço! I should not have said that. The oil is there behind that *cuya*. But first let us bury Luis while it is yet day. We have not much time."

After some difficulty, we found a place where the dead man could be laid at rest. Then we went to the store, where we found men growling because we had buried Luis so quickly instead of burning candles over him all night and giving the townsmen an excuse to sit up and get drunk, as is usual when someone dies. They hushed, though, when we gave them hard looks and then bought many cartridges.

"Are you indeed going on this wild trip of which men talk?" asked Joaquim, the trader. When we said we were, he added:

"Then talk with my old father, who traveled much in his younger days and knows something of the Juruá. You will find him in the family-room behind that door."

In the room to which he pointed we found an old man lying in a hammock and smoking a long pipe.

"Greetings, *compadre*," said Pedro. "We go to the Juruá. Joaquim says you can tell us something of that river."

The old man blinked up at us, took out his pipe, and cleared his throat.

"And so I can, my sons," he answered. "What do you seek on the Juruá?"

"We know not, father, whether we seek men or beasts or demons; they may be all three. We would find things with tails which have tortured my old friend, Luis Pitta. The tailed men of the Juruá, he called them."

"*Si*. I have heard of the death of Luis."

He began puffing again, gazing through the smoke as if seeing something far off. We said no more, but waited. After a time he spoke again.

"The Juruá is bad. It is long and more crooked than a snake, and on its banks live evil things. I would advise you not to go there, but I see that your eyes are hot and your heart burns for your friend, and I am not so old that I have forgotten my own youth. You will go. But I hope, my sons, that you will not find those things you seek, for if you do you may not come back.

"I have not seen those *demônios*, but I have heard of them. They are far up the river and they are beasts which walk like men. To reach them by going up the river would take many days and you might not live to enter their country, for the Arauas would murder you if they could. These Arauas live eight days' journey from the Solimões and they are not to be trusted.

"There are also the Catauxias, but these are not so bad. Above these were the Canamaris, but the Canamaris have nearly died out through war with the Arauas. And much farther up are the Culinos and Nawas, of whom I know little, for it takes two moons to reach their region from the Amazon. Above all these are the Uginas. They are the tailed men.

"Yet you can avoid the tribes lower down the river, and shorten your journey to the Ugina country, by paddling up the Tecuahy and following a *furo* to the south."

"That was our plan," Pedro nodded. "I know there is a *furo*, but I do not know where it begins."

"It is in the Red Jungle. Far up the Tecuahy you will find it—a great forest of *massaranduba* trees. Soon after you have entered it you will see opening at the left a long *enseada*. Go into this bay and you will find it narrowing to a *furo* which will run almost straight for a time and then will become more winding. Where it ends I do not know, but it leads toward the land of the tailed *demônios*. *Adeos*, my sons. Go with God."

As we strode out Pedro turned and looked back at him. And when we got into our canoe he said:

"There, Lourenço, is the first real man I have seen this day, except yourself. Did you notice how his old eyes followed us when we came away? He has been an adventurer in his day, and even now he hungers to go with us. It is a pity he is so old and feeble."

Back to our *barracão* we went, stowed our equipment in our canoe, cleaned our guns, curled up in the hammocks, and slept. As soon as the black night turned to gray day we rolled out again, ate, and started.

Days of paddling followed. On our first night out we found ourselves very tired, for the loafing at the town had softened us and shortened our wind, and the next morning we were sluggish and stiff. After that, though, our muscles hardened, and we swung along at a stroke that put the miles steadily behind us. We talked little, for Pedro brooded on the fate of his old friend Luis, so that for a time he was not the lighthearted fellow I had usually found him. He did not seem like himself again until we reached the Red Jungle.

Late on a day of rain we found it. The dense green wall of jungle along the banks of the Tecuahy thinned out. Then the huge reddish trunks of *massarandubas* began to slide past us, their lofty crowns matting together so thickly that they seemed to make a solid roof. Soon we were in the midst of them. To right and left and up ahead they towered out of the flood waters. Through them we paddled on fast, looking to the left. And before long, as the father of Joaquim had told us, a long *enseada* opened out toward the southeast.

In among the giant trees we pushed until we reached a hill where we could land. There Pedro took from the canoe his *machadinha*—the little hatchet which we use in tapping rubber trees—and cut into a big trunk until milk came pouring out. As you know, *senhores*, the *massaranduba* is a "cow-tree," and its milk is good to drink if taken fresh, though it soon thickens to a tough glue if exposed to the air. We were hot and thirsty, and each of us drank a cupful of milk. Then, much refreshed, we made camp between the root-walls of that tree and ate our evening meal.

Though the day had not quite ended when we finished, it was very dark under that thick roof of branches and leaves. But the rain had stopped, and now the low sun suddenly flashed out, shooting its long rays in from the bay and making the wet reddish trunks glow like dull fire.

"This is a solemn place," I said, gazing at the great columns standing out against the farther gloom. "It seems weird and unnatural. No Indians would ever live in such a place; they would believe it to be the home of the Caypor*, that great jungle-demon with the flaming red hair."

He nodded and opened his lips to answer. But no words came. His eyes widened, then narrowed, as if a strange thought had come to him, and he looked sharply at the nearest tree. I looked too, but saw nothing odd.

"What is it?" I asked.

"The women—" he said slowly, "the women of the *caboclos* make red dye from the bark of the *massaranduba*."

"Yes. But what of that?"

Still he studied the tree. Then, for the first time since Luis Pitta came floating down the river, he laughed. But why he laughed he would not tell. So, knowing him well, I asked no more questions.

As suddenly as it had come, the sun left us. At once it grew so black that we could see nothing at all. Tree frogs and crickets burst out into their usual nightly hammering. Their racket made us feel more at home here, and we soon slept

In the morning we drank again of the tree-milk, and before we left the hill Pedro cut off chunks of the rough *massaranduba* bark. These he stowed away in the canoe. Seeing my questioning look, he grinned.

"Perhaps I will make a red dye and paint the tails of the Uginas with it," he joked. "Who knows?"

"If we find them, I think we will paint them with red from their own

---

* Bush spirit, Amazonas.

veins," I replied.

His face hardened, and he grunted agreement. We left the hill, paddled away through the trees to the open water, and went on until we found the *furo*.

In the next three days we journeyed far and fast. The *furo* was narrow, but straight and deep, and there was neither current nor low-hanging bush to hold us back. The Red Jungle still rose around us, and its thick roof prevented the usual small stuff from growing around its trunks. In the dim shadows among those tremendous trees we saw no living thing, and heard no sound except that of frogs and bugs.

Then the big trees ended, and again we met the tangle of undergrowth and hanging vines. Here we had to travel more slowly. In some places we had to use poles instead of paddles. Snakes dropped down around us from branches overhead. Swarms of *piums* and *motucas* attacked us and bit until blood dripped from us. At night we heard jaguars roaring nearby, and once we had to sleep almost buried under our supplies to protect ourselves from vampires. But we made good speed along the narrow canal in the daytime, and at length we shot out into a clay-colored water which at first we took for the Juruá.

We soon learned, however, that this was not even a river. It had a slight flow, but it was only a winding maze of flood waters in which we wandered for days. And in this wandering we lost the *furo*. When we found that we were not on any river we sought it again but could not find it. But we did find a small river flowing in from the south, and up that stream we went.

Before we had gone far on this river we were attacked. Shrill yells sounded in the bush, and arrows dropped around our boat. We snatched our rifles, but could see no men—only the heavy arrows rising slowly from the farther shore, curving in air and plunging straight down. Several struck in the canoe.

"Drop as if you were hit," snapped Pedro. Even as he spoke an arrow fell down my back, scratching my shoulder muscles and catching in my shirt. I slumped forward, thinking that now I was a dead man in truth—for if that arrow was poisoned I could not live long. A second later Pedro gave a groaning cry and flopped backward.

At once the arrows stopped. The yells became screeches of savage joy. We lay quiet, our boat drifting downward, until Pedro gave the word. Then we popped up and found naked wild men in plain sight on the bushy bank. Before they realized we were alive our bullets were striking them down.

At the belch of our guns they screeched again—this time from fear. They jumped away, but not before three of them had fallen dead and a fourth had tumbled into the river. We slammed several more bullets into the jungle, and heard their yelps grow fainter as they fled. Then I yanked that arrow out of my shirt and looked at its point. There was no stain of poison on it, and so the scratch across my shoulders meant nothing.

"Let us get that man," said Pedro, and I saw that the Indian who had fallen into the water was alive and trying to crawl out. We drove the canoe at him, caught him, and dragged him in. Then we crossed the river again and hung to bushes while we questioned him.

He had been shot in one leg but he paid no attention to the wound. He was more afraid of what we might yet do to him than of what we had done. His face was dull and stupid but his beady eyes showed his fear. We took care that he should keep on fearing us and tried to make him talk.

It was hard to make him understand. We spoke in Tupi, the *lingoa geral* of the Amazonian Indians, but he seemed to know only a few words of it. From this we judged that he belonged to one of those small tribes often found far away from the Amazon, who have lived in one place so long they have almost forgotten the language of others.

Yet we learned a few things. We had been attacked because we were strangers, and these people feared all strangers. They would not assail us again, because now they would be too much afraid of our guns. The river we were following came out of a chain of swamps, and at the other end of that chain another stream ran south. This was what we most wanted to know, for it meant that we were on a route that would bring us out on the Juruá. We tried to find out something about the tailed men, but he could not—or would not understand; he seemed to think we spoke of monkeys. So, having learned all we could from him, we let him go.

Back across the river we took him and put him out on the bank, knowing the others would find him there when they came back for their dead. Then we continued up the stream.

Our prisoner had told the truth; perhaps he was too stupid to lie to us. At the head of the river we came into great dismal *lagos*. After crossing these dead waters we found a flowing current which took us down another small stream to the south. This widened into a good-sized river, and at length it carried us out into a big, slow, dark water which was wider than anything we had seen since leaving Remate de Males. We had reached the Juruá.

" 'The Juruá is long and more crooked than a snake, and on its banks live evil things,' " said Pedro, gazing out across the dreary river. "So spoke the father of Joaquim. In truth, this looks to be an evil water. Now shall we go up or down? We do not know where Luis was held prisoner."

"Up," I judged. "We were told that these Uginas live higher up than the other tribes. And Luis, in escaping, would naturally go down the river so that the current would aid him. The place where he was held must be above here."

So we turned to the right and journeyed up the dark water.

For two days we found nothing. By day we stole along through flooded swamps, keeping near shore, watching the bush and listening. By night we hid our canoe and slung our hammocks at the top of some hill, lighting no fire. We shot no game, made no noise we could avoid, and slept lightly with our guns beside us. But we neither saw nor heard anything except the usual animal life.

Then came storm. The sky had been dull for days, and rain had fallen often, but not hard. Now, as we scouted along a steep bank rising several feet above us, Pedro stopped paddling and looked behind him. I too looked backward, finding that the sky was swiftly growing black. As we held our paddles there came to us a dull roar of wind.

At once we snapped into swift strokes, seeking an inlet. Before we found one the wind had struck us, and the storm-waves were slapping heavily against our boat. But as we sped onward the bank grew lower, and then a small cove opened. We swerved into it. As we tumbled out on shore the storm broke.

Blinding lightning, crashing thunder, and drowning rain came all at once. We dragged the canoe up as high as we could, then squatted beside a tree until the squall should pass. But it did not pass as soon as expected. The wind and the deluge of rain swept onward after a while, but the thunder and lightning continued. So we stayed where we were, our eyes nearly closed to lessen the glare of the light-flashes, and waited.

Suddenly I felt Pedro's hand on my wrist. His lips moved, but a roar of thunder swallowed his words. He had come out of his squat and was sitting straight up on his heels, and his eyes were wide-open. Following his stare, I saw, peering at us from behind a tree, a face.

It did not move. It hung there as if it grew from the tree, and the swift lightning lighted it up time after time. It was the face of an animal, but yet the face of a man. Heavy black hair hung down over its low forehead. Little black eyes glimmered at us. The nose flared so that it seemed a snout. The thick lips were drawn back, and yellow teeth gleamed in a soundless snarl. The whole face was bestial—such a face as a man might see in a bad dream.

The rapid flicker of lightning suddenly stopped. With the end of that winking glare the jungle seemed black. Pedro pushed me, and I lost my balance and toppled sidewise. He shoved me again, and then I caught his idea—that we should move away from that spot. We crawled several feet, got behind a tree, and stood up with rifles cocked.

Another flash whitened the bush. We saw the beast-man again. He too had moved, though only a little. He had slipped out until his arms and shoulders were clear of the tree, and he held a bow with the arrow aimed at the spot where we had been.

Though that space now was empty, he loosed the arrow before he realized we were gone. In the same instant he fell with two bullets through his head.

The lightning vanished, but we jumped through the gloom to his tree. Beside it we found him huddled as he had fallen. While other flashes came and went we squatted there, peering around to learn whether this man had companions. Seeing none, we dragged him out to the canoe.

There we looked him over. We had dropped him face upward, and we saw that he was small, scrawny, filthy, and totally naked. Now Pedro took one arm and flopped the body over. We both recoiled.

"*Deos meo!*" cried my comrade. "It is true! Look! The tail!"

Yes, *senhores*, that dead man-animal had a tail. It was a long, naked, blackish tail like that of a great rat. It was not a thing fastened to him by rods or glue, either, but a real tail that grew from his body. And in spite of the dying screams of Luis Pitta, in spite of what the father of Joaquim had said of the Uginas, the sight of that bare, repulsive thing hanging from the dead man struck us dumb.

We stood staring at it until Pedro stooped, grasped it, and lifted. The body rose from the ground and dangled in air like that of a monkey. Dropping it, my partner rubbed his hands on his breeches as if to get rid of a snaky feeling.

The thunder died to a dull mutter before we spoke again. Then Pedro said:

"We have sent one of Luis' *demônios* down the road to hell. But yet this thing is no demon. It is hardly more than a *bicho do mato*—a beast of the forest. Either of us could kill two of these creatures at once with our bare hands. I wonder that a strong man like Luis let such things overcome him."

"They must have caught him asleep, or trapped him in some way," I reasoned. "And any one man, no matter how strong, can be overpowered by many others. You know how it is when we meet a horde of ants—we can crush a score of them at one step, but the others will swarm upon us and bite us horribly. And an ant is a tiny thing compared to this brute."

"True," he agreed. "I should not have spoken so of Luis. Let us see how bad the bite of this misbegotten creature would be."

We went over to the arrow sticking in the ground, pulled it up, and examined it. It was poorly made and had no barb, seeming to be only a straight stick with one end badly notched and the other fire-hardened and scraped to a point. Looking closely at that point, we could find no sign of poison.

"They are so ignorant that they do not know how to make poison," said my partner. "Yet we must not make the mistake of holding them too lightly.

This arrow was shot hard enough to kill one of us. And no doubt they are cunning, like an alligator or any other low beast. Ah, the sun shines again. Let us see where this man came from."

As he said, the sun had blazed out. By the new light we went back to the tree where the man-beast had lurked, and there we found a few more arrows and his bow. The bow was as poorly made as the arrow we had inspected, but was strong enough to kill. Working away from the tree, we sought a path, but found none. In the mud, however, we spied the tracks of the dead man's feet. This trail we followed back through the bush.

It was not easy to track his course, for the footmarks were few and scattered, and he seemed to have rambled in a winding, purposeless way. But when we lost it we always managed to find it again, and gradually it led us back some distance from the river.

We judged that he had been hunting, for we found spots were he had stopped and stood, making several marks in one place as he shifted his feet. On and on we crept, watching everything, saying nothing, until we came into what seemed a very faint path. There the wet earth was pressed down more firmly, and by looking along its edges we found a few marks of human toes.

Along this vague track we went with our heads up, glancing at the trail only now and then to make sure we did not lose it. All at once I stopped and threw up my rifle. Ahead of us a dark shape was swinging down along vine hanging from high branches.

But I did not shoot. The moving thing was only a big monkey. It showed no fear of us, but came down until it could get a good view of us. There it stopped, gripping the vine with all four of its paws and, swinging slowly, watched us. We stood still, staring back. After a time it climbed deliberately up again until it reached the tangle of limbs. Then we saw it go jumping and swinging away through the trees.

"He goes toward the place where this path leads," whispered Pedro.

"A pet monkey, perhaps," I guessed.

"Perhaps."

He smiled oddly, then motioned for me to go on.

We advanced for some distance before we saw or heard anything more. Often we stopped to listen; and it was at one of these still moments that we caught a sound ahead—a low mutter like a man's voice. At once we slipped aside into some thick bush and squatted.

Soon we heard a slight rustle of leaves. Then a man came stealing past. Another followed, and another—four in all. They might have been brothers of the one we had killed on the river-bank, for each had the same low, brutal sort of face. I thought I saw tails too, but could not be sure, for their bodies were partly hidden by the undergrowth. All were armed with bows and arrows, and all were peering ahead as if hunting something.

When the last man had passed I started to creep forward, intending both to look after them and to see whether more were coming. But I stopped where I was. High up over us broke out a noise.

Glancing upward, I saw the big black monkey which had watched us and gone away. He was hanging from a branch, looking down at us and chattering loudly. Low grunts came from the path where the savages had disappeared.

"Do not shoot!" whispered Pedro. "Use your *machete*!"

Silently we drew our bush-knives. With our legs tensed under us, ready for a spring, we waited. In the path a man reappeared, scowling into the tangle on both sides of the trail. On his heels crept another. Before we saw the other two, the first man spied us.

The instant his eyes met ours we leaped up and at him. My *machete* chopped him across the neck, and as he reeled I heard the cutting crunch of Pedro's heavy knife killing the savage next to him. Clutching my man about the body, I swung him around as a shield as I faced the two left alive. It was lucky that I did this, for one of those *bárbaros* had drawn an arrow to its head, and now he shot. The arrow plunged into the body I held. Throwing the dead man from me, I jumped at my enemy and, before he could put another arrow to the bow, struck him down. Then I turned toward the fourth man.

He was stabbing at Pedro. My comrade jumped back like a cat, and his red *machete* whirled up sidewise against the other's wrist. A snarling grunt sounded in the throat of the Ugina. His knife flew aside. An instant later his whole body rose from the ground as Pedro drove his *machete* into his stomach and lifted.

A short, gasping wail burst from him. After Pedro threw him to the ground he writhed a moment, then lay still. We looked all around us, but saw no other man. Except ourselves, the black monkey overhead was the only living thing in that place.

We kicked the dead men over on their faces. Each had a tail.

"Four more gone to whine to Luis for forgiveness," said Pedro grimly, as he wiped his *machete* on a leaf. Then he stood scowling thoughtfully at the one he had just killed.

"He had a knife," he went on. "I chopped his bow, and then he drew— See! He wears a belt! A black leather belt and a knife-sheath! Where could such an animal get a knife, belt, and sheath? Where is that knife?"

Searching the undergrowth, we found it. It was long, with a sharp point and an odd handle—a handle of white bone, carved to fit the hand, with a knob at the upper end.

"It is as I thought," said Pedro, nodding. "This is Luis' own knife. I remember it well. It is a North American knife, and was given him by a man from Nova York who stayed for a time at Santarem collecting birds and insects for a great *museu*. He was very proud of it, for there was not another like it on the Amazon. Poor Luis!"

"These are the fiends who tortured him. This one must be the very man who cut him with his own knife—the one of whom he screamed as he died. I am sorry I did not know it sooner, for then this beast would have died more slowly."

He glowered down at the dead Ugina. Then he plucked big leaves from the bush, wrapped up the knife, and tied the bundle with bush-cord.

"I do not want the belt and sheath, now that this vile creature has worn them," he said. "But the knife Luis loved so well shall stay with me. Now let us throw these brutes out of the way."

We did so. After that Pedro turned back toward the river.

"Come," he said. "I have a plan which is better than going straight ahead now. And we had best get more cartridges."

It was not until then that I realized we carried no cartridges except those in the magazines of our rifles. So, picking our guns from the undergrowth where we had hidden them, we returned as we had come. We took no care to conceal our trail, for our feet were bare and made no strange marks in the path.

In the river-bank Pedro stopped short, staring at the ground.

"Lourenço!" he muttered. "We killed that *demônio*, did we not?"

I looked for the dead man. He was gone.

Our canoe was there, and nothing in it had been touched. There was no sign that other men had come while we were away. The bush around us was silent and empty. Yet that tailed thing with the top of its head blown off had disappeared.

The sun had gone under clouds again, and the light was dim. Stooping, we scanned the ground where the Ugina had lain. Then we saw signs that something had been dragged from the spot. The signs led toward the water. In the mud at the edge of the water was the trail of a big alligator.

"Ah, that is more natural," Pedro said in a relieved tone. "I was almost ready to believe that the man-devil had stuffed his brains back into his head and walked off. I think I am losing my own brains. Let us go somewhere else for the night. It is too late to do anything more today."

So we left the inlet, paddled back downstream, crossed to the other side of the river, and camped there.

As you may suppose, we argued that night about the tailed men. We agreed that they were not much more than animals, but the question was how they got tails. They might be monkeys turning into men, or they might be men becoming monkeys; but still they did not seem monkey-like, except that they were hairy and had the tails and faces of brutes. Their feet were the big flat feet of men, not monkey paws; and their tails seemed useless. Finally Pedro said:

"The things of which we are sure are that they have tails and that they are vile and cruel. They have no human hearts. And my idea about them is that they are men, but so low that they breed with monkeys.

"You remember the *bárbaros* who attacked us before we passed through the swamps, and what a stupid fellow that one was whom we caught. He was not much higher than these Uginas, though he had no tail. You know how some of these small tribes who live in one place breed among themselves until their brains become hardly better than those of animals. They sink lower and lower until they are beasts, living only to eat and sleep and do vicious things. And you remember that black monkey we met, which looked at us and then brought those four men to seek us. He was a *coaita,* the tallest and most knowing monkey in our jungles—you have seen *coaitas* kept as pets along the Solimões. Why, then, should a tribe so low as these Uginas not breed with *coaitas*? And why should not that breeding give them tails?

"Who knows where men came from in the first place? Who knows whether the first men on earth did not have tails? If they did, would it be strange that such people as these, by mixing with monkeys, should grow, them again? Lourenço, I think this is the true reason why these tailed men exist.

"I believe that *coaita* who spied on us was not only a pet, but a blood-brother—or perhaps a father—to some of those creatures who came to hunt us! And I believe that when we enter their town—if they have a town—we shall find other *coaitas* there."

"You may have it right," I admitted. "Now that I think of it, I remember something I once heard said by a college professor from North America—Senhor Grayson, who stayed at the *coronel's* place for a time to study jungle creatures, and whom we named the Jabiru because he looked so much like that bird.

"He said there had been a time, far back in the early days, when men lived in trees like monkeys. He did not say they had tails, or even that men and monkeys ever were the same. But if they lived like monkeys perhaps they were like monkeys in other ways—I do not know any reason why they should not be.

"But the question now is not so much where these men got their tails as what we shall do to them tomorrow. What is your plan?"

"My plan now is to sleep," he said. And sleep he did, so that I could do nothing but wonder a while and then sleep also.

In the morning Pedro made the first fire we had lighted since reaching the Juruá. The place where we had slept was up a narrow creek concealed by thick bush, and we could find no sign of human life near it. My partner set water to heat in a cooking-vessel, broke up the *massaranduba* bark he had cut in the Red Jungle, and put that also into the pot. Then, leaving me to watch the fire, he went away.

He was gone for some time. When he returned he brought an armful of light-colored strips of thin bark and a number of small springy withes. While I kept the water boiling he untied the knife of Luis, which was more thin of blade than his *machete*, and with this he shredded the light bark into fibers hardly bigger than hairs.

At this work he spent most of the forenoon. When it was done we pulled the boiled chunks of *massaranduba* bark from the pot. The water in that vessel now had become a red dye. Into this we stuffed the hairy fibers, leaving them in until they became red, then taking them out and putting in others, until at last all were dyed.

All this time I had asked no questions, for Pedro had plagued me many times in the past when I sought reasons for what he did, and had always found that behind his actions was an idea. But now I could no longer keep still.

"If it is not a great secret," I said, "may I ask what you are making?"

"Hair," he grinned. "Red hair. Is it not beautiful?"

"It is red enough, if any one loves red hair. But what has this to do with killed tailed men?"

"I am surprised that you have not guessed it," he mocked. "We shall make ourselves so handsome that when the Uginas see us they will drop dead from admiration."

I said no more. When he took some spare clothing and rubber-covered pack-sheets from the canoe, however, and began to shape them over withes bent and tied into the shape of a large head, I caught his idea. Back came the memory of my idle remark in the Red Jungle about that demon of the Indians—the Caypor. Now I saw why Pedro had brought along the red bark and why he made red hair. At once I went to work helping him.

Over the frameworks of springy branches we built up trunks, shoulders, and heads, weaving bush-cord through holes in the cloth and rubber and tying them into the right shape. Around the great heads we bound that red hair which we had just made. On the dark rubber we made awful faces, using bits of fungus, daubs of clay and streaks of red dye, and cutting slits for mouths, into which we fastened bits of wood like jagged yellow teeth. When we lifted the things and set them on our shoulders we became the most horrible monsters I have ever seen, except in nightmares.

We seemed misshapen giants whose arms grew from our waists, whose hair had been dyed in blood, and whose huge red-smeared mouths were stretching open ready to tear men into mangled corpses. Even a civilized man would have started with fear at first sight of us. And we believed that such low-brained creatures as the tailed Uginas would take us for real and deadly fiends.

Making sure that the frameworks fitted well over our shoulders and that the holes cut for our eyes would not slip aside and leave us blinded, we took them off again and emptied our canoe. After hiding our equipment where nothing could disturb it while we were away, we ate and smoked.

"Our arms are stained red from that dye," I said.

"They will be more red before we return," Pedro answered. And he spoke truth.

No rain was falling, but the light was poor. This suited us well. Carrying with us only those weird false bodies, full cartridge-belts, and our weapons, we slipped the canoe down the creek to the river, crossed over, and stole along up the northern bank until we reached that little inlet where we had shot the first Ugina. A short scouting trip proved that this time no enemy lurked there. So we bound on our terrible masks, looked again at our rifles to make sure they were full, and took the trail toward the lair of the tailed men.

We soon found that, though our towering masks were not heavy, they were awkward and uncomfortable. Before long we were dripping with sweat, and we had to walk in a stooping posture and step carefully to keep our false heads from butting against low branches.

But we knew that unless the Uginas lived in different fashion from all other tribes their village would be in a cleared space, and there we could stand erect. We knew, too, that they probably would be dozing now, for it was midday and the muggy air was sweltering hot. Our plan of attack was very simple—to walk in among them and start shouting.

At the place where we had hidden yesterday and fought the four men led by the monkey, we found signs that other men had been there since we left. The bush was beaten aside and broken, and fresh footmarks showed in spots where the soil was soft. Though we stayed in the path, we knew the bodies which we had thrown aside had been found and taken away.

"We had best go slowly," I advised, "or we may fall into a trap. They must be hunting us, now that they have found those bodies."

But he snorted.

"You forget that we are demons," he objected. "Who ever heard of a demon slinking along cautiously? We must go in with a roar. If a few lurk in ambush, they will run when they see us. And I do not believe they are waiting for us—they have no reason to expect us to return, and it is so hot now that they are probably sleeping in their dens."

He was not wrong. We saw no man until we opened our fight. Abruptly the jungle ended and we emerged into a clearing. Trees grew there, but they were few and large and scattered, and the smaller growth had been hacked or burned away. We saw no houses of any kind. Surprised by this, we halted.

Then out rang a scream, so near us that we jumped. From the base of a huge tree close at hand sprang a naked figure which ran shrieking down the open space. We threw up our rifles, but did not shoot; for the long hair flying out behind that form showed it was a woman. Later I remembered that she was not a tailed creature. Now we glanced at the place whence she had jumped, and saw that it was a tangle of sticks with a door-like hole in it.

Out through that hole scrambled two other figures. One was a big *coaita*, which looked at us and then fled up into the tree. The other was a squat, scared-looking beast-man who rose to his knees and threw a spear at us. Pedro's rifle barked, and the Ugina flopped on his face.

Then we saw the others. From the butts of those big trees they came popping out like ants. The woman was still running, still screaming, and as they saw us they too began to jabber and yell. In our deepest tones we roared an answer. Then, our guns spitting death, we advanced on them.

For a moment it seemed that they would run for the jungle. I hoped they would stand and fight, for I would dislike to shoot even such beasts as these in the back. But I need not have troubled about that. They ran only to get weapons. If they had known we were merely men they probably would have swarmed on us. As it was, they bunched around their trees and shot arrows and threw small spears, fighting as a beast fights—because he is too much scared to do anything else.

We stopped before we came too close, bellowing as fiendishly as we could and moving from side to side while we reloaded our guns. Arrows fell around us, some striking fire-charred stumps and bouncing off, some slithering through the grass, some chunking down into pools of water. Many of these might have hit us if we had stood still, but by our irregular movements to the side we evaded most of them. Besides, the Uginas were shooting and throwing with the hurried aim of fear, and their spears fell short and their arrows flew high. No doubt those who took any aim at all shot for those terrifying false heads of ours. At any rate, the few missiles which hit us went into the hollow framework of our masks, leaving our own heads and bodies untouched.

Shooting swiftly but carefully, we poured another magazine of lead into a knot of snarling savages around the butt of the nearest tree. Some yelped as they fell. Others dropped silently. One or two squirmed on the ground, then lay still. The note of terror in the yells of those still standing became sharper. And when, our guns once more emptied, we began advancing toward them as we reloaded, panic swept them into howling flight.

A couple of dropping arrows had caught in my shirt and stuck there, scraping my skin but doing no harm. From our false heads and shoulders several other arrows protruded. And the Uginas, seeing this and finding that we showed no signs of hurt, must have believed it was impossible to kill or even wound us. Yelling hoarsely, they turned and ran for the bush.

But it was only the first tree that was deserted. From the other butts more Uginas ran out and joined those seeking cover, but these seemed to be mostly women and children—or, perhaps, monkeys. The men stayed, bunching together and sending a few more arrows at us. One of these, falling slantwise, pierced my left foot.

I was glad then that those arrows had no barbs, for it was easy to pull out that one and throw it aside. I tried to do this carelessly, as if it did not hurt. But I must have shown some sign of pain—perhaps I had jumped when the shaft struck me—for the shouts grew louder and arrows came more thickly again. We paid no attention to these, moving on as if we scorned them until we came into the shelter of the big abandoned tree.

There, partly covered by the huge trunk, we shot steadily into the knots of savages around the other trees. We divided these between us, Pedro taking those to the left while I attacked those to the right. And now we did not concentrate on one spot alone, but shifted our fire from butt to butt, striking men down here and there so rapidly that it must have seemed we were killing the whole tribe at once. Yet the Uginas fought on, though their fight seemed to be weakening and their noise died down.

If they had known enough to keep quiet we might have died suddenly. Nothing had threatened our backs, and our enemies were in front, so that we never glanced behind. But now new cries began to come from the line of trees, and we saw the beast-men looking beyond us. Wheeling, we found several stealthy forms crawling up on us among the stumps.

They were on hands and knees, partly hidden by stumps and grass, but we could see their heads well enough. Into two of those heads I sent bullets. Then my hammer snapped down without an explosion. Dropping the empty gun, I yanked my *machete* and jumped at the rest of them.

But they did not wait. Their only weapons were short spears, and as we bore down on them they rose, threw their weapons, screeched, and ran for their lives. One just ahead of me fell over a stump, and another tripped over his outflung arms. I got both of them with slashing blows across the back of the neck. Pedro, too, caught one of the fleeing creatures and killed him, and later I found that he had shot another as he charged at them. Only two were left, and they went bounding away, howling fearfully.

We turned back, sweeping the line of trees with our eyes to see whether other Uginas meant to rush us. But none did. Instead, more were sneaking for the bush.

"My cartridges are running low," said Pedro, as we reloaded. "Let us advance on them before we use up all our bullets."

With our deepest yells we left our tree and advanced at a trot. The beast-men could stand no longer. A few sprang out from each butt and fled. The rest wavered an instant and followed. Halting, we shot fast and straight, downing several more of them. Then the clearing was empty.

"Now that they have quit, they will keep on running until they think themselves safe," said Pedro. "To help them on their way I will scream a little."

And scream he did, horrible wailing screams that sounded as if some wounded man were being torn apart and devoured by those yellow teeth in our false faces. They made me cold, even though I knew who made them and why. And the fear-ridden fugitives must have fled deep into the bush on hearing them, for we saw none of them again.

Roaring and screaming by turns, we passed along the line of big trees, seeking any living thing that might remain. We found only two. In the doorway of one of the miserable hovels built between the root-buttresses we spied a wounded savage. As we stepped toward him he gave one snarl of terror, lifted a spear, and plunged it into his own heart. In another hut we found a sick *coaita* monkey which squatted and watched us without moving. Nothing else was under those trees except bodies.

Some of the dead men, we noticed, had no tails. But, tailed or tailless, all had the same brute faces. We paid little attention to them, except to make sure they were dead and could not kill us from behind. When we reached the end of the open space we stopped yelling and stood looking at each other.

Pedro's mask was pierced in several places, and one arrow jutted out only a few inches from his eyes.

"Are you hit?" I asked.

"No. This arrow scraped my head and may have torn my scalp, but it is nothing. Your foot wound is much worse than that. Let us finish our work and go."

Out from a pocket he drew a small package carefully wrapped in rubber, and from this he produced matches. We pulled a few dry sticks from inside the stinking hut nearest us and set fire to them. Soon we had all the shelters around that tree going up in smoke. Then we passed back as we had come, firing the filthy hovels until each tree was ringed with flame.

After leaving the tree where we had made most of our fight, we stopped a moment to look down at the bodies of those whom we had shot while they were creeping up on us from behind. They lay face down, and they were tailless and had long hair.

"*Nossa Senhora!*" exclaimed Pedro. "They are women!"

I shoved one over with my foot. It was true. The other two whom we had shot were women also. Their faces were as vile and their bodies as scraggy as those of the men, but women they were. Wondering whether the others also had been females, we went on and looked at the three whom we had killed with our *machetes*. We found them to be men.

"That explains it," nodded Pedro. "I wondered how they dared to come so near us. The women were the leaders. Perhaps we had killed their mates. The men had sense enough to fear us, but a woman crazed with fury loses all fear and all sense. I am glad we did not fall alive into their hands."

Remembering the scarred body of Luis Pitta and looking into the faces of those she-devils, I grunted agreement.

We left them there and went our way. At the edge of the bush, where the faint trail began, we turned and looked back. The dismal clearing, with its blackened stumps and its few gaunt trees, now was blue with low-crawling clouds of smoke through which glared the belts of flame eating up the habitations of the *bichos do mata*. Around those fires, we knew, lay the bullet-torn corpses of many tailed creatures who never again would torture a prisoner. The jungle around us was empty and silent, and the only sound was the sullen crackle of the fires. We had come as demons to fight demons, and we left behind us a death-strewn hell. Our work was done.

Back along the vague path we passed to the river. There we cut off our monstrous disguises, pitched them into the canoe, and breathed deep of the damp air.

"Luis, old comrade, we have done our best for you," Pedro said soberly. "So far as two men could destroy these fiends we have destroyed them; and into the others we have put fear that will abide. Now sleep in peace, Luis *meo*."

And we got into the canoe and paddled away toward the creek where our supplies were hidden.

Excerpt from The Camp-Fire

Something, in self-defense, from Arthur O. Friel as to the tailed men in his story in this issue. I wish he'd "burden" us more.

As a general thing I don't believe in burdening the Camp-Fire with dope concerning my yarns. This tale of "The Tailed Men," however, is so unusual that I can anticipate this derisive query by sundry gents from Missouri: "Men with tails? Say, Friel, where the merry heck do you get that stuff?" So I'm going to get the jump on these members of our sewing-circle by telling the world just where I get that stuff.

First, a few remarks by Padre Noronha, a priest of the Amazon, as quoted by Count de Castelnau, French explorer, and requoted by Lieut. William Lewis Herndon, U.S.N., who descended the Amazon in 1851, in an official report to the Secretary of the Navy, who in turn passed it to the United States House of Representatives, Thirty-third Congress:

"The Indians, Cauamas and Uginas, live near the sources of the river. The first are of very short stature, scarcely exceeding five palms (about three and a half feet); and the last (of this there is no doubt) have tails, and are produced by a mixture of Indians and Coata monkeys. Whatever may be the cause of this fact, I am led to give it credit for three reasons: first, because there is no physical reasons why men should not have tails; secondly, because many Indians, whom I have interrogated regarding this thing, have assured me of the fact, telling me that the tail was a palm and a half long; and thirdly, because the Reverend Father Friar José de Santa Theresa Ribeiro, a Carmelite, and Curate of Castro de Avelaens, assured me that he saw the same thing in an Indian who came from Japurá, and sent me the following attestation:

" 'I, José de Santa Theresa Ribeiro, of the Order of Our Lady of Mount Carmel, Ancient Observance, &c., certify and swear, in my quality of Priest, and on the Holy Evangelists, that, when I was a missionary in the ancient village of Parauau, I saw a man called Manuel da Silva, native of Pernambuco, or Bahia, who came from the river Japurá with some Indians, amongst whom was one—an Infidel brute—who the said Manuel declared to me had a tail; and as I was unwilling to believe such an extraordinary fact, he brought the Indian and caused him to strip, on pretense of removing some turtles from a "pen," near which I stood to assure myself of the truth. There I saw, without possibility of error, that the man had a tail, of the thickness of a finger, and half a palm long, and covered with a smooth and naked skin. The same Manuel assured me that the Indian had told him that every month he cut his tail, because he did not like to have it too long, and it grew very fast. I do not know to what nation this man belonged, nor if all his tribe had a similar tail; but I understood afterwards that there was a tailed nation on the banks of the Juruá; and I sign this act and seal it in affirmation of all that it contains.' "

Second, a remark by one M. Baena regarding the Juruá:

"In this river there are Indians, called Canamas, whose height does not exceed five palms; and there are others, called Uginas, who have a tail of three and four palms, according to the report of many persons."

Third, something by the Count de Castelnau himself:

"Descending the Amazon, I saw one day, near Fonteboa, a black Coata of enormous dimensions. He belonged to an Indian woman, to whom I offered a large price, for the country, for the curious beast; but she refused me with a burst of laughter. 'Your efforts are useless,' said an Indian who was in the cabin; 'that is her husband.' "

All right, laugh! When you're through snickering I'll spill some more dope for you. Here it is:

The coaita (or coata) is the tallest of the Amazonian monkeys, and is considered by naturalists to be the highest development of the American type of apes. Its disposition is mild and affectionate, and the Indians are very fond of it as a pet. And its most striking feature is its tail, which is highly prehensile—so much so that a coaita shot out of a tree can, in falling, catch a bough with its tail alone and crawl back on the limb. If there be anything in heredity, is it not possible that any creature fathered by a coaita would be likely to have Daddy Coaita's tail?

In this connection let's proceed to another point. I'm no embryologist, but in days gone by I've dabbled in a few other -ologies, and in so doing I came across the following scientific fact: During the process of gestation, the human embryo passes through successive stages of development in which it closely resembles the embryos of lower forms of life. And in one period of this development the human embryo has a rudimentary tail. Furthermore, there are cases on record in which this tail persisted in children after birth, and even in full-grown adults. I'm not talking about Amazonian Indians now, either, but about folks right here in the U.S.A.

You don't have to take my word for this. Ask some expert embryologist. I did that very thing myself, just to make sure that my memory hadn't warped with the passage of years. And I was assured not only that I was correct, but that at least a hundred cases in which "caudal appendages" remained after birth are recorded in medical literature.

There, gentlemen, that's where I get that stuff. I could ramble along to the extent of several hundred words more on this subject, but I'm cutting this oration as short as possible. Paper costs money these days, and you can fill in the gaps in this sketch for yourselves.

—A.O. FRIEL.

Wild Women

So the first Amazons were women warriors of Europe who cut away their right breasts in order to handle their bows more freely and so were called A-mazos, meaning "without breast." And this river Amazon got its name from the fact that old Orellana*, the first white man to descend it, had a fight with a Tapuya tribe whose women fought beside the men, and named the river for those women warriors.

Yes, I heard that tale before about Orellana, *senhores*, and it may be true; for rivers and towns often are named for people. This upper Amazon where we now are is known to us Brazilians as the Solimões, because an Indian tribe of that name once lived here. And the town of Manaus, toward which this steamer is carrying us, is so called because the region near the Rio Negro was the country of the Manaos savages. But my own idea about the name of this river is that neither Orellana nor those fighting women had anything to do with it, and that it really comes from our Indian word *amassona*. That word means "destroyer of boats." And if you know the Amazon, with its sudden storms and great floods and *terras cahidas*—falling banks which topple thundering into the water and crush or swamp any small boats near shore—you will see how well that word fits.

Yet it does not matter. The thing which most concerns us is that we are outward bound, you two *senhores* sailing back to your North America and I to my old home below the Black River. You have spent months exploring the jungle of the Javary, and I have passed years there as a rubber-worker, and now we all are interested more in what lies ahead than in what we leave behind us. But your talk of those ancient Amazons interests me much, for it brings to me the memory of a queer thing that happened not long ago. And now, since you have told me a tale of wild women, I will repay you in your own coin.

This thing came about, *senhores*, not on our own Javary, but on the Juruá, a sluggish and very crooked river to the east. When the flood-waters were high I had gone there with my comrade Pedro, a rubber-worker like myself, who burned to avenge an old friend tortured and crazed by a tribe of beast-men called Uginas. We had found the lair of these brutes, shot down many of them, driven fear deep into the rest, and burned their filthy huts. And now, after sleeping a night at a secret camp of ours farther down the stream, we packed our canoe for our journey back to the Javary.

This was easy work for Pedro, who had come unhurt through the fight

---

* Francisco de Orellana, 1541. See introduction to Volume 1, pgs 5-6.

with the Uginas. But it was not so easy for me because I had been struck in one foot by a dropping arrow, and this morning every step hurt me. When all was ready my partner stood looking thoughtfully at me. Then he said:

"Lourenço, let us stay on this river a few days before going back. The rubber-forests are drowned, and we can do no work there. The journey back is hard, and the strain of paddling and moving about will not do your sore foot any good. We have plenty of food and nothing to do, and we have never been on the Juruá before. So let us drift downstream a while and see what we may see."

"But we shall lose the channel on which we came across from the Tecuahy," I objected.

"We can probably find another," he said. "Those flooded *furos* are common enough when the water is so high. If we can not find one we can come back to the one we used before."

My foot gave a sharp twinge then, and I agreed. We paddled down a little creek, swung into the winding Juruá, and floated away westward.

In the next few days we found nothing new. The country around us was mostly swamp, and both the low-lying *igapó* and the higher *vargem* lands now were submerged under many feet of water. On each side the usual matted wall of trees and vines rose out of the flood, and the only soil remaining uncovered was the highest terra firma. The weather was that usual in the wet season—dull sky or tremendous rains or bursts of blinding sun. Through this we floated on around the twists and bends of the slow-moving stream, sleeping wherever we could, eating *chibeh* or dried fish, watching lazily for anything that might come and giving my bad foot a chance to heal.

This, of course, grew tiresome. We could not even hunt, for the trees seemed to hold little life, and whenever we found a *restinga*—a neck of land running back between two stretches of flood-water—the thick bush and my lameness prevented us from going far along it. So as soon as my foot became better we decided to seek a channel on the northern side and start working back toward our own country.

Then, as we were turning our backs on the Juruá, something happened.

Behind us sounded a long soft whistle. We turned and looked. At that point a *restinga* stood up from the waters, and the sound had come from that land. As we listened it came again..

"A *mutum!*" muttered Pedro, his eyes shining. "And it is down on the ground instead of overhead. What luck!"

It seemed luck indeed, *senhores*. The *mutum* is a fine big bird, and after living for days on fish and *farinha* the thought of broiled fowl made our tongues drip. Turning the canoe, we went back with swift but silent strokes.

As we reached the land we heard the same whistle, and then another one in answer. Both seemed near, but the bush was rather thick and we could see no life. I pointed to my foot, shook my head to show Pedro I would not go ashore for fear of stumbling and making a noise, and motioned for him to go after the birds. He nodded, stepped out, and slipped smoothly away into the tangle.

Holding the canoe still, I waited. The whistles sounded two or three times at intervals, and they seemed to be going away from the river. I could picture the birds poking along and seeking food, and Pedro stealing after them with rifle ready, but I could neither see nor hear anything to tell me how the hunt went. It seemed that my comrade had been gone for some time when finally I heard a shot.

The bark of the rifle came from some distance back in the bush. I listened eagerly for another shot which would tell me that the second *mutum* also had been killed. None came. Instead I heard a confused noise as if a struggle were going on, and then sounds like voices.

Grabbing my rifle, I jumped out, yanked the canoe up on shore to prevent its floating off, and worked into the bush as fast as I could go.

In doing this I could not help making some noise; and, knowing that any one there could hear me coming, I decided to make as much noise as possible. I shouted to Pedro several times, changing my tone to make my voice sound as if more than one man were calling and purposely shook the undergrowth as I passed through it.

I had no idea as to what was happening, or whether anything really was wrong. But the thought of savages was in the back of my head, and if any were there I wanted to make them think a number of men were coming to aid Pedro.

The only effect this had was to prevent me from hearing anything ahead. And I soon learned that it did not deceive any one. Coming out into a place where the bush was not so thick, I saw three figures rise suddenly from the ground.

I threw up my rifle, but did not shoot. Just as my trigger-finger tightened I saw that all the strangers were women.

For a minute I stood there staring at them along my rifle-barrel. They were nearly as tall as I, and, though slender, they were full-breasted and fairly broad of shoulder and looked strong. They were lighter than most Indians, for their smooth skins were not copper-brown but of a reddish tan color. Their hair, I noticed, did not hang loose, but was coiled snugly around their heads, making them look somewhat like men. Their faces, too, were strong and resembled those of men rather than of women. And their attitudes quickly showed me that these were no shy, shrinking maidens.

Each held a bow ready to shoot, and each arrow pointed straight at my body. Yet they did not seem hostile. They held back those arrows just as I held back my bullet; but it was perfectly plain that if I should shoot one of them the others would strike me down.

Much puzzled, I lowered the rifle and uncocked it. They in turn let their weapons sink, though they still held them ready. We stood watching one another for a moment longer. Then the whole thing suddenly seemed funny to me, and I laughed.

They smiled in answer, and the smile softened their expressions so that now they did not seem like men at all. One motioned for me to come farther back into the bush. Knowing that Pedro must be somewhere behind them, I nodded and went straight ahead.

They waited until I passed, and then followed close behind me. I had taken only a few steps when a sudden blow struck my rifle and nearly knocked it from my hand. The woman at my heels had done this, and as I turned she seized the gun and tried to yank it from me. But I kept my grip and twisted it out of her hands. Then, angered, I told them not to try that trick again.

They laughed as if it were only a joke, and one of them spoke in a sort of Tupi dialect. She asked if I was afraid to be among women unless I had a gun, and the other two laughed again in a way that made me uncomfortable. But if they thought to shame me into handing over my rifle they were dealing with the wrong man.

"I am no fool," I growled. "And if you would be treated like women you had best behave like women. If you act like men I will treat you as men, and it may not be pleasant for you."

Two of them frowned, but the one who had teased me smiled again and looked at me with eyes dancing. They were big brown eyes, and I noticed now that she had very good teeth, and with that smile brightening her face she was not at all bad-looking. Her figure, too, was almost perfect. Like the others she wore only a *tanga*—a wide strip of bark-cloth around the hips. This was not much, but it was far more than some savage women wear; and from this and their intelligent faces and shapely bodies I knew these people were of a higher type than some I had seen.

I did not smile back at the brown-eyed girl—indeed, I scowled all the more; for it does not always pay to let a woman know you approve of her. Nothing more was said, and I turned away, keeping a tight grip on my gun. I need not have been so careful, though, for they tried no more tricks. The four of us passed quietly onward until we came to Pedro.

He was leaning calmly against a tree, with the butt of his rifle resting on the ground, and talking with four more women. When he saw me he laughed.

"Greetings, old hater of women," he said. "I am glad to see that you are safe. You were bawling so loudly that I thought all three of your girls must be kissing you at once."

"They are not my girls," I disputed. "And do not call me a hater of women, for how can a man hate a thing in which he feels no interest whatever? Perhaps I did bawl, but I was not so much afraid that I had to shoot, as you did. What is the meaning of all this? And are no men here?"

"Yes, there are one and a half men—myself and you," he answered teasingly. "It took seven women to capture me, while three were too many for you. There are no other men that I have seen. And this means that we have been tricked and are prisoners at the mercy of these strong-armed ladies. I do not know what our fate is to be. Perhaps they will love us to death. That would be a sad end for you, but I think I could die happy."

He glanced at the girl nearest him. I looked at her and saw that she was quite handsome. When I say that, I mean that she was not pretty in a girlish way, but handsome as a man would be, and as Pedro himself was; tall and straight, deep-chested and firm-breasted, with strong arms and shoulders, regular features, and a straight steady gaze. She was much the best-looking woman there, and it was easy to see why Pedro's eyes turned to her. At the same time I thought that if she should take the notion to "love him to death," as he said, he might not find it so funny after all.

"I do not quite see how we were tricked as you say," I told him. "Where are the birds we heard?"

"These are the birds," he explained, nodding toward the women. Then he spoke in Tupi to the handsome one, telling her to make the call of the *mutum*. She lifted her hands and whistled between them, and the call was perfect.

"They drew me back here with those whistles," he went on, "and then six of them hid and jumped on me all at once while I was following the sounds made by the seventh, thinking she was the *mutum* ahead of me. The shot I fired was an accident—they startled me so that I pulled trigger and hit nothing. After that we danced around together until I saw they were women, when I stopped trying to fight and began to talk. Any woman would rather talk than fight, so we were becoming quite friendly when we heard you howling. Then three of the girls went out to welcome you."

"I see," I said. "And now that I am welcomed, what happens next?"

This he did not know. So he asked the woman beside him, and she answered that we were to go with them to higher ground some distance away. I asked what we should find there, and she told me that in that place were more people. Then I inquired where the men of the tribe were, and got a surprizing answer. Her tribe had no men at all.

When we asked more questions about this we got no satisfaction. They became impatient, said we should learn about that later on, and told us to come.

I did not like this for three reasons. First, it displeased me to be told by women what I should do. Second, I had hurt my foot again in my haste through the bush, and the thought of traveling far on it was not attractive. And last, it would not do to leave our canoe where it was for any length of time, for a storm or a rise in the water would sweep it away. So I said rather shortly that I would not go; that Pedro could visit that place if he wished, but that I was going back to the canoe.

At once their faces grew cold. Three of them stepped back and lifted their bows. The handsome one beside Pedro spoke sharply, telling me I must come. And then Pedro added:

"Did you not hear me say we are prisoners? This is not so much of a joke as you think. True, we have kept our weapons, but we are outnumbered and they are determined to make us do as they wish. More than that, they are women, and we are no woman-fighters. If we do fight it will be no matter of scratching and pulling hair—there will be no killing. And they are only asking us to come with them. Now do not be sour. Let us go and see whatever we may."

I grumbled about my foot, but before I made a flat refusal I happened to glance at the brown-eyed girl who had first spoken to me. She had not raised her bow, but stood quietly watching me. Now she smiled again. And without thinking why, I suddenly decided that Pedro was speaking sense and I ought not to be sour about the matter. So I said I would go, but insisted that first the canoe must be put in a safer place.

Pedro agreed with me on that point, and, after looking keenly at us, the handsome one also agreed. But she said both of us need not go back for that, and as I had a bad foot I should stay here while Pedro attended to the canoe. So she and two others went with him, leaving four to watch me.

Having nothing to do but wait, I knelt and examined my foot. As usual, my feet were bare, for I do not wear boots in the bush unless there is some particular reason for it. The arrow-wound, which was partly healed, had been torn by something I had struck on my way from the river, and now it was bleeding. Seeing a tiny pool of rainwater near me, I limped over to it and bathed the wound. While I was doing this the women talked, and then the brown-eyed one slipped away into the jungle.

Soon she returned with some *isca*, a tough substance made by ants, which is good to stop bleeding. Kneeling beside me, she placed this on my hurt, wrapped some leaves around it, and bound it on firmly with bush-cord. Still resting on one knee, she asked me how I had received that injury. So I told her of our fight with the Uginas.

All listened closely, and when I finished the tale they nodded approvingly.

"Such men breed fighters," one said in her Tupi tongue. Again the others nodded. I asked what the speaker meant by that. They all laughed and made no answer. And then Pedro and his four escorts came back.

"So they are kneeling to you already," he said, his eyes twinkling. "I should have known better than to leave you alone with them. You pretend to despise women, but when you have them all to yourself it is a different thing."

I promptly told him he was a liar, and he laughed as if I had said something funny. The brown-eyed girl rose hastily, but with a graceful ease that told of lithe muscles, and, pointing to my foot, spoke to the handsome leader. The tall woman nodded, but I saw that she gave the other girl a rather sharp look. Without speaking, she motioned for us to march.

With three girls ahead of us and four behind, we filed away into the jungle. The undergrowth was not so thick here, and I went on without much trouble. But I could not help limping a little, and I felt like a clumsy cripple as I watched the women ahead, who swung along with a velvety stride and smoothly swaying bodies, making no sound except a slight rustle of leaves. Pedro, watching them too, spoke over my shoulder.

"Lourenço, a man is an awkward, heavy-footed creature when compared with a woman."

"Yes," I admitted. "But a woman is not the only creature that travels smoothly. So does a cat. So does a snake. So does a vampire bat."

As I spoke the brown-eyed girl turned, looked down at the foot she had bound for me, and asked whether it hurt much. I said no, and felt a little ashamed of my last remark. Pedro chuckled.

"Be sure you speak in Portuguese when you make such answers," he said. "Your friend will not love you if she knows you call her cat, snake, and vampire."

I snorted, but said no more.

The ground, I noticed, was gradually rising. I expected that on the highest point we should find the place where these people lived. This proved true. After a time we entered a cleared space, and in this stood a long, low house.

It was much like the *malocas* of certain savages in our own Javary region, but not so large. Its walls were not more than eight feet high, and its roof was low, without much of a slant.

Knowing how close to each other the inhabitants of such houses usually slept, I judged that there might be a hundred women living here. But later I learned that this was too large an estimate, and that there were hardly more than half that number.

Several women were working at something near the one small door of the *maloca*, and as we came out of the bush they stood up and stared. The girls around us called to them, and I caught the words *apuyáh* and *camarâh*, meaning "friendly men." At once the others began to cackle like a bunch of hens, and I saw heads appear in the doorway.

Our guards spread out now, and we walked nine abreast toward the house. I tried not to limp, with the result that I walked stiff-legged, and I must have looked about as dignified as a jabiru crane with his toes bitten off. But the women ahead stared at us as if we were the most wonderful things they had ever seen.

By the time we reached the house at least twenty women were waiting, and more were coming out. The chattering increased so that we could make nothing of it except that all wanted to know where and how we had been discovered. While this went on we stood quietly looking them over, noting that all seemed fairly young and that there were neither any very old women nor any small children. I tried to pick out some one of them who might be in command as a *tushaúa* or chief, but could see none. So I touched the arm of my brown-eyed friend and, shouting to make myself heard, asked whether they had a chief.

She nodded and shouted back that we should see the chief, who was very great. Just then a commotion started at the back of the crowd facing us, and she said the chief was coming now. I looked, expecting to see a magnificent woman decked in a brilliant feather dress and grave and stately of manner. But as the others gave way to let the ruler pass I found myself mistaken.

The chief was great indeed, but not as I had thought. She was great with the greatness of a tapir. The best way I can describe her to you, *senhores*, is to repeat an expression I heard one of you use a while ago—"big fat slob." That woman was a big fat slob.

She waddled like a pot-bellied duck, and the rolls of fat on her flapped like jelly. Out of that fat oozed beads of sweat, and her face was greasy with it. Her *tanga* was askew, and looked like a rag stretched around a barrel. And her feet—*senhores*, I never saw such feet in my life. They looked more like a pair of shovels.

And not only was this dainty creature so charming in appearance, but she was drunk. She staggered in her walk, and how she managed to swing those huge feet without kicking herself I do not know. When she stopped before us and squinted at us through twitching lids I caught a whiff of her breath that reminded me of a jug of rum.

She stood there a minute, swaying on her thick legs and looking us all over. As I gazed back at her and remembered what a splendid savage queen I had expected to see I could not help grinning. And whether she thought I grinned because I liked her I do not know; but after staring tipsily at me a minute she wrinkled her fat face in an answering smile. Before I guessed what she intended she lunged forward and embraced me.

I tried to shove her away, but her hold was too good. Both those huge arms were around me, squeezing so hard that I felt as if my stomach would pop out of my mouth. She buried her face in my neck, snorting like a dolphin coming up for air and rubbing her cheek against my jaw. And when I tried to kick her fat shins and make her break away I found I could not—she was standing on my feet.

I heard Pedro yelping with laughter, and the sound maddened me. I managed to get an arm under her chin and force her back. Then I clawed myself loose.

My rough work angered her. She glared at me. But my brown-eyed girl began to talk rapidly, pointing to my bad foot and telling the ruler she had hurt me. The fat one stared at the foot, then at my face, and her thick lips twitched. Then her eye went to Pedro. And suddenly she swept an arm out and caught him as she had caught me.

He too sprang back, but not in time. It was my turn to laugh, and I did.

"You said if you were loved to death you could die happy," I reminded him. "Now die like a man, and do not look so miserable."

"Pull her away!" he gasped, wrestling with her.

"Not I," I refused. "She is dying for love. Take pity on the poor little thing, comrade, and treat her tenderly."

He gave a despairing gurgle, and I doubled over with laughter. Others laughed too, and I saw that my brown-eyed friend was shaking with mirth. The tall handsome girl who had brought us there, however, was not laughing at all. She was biting her lips, and her eyes showed anger. But as my comrade still strove to free himself, she prodded him with a finger and gave him a warning shake of the head. So, though his mouth was twisted with disgust, he stood still and waited for her Royal Fatness to release him.

But she kept her grip, and I became sorry for him. Also, I thought of a plan that might give us a breathing-spell. So I suggested:

"Tell her we want rum. She will drink with us, and she is so unsteady now that a few more drinks may put her to sleep."

He did as I said. Her head was on his shoulder, and he spoke into the ear nearest his mouth, telling her we were glad to find ourselves so welcome here, and that we should like to show our friendship in a little drink of *cauim* if there was any. With another hug that nearly broke his back she straightened up and laughed in a throaty way. There was *cauim* in plenty, she said, and we should have all we liked. With that she turned around carefully, got her feet pointed toward the door, and lurched away into the *maloca*.

Pedro drew a long breath, as if he had been under water a long time and had just come to the top. Seeing that the women expected us to enter the house, we followed the fat one through the little doorway and down the long room to a huge hammock.

She flopped into this, lay there grinning, and then called for liquor. Some one brought a big jar of strong-smelling stuff and gourd cups. I poured the liquor, and I took care to give her the biggest cup and fill it to the brim, while I left our own only a little more than half full.

We found the rum strong and fiery, but we pretended to swallow it eagerly. She gulped down the whole gourd in a noisy, thirsty fashion, and reached for more. I gave her another good measure, and then we sat down in nearby hammocks and talked.

She asked whence we came and why, and we told her. We spoke slowly, swallowing a little now and then from our cups and filling her gourd as often as we could. Once I spied a smile on the face of the tall handsome girl, and knew she understood our plan and was amused by it. Some others smiled too and nudged one another, watching the fat one.

She drank a surprizing quantity of the *cauim*, but at length it overpowered her. The gourd fell out of her hand, she laughed foolishly, her eyes closed and opened a few times, and she began to snore.

Then we drained the cups we held, threw them aside, stretched ourselves and grinned at the other women. They laughed, looking with some contempt at their stupefied ruler.

"Now, girls, let us become better acquainted," said Pedro. Speaking to the tall girl, he added: "I have told you that I am Pedro. Who are you?"

"Tata," she answered with a calm smile. I thought the name did not fit her well, for the Tupi word *tata* means "fire," and she did not seem at all fiery. But then the thought came to me that fire is not always quick and fierce—it may burn quietly; and smoldering flame is the more dangerous because it is hidden. Remembering how she had bitten her lips while she watched her chief slobbering on Pedro's shoulder, I said—

"You had best be careful, or you may be burned."

"I would rather be burned than drowned in sweat," he answered, glancing sourly at the sleeping chief. "Tata, what is the name of this one?"

"Amuy—the rain."

"*Por Deos!* It is a good name for her. She leaks at every pore. Bring me some water, that I may wash the grease of that creature off me."

Tata smiled again, but replied that she was not a carrier of water, and that if he wanted some he could get it for himself. He frowned at her, but she made no move. But then some other woman brought up a jar of water for him, and he began bathing his face and arms. While he did this I asked the girl who had bound my foot what her name was.

"Jahy," she told me.

At first I thought that name badly chosen, for *jahŷ* is the moon, and this brown-eyed maid was slender and graceful. Yet there are few things more beautiful than a slim young moon sailing up in the night sky, and as I realized this I told her she was *jahŷ ahûh*—the new moon.

"Ah, what a change!" Pedro gibed. "A while ago women were snakes and vampires to you, and now you rave of the new moon! Do not tell me again that I am likely to be burned. You are moon-struck!"

"The moon does no harm to men," I retorted.

"No, oh no. It only twists their brains and makes them mad."

I told him I could take care of my own brains. And then, to show him how little I cared about his teasing, I did a thing which otherwise I should not have done. Jahy, smiling over my compliment and looking very girlish and winsome, was standing close beside me; and I put an arm around her, drew her to me, and sat down with her in the hammock.

The result of this astonished me. Jahy pushed me in a startled way, then sat quiet, looking at me with eyes wide and shining as if surprised but pleased. A sudden murmur went among the other women, and many of them stared at us sourly. As they muttered to one another I repeatedly caught the word *erekuâhn*. And that word, *senhores*, means "husband."

Then Tata spoke. She told me that this thing could not be unless the chief gave consent.

"*Ani akuân*—I do not understand," I said. "This concerns Jahy and nobody else. If she is willing to sit by me the consent of that fat drunkard is not at all necessary."

The women murmured again, and Tata looked at me searchingly. Then she quietly said that truly I did not understand. By taking Jahy into my hammock, she explained, I had made her my wife.

And this was not all. The chief, she told me, would say who should be my first wife, and would decide the order in which the other wives should follow that first one. It might be that the chief herself would want to be first wife. And whether that were so or not, I had nothing at all to say about it. All would be settled by the chief.

"*Por amor de Deos!*" I gasped. For the moment I could say no more. My arm still was around Jahy, and I felt that she had grown tense. She was sitting straight up, and she did not appear girlish now. Her face was cold and her eyes hard, and she looked defiantly at all the other women. Her attitude was exactly that of a man who has walked up to a village belle, kissed her, and then swung on other men and asked them what they intend to do about it. She said no word, but it was plain as day that any woman who wanted to dispute for the place of first wife to me would have to fight for it.

I glanced at Pedro. He put a hand to his head as if he were dizzy, and said nothing at all. And after staring around me a minute I told Tata neither of us understood this matter well; that we wanted to know who they were, why they had no men, why we were brought here, what she meant by a number of wives for us, and so on. So she told us all there was to tell.

They were women of the Passés, one of the highest tribes of Indians found in this Upper Amazon country. These are a peaceable people who live quietly in groups scattered along the interior rivers, building small villages where they can raise crops and have permanent homes. The group to which these women belonged had lived in a village over to the west of the Juruá country, and there they had been happy and content.

But then had come upon them from the north and west a horde of those fierce *bárbaros* who roam the jungle like wild beasts, killing and plundering wherever they find the settlements of quieter tribes. There are many such bands of killers in the unknown depths of our great southern forests—bloody brutes who spend their lives roving and fighting, crossing rivers by making bark boats and sweeping onward into regions where they have not been before. When they come there is only one thing to do—kill them.

Now the Passés, though peace-loving folk, are no cowards or weaklings. And so when one of their hunters came staggering in one day with an arrow in his chest and the news that a horde of murderers was coming, the men seized weapons and went out to fight to the death.

Even the little boys, except those too young to be of any use, were taken along; for a small boy, with his little *zarabatana* blow-gun and poisoned darts, often can kill men, and the Passés knew they would need every ounce of their power against those invaders. But they did not take their women, for it was not the custom among them for the women to fight. Instead, they ordered them to take their babes and flee southward in canoes, promising that if they won the fight they would meet them again at a place agreed upon and bring them back home.

The women never saw their men again. Only a half-grown boy, badly wounded, managed to reach them after the battle. He told them all the other men were killed, their homes were ravaged and destroyed, and the *bárbaros* now were searching the bush for the women. They must go on at once, he said. Then he died, and the women and babes fled far and fast to escape the brutes behind them.

In this hard flight all the babies died. The only children to survive were those old enough to endure the hardships they met; and these all were girls. When at last they reached this place and stayed here, it happened that the babes born of dead fathers all were girls also. And so the years passed and the young people grew up without a single boy or man among them.

There were men among other tribes around them, they knew. But the Juruá is an evil river, and the tribes living at its headwaters are either low, vile creatures or brutal savages; and the Passé women, roving the jungle and learning what sort of men were there, had carefully kept away from them and allowed no man to approach their hidden home. Having no men to hunt and fight for them, they themselves had become hunters and fighters; and when any men of the Juruá tribes stumbled on their *maloca* they promptly fought and killed them, so that they should not go back and bring others to overpower them and make them slaves.

Yet, though they lived without men and protected themselves against all dangers, they knew well that in time they would all die out unless men came among them. They had talked of going back to the country whence they came, where they could mate with others of their Passé tribe. But this they had not been able to do because their mothers, who had brought them here, grew too old and infirm to make that long journey, and the girls would not abandon them. So they had agreed among themselves that they must stay here until the old women all were dead, when they would be free to return to their own region and themselves became mothers.

They had also agreed that if by any chance there should come into this place men fit to unite with them, these men should be made the husbands of all. Their ruler, Amuy, who governed them because she was descended from the chief who had died fighting the *bárbaros*, should decide the order in which they should mate with any such men. In this way each woman would have a man for a time, and thus no one of them could keep him all to herself and cause the others to be neglected. And now that we had come they would follow this plan. As soon as it should please Amuy to make her decisions in the matter, the mating would begin.

As you may suppose, *senhores*, I was speechless for a time after this. I looked around the *maloca* and saw that, although death had taken away all the older women except two who lay in their hammocks, there were at least fifty waiting to be our wives. I looked at the fat Amuy, and remembered Tata's statement that perhaps Amuy herself would choose to be first wife. From what I had seen of her I was quite ready to believe it; and at the thought my stomach squirmed. After thinking a while I said:

"But two men are not enough to be the husbands of half a hundred girls. We will go out and bring back some of our comrades."

The women laughed scornfully. Tata told us we were not going out. From her tone I gathered that if we did not choose to stay here alive we would stay here dead. And when Pedro found his voice and asked how long they expected us to remain, she said we would never go; that we would pass our lives here and become the fathers of many strong fighting men.

Watching her eyes as she answered him, I thought again of smoldering fire. I thought too that though she spoke so quietly, she was as much determined to be the first wife of Pedro as Jahy was to be mine.

"But we have wives in our own Javary country," Pedro objected. "Wives and children who need us. We must return to them."

Tata looked him straight in the eye. Whether she saw that he was lying I do not know, but it made no difference. She coolly said those wives of ours could get other men to take care of them. We were here, and here we should stay.

Then she told Jahy to leave my hammock. Jahy snapped back that she liked this hammock very well and intended to stay in it. Tata looked steadily at her, then lifted her brows, glanced at the sleeping Amuy, and smiled in an irritating fashion. But she said only that now we should eat. And the other women, also glancing at Jahy and at Amuy, turned and brought their *tupé* eating-mats and food.

Pedro and I looked at each other hopelessly, grinned, and squatted beside the mat that was laid before us. Jahy and Tata took places on each side of us, and the women who brought the food to our mat also squatted around it. The food was plentiful and good—fish, fowl, and fruit—and we ate heartily. Then, as usual, we made cigarets for ourselves and lighted them.

The women looked rather scornfully at these little smoke-rolls of ours. One of them arose, went somewhere, and came back with a cigar in her mouth. It was a huge, clumsy thing, looking more like a club than a cigar, for it was as thick as my two thumbs and nearly a foot long. She dropped several more of these on the mat, and each of the girls took one. When all were puffing away the smoke was so strong it nearly knocked us over.

"*Nossa Senhora!*" muttered Pedro, watching a woman dip up a gourd of that fiery *cauim* and drain it without a quiver. "These are weak, helpless creatures indeed! Perhaps I spoke truth when I said we should be loved to death."

"Have courage," I said. "It is nearly night, and we may find a chance to reach our canoe before dawn."

"Yes, a fine chance!" he sneered. "If you had ever tried to evade a woman you would not be so hopeful. We have just as much chance of escape as if we were two mice surrounded by fifty cats."

I made no answer, for, though I was sure the women did not understand Portuguese, I thought they might read our faces. Yawning, I told them we would like to walk about and see more of the clearing. They assented, and we all went outside.

I limped along rather slowly, and they surrounded us closely all the time, so that we did not see as much as if we had been alone; but we found that they knew well how to take care of the plants and trees. Between the growing fruits and mandioca, the fish of the river and the birds and beasts of the forest, they made a very good living for themselves here, and we should not be likely to suffer from want of food. But food is not everything; and the thought of spending my life in this one small spot was not endurable. I took care not to show this, though, and waited for a time when Pedro and I could talk and agree on some plan.

Night came soon; a night of blackness so dense that no man could see anything his length away. Returning to the *maloca*, where the women barred the door with stout poles, we asked where we should sleep. Two hammocks were given us—not the same ones where we had sat before, but others nearby—and this time I did not take Jahy into my bed.

She stood beside me, waiting while I sat and smoked another cigaret. Then she asked if I did not want her.

"Little New Moon," I said, "you are very pretty and graceful, and I see no other girl here whom I would sooner have. Yet since an agreement was made among you girls before we came, it is best to abide by that agreement until Amuy shall say what is to be done. I have taken you once into my hammock, and I do not regret it. But to do so again now would only make bitterness and trouble between you and your sisters, and that would not be well. Let us wait and see what the new day may bring."

She nodded slowly and turned away. But soon she was back with a clay pot and some leaves. Stripping the other leaves and the *isca* from my lame foot, she dipped a sort of paste from the pot and covered the wound with it, then bound up the foot again. After that she lay down in the hammock next to mine and began smoking another of those big cigars.

I lay for a while watching the shadows thrown by the little fires burning here and there in the big house. As I thought of our position I wanted to laugh and to curse at the same time. Finally I spoke to Pedro.

"Comrade, I have been in queer places, but never in one like this. And I am not anxious to remain in it. Are you resigned to your fate?"

"No, I am not," he admitted. "If I could pick one wife and ignore the rest of them perhaps I could be content here for a long time. And I think that you and Jahy too could be quite happy if you were let alone. But to be passed around from one to another is not to my liking, and to have no choice in the matter is worse. And worst of all is the fact that we shall be nothing but slaves, without any liberty whatever. They treat us with some consideration now because we are new to them, but after the newness has worn off we shall be no better than dogs."

"You have it right," I agreed. "To take a woman because you and she want each other is one thing, but to be forced into a mating is much different. And to pass a lifetime as a slave is not to be thought of. I care more for my liberty than for my life, and so do you. Yet I do not see how we are to free ourselves. If only they were men instead of women we might succeed by killing a few when our chance came; but we can not do that."

"No, we can not do that. Yet I can see two possible ways for us to go. See if you can think of one."

Of course, I thought first of trying to slip away in the night. But, looking around me again, I saw that a number of women were squatting around a little fire between us and the one door. They looked as if they meant to stay awake until morning. I knew, too, that outside it was so dark we could not find our way through the jungle even if we could leave the house.

Then my eye settled on Jahy. She was watching me, and as I gazed at her she smiled. I thought of all that had passed since we first met. And I thought that since I had made her my wife I would abide by what I had done, if she wished to flee away from this place with me. Leaning out of my hammock, I asked in a low tone:

"*Jahŷ ahûh, apotáre hahóh heiruhm*? New Moon, do you want to go away with me?"

She shook her head. Quietly but firmly she told me she would not leave this place, and that I had best not try to leave it either. Since I did not care enough for her to take her into my hammock the second time, she added, she now would wait and see what Amuy would do. I said no more, but lay back, feeling as if I had been slapped in the face.

"You have thought of one way, and it is not good," laughed Pedro. "If your Jahy will not run away with you tomorrow I am quite sure Tata would not go with me, so I shall not ask her. But unless I am mistaken in the ways of women we shall see something interesting in the morning. Now we may as well sleep."

We did sleep. I knew nothing at all until day came again. The first thing I heard was fat Amuy groaning because her head ached.

She was sitting up in her hammock, looking frowzy and stupid and calling for water. A younger woman brought a jar of it, and she drank noisily and then poured the rest on her head. After that she swallowed a gourd of rum and seemed to feel better.

Every one else in the *maloca* had risen and was busy making the morning meal. We got up and stretched ourselves. I found my foot much better, and, though I still limped a little, I walked about quite easily. Amuy blinked at us in a puzzled way, then smiled thickly as she remembered us. But she said nothing until after she had eaten a big breakfast, taken another drink, and begun smoking one of those huge cigars.

By that time the rest of us also had eaten, and all the women gathered around us and the chief to learn what should be done.

Amuy stared steadily at us through the rank smoke she was making, and then asked some questions which showed she had forgotten most of what we had told her about ourselves. We answered them coolly, saying nothing further. We did not remind her of her warm welcome to us, nor tell her of my taking Jahy into my hammock. But she soon learned of this.

A bold-faced woman to whom we had paid no attention now shoved herself forward and pointing to me and Jahy as she talked, told how I had made myself the *erekuâhn* of the Moon. She also argued that this must not be allowed; that she herself or any of the others had as much right to be my first wife as Jahy had.

Amuy scowled. But before she said anything Jahy spoke for herself.

She had a better right to me than any one else, she declared. She had been one of the first to find me, while this other woman had not even been in the party that caught us. She had attended to my wound when nobody else offered to do so, and I myself had preferred her above all the others and had taken her into my bed. Besides this, she had recently found and killed a *uirá-pará*, and our coming so soon after that showed that one of us was meant to be her man.

Perhaps you do not know the *uirá-pará, senhores*. No? Then let me explain. You may have noticed that the small bug-eating birds of our jungle usually do not travel singly, but come in sudden swarms which swiftly search the trees for insects and then are gone. The Indians all believe that these flocks are led by a mysterious little gray bird, the *uirá-pará*. And the Indian maidens—and many white girls too—believe that if they can get a *uirá-pará* and keep its smoke-dried little body it will draw many men to them, even as it draws the bird-swarms after it in life.

Jahy had one of these little birds, as she said. She drew it out from a fold of her *tanga* as she spoke, and insisted again that by all rights I was her *erekuâhn*. Amuy looked rather sourly at it. Then she glanced at Tata.

Tata stepped forward and spoke. She too had a *uirá-pará*, which she had killed before Jahy found hers. And she had been leader of the party which found us, and she had given the deceptive *mutum* calls that brought us ashore. So she had the best right to take the first choice, she asserted. Yet she would not dispute Jahy's claim to me, for she did not want me. She would be the first mate of Pedro.

Amuy said nothing, but puffed away and looked at us both. Perhaps she waited for other women to speak, or perhaps she was only thinking. But other women spoke—indeed they did! A dozen of them at once began to argue, and others quickly joined in, each yelling and screeching to make herself heard. In no time at all the place was a riot of dispute.

Pedro laughed and shouted into my ear.

"I thought it would be so. It is easy for women to make an agreement but not so easy to keep it—especially about men. Are you not flattered to see them wrangle over you?"

"I might be if they were in love with me," I shouted back. "But not one of them really cares about us. They quarrel from selfishness, not from love. Each wants to beat the others by being first."

He nodded quickly and made some answer. But I lost it because I was watching the start of a fight.

One of the women, arguing with her mouth and both hands, shoved Tata roughly aside. Tata swung an elbow into that woman's stomach and knocked her backward. The woman sat down hard on the pot of rum, which tipped over and sent her sprawling. She bounded up, screeching in fury, and leaped at Tata. But then Amuy stopped it.

She lurched up between the two, and her solid bulk threw them both back. And in a tone that cracked like a gun-shot she commanded—

"Quiet!"

Tata and the other glared, but they obeyed. The others, too, stopped their noise so suddenly that it seemed still as the grave. Amuy was scowling, but I noticed that her eyes gleamed as if she were pleased by the trouble. I soon learned why.

"The men are mine!" she said.

We all stared. Nobody spoke.

"They are mine," she repeated. "They shall both be my mates. Later you shall have them in turn."

Black looks went among the women.

"No! That was not the agreement!" cried one.

"The agreement is broken!" Amuy answered instantly. "You have broken it yourselves. I, Amuy, am chief. It shall be as I say."

Angry murmurs followed. Jahy and Tata stood biting their lips, and their eyes burned. But no open revolt came, and Amuy, looking very well satisfied, turned to us.

"Smile, Lourenço, and try to look pleased," whispered Pedro. It was hard for me to do so, but I managed to twist my face into a grin. He smiled also, and said:

"The matter is well arranged, Amuy. And now that it is settled, should we not have a celebration? Let us drink and dance the *pira-purasséya* and make merry."

All except Amuy heard this in sullen silence. But the chief, much pleased with herself, accepted the suggestion at once. It should be a day of feast, she said, and all the *cauim* they had should be brought out. At her command the women went slowly away, muttering to one another, and began to bring big clay jars from the end of the *maloca*. These were carried outside.

"If you think they will all drink themselves stupid you are mistaken," I grumbled. "There is not enough rum for that."

"I know it," he answered. "But there is enough to make us all quite lively. Be cheerful, comrade, and show how joyous you are at being made half-husband to this lovely lady."

I looked sharply at him and saw that he had something in his mind, so I said no more. Noticing that he took his rifle, I picked up mine, and we moved to the door. We were outside before any one noticed that we carried our guns. Then Amuy eyed us suspiciously and asked why we had brought our weapons.

Glancing down at his gun in a surprized way, Pedro said he was so accustomed to carrying it that he had taken it without thought. He dropped it carelessly beside the wall, and I followed his example. Then he stepped to a jar of *cauim*, dipped up a gourd, and said:

"Girls, let us all drink and try to be satisfied with the arrangement that has been made. It is not what you agreed on, and in my own country we should do differently; but you know best what you wish to do."

"What would you do in your country?" asked a big woman.

"If two women were to be the wives of many men they would go first to the strongest fighters," he told her. "But of course you are only women, and so you can not settle it in that way."

The women, all proud of their hunting and fighting ability, looked at him and at one another with faces hardening. They drank in silence, pouring the liquor down their throats in a way not at all gentle or womanly. Before Amuy's fat brain sensed the feeling his words caused he added:

"Now let us form the circle. Who will be the first fish?"

The "fish" in this *pira-purasséya* or fish-dance, as you *senhores* know, is the person who stands in the center of the ring, answers questions, and finally rushes at the others circling around and tries to break through. If the fish escapes, then the one who let him out has to become the fish. And now no girl wanted to be fish. They were not in the mood for play.

"Then I will be fish," he said. "And since a fish does not like to be dry, let us all drink again."

Some of them smiled at this, and all dipped deep into the jars. With another gourd apiece under their smooth skins they formed a ring, joined hands in a rather unwilling way, and marched around my partner. Because of my lameness, I stood outside the circle.

"Fish, what kind of fish are you?" called some one, according to the custom.

"I am no fish, but a lizard," was his answer. It was a good one, for he was tall and slender.

"What do you here, lizard?" asked somebody else.

"I came to warm myself at the fire—*tata*."

"And does the fire comfort you?"

"No. I can not reach it because I am drowned by the rain—*amuý*."

There was laughter at this, but it sounded unpleasant. And a voice called—

"Why do you not push the rain aside to reach the fire?"

"Because the rain is too thick."

This time the laughter was very loud. Amuy looked ugly. And she looked still uglier as the other women began to sing of the lizard which came seeking the fire but was swallowed up by the thick, heavy rain. But before she could say or do anything Pedro dashed toward me, broke through the circle, and slapped my shoulder.

"Be the fish now," he said rapidly. "Do you see my plan?"

I nodded, told the women I was next fish, and suggested another drink. After that the circle started again, and they asked me what sort of fish I was. As I am rather broad, I said—

"I am not a fish but a turtle."

"And why does the turtle come here?"

"I am here because I followed a *uirá-pará*."

"And what did the *uirá-pará* tell you?"

"It said that here I should find the new moon."

"Do you like the new moon?" asked Jahy herself.

"I like it very well. But the wretched rain has come between us."

There was silence. Then one said—

"A turtle should not fear the rain."

"The turtle does not fear the rain," I denied. "Yet the rain prevents the sun from shining on us."

A low murmur of agreement went around. But some woman called—

"The rain will pass."

"How do I know it will pass? It may hold me from the moon until I am dead."

Again came a murmur. Then they sang of the rain which kept the sun from them, and said the rain must not last too long. The singing had a defiant note. And the next "fish" carried the defiance much farther.

That fish was Jahy. She caught my eye, moved her head, and when I approached she broke the circle and let me through. Then, after another drink of that fiery rum, she took her place in the ring.

This time Amuy would not march. Hard-faced, bad-eyed, she stood glowering at us and all the rest. The women ignored her and marched around as before.

Asked what she was, Jahy answered loudly—

"I am a sting-ray."

"And what seek you here?"

"A turtle with a hurt foot."

"But your turtle," some woman laughed, "is lost in the rain."

"It does not matter. The rain must give him up."

At that, all looked hard at Amuy.

"But what if the rain does not give him up?" called Tata.

"I am a sting-ray!"

"Is your sting sharp?"

"It is sharp and long. When I sting, I kill!"

She said it clearly and boldly. Again all looked at Amuy. And Amuy stood staring, her mouth open, as if she could not believe she really heard such a threat.

"But perhaps the turtle will learn to love the rain," some one said mockingly.

"Then the turtle will die!" Jahy cried. And now every one looked at me.

I said nothing. The circle moved on, and this time they did not sing. Neither did any one speak. Somehow the tread of those women reminded me of a war-party swinging out on a death-trail.

"Lourenço, I think your new moon is growing full," said Pedro. Watching Jahy, I saw that the ugly recklessness of drink showed in her face. Then I studied Tata also.

"You are right," I agreed. "I do not admire the moon as much as I did. And I think also that your fire will soon break out into open flame."

Tata did look dangerous. So did all the rest. Between their anger over the selfishness of Amuy, the powerful *cauim* they had drunk, and our goading answers, they were in a bad mood. Storm was near.

The storm nearly broke when Jahy threw herself at the others in her attempt to leave the ring. Perhaps it was accident, perhaps not; but she sprang at the bold woman who had first disputed her claim to me, striking her so hard that both fell to the ground.

As Jahy rose the other woman screamed in rage and clawed at her legs. Jahy also screamed. Then she kicked the other in the stomach, kicked her again in the mouth, and jumped on her face with both feet.

Some one pushed Jahy away. Several others jumped between her and the woman on the ground. Jahy fought all of them, but they overpowered her and dragged her back. The other woman arose in a dazed way and staggered toward the *maloca*.

"Kill! Kill!" she muttered as she neared us. And we knew she was going for a weapon.

We stepped before her and blocked her.

"You will not kill Jahy!" I declared loudly.

At that the others all crowded up. Amuy came shoving roughly through them.

"Who talks of killing?" she demanded.

"This woman says she will kill," I answered. "There will be no killing."

With an evil gleam in her eyes Amuy squinted at me, at Pedro, at Jahy.

And then, partly drunk with rum and wholly drunk with rage, she said hoarsely:

"There will be killing. The rain may be heavy, the rain may be thick, but the rain rules. The lizard and the turtle who would end the rain shall die—and the sting-ray also. Kill these men! Kill!"

The women surged toward us. Then, realizing what that command meant, they halted. Pedro spoke.

"You see how it is. Rather than give us to you, this woman would have you kill us. Dead men can not be your mates. Shall we be killed?"

"No!" rang the answer. Instantly he went on.

"No. And you see what sort of chief you have. A chief should rule for the welfare of the whole tribe. A chief who rules only for herself is no chief. Why do you follow such a leader? There are others among you far more worthy. Here is one!" He pointed to Tata. "Are you weak, watery women who should obey the rain? You are women of red blood and fire! Then let the fire rule!"

A shrill yell went up.

"Tata! Tata! A real chief!"

Tata was not slow. She leaped forward, her eyes flashing.

"You hear!" she snapped at Amuy. "I am chief!"

The Fire and the Rain faced each other. Then the storm broke in earnest, With one screech of fury Amuy heaved herself at Tata. The tall girl leaped aside and tripped her. Amuy dropped heavily. Tata jumped on her as Jahy had jumped on the other woman. But her feet slipped off that greasy skin, and she fell.

Others sprang on them both. In no time there was a kicking, clawing, biting heap of women struggling on the ground and knocking other women off their legs.

Out of this heap rose Amuy, bloody-nosed and blubbering. Head down, she plowed through the rest toward the *maloca* door, howling—

"I will kill!"

Then Tata fought her way up and plunged after her. Both disappeared inside the house.

The others swarmed after them, fighting madly to squeeze in at the small opening and get their weapons. Before half of them were through it, more fighting screeches sounded inside, and those still around the door strove even harder to get in. Soon all had jammed themselves through and thrown themselves into the riot, and only we two men stood in the open air.

Pedro strode to the wall, snatched up our rifles, and ran for the jungle. I followed, and I did not let my lameness slow my steps. Through the bush we sprinted toward the river.

"Over here!" he panted, halting beside a twisted tree and whirling me to the right. We squirmed through the tangle as fast as we could, stumbled out at last at the edge of the water, and found the canoe lying snugly in a tiny cove where he had fastened it. Shoving out, we grabbed our paddles. Then I sat back and laughed.

"We had best move out of arrow-shot before we laugh too hard, comrade," he said. "Listen!"

Out of the confused noise of fight away behind us grew sharp cries of rage which quickly became more loud and clear. Some one had found that we were gone, and pursuers were rushing after us. We were up a narrow *enseada*, and the point where we had first landed was beyond us. Until we cleared that point we could easily be shot, and we had little doubt that we would be. Stroking hard, we slid away toward the open river.

We got away none too soon. Before we passed the point of the *restinga* baffled screams rang out from the little cove which we had just left, and arrows plunged into the water close behind us. And when we were out on the slow current of the Juruá more screams and more arrows came from the spot where Pedro had gone ashore yesterday to seek the false *mutum* birds. But the missiles fell short, and we rested on our paddles and looked back.

At the edge of the bush we saw faces twisted by fury and drink, but whose they were we could not tell. Voices shrieked to us to come back and be killed.

"We thank you," called Pedro, "but we would rather return to our weeping wives and suffering children—ha ha ha! *Adeos*, girls! Kiss Amuy for us!"

And we waved our hands and went away from there.

Whether they followed us in canoes I do not know. We had seen no boats there, and perhaps they had none except the old, worm-eaten dugouts in which their mothers had come there years ago. However that may be, we never saw them again.

And let me tell you, *senhores*, I do not want to see them again. Wild women may be interesting, but I do not want to live with girls who smoke suffocating cigars, drink rum that would paralyze a tapir, and kick off the faces of those who anger them. I would rather be among the snakes and jaguars and man-eating savages of my own Javary jungle, where I can be safe.

The Trumpeter

Deos Padre! Hear that war-horn!

Hand me your field glasses quickly, *senhor*! Something is happening over there on the southern bank of the river, and I can not see it plainly. If it is an attack there will be rifle shots, unless the settlers are overpowered at once. Listen!

Ah, it is nothing. Only a celebration. I can see Indians with great false heads doing a devil-dance before the house of some planter, who stands there with his woman and laughs. Probably he is their *patrão*, and has given them a holiday to keep them in good humor.

If the harsh blast of that *turé* had not struck my ear so suddenly I might have realized that it was blown only in merrymaking, for the days when hordes of bloody *bárbaros* attacked settlers here on the Amazon are long past. Past, I mean, on the Amazon itself. Up the great wild rivers which flow in from the south there are still plenty of savage killers, and we Brazilians who rove the unknown jungle know well what the *turé* means. It is the voice of death.

You can not blame me, then, for leaping up so suddenly just now. That jarring note made me forget for an instant that I was safe on the deck of a steamer instead of back in the wilderness of the Javary. Moreover, it is not many months since I heard the *turé* blown in deadly earnest, and I have not forgotten what followed.

Certainly, *senhor*, I will tell you the story if you care to hear it. Wait a moment until I make another cigaret. The one which I was smoking must have dropped overboard when I sprang up.

Now this thing of which I speak came about while the waters of the great yearly flood were sweeping over the lowlands of the Javary region, where I was a rubber-worker for Coronel Nunes. As you know, there are really two floods each year here on the upper Amazon, but only one of these is the great rise. Then the water overwhelms all except the highest places, and our work in the swampy forests must stop until it drains away to the far-off ocean. And it was at this time that I met the Trumpeter.

With my comrade, Pedro Andrada, I had paddled southward through flooded channels to the upper reaches of the river Juruá. There, after escaping from a band of fighting women who had no men and were determined to make us husbands to all their tribe, we found a *furo*, or natural canal, opening out of the river toward the north. On this we started back to our own section, moving at our usual cruising speed. We were in no hurry, for we thought there would be nothing to do when we should reach our journey's end. But two days after leaving the river, as we were looking about among the half-drowned trees for a solid spot fit to sleep on that night, Pedro spoke in a tone of concern.

"Lourenço, we had best paddle a little harder tomorrow. The *enchente* has ended and the *vasante* has set in."

As he said, the great rise had reached its height. On the trees around us were wet stains showing that it was beginning to ebb. From now on the waters would drop steadily until they were fifty feet or more below their present level. We had never traveled on this *furo* before, knew nothing of its depth ahead of us, and were not even sure that it ran all the way to the Javary region. So, though we did not worry, we knew it would be well to waste no time and take no chance of finding ourselves stranded in unknown country.

When we found firm land and went ashore to sling our hammocks I nicked a tree with my *machete*, making a mark just at the waterline. The next morning that mark was more than the width of my hand above the surface. And all that day, as we swung on homeward, we saw the wet stains lengthen on the big trunks towering around us and knew we were sinking toward the thick bush submerged far below. So we talked little, ate without delay, and kept going until darkness was near. When we landed again we were tired.

"A good day's work, comrade," Pedro said. "I do not know where we are, but we are nearer to the Javary than last night. It is good that the dull skies of the rainy time have gone and the sun shines steadily. Now we can tell better which way we are traveling."

"Yes," I agreed. "And now that the sunny *verão* has come we should hear birds calling more often. This country has been too still to suit me. I should like to hear the sweet song of the *realejo*—the organ-bird—or the long piping of that fifer, the *uirá-mimbéu*."

Just then, as if in answer to my wish, a long clear call came floating through the forest. It died so softly that it seemed to hang in the air when we could not hear it more. As we stared at each other it came again. Three times in all it sounded, neither rising nor falling—just the one note, long and slow. Then we heard nothing further.

"That is not a fifer, and it certainly is not the *realejo*," said Pedro. "It must be a trumpeter. You have heard that bird, of course."

I nodded. I had not only heard it, but I had seen it. The trumpeter is that blackish bird which the Peruvians call *trompetero*—a creature about the size of a big hen, but with longer legs and neck. It is a fast runner but a poor flyer, and the Indians sometimes tame it. I had known one *caboclo* who kept such a bird, and when it died I carefully cut it open to see how it made its trumpeting cry. I found that its windpipe was very long, running down under the skin almost to the tail, then doubling around and rising again to the chest, where it went inside the breastbone to the throat.

The sound which had just come to us was much like the call of that bird I had known, and yet it did not seem quite the same. If I had heard it anywhere else I should have said it was made by a man with a horn. But here in this desolate region such a thing seemed not possible, unless the man were an Indian; and a blast from an Indian trumpet would never have such smooth sweetness.

"Yes, it must be the trumpet bird," I agreed. "If it would only stay where it is until tomorrow we might see it, for it is over to the westward. But probably we shall not even hear it again."

I was wrong. We were to hear it once more that day, and several times in the days to come.

We built a little fire, ate, got into our hammocks, and lay back smoking. Around us it was quite dim; but high up overhead, where were scattered openings in the tangled roof of branches, the sunshine still glinted. Then suddenly it was gone. Darkness swallowed everything but our tiny fire.

With the passing of the sun the distant trumpeter spoke again. And this time the sound was not one unchanging call. Slowly, sweetly, it rose and fell, going higher on each long note, quivering on the highest, and then sinking to the one on which it had begun. There it died away. And we lay there silent, *senhores*, silent with surprise, and silent with a feeling of loneliness and sadness which that strain left in our hearts.

At last Pedro spoke.

"That is no bird, Lourenço. It is no wild man of the bush, either. Then what can it be?"

"I do not know," I said. "Some things happen in the jungle which can not be explained. But listen. Perhaps it will come again."

We listened long, but heard only the usual night sounds. After a time these noises blurred and faded into nothing. I slept.

Morning brought the trumpet call again. While we were making our coffee we stiffened into listening. The sound was the same one we had first heard—three slow notes in the same tone. But somehow it seemed to us that this time they were weaker than before, and that in them was a note of despair.

We said no word. We only looked at each other. But we hastened our meal, rolled up our hammocks speedily, and paddled away with swift strokes. As we went we searched the jungle with sharp glances. The *furo* was leading us straight toward the place whence those sounds must have come.

After a time we halted. We had heard nothing more, nor seen anything alive. Yet we knew we must be near the spot we sought.

"It can not be a bird or a beast," said Pedro. "If it has a body it can be nothing but a man." Then, breathing deep, he roared out the call we give in our own region when approaching a house—

"*O da casa!*"

For a moment no answer came. We heard only the slight sucking sound of water around the tree trunks. Then, not far away to our left, the trumpeter answered. And now the notes were not long and slow. They were quick, urgent, discordant—as if a man were blowing a horn in a frenzy of hope and fear lest we go past and leave him.

We yelled together, swung our dugout, and passed in among the trees toward the noise. Soon we found land. We called again, but no voice answered. Several small sounds came to us, though, and we stepped ashore and moved toward them.

Suddenly we stopped, staring at the ground.

A man was dragging himself along toward us. His head hung down so that we could not see his face—only a thick mass of long blond hair. He moved on both hands and one knee. The other leg dragged behind him as if useless. At each forward lift of his knee he grunted as if the movement cost him a mighty effort.

"Stop, friend," I said quietly. "We are here."

He stopped. His arms quivered under him, then suddenly bent and let him slump down. But as we dropped on our knees beside him he turned his head and, lying quiet, peered up at us. We looked into blue eyes gleaming in a tanned face overgrown with short yellow beard. The face looked drawn and pinched.

"Howdy!" he said hoarsely. "Got any grub?"

"We have plenty of food, *senhor*," Pedro said. "Have you hunger?"

"You said it. That's all I've got—hunger and a busted leg. For the love of God, slip me some eats!"

"*Por amor de Deos*, we will do so," smiled Pedro. "Lie still." And he arose and strode back to our canoe.

While he was gone I looked the man over more deliberately. His speech and his dress—pocketed shirt, khaki breeches, knee boots, web belt and flat pistol—showed him to be American. The clothing was not so badly worn and stained as it would be if he had been long in the bush. The right leg was unbooted, and rough splints were tied to it below the knee. Glancing again at his face, I saw that his teeth were set and the sweat of pain was on his forehead.

"You have hurt that broken leg by your crawling," I said. "Why did you not lie still and let us come to you?"

"Because that would be the sensible thing to do." His voice was weak, but he grinned gamely. "I never show any sense. If I did I wouldn't be here at all. Besides, I've been on my back for a week, and I've learned what it is to be lonesome."

"What! You have been lying here a week?"

"Yep. Not here, but back in my tent."

Before we could talk more, Pedro came hurrying back with a gourd of *chibeh*. At sight of it the man tried to scramble up, but groaned and sank back. I scolded him, telling him to keep quiet. Then we fed him.

It was not until the gourd was empty that I thought to ask him how long he had been without food. He said it was three days. Then I wished we had fed him more sparingly at first. But since *chibeh* is only a mush of *farinha* and water, I decided that it would not hurt him. This proved true.

"Now if I only had a bucket of coffee and a smoke I'd be all set," said the stranger. "Got a cigaret on you, buddy?"

I quickly made a cigaret for him, and we promised him coffee as soon as we could make it. But first we decided to take him back to his tent and make him more comfortable. So, when he had finished his smoke, we lifted him as gently as possible and carried him back through the bush.

The distance was short, but the traveling was not easy, and in spite of our care we knew we must be hurting his bad leg. Yet he made no sound. Keeping his teeth locked, he stared straight upward until we brought him to his camp.

Beside a huge *itauba* tree we found his little tent. Inside this, his hammock hung. On the ground lay his mosquito net. We laid him down easily and picked up the net to drape it over him again. On the earth under the net we found a battered bugle.

"So it was this we heard, not a bird," I said, picking it up and glancing it over. "At first we thought you were a trumpeter."

He lay quiet a few minutes, his teeth still set. Then, as the pain in his leg grew easier, his jaws unlocked and he grinned in a tight-lipped way.

"I am," he said. "Been fooling with tin horns since I was a kid. Maybe it's my name that makes me that way—Horner. Folks used to call me Little Jack Horner, though my first name really is Jerome. How about that coffee, buddies?"

"You shall have it," I promised. We left him there and returned to our canoe, where we got our coffee and other things and started back.

"A brave fellow, Lourenço," said Pedro, as we neared the tent. "No fuss, no groan or whine, though he is broken and starved and has been alone with no help in sight. *Por Deos*! Look there!"

On the ground were jaguar tracks. They were more than tracks—they made a path, showing that the beast had circled for hours around the tent. The marks seemed fresh.

"You were not alone last night, *senhor*," I said, entering the little cloth house.

"Huh? Oh, you mean the big cat. Sure, he did sentry-go around here most of the night. He wouldn't come in, so I kept still and let him prowl."

"Your tent saved your life," Pedro told him. "He could smell you, but he did not know he could force his way through these strange cloth walls. If he had—"

"If he had I'd have eaten him," Horner cut in. "Did you bring the coffee?"

We made the coffee, and we made it strong. The hot black liquid gave him new vigor. When he had swallowed all he could hold he gave a long sigh.

"Oh boy!" he said. "That's better than a bushel of that sawdust you fed me. How do you guys live on that *farinha* stuff, anyhow? It takes pork and beans or ham and eggs to put hair on a fellow's chest. Now say, while I'm feeling husky I wish you'd straighten out my leg. It feels twisted."

It was twisted. Working carefully, we reset the broken bone as well as we could and bound new splints on it. As before, he made no sound. When the work was done he calmly asked for another smoke. And then, with the cigaret glowing, he told how he had come there.

He had been a soldier of your United States in the great war in Europe. When the war ended and he returned to his own country, he said, he made the same mistake that many other released soldiers made—he lingered in the vast city of Nova York, quickly spent all his money, and then found himself unable to get work. So, when a chance to make money came unexpectedly to him, he grasped it eagerly.

While he was sitting with other penniless soldiers in a place called Union Square, a tall bony man with strange eyes passed by several times, looking sharply at him and his mates. Then this man asked him and four others to come with him. Being curious, they did so. He led them to a big hotel some distance away, took them to his room, and there made them an odd offer.

He wanted trusty and fearless men to go with him into South America and help him seek something of which he would tell them later on. They would be handsomely paid, and if he found what he sought they would all be made quite rich. There might be danger, he said, but they would be well armed, and the reward would be worth any risk. He had already obtained the promises of other war veterans to go, and he intended to get more. All they had to do was to come along, obey orders, ask no questions, and take their chances of success.

With nothing to lose except their lives, all five of them accepted. Soon afterward they sailed southward with more than a dozen other soldiers whom the bony man had got in the same way. They came up the Amazon and turned into a smaller river, where Indian paddlers in long canoes carried them southward for many days. And in all this time their queer leader never told them where they went or why.

He had been acting oddly for some time, and naturally the men had been talking much among themselves. Now at last they demanded the reason for this long journey into dismal and flooded jungle. Still they got no satisfaction. They were told that they would soon know, but the time had not yet come. Quarreling followed.

The men said they would go no farther. Finding them determined, the bony man suddenly began to rave and shriek. He screamed that he was somebody named Midas, and that he could turn all things to gold by touching them. Then he jerked out a revolver and began shooting at the men.

His bullets killed two soldiers before they downed him. Somebody fired back, and he toppled overboard and never came up again.

After that the men disputed among themselves over what they should do now. None of them had a clear idea as to where they were. Some were for going back as they had come, while others believed that by keeping on they would soon reach the Andes and could then cross the mountains and so reach the western ocean. Before they could settle the question their paddlers brought them to a small Indian settlement where the people gave them welcome. And since all were tired of so much boat travel, they agreed to stay at that place for a few days while they rested and determined what should be done next.

Two days of this were enough for Horner. In spite of much argument, his mates could not yet agree, and he grew too restless to stay idle any longer. So, quietly taking a small canoe, a tent, a little food, his guns and his bugle, he slipped away by himself on an exploring trip to the eastward.

He did not intend to desert his comrades, but only to see what he might see and then return. But he found it so pleasant to be alone that he traveled onward for five days before he tired of it and decided to turn back. Then he became confused among some winding waterways, and before he could find the right one again he met more misfortune. He lost his canoe and broke a leg.

The boat drifted away in the night. While seeking it, he tripped among some vines and snapped his leg over a projecting tree root. Then he could do nothing but crawl back to his tent, lie there, and blow his bugle in the hope that some of his comrades might seek him.

He knew well that his chance of rescue was slight, for he had left the settlement without telling any one where or why he was going, and the other men probably would think he had gone along the river. And yesterday, he said, his courage had almost failed.

. . .

"It's the loneliness that gets you," he added. "Being hungry and busted up is no joke, but knowing that you've got less than one chance in a million of coming through is a lot worse. I've lain out in No Man's Land for two nights and a day, with five shrapnel holes in me and all—rip-roaring around, and I thought I was out of luck. But I'd rather be there than here any time. A fellow has lots of company out there. Last night I got so down in the mouth I blew taps over myself."

Seeing that we did not quite understand, he lifted the trumpet which we had laid beside him and blew the sad, sweet song we had heard at sunset.

"That's taps," he explained. "They blow it over dead soldiers. I didn't know but I might go west before morning, so I did the honors beforehand."

"But how could you go west without a canoe, *senhor*?" I asked. He laughed, and explained that by "going west" he meant dying. So then I told him he was going west indeed, but not as he had thought.

Whether we should be able to find the Indian town over to the west we did not know; but if we did not find it, I told him, we would carry him with us all the way northwestward to our own country, where our old *coronel* would do everything possible for him. And since it was best for all of us that we lose no time, we would get underway at once.

Carrying him and his hammock together to the canoe, we left him there while we took down his tent. On our return we folded the canvas to make a bed in the bottom of the boat, stowed our supplies differently, and helped him in. When he was comfortable he gave a long yawn.

"Guess I'll rip off a few yards of sleep," he said. "I'm about all in. Haven't had a real solid snooze since I cracked my shin." His eyes closed.

After we had paddled a while Pedro said:

"He spoke truth when he said he would rip off his sleep. Hear him snore!"

I grinned, for the blond trumpeter certainly was a noisy sleeper. But as I thought of the long black nights of pain and hunger and hopelessness that lay behind him, his snorts and gurgles did not seem funny at all. Indeed, I marveled that he had not gone mad or ended his torment with one of his bullets.

All the rest of the day he slept while we paddled on. Near night, as we were seeking a sleeping place, he opened his eyes and blinked at us, the canoe, and the trees.

"Aw shucks!" he grunted. "I'm back here again!"

"Where have you been, Senhor Trumpeter?" laughed Pedro.

"I was back home, playing ball and cussing the umpire because he called me out when I never even offered to swing. Home was never like this. I'll say not! Say, when do we eat?"

"As soon as we land," I told him. "Are you ready to eat more of our sawdust?"

"I'll eat anything, buddy. If you don't get ashore pretty quick I'll start chewing your leg."

Then, lifting his bugle, he blew a loud, lively air, much different from anything we had heard before.

"That's reveille," he said. "It means 'wake up—snap into it.' Put a hop on your stroke and land me before I get violent."

"Calm yourself and spare my leg awhile longer, and we all shall eat," I promised. "But I would not blow that trumpet again, *senhor*, until we reach some place where we know we are more safe. We are few, and it would not be well to let any savage Indians know we are here. Did you blow a bugle in the war?"

"Nope. Not so anybody could hear it. I knew all those army calls before any war came along. Then I wanted to fight, and the only way you can be sure of fighting these days is to make the personnel sharks think you don't know anything."

"How is that?" I wondered.

"If you can do anything they try to make you do it in the army. If you're a mechanic they keep you tinkering on bum motors. If you're a newspaper man they make you a censor. If you know a shirt from a sock they shove you into quartermaster work. If you're a cop they make you an M.P.—and then you're popular, I guess not!

"It's the same way all along the line. So when my turn came I didn't know a thing. If they'd learned I could blow a horn they might have made me a bandmaster or something. But seeing I was dead from the neck up, they gave me a gun and let me in on the big show."

This seemed very queer to us, for we had always thought that in an army everybody was expected to fight. He grinned as he talked, and it may be that he did not mean just what he said. But we spoke no more of the matter, for then we spied a good camping spot and went ashore. And after eating and smoking, we all slept soundly.

The next day Horner found himself. Without realizing it, we strayed off the *furo* into another channel, along which we paddled for some distance before the slant of the sun-thrown shadows warned us that we were off our course. Then, as we slowed and told each other we must go back, the Trumpeter spied an oddly bent tree leaning out over the water ahead.

"Say, this is the way I came!" he told us. "I know that tree. There was a big snake on it. I shot him off, and he kicked up such a riot he nearly upset me. Gee, he was a regular whale! Keep on going, and you'll hit the burg where the rest of my gang hangs out."

So we kept on, and as we went he recognized other things along the way.

Two days later we came out into a rather large river flowing northeastward. And there our passenger blew again that dancing reveille tune.

"Home again!" he laughed, when the last note had pealed away through the jungle. "Injun Town is only about half a mile upstream, and the rough old tough old bunch is waiting for us up there. Snap into it, buddies!"

We snapped into it. We knew how eager he was to meet his comrades again, and it had been some time since we ourselves had talked with white men. So we went upstream fast.

The Trumpeter was much stronger now after the long sleeps and hearty meals of the past few days, and as we surged on up the river he sat leaning forward, grinning and waiting for a sight of his mates. But as we swung around a bend, his smile faded and his jaw dropped.

A little way ahead, under tall trees where little bush grew, a number of Indians were standing at the water's edge. Several small canoes also were there. But we saw no large boat nor any white men.

"——'s bells!" groaned Homer. "The gang's gone!"

It was so. Only the Indians waited for us there. They held weapons, and at first they seemed unfriendly. But when we came near and they saw Horner clearly they grinned at him, and as Pedro and I stepped out on shore they greeted us cordially.

A tall, grave man who seemed to be chief spoke in a Tupi tongue, saying they were glad to see again the blower of the horn, and that they had thought him gone forever. I explained why he had left them and why we now came with him, and asked where the other white men were. He said they had gone two days after Horner disappeared; that they believed he had gone up the river, and so they had decided to go that way also. He added that he was sorry to know the blower of the horn had hurt himself, but that a broken bone would soon mend, and all of us were welcome to his village.

"When you guys get through making a noise with your mouths maybe you'll give me the lowdown," said the Trumpeter. "It don't make sense to me."

So I said it all over to him, and asked how he and his fellow soldiers had been able to talk with these people if they knew no Tupi. He said the talking had been done through one of their canoemen. The thought came to me that if he could not speak their tongue he might find it hard to get along with them after we left, and that we had best take him on with us. But I said nothing of this just then. We helped him out and followed the Indians.

They led us only a short distance back from the water, and then we found ourselves in a small town of little low houses. The chief took us to one of these, ordered a man and woman living in it to go elsewhere, and told us it was ours. Then he went away, and his men with him. But before he left us he looked shrewdly at our guns and asked whether we could make them speak many times.

Of course we told him yes, we could make them spit death at a whole tribe. This was not true, for we had used up many of our cartridges in a fight with some beastly *bárbaros* back on the Juruá, and now we had not a great number left. But it is not wise to let Indians think you to be weak, even though they are friendly; so we were prompt in our answer. He said it was well.

After we put up our hammocks I told the Trumpeter he had better come on to the Javary with us. Before this he had been one of a score of fighting men, I pointed out, but after we went he would be alone among these Indians, and perhaps he would not be so well-treated as before. So, though the journey to the Javary might be hard, he might come out better in the end than by staying here. But he only laughed.

"Oh, they're good skates," he said. "They wouldn't pull anything raw. You don't know 'em as well as I do."

"Perhaps not," Pedro answered him. "But we have ranged the bush far more than you, *senhor*, and my comrade here speaks sense. It takes more than a few days to know Indians well; and the ways of Indians toward twenty strong white men and toward one broken white man may not be the same. And these people came to meet us with weapons and their leader just asked us how strong our guns are. True, they seem peaceable, but—you had best go on with us."

"But I tell you they're all right," he insisted. "They're only a bunch of hicks, and they don't want trouble with anybody. They raise crops and kids and take it easy, and they're regular fellows. Walk around and look 'em over. Me, I like 'em fine."

Still rather doubtful, we did walk around and look over the place and the people. And we found that it was as he said: the Indians here seemed to be quiet and honest, happy in the peace of their town and content to toil on the plantations beyond it, where the trees had been thinned to let the crops grow. Still, we noticed that here and there were men with weapons, watching the women work and occasionally scanning the thick bush beyond.

Stopping beside one of these armed men, we talked for a time about hunting and such things, and then asked why he and his mates stood guard in this way. In a quiet, respectful manner he replied that they watched lest the place be attacked. And when we asked further about this, he said they had heard that a band of fierce savages was somewhere in the region round about.

Who the bad men were he did not know, nor whether they would come this way. This flood season was not the time for such attacks, he said, for usually those roving bands of warriors were not boatmen and so were more likely to come at the time of low water; but of course one could never know when creatures of that sort would take it into their heads to run wild and kill. He spoke of them as if they were jaguars or other beasts—dangerous animals against which his people must guard themselves but which they considered unworthy of any respect.

Thinking this over, I saw why the chief had asked about the strength of our guns. I thought, too, that this might be one reason why we were so welcome here—three men with rifles would be a great help to him if an attack should come, even though one of us was crippled. I wondered, too, why he had not planned to keep the other Americans here until he knew whether the *bárbaros* were coming this way. So I asked the guard whether they had warned the white men about these savages before they left.

He said no. They themselves had not heard of the wild men until yesterday, he said, and the white men then had been gone for days. He added that he hoped the whites would meet the marauders somewhere up the river, because then there would be a fight, and of course the men with guns would kill all those brutes.

I had some doubt about this, for I thought the soldiers would find fighting in thick jungle to be far different from what they had been accustomed to in Europe. But I told him the white men would surely kill every one of the savages if they met them. Then we went back to Horner, much better satisfied with these people than we had been at first.

"Sure, I knew you'd like these brown boys after you got their range," said the Trumpeter, when we told him we had changed our ideas. "When you thought they were sneaks you were overshooting. I'm satisfied to stay here until I'm ready to go down river. So you guys needn't worry about me, and if you want to move on don't let me block you."

We urged him again to come with us, but he flatly refused. Then we went to the chief and asked him whether he had any real reason to expect an attack. He seemed a little surprised that we had learned of this; but he said there was nothing to show that their enemies were coming here, and his men were watching only because they always did so when they heard that bad men were near. So, since the blond American would not go with us, and since we could not dally here long, we decided to continue our homeward journey the next day.

But the next day brought squalls. Soon after our morning meal, while we were talking with Horner and the chief and preparing to go, the sunlight was blotted out. Thunder crashed and sheets of lightning dazzled us. A flood of rain fell, driven slantwise by a fierce wind. And when the storm had passed, the chief advised us to stay over for another day.

He said such sudden storms were not uncommon here at this time of year, and that a squall so early in the day would be followed by others. If we went on now we should meet worse weather before long, he told us, and if we were not swamped by some sudden blast of wind we should at least sleep wet and uncomfortable that night. He added that the rains today would make the waters rise, so that we should gain rather than lose by waiting. So why not remain here and be comfortable and visit his people, whom we might never see again?

This sounded sensible, and we were pleased by his honest way of speaking. So we decided to stay until the next morning, and then start early. And we were glad we tarried.

For one thing, we found that he knew the weather. More squalls did come, and they were heavy. Besides this, the people were agreeable companions, and they brought us fresh food, which was a welcome change from the rations we had recently been eating. So, between watching the lightning, eating huge meals, listening to the Trumpeter's bugle, and talking with the chief and others, we spent the day very pleasantly.

While we talked we cleaned our rifles, which had grown rusty. The chief was much interested in these weapons, partly because he knew little about them and partly because Pedro's gun and mine were different from that of Horner. Ours were the American repeating rifles generally used in our region, with the lever behind the trigger and a bore of .44 caliber. The Trumpeter's gun also would repeat, but it looked much different and its action was not the same. The wood under the barrel ran almost to the muzzle, and it was cocked not by a lever but by a sort of handle on the bolt. The bore was much smaller than ours, but Horner insisted that the power of his gun was far greater than that of our big-bulleted weapons. We did not believe him until he told us his was an army rifle. Then we knew it must be high-powered.

The bony man who led him and his comrades here, he said, had managed to get enough of these rifles to arm every man in the party, as well as the flat pistols to which they were accustomed. He added that besides these guns he had something more deadly than any bullet. Then, twitching from his belt a long knife which we had taken for a sort of *machete*, he snapped it onto the gun under the muzzle.

"That's the real killer," he said. "A guy can get all shot up and still live, but when you slide this little old toothpick into a man he's through. Hot lead is all right, but the cold steel is the stuff that mops 'em up."

Dropping the blade into a line with my stomach, he made a playful jab upward. I fell over my own feet and knocked Pedro down in dodging away from it. Then Horner chuckled, the chief grinned, and I laughed rather foolishly.

"Don't feel very good to see that thing start for your lunch basket, does it, even though I'm only a one-legged crip sitting down?" asked the blond man. "Then figure out how Fritz felt when he saw hundreds of 'em coming over.

He sure made himself AWOL, and then some."

After he explained what AWOL meant, I said I did not blame Fritz for going somewhere else without orders. I added that in this thick jungle of ours such a weapon was likely to be more useful in a fight than a far-shooting gun. His answer disturbed me a little.

"Yep, and if I hook up with any tough nuts before I hit the Amazon I may have to use it. The gang carried off all the ammunition with them, and all I've got left is two clips for the rifle and one for the pistol. But when I get my legs under me again I can show anybody that wants a row some wicked bayonet stuff."

Pedro and I glanced at each other, but said nothing. Our cartridges would not fit his gun, so that even if we could have spared any they would have been useless to him. We could do nothing to help him—or so we thought. Yet before we were many hours older we were to help him much.

With one final ripping squall the day ended. Before the rain stopped the light had gone. A moonless night followed. As we intended to start early the next day, we soon got into our hammocks. Before we slept the Trumpeter blew again, loud and clear, that song of taps.

"Why do you do that, *senhor*?" asked Pedro. "There are no dead soldiers here."

"Right. But Taps isn't just a dead man's tune. It means 'good night—sleep tight—all's well.' I'm just saying good night to that bunch of gorillas that beat it upstream while I was away. They can't hear it, but they're getting ready to snooze now somewhere up there, and maybe they're thinking about me."

Though he spoke lightly, we could see that his heart was lonely for the companionship of those "gorillas." We said no more. Soon we slept.

Before daybreak Pedro and I awoke and arose. Around us it was very dark, but not silent. Horner was trumpeting through his nose, and from other little huts nearby the snores of sleeping Indians came back like echoes. Outside we could see nothing but the vague loom of the jungle against the star-spattered sky. So, since it was too dark to take down our hammocks, we sat down in them again and smoked, waiting for the shadows to lift.

Soon a wan light dawned on the clearing. The trees became trees instead of a black blot. The sun was not up, and a thin mist blurred the air, but day had come. We snapped our cigaret butts through the doorway, and stood up.

Then came war.

A long harsh trumpet-blast tore across the gurgling chorus of snores. A roar of yelling voices followed. Out from the edge of the jungle sprang naked warriors. Through the mist they came bounding toward the huts, howling and brandishing spears and clubs and bows. Other cries answered them: shouts of men springing awake, screams of women terrified by that awful trumpeting—the deadly blare of the *turé*, war-horn of brutal murderers.

We swooped up our guns, sprang outside, opened fire. The leaping brutes nearest us swerved and fell. Others screeched sharply in shocked surprise and stopped. They had not expected to find men with guns here. For an instant they wavered. While they hesitated we dropped several more of them. Then our hammers snapped down on empty chambers. But as we turned toward our door, the *bárbaros* also turned and ran.

It was only those fronting us, though, who fled. The rest, though they slowed and looked toward the roar of our rifles, came on. But now they ran into a rain of arrows shot by the Indians who had sprung from their houses, and more of them fell. We saw nothing further just then, for we dashed into our hut to get more cartridges.

The American was sitting up, and he asked no questions—he was a soldier. As we swiftly reloaded and shoved our remaining cartridges into our pockets, he said with a tight-faced grin:

"Go to it, buddies! Blow 'em wide open! Get around behind the house! I'll handle anything in front."

He was sitting on the edge of his hammock, with his crippled leg resting in it and the other foot on the ground to steady him. On his lap he held his rifle, pointing toward the door, and the long hungry-looking knife gleamed at its muzzle. We saw this in a flash, and then we were outside again.

Even as I left the door I met a big savage running toward it. He hurled a short spear, but I ducked and shot him in the stomach. Pedro's rifle cracked twice, but I did not look around, for I knew he had killed his men. The American's order to get behind the house was a good one, and I followed it. At a rear corner I halted and looked about.

The *bárbaros* had swept in from all sides at once, and fierce close fighting was going on everywhere. A few arrows darted out from the houses, but the combat was mostly hand-to-hand. Stabbing, clubbing, choking and clawing and breaking bones, small knots of men struggled desperately for mastery. Caught by surprise and perhaps outnumbered as well, the townsmen seemed to be getting the worst of it; but they fought furiously to protect their women and children, who kept screaming as if they were already being murdered.

Picking my men, I fired again and again into the battling *bárbaros*. Behind me, on the other side of the hut, sounded Pedro's gun. Then from the house itself came a shot—a sharp crack not like the blunt bark of our own weapons. Twice more that army gun cracked, and then it was still.

When my gun was empty again I shouted to Horner, asking if all was well. In answer his bugle rang out. Above the screams, the fighting yells, and the hoarse bellowing of the savage *turé* it sounded—quick, sharp blasts on the same note, lifting suddenly to two higher ones, dropping back then to the same tone as before. And it did not stop. Over and over it blared defiantly, hammering away at our ears until the men defending their homes seemed to gain fresh strength from it.

Whether the urge of that trumpet really did give them new power, or whether it and our bullets together brought fear into the minds of the wild men, I do not know. But I do know that soon the fighting died. While I was emptying my gun once more I saw that the attackers were giving way toward the bush and our friends were battling harder than ever. Before I had filled my magazine again the savages on my side of the town were gone.

Running around to the front, I found that there too the space was clear except for the townsmen and a few men grappling on the ground. The battered defenders pounced on these small groups, and when they turned away the *bárbaros* who had been fighting there were dead.

The war-horn had stopped blowing. The cries of the children too had ended, and the yelling men were still. Only the bugle sang on in the same quick tune. Then, with one long flare, it became silent.

"Pretty slow stuff!" grumbled the Trumpeter as we stepped into the hut. "If that's the best your South American badmen can do I don't think much of them. All I had to do was to pot two or three out front here and then toot my horn to pass away the tune."

"You did not see much of the fight, *senhor*," Pedro reminded him. "You are inside, and the walls shut out most of it. Yet it was not such close work as some I have seen—at least not for us three. Our friends had their hands full beating them off."

"Slow stuff," Horner repeated, yawning. "Did the chief come through all right? If so, tell him I'm hungry."

We laughed, went out, and looked about for the chief. But we did not see him anywhere. Some of the Indians were picking up their dead and wounded, while others stood watching the jungle where their enemies had disappeared. We passed along among these, glancing at the bodies and noticing that there were more dead townsmen than savages. The wounded, of course, were defenders, for the injured attackers all had gotten away into the bush or been killed when their mates retreated. Without trying to count the dead, we could see that without our bullets to aid them our friends would have been quickly overwhelmed and butchered.

We could not find the chief among either the living or the dead there in the clearing, so we asked men what had become of him. They told us he was hurt and now was in his own house. They said also that, armed only with a club, he had killed three of the *bárbaros*; and they showed us the bodies, each with its head crushed.

When we entered the chief's hut we found that he had not fared any too well. His left shoulder was badly torn by a spear-thrust, and a long arrow stuck out from one leg. A little old man whom we had not seen before was working to pull out the shaft, but its head was buried so deeply in the muscles that he was only hurting the chief, who sat silent but with lips drawn tight.

Looking up and seeing us, the chief motioned for me to draw that arrow out. I did so, but I had to pull hard, with one foot against the leg to brace it. When it came away the chief rocked in his hammock with pain, though he still gave no whimper. A look at the arrowhead showed me why it had stuck so stubbornly. It had double barbs, pointing both forward and back, which tore the flesh when they went in and when they came out, and which would prevent the shaft from being removed by pushing it on through the wound instead of drawing it out backward.

It was one of the most cruel weapons we had ever seen, and the sight of it angered us. Until now we had not felt any great hatred for those wild men; we had fought only because we were attacked, and so must kill or be killed. But those barbs, deliberately placed so that they would torture a man wounded but not killed, made us hot.

"If the brute who made this is still alive I hope he has one of my bullets in his bowels," I growled.

"And I wish I could shoot a few more of them," said Pedro.

We talked in our own language, but the chief was watching us while the little old medicine man worked on his wounds, and perhaps he understood. He spoke, telling us to keep our guns ready for quick use when the time should come. The *bárbaros*, he said, probably would attack again.

Somewhat surprised, I said we thought the fighting had ended. He shook his head, saying that it was not the way of those fierce men to quit while many of them were left alive. They had expected to overpower him and his people by attacking while the town still slept, but our prompt and deadly fire had surprised and confused them so that they could be fought off. But now they were preparing for another assault, and when they were ready they would come in spite of our guns, and the next fight would be to the death.

He added that unless we and our guns were strong the wild men would win. Many of his best men were dead or hurt, and he himself could not fight so well as before. He spoke very calmly, as if only saying that it might rain before night; but his eyes went to his two small children, who stood close by and watched the medicine man. We too looked at them—chubby little fellows with round faces and wide eyes—and shut our teeth. And though we knew our cartridges now were far too few, we told him our guns were strong enough to wipe out those beasts of the bush if his people would fight as bravely as before. He answered simply that they would fight until they died.

Soberly we went back to the Trumpeter, taking with us the bloody double-barbed arrow. We told him all there was to tell, and gave the arrow to him. As he studied it his face hardened.

"Dirty mutts!" he said. "If they'd shoot a thing like that into a man what would they do to the women and kids? Blast 'em, I hope they do come back—I want another crack at them! And say, if they come don't stick around this shack. Pick a couple of places where you can get a crossfire and make your bullets count. I'll take care of my end of the riot."

Then he grinned.

"Gee, but wouldn't the gang be hopping mad if they knew they'd missed a regular row! By this time they must be halfway to Borneo, or Bolivia, or whatever you call that spiggoty country down south, and wishing something would happen. And here squats little old Jack Horner, the poor crip, with a real rough-house coming off and not another Yank to see it. If I ever meet up with that bunch of gorillas again won't I rub it into 'em! Say, when do we eat?"

We did not eat at once, but after a time food came to us. Armed men watched ceaselessly, and nobody went close to the bush, but otherwise life went on much as usual in and around the houses. We breakfasted heartily, talked more with Horner, and tried to pick places for that crossfire he wanted. But this we could not do with any certainty because we could not guess how the next attack would be made.

All around the clearing rose the jungle, and the *bárbaros* might burst out from any part of it. They might come as they had come before, from all points at once, or they might divide into parties and charge from several different quarters. If we fixed any particular spots for our firing we might find ourselves in the wrong places when we were needed. So, after some argument, we decided simply to take things as they came and do our best to meet whatever plan our foes had.

"One thing is pretty sure," said Horner, "and that is that they won't come just the way they did the first time. They attack by trumpet signal, and that shows they've got some idea of teamwork. Fighting men with any brains don't pull the same stuff twice running, and you've got to watch out for a trick this time. Tell the chief not to let all his men go piling into the first bunch that shows up, but to hold some in reserve until he sees where he can use them best."

That was sense, and I took the message to the chief while Pedro stayed and watched. I found the tribal ruler now sitting quietly with his leg and shoulder bandaged with pads of bark-cloth, and talking with several of the older men. He agreed that the advice of the white soldier was good, and gave orders to those with him that certain men should be held back for a time. He asked me also whether I would direct the fighting of those men. But I refused, for I wanted nothing to think of but my own work, and I knew his

men would understand their own leaders better than me. Then I returned to
our hut.

A long time dragged past. The sun rolled high and hot in an unclouded
sky. We talked little and smoked much—I do not believe I had ever smoked
so many cigarets in one morning. Around the other huts hung the strained
silence of tense waiting. At the edge of the jungle no life showed, and from
it came no sound. Between houses and bush the only living things were the
vultures that had swooped down and were stripping the bones of the dead
wild men.

"Ho-hum!" yawned the Trumpeter. "This is the hardest part of war—
waiting for the other guy to start something. I'm getting sleepy. Might as
well have a little music. Guess I'll give those roughnecks out yonder the
reveille and wake 'em up."

As his rollicking tune ended Pedro leaned forward, listening. A confused
noise, muffled by the bush, sounded and died.

"The *bárbaros*!" I said.

"Perhaps so," he replied doubtfully. "It seemed like the voices of men
shouting together, but I did not think our enemies were so far away."

Again we listened, but no further sound came. We settled back into
waiting.

"Lourenço," my partner said softly after a time, "do you see something
climbing in that tall slim tree over yonder?"

Following the line of his pointing finger, I glimpsed a dark body moving
upward at the edge of the bush. The leaves between it and us were so thick
that I could notice it clearly, and soon I lost it altogether.

"Yes. I saw it. But I can not see it now."

"I can. It has stopped and is resting on a limb. Perhaps, Senhor Trumpeter,
your music has made the blower of the *turé* jealous. If that is he, I will play
him a tune on this little steel pipe."

Lifting his rifle, he rested it against the side of the doorway and stood
aiming steadily at the thing in the tree. And soon his joking remark proved
truth.

Out from that tree broke the bellow of the war-horn. Pedro's rifle spat.
The blare of the *turé* ended abruptly. The dark form fell crashing down
through the branches.

Yells sounded behind our hut. Pedro and I jumped around the corners. A
mass of savages was charging straight at us.

As we threw up our guns the mass split into three bodies. One swerved
to the right, one to the left, and the third came on. At the head of this middle
force ran a huge brute smeared with red paint, wearing a belt of human
hair and a necklace of human teeth, howling like a madman and carrying a

tremendous club.

We both shot him at the same instant. He pitched on his face and lay quiet. Over his body the others jumped, and we fired so fast that we killed some while they were still in the air. A small heap of corpses grew between us and the dead leader. Other warriors stumbled over these bodies, falling themselves and tripping more men behind them. By the time our guns were empty the force of the rush was broken.

But we got little time to reload. I managed to get two more cartridges into the magazine before the first *bárbaros* reached me, and I fired these straight into their faces. Then I swung my gun, braining one man with the barrel, and dropped the empty weapon. Seizing the warrior I had just killed and holding him up before me as a shield, I pulled my *machete* and set my back to the wall.

Just what happened after that I can not tell you. It was stab—slash—dodge aside—stab and slash again, always holding that dead man in front and keeping the wall behind. All I can remember is snarling faces, stinking breath, grunts and groans and screeches, blood and brains and entrails. At last, gasping and dizzy with exhaustion and half-blinded with blood from a gash on my forehead, I leaned against the wall and found no man attacking me.

On the ground near me four men were heaving and wrenching, and out of the tangle a red *machete* rose and fell. By the time I got my wind and stood away from the wall their fight was over. Up from among the bodies rose a half-naked, red-smeared figure which reeled toward me. I lifted my *machete* to attack it. Then I recognized the bloody man as Pedro.

He stumbled against the wall and slouched there, sick from fatigue and blows. When he could breathe naturally again he twisted his split lips in a grin.

"Drop it!" he wheezed, looking at the dead savage still clutched in my left arm. After a glance at it I dropped it. Its head was no longer a head but a crushed pulp, battered in by club blows aimed at me. Its trunk, too, was full of gaping wounds, and several short spears stuck out from its ribs.

We picked up our guns and reloaded. The cartridges were our last, and so few that neither of us could fill his magazine. We looked at each other and at the fighting around us. And Pedro said—

"We must keep these for our last stand."

It was so. The townsmen were being beaten down. Near us no man lived, but we knew our turn would come again all too soon, and that then our rifles and *machetes* would not save us long. The women and children were screaming again, and the yells of the savages spoke brutal exultation. Already some of them had stopped fighting and were butchering the wounded.

Behind us the army rifle cracked twice. Horner still lived. Dimly I remembered hearing him shoot several times while we fought. Now we ran back to the front of the hut, and there we found another fierce fight going on all along the line. The wild men had charged from the bush on this side also, and only the American's foresight in providing for reserves had prevented them from catching the chief's men from behind. These men, held back from meeting the rush at the rear, had stopped the one in front. But here too they were being killed faster than they were killing.

The end of all of us was close at hand, and we two stopped at the corners and held our fire for our last fight. But then a pair of red-streaked brutes went plunging into a hut close by, and out from that house a long scream rose high over the other cries around us—the shriek of a woman in an agony of fear. It was too much for me.

I dashed down to that place, shooting down a savage who got in my way, and attacked the murderers inside, who had seized a woman and a child. Two more of my bullets were gone when I came out; but the woman and child still lived, while their assailants did not.

As I left the doorway another wild man came bounding at me. Firing from the hip, I shot him in the body. He fell, writhed, clawed the ground, went limp and was still. The downward yank of my lever brought up only an empty shell. My last shot was gone.

A thrown spear thudded into the wall. Several more *bárbaros* were coming at me. I sprang back into the house, where, with *machete* drawn, I waited just inside the door. But most of those killers never reached me.

A sudden crash of gunfire ripped out. Two of the charging savages toppled sidewise. The others stopped, faced to their left, poised there staring. At the same instant the wild yelling ceased. It seemed still as the grave.

CRASH! Another volley.

One of the wild men before my door doubled in at the middle and dropped. Another fell backward, the top of his head gone. Only one was left standing. He whirled about, looked this way and that, and bolted for the shelter of the hut where I stood. As he came I saw that now his face was drawn with fear.

I stepped aside. As he plunged in at the doorway I swung my *machete* hard to his throat. He flopped down, his head cut almost off. The woman and child cowering behind me screamed again, but I gave no attention to them. I popped out into the open.

No more volleys came. Instead, the firing now was a steady crackle. Naked men were dropping dead. Other savages were running—some toward the bush, some toward houses, some straight at the place where the shooting sounded. That place was near the river, and there among the shadows I saw gleaming steel, spurts of flame, yellow shirts and broad hats.

The Trumpeter's "gorillas" had come back.

• • •

Shouting in wild joy, the desperate townsmen sprang again on their confused enemies. With spears, clubs, bare hands, they fought as if suddenly given new life. Then a whistle shrieked, out—one long blast—and at once the firing ceased.

With the end of the shooting, wild men who had taken cover came running out again and rushed toward the yellow shirts. They thought—and so did I—that the bullets were used up. But the riflemen had not stopped fighting. They had only begun. With a roar they came lunging forward, the long knives on their guns flashing in the sunlight.

Then, while I stood there staring like a fool, I saw what those knives could do in the hands of men trained to their use. I had thought the bayonet must be a slow weapon, but I learned otherwise. Those grim-faced Americans seemed hardly to be really fighting, but only to be jabbing and dancing about; yet the savages swarming at them dropped, dropped, dropped, and the soldiers kept coming on.

But they came more and more slowly, and soon they were stopped. Heaving, hacking, stabbing, spearing, white and brown men were locked in a solid mass. And then, with the *bárbaros* jamming together, the shooting started again.

The shots sounded dull and muffled now. Later I learned that this was because the muzzles were almost against the skins of the *bárbaros*, and also that each of those bullets tore through two or three men. The firing did not last long, but it seemed to blow the wild men off their feet. So many fell dead at once that they blocked and bore down the others, and what had been a tangle of raging warriors became a heap of flesh.

Out of that pile squirmed men yelping with terror, who tried to break loose and run. And into that pile plunged the soldiers, reaching the struggling *bárbaros* with tremendous long thrusts and spearing them like fish. Here and there a savage managed to pull himself out of the welter and run, but none of these ran far. The townsmen cut them off and slew them before they could reach the shelter of the jungle.

"Lourenço! To the rear!" called Pedro's voice.

I started, looked around, could not see him, and got around the hut quickly. I had forgotten all about the fighters on the other side of the houses. There too I found white men battling hard, and these had not overcome their foes. There seemed to be fewer soldiers and more savages on this side, and the two forces were not locked together but broken up into scattered groups, every white man fighting his own battle against a number of copper-skins.

Pedro, after his shout to me, had thrown himself into this fighting and was swinging his *machete* on wild men who were swarming on a lone soldier. As I ran I picked another group doing the same thing, and a few seconds later I was hacking at their necks. For a while I was very busy. Then I found a limping townsman helping me with a spear, and between the soldier in front and us two in the rear we cleaned up that group.

Shots cracked around us as the last wild man fell at our feet. New yells rang out. *Bárbaros* ran for the bush. The soldiers and village Indians from the other side of the town had swept in here to finish the battle. With their coming the wild men had bolted, and they found nothing to do but stand and shoot rapidly. When the crackle ceased no living enemy was left in sight.

"Phooey! 'Tis a hot day for workin'!" panted the soldier whom I had helped, mopping his broad face with a sleeve and grinning at me. "Thanks for carvin' up them guys the way ye done. I been gittin' fat, and me wind ain't what it was."

"And I thank you, *senhor*, and your comrades, for coming when you did," I said. "My last shot was gone."

"Was it so? I wouldn't think ye'd need a gun anyways, feller. Ye sure can sling a wicked knife."

Then up came another soldier—a long, lean, easy-moving, red-spattered man.

"Howdy, mistuh," he drawled, looking at me. "Have yuh seen a good-fo'-nothin' rapscallion named Hawnuh—a li'l cuss with a brass hawn an' a lot o' gall?"

"He is in that house, *senhor*," I nodded. "My partner and I found him with a broken leg and brought him back here."

The tall man lifted his brows slightly.

"Laig busted, huh? Reckon we bettuh mosey ovuh an' see how he come through this li'l pahty. Nawthin' mo' to do heah—these town boys will do the moppin' up. Come on, Mike, yuh fat Dutchman."

"Dutchman!" snorted the broad-faced man. "Ye slab-sided skeleton of a down-South hookworm, if I'm a Dutchman ye're a greaser."

The lean man grinned a slow grin, but made no answer, and we moved toward the Trumpeter's hut. Other soldiers joined us on the way, looking curiously at me.

"Friend of mine," said the man Mike, noticing these looks and moving his head toward me. "Who he is I dunno, but he's there wit' the rough stuff. Anybody cashed in?"

"All present or accounted for," answered a stocky soldier with bow legs. "Tim Moran is busted up some, and so are Chicago Tony and Scotty McLeod, but nobody's gone."

"Arrugh!" grunted Mike. "Tim and Scotty need a swift kick for mixin' in at all—they're both rotten wit' fever. And that little fightin' fool of a Chicago wop— Holy Mother! Whaddye know about this!"

We had come around to the front of the house of the Trumpeter, and we stopped and stared. Its doorway was choked by a heap of dead *bárbaros*.

"Hey you, Jack Horner!" some man snapped. "You all right?"

"Sure, I'm all right," came the Trumpeter's cool voice. "Kick that stuff out of the door and come on in."

We threw the dead aside and entered. Horner stood on his one good leg, with the other knee supported by the hammock. His rifle-butt rested on the ground, and the long bayonet sticking up near his shoulder was dyed red.

"Who gave you guys any license to horn in on my party?" he complained. "Here I'm getting a lot of good bayonet practice and you bust in and shoot up the whole works just when I'm going good. What you doing here, anyhow? Did the spiggotys down in Borneo give you the gate?"

"Listen at him, will ye!" rumbled Mike. "Talkin' like he was a growed-up man! And him blowin' the guts out of his tin horn a while back, tryin' to git reinforcements!"

"Not by a jugful!" Horner denied. "I blew the charge, but I did it just to make a racket and give these boys out here a little pep. Where were you guys, anyway?"

"Upstream a ways. We found it bum goin', so we turned around and come back. We camped above here last night, and heard ye play taps. When yer charge come to us this mornin' we took our foot in our hand and come on. Didn't ye hear us yell when ye blew reveille?"

"I heard shouting, *senhor*," said Pedro. "But we thought it must be *bárbaros*."

" 'Twas a bum guess—there ain't a barber in the gang," said Mike. "But now listen here, Kid Horner. We got to slide right along downstream before anymore of the bunch kick off wit' fever. Eb Peabody, that New England feller, cashed in a couple days ago, and Tim Moran and Scotty are gittin' bad too. I hear they come ashore here wit' the rest of the gang and got mauled, and that won't do 'em no good. So we'll move as soon as we can git them lousy paddlers back—they was that scairt of the wild guys they beat it acrost the river as quick as we landed.

"I'll go git 'em now. When we're ready we'll give ye a yell. Slim, stay here and help Jack frog it down to the water. Fall in, the rest of ye."

He turned and went, followed by all except the lean man with the slow drawl, who stood calmly chewing tobacco and spitting in the eye of a dead savage who lay face upward.

"Yuh li'l hawn-toad, yuh!" said Slim. "Yuh sho' did tickle these felluhs' ribs some. Whyn't yuh jab 'em lowuh down? Yuh might of busted the steel on them rib-bones, an' then whah'd yuh been?"

"Had to take 'em any way I could get 'em, Slim," replied Horner. "They rushed the place after Pedro here left, and if I hadn't plugged a couple and sort of choked up the door with them they might have got me. Then I jabbed straight and withdrew quick. You can't do any footwork when you've got a dead leg. Ho-hum. I sort of hate to leave this town, it's so quiet and peaceful."

Slim grinned, and we laughed. After looking at the dead men a minute Pedro strode out, crossed the clearing, and disappeared into the bush. Soon he returned with a long tube.

"Perhaps you would like a remembrance of the peace and quiet of our Brazilian forests, *senhor*," he suggested. "Here is the *turé* of the *bárbaros*."

"Say, that's mighty white of you!" cried the Trumpeter, reaching eagerly for it. After turning it over and examining its wooden barrel and crude mouthpiece he unfixed the bayonet from his rifle and passed the gun to Pedro.

"It's a fair swap," he said. "You guys will likely need a gun before you get home, and yours are no good with your ammunition all gone. The gang will give you plenty of shells. I won't need the gun anymore."

Knowing we were indeed likely to need a gun before reaching the Javary, we took the weapon thankfully. Then came a yell from the river, and Slim came in, took Horner's arm around his shoulders, and started with him to the stream. We took down the hammocks and followed.

At the house of the chief we stopped to say farewell, and from him we learned that about a mile down the river we should find a channel which would take us on toward our own country. Then, with a final wave of the hand to the townsmen who had been our hosts and fighting mates, we went on to the water.

There we found two, big *igarités*—long canoes with arched cabins—manned by stocky *caboclos*. And there we found waiting for us another of those heavy army rifles and many of the queer bottle-necked cartridges that went with it. The gun, we learned, was that of the man Peabody who had died of fever, and we were welcome to it. After big Mike had shown us how to work the bolt action and explained what he called a "safe" and a "cut-off," we got into our own canoe and took up our paddles.

"All set back there, Brazil?" someone called.

"All set, North America," we answered.

Our little fleet pushed off and swung away toward the far-off Amazon.

Though our canoe was lighter and faster than the big *igarités*, we had to stretch our muscles to keep up with them. Perhaps because of the sick men aboard, but more likely because they themselves were homeward bound, the *caboclos* heaved their craft along with swift, hard strokes. It seemed that we had gone much less than a mile when we spied at our left the channel of which the chief had told us.

"*Adeos, senhores!*" we shouted then, and swerved toward the bank. But a roar of protest followed. The big canoes stopped, and the soldiers yelled to us to come on. When we did so they told us they had thought we would camp with them a few times, and urged us to continue on with them for a day or so. But we said no, the water was ebbing and we must cut across country here.

One by one they shook our hands, slapped our shoulders, and wished us well. When the Trumpeter's turn came he said less than any of them, but there was that in his eyes and his grip that spoke louder than all the jovial voices of his mates.

"So long, buddies," he said simply. "I want to take back what I said about that sawdust grub of yours. And any guy that I ever catch knocking Brazilians is going to get one stiff clout in the jaw from little Jack Horner."

I grinned, but my thoughts were back in the jungle behind us. Somehow I seemed to see him again as on that first day—hunching himself along on hands and knee, sick and starved and broken, yet unflinching and brave clear through. And, though I too said little, when my hand left his it was numb.

With one final chorus of farewells the big boats moved away. We wriggled our fingers to bring back the blood driven out by those parting grips and paddled back to the place were the *furo* opened. And there, as we turned into the bush, we heard our last of the Trumpeter and his comrades.

Out broke the hoarse, menacing blare of the *turé*, now blown only in fun by some homeward-bound soldier. As its growl died, the clear, smooth notes of the bugle rang again in that swift "charge" which had brought the fighting men of North America that morning to pull us out of the jaws of death. Finally, when the bugle in turn was still, there came to us a roaring, rollicking song.

> "HAIL! HAIL! The gang's all here!
> What the —— do we care?
> What the —— do we care?
> HAIL! HAIL! The gang's all here!
> What the —— do we care now?"

The Barrigudo

Have you noticed, *senhores*, the big, slow-moving monkey which that oily-faced trader over yonder is taking down the river with him?

It is a *barrigudo*—the "bag-belly" monkey—and one of the largest I have seen, though I have met many of those big fellows during my years of service as a rubber-worker in the Javary jungle. From the end of its solemn nose to the tip of that strong tail, which it can use as a fifth leg in the trees, it must be more than four feet long.

The trader tells me that he intends to sell it as a pet in Para. But unless he is very lucky his monkey will be dead long before the end of his journey. For the *barrigudo*, *senhores*, is a creature of this upper Amazon alone, and when he is taken away from his own country he dies.

Why this is so I can not tell you. Looking at his bulky body, you would think he could endure almost anything. Yet he is *mortál*, as we Brazilians say—delicate, not hardy. It may be that in his silent way he grieves himself to death because he has lost his own land and his old friends. You can not always tell, by looking at either monkey or man, what sort of heart is hidden in his breast. And, after all, the heart is the only thing that really counts.

This may seem, *senhores*, like idle talk, but it is not. I have a tale to tell you—a tale of the most surprising *barrigudo* I ever met.

I came upon this creature at the time when the great yearly floods had passed their crest and were going down again. Indeed, they had gone down so far that I was worried; for I was far from where I ought to be, and in strange country where I might soon find myself stranded in the midst of unknown jungle.

With my comrade Pedro Andrada, I had paddled across country from our Javary region into the upper reaches of the Juruá, a low-lying and very crooked river to the south and east. Then, after meeting with queer experiences and traveling some distance down the river, we had turned homeward, journeying along a flooded *furo* until we met a number of roving North American soldiers who saved us from death at the hands of a horde of fierce savages. Now these men had left us and gone back toward the Amazon, whence they had come; and we were trying hard to reach our own territory before the ebbing waters should leave us trapped in some blind flood-channel.

As I say, I was worried. If we had known where we were I should not have cared so much, for then we should have been able to judge our course.

But neither of us had passed this way before, our only guide was the sun, and we had to trust to that and to luck to carry us through the maze of twisting water-courses opening around us on all sides.

The *furo* itself, which had been fairly plain, now was becoming harder to follow, winding here and there in a confusing way; and already we had blundered off it more than once and lost much time in learning our mistake. Besides this, our food supply now was none too plentiful, and we found little game to shoot. And inch by inch, day and night, the thick tangle of bush was rising steadily around us as the waters slipped away.

Yet these things, serious though they seemed, suddenly became nothing at all. They were swallowed up by something far more grave.

Pedro fell sick.

It must have been the Spotted People who gave the disease to him. We came upon them in the morning of a sweltering day when no breeze stirred. We were stripped almost naked, breathing with mouths hanging open, gasping now and then for the air which it seemed we could not get, but shoving steadily onward. All at once my comrade, up in the bow, held his paddle and called sharply:

"*Quem vai la*? Who goes there?"

No answer came. No sound of any kind followed his hail. He was peering at a tangle of trees rising from the water at his left.

"Do you see anything, Lourenço?" he asked.

"Nothing," I replied.

"Yet I thought I heard— Let us go and look."

We turned the canoe into the trees. As we neared them a figure rose behind a big blown-down tree-trunk. It held a bow and arrow. Instantly we backed water and snatched up our rifles.

For a moment we hung there, the man menacing us with his arrow but not daring to loose it with our gun-muzzles covering him. He was a naked Indian, and seemed to be standing on the water.

"*Báah derekôh*? What is the matter with you?" he growled sullenly in the Tupi tongue.

"*Anîh báah*. Nothing," I answered in the same language. "Put down that arrow if you would not be shot."

He lowered his weapon in a surly way.

"What are you doing here?" Pedro snapped.

For answer the man stooped and held up a spear, on which a fine big fish hung quivering.

Laying down our rifles, but keeping them within instant reach, we pushed up to him and found that he was in a small canoe hidden by the prostrate tree. He still held the spear, and the water on its shaft showed that he had plunged the barb into the fish just before Pedro shouted. We saw that he was peaceable enough, and that he was a very ordinary-looking fellow except for one thing. His face was blotched with hard, rough, black spots.

After telling him we meant no harm to him or to any other man who did not attack us, we asked him whence he came. In a slow, heavy manner he replied that his people lived close by, up on a little hill above the reach of the floods. We asked him if they were many, and he said no. Then, without questioning us in turn, he dropped spear and fish into his canoe, picked up a paddle, and began to move away.

"Wait," said Pedro. "Will you sell that fish?"

He stopped, squinted at the fish and at us, and said he would barter for beads. But we had no beads, for we were not on a trading trip. We offered him some empty cartridge shells, though, telling him they were lucky bells which would keep demons away. He hesitated so long that we thought the fish was ours. But then he grunted, "No," and started on.

"Wait," Pedro commanded again. "Is there fruit at your town?"

The fellow said there was much fruit. So then we told him that if he would give us fruit he could have the lucky bells. At once he consented. We followed him a short distance through the watery forest to the hill where his village stood.

It was a miserable little place of a few scattered huts, and the people in it seemed as wretched as the town. When we walked boldly in among them, following our guide, they gathered around us in a sluggish way and looked us over without saying anything. Their eyes were dull, their expressions blank, their movements lifeless and their skins spotted with those same black patches which disfigured the fisherman. Every one of them—men, women, children—was spotted.

The older they were, the worse they looked. The children had only small spots, with lighter rings around each blotch. But the grown people were crusted with hard patches, and among them I saw a withered man whose face was one great black scab. And not only the people, but the town itself, seemed sick; for there was a smell in the air—a heavy, depressing odor of disease which made me wish we had not come.

"Let us get our fruit at once and go," I muttered. "I can not breathe well."

"Nor I," my partner agreed. "But I want something fresh to eat, and I will have it. Here, stabber of fish! Fetch the fruit quickly, or we will go and keep our demon-bells."

The fisherman grunted, moved his head for us to stay there, and went away. He was gone for what seemed a long time. We stood still, and all the others stood still, staring without a blink. And the odd thing was that they stared not so much at our guns and breeches as at our skins. After a time it dawned on me that they marveled because we were not blemished as they were.

"*Por Deus!*" muttered Pedro. "When we leave this place I shall take a bath. These people make me feel slimy."

"I feel the same way, and the smell here makes my stomach squirm," I said. "But here comes our man."

The fisherman was returning, bent forward under a long *atura* basket which hung down his back. We turned at once toward the water. He followed, and at the canoe he put basket and head-line and all into the bottom.

Handing him the empty shells, we pushed off and away, leaving him jangling his "demon-bells" in his palms. No doubt he thought we were great fools to give such a charm for a simple basket of fruit. And the time was not far off when I was to believe we had indeed lost our luck at that place.

We paddled away fast and traveled some distance before we either ate of the fruit or took the bath we had promised ourselves. Somehow the sickly smell of that village seemed to stay with us long after the town itself had disappeared behind us. A thin mist had hung over the place of the Spotted People, and the same vapor was crawling along the water and keeping up with us. Not until we finally got clear of it and breathed clean air once more did the odor fade away.

"Phew!" whistled Pedro, his nose wrinkled. "What an unwholesome hole! Now that we are quit of it, let us bathe and eat."

So we found a firm bare spot where we could stand and pour gourds of water over ourselves. We wanted to take a swim, but the water did not look inviting and we knew well that under its surface might be lurking death in the shape of fish or reptile, so we bathed on land.

When we felt clean again we ate heartily of the fruit, which tasted very good. And as we paddled onward after that we munched now and then at other fruits taken from the basket.

That night neither of us ate well. Our stomachs did not want the usual ration of dried *pirarucu* and *farinha*. So we devoured the rest of the fruit and were satisfied.

Before dawn I awoke to hear Pedro moaning softly in his sleep. He had a bad dream, I thought. So I yelled and roused him, grumbled that he was disturbing me, turned over in my hammock and shut my eyes again. He said nothing, and I slept almost at once.

When next I looked around me it was day, and my partner was sitting up and holding his head in his hands. He only grunted when I spoke.

I got breakfast, but he would eat none. This was so uncommon that I looked sharply at him, finding his skin pale and his face drawn. But when I asked him what ailed him he said only that he had not slept well.

We paddled away as usual, and all through the hot, sunny morning he said no word. His stroke lacked its regular power, and several times he stopped work and bent forward as if to favor his stomach. I grinned, thinking he had a touch of colic from eating too much fruit and was too stubborn to admit it. At last I snickered outright.

"Poor little man!" I mocked. "Does his little belly ache? Perhaps he needs a little drink—"

I did not finish. He groaned, wavered dizzily, and slumped into the bottom of the boat.

This scared me. He was not the man to let anything overpower him as long as he had an ounce of fight left in him, and I realized that he must be very sick.

As quickly as possible I got the boat to shore. There I found that his illness was not a mere ache of the stomach.

He had fever. And it was not the ordinary jungle swamp-fever—which is bad enough—but a deadly sickness which burned and froze and griped and turned him inside out. When at last his spasms ceased he lay so limp that I thought him dead.

He could not even whisper. He could not move. He lay like a corpse and he looked like one, and only the feeble throb of his heart and his shallow breathing told me that he still lived. And there was not a single thing that I could do to help him, for we had no medicine—not even a mouthful of rum to strengthen his heart.

Squatting beside him, I tried in a dumb, dazed way to think of something I could do.

He was more to me than any one else in the world. He was far closer than a blood brother—he seemed a part of myself. A handsome, happy-hearted, boyish man, strong of hand and quick of thought and action, he had been my comrade in fair weather and foul, in times of merriment and times of deadly fight. Either of us would throw away his own life to save the other—yes, or endure torment worse than death, if by it the other might escape.

And at that very moment I was in such torment of mind as I hope will never come to me again. I could not let him die, but it seemed that I could not aid him to live.

At last I thought of a thing, though it seemed of little use. If I could find some *pajémarióba*, a bitter medicinal herb sometimes used by the Indians to make a sort of tea, it might start him to sweating and drive the fever out. The *pajémarióba* grows wild in many places, and some might be there.

I started at once and hunted all about the spot where we were. But I found none.

I came back to him just in time. He lay on the ground as I had left him, limp and motionless. And halfway out of the water, crawling up toward him, was a big alligator.

I leaped at the beast in fury. It slewed and slid back under the surface. Then, lifting my partner, I laid him in the canoe and stroked swiftly away from that accursed place.

As we went onward I watched along both sides, hoping to see a patch of *pajémarióba* on some point of land. The chance of finding it was poor, I knew, but it was all I could do, and at any rate I was doing something. So, hunting desperately for some sign of that herb, I kept on for I know not how long.

At length I came into a place where the water widened out and met open shores covered with fine *matupá* grass, beyond which grew ferns and slim *açai* palms. I paddled slowly near one bank, thinking that here I might land and seek again for the *pajémarióba*. And while I looked around and thought it over, an astonishing thing came about.

On the empty shore, a few feet from me, a voice spoke.

"*Kô tam bahéh*? What is that?"

I started, looked at the spot whence the words had come, and saw no man. Nothing was there except thick tufts of grass, and the grass was not tall enough to conceal any one unless he were lying down. Yet I was certain the voice had spoken at that place. Watching it steadily, I turned the canoe straight at it.

But just as the bow touched shore the voice came again from another spot.

"*Bíh pendé hoh*? Where are you going?"

The question came from a small bush standing a foot or so above the grass and a few feet to my left. As before, no living thing was there—no living thing with a voice could be there. The bush was so thin that I could see through it, and beyond it was nothing except grass and trees.

I felt a little chilly. Then I grew angry. If some man was there and making sport of me I would spoil his joke. Picking up my gun, I stepped ashore into mud that rose over my ankles, and through this I plowed straight to the bush.

I found nothing at all. No man was there and no man had been there, for the mud held no tracks but my own.

Then, as I scowled around me in wonder, a new thing came. It was a sound of singing.

It seemed to be far away, yet very near—almost over my head, a clear, sweet song without words, up in the blank air above me. I stared upward, and, seeing that nothing but the sky was over me, I grew chilly again. Was I going mad? Was I, too, about to become delirious with fever? Was this a place of demons, where grass and bushes spoke and the air sang? I did not know. But I did know I wanted to get out of there. Turning, I sloshed back through the soft mud to the canoe.

As I got into it the voice spoke once more. From the water near me rose the same question the spotted fisherman had asked:

"*Báah derekôh*? What ails you?"

For the first time I answered. With my eyes on Pedro I growled in Tupi: "*Herakû.* Fever."

Then I shoved off. But a reply came that stopped me.

"*Ehé ahráhm. Ché ahôh apuh ayuk.* Wait. I will cure the sickness."

This time the voice seemed to be heavier, more like that of a man; and it came from a place near the edge of the trees. I looked sharply at that spot, but saw no man there. For that matter, I did not expect to see anything human, after what had happened.

But this weird voice had said it would cure Pedro, and if the great horned devil himself had risen beside me and given me that promise I would have embraced him. Holding the canoe still, I told the Thing to come to me.

It answered that it could not come, for it had no body but was only a spirit. But if I would go and find a man who now was sleeping on the shore of a narrow neck of water beyond us, and would follow him, the fever should be driven out.

That was all. I asked the Thing just where this man was, but got no reply. No sound of any kind came to me. The *matupá* grass, the bush, the water, the trees—all were vacant and silent. I drove my paddle into the water and heaved the dugout ahead.

Pedro moaned, squirmed a little, and lay still. Looking at him, I shut my jaws and began watching along shore for any narrow water such as the Thing had told about. And soon, *senhores*, I found it. And I went into it, and under a tree I found a sleeping man.

He was half-lying, half-sitting with his back against the tree trunk. His mouth hung open, and from it came a gurgling snore. But after I looked at him, I came near turning about and going away. No such creature as he, I thought, could ever cure Pedro.

He was a greasy, bag-bellied *barrigudo* of an Indian. Hairy as a monkey he was, too, and the black hairs of his whole body were matted with clay, plastered on thickly to keep biting bugs from reaching his hide. The long, stringy hair of his head hung down over his face so far that I could see little of it, but what little I could make out looked blank and stupid.

As I have said, I would have welcomed the devil himself if he had offered aid to my comrade; but the devil, *senhores*, has brains, while this creature looked as if he hardly knew enough to scratch an itch—a mere mass of fat, hair, and dirt.

I grunted with disgust, and half-moved my paddle to push out and away.

But just then the queer voice spoke again.

"*Hémba éah hŷ*," it reminded me. "You are sick."

It came from the tree, a little above the sleeping man. I looked first at the tree trunk, on which was nothing alive. Then my eye swerved again to Pedro. And instead of going away I drove the dugout to shore, stepped out, and prodded the human *barrigudo* with my paddle.

His snoring ended. I caught the glint of eyes staring through his hair. He grunted, and the sound seemed to come from the depths of his belly. Then he sluggishly pushed himself up higher against the tree, yawned with a wheezing noise, and growled—

"*Báah derekôh?*"

"My mate has fever," I answered, pointing at Pedro.

He sat bunking. Then he yawned again.

"*Hémbara ahretéh.* I am very tired."

And his head drooped as if he meant to go back to sleep.

His callousness angered me. In one long stride I was at the canoe. In another I was back, with my cocked rifle in his face.

"Get up, you filthy beast!" I snarled. "Get up and take care of my comrade, or the next alligator that comes here will find a fat feast awaiting him."

He got up. Slowly, as if afraid he might touch the gun and discharge it, he rose and stood against the tree. When I lowered the weapon he waddled past me and stared at Pedro. Then, with a sour grunt, he pointed a thick finger and moved his head to show I was to pick up my partner and go somewhere with him. After scowling at him I did so.

He led me for some distance back into the bush—so far that before we stopped I was breathing hard, for Pedro was no lightweight to carry. Yet I would rather carry him myself than have that dirty Indian do it, even if he had offered to.

As I look back at that time I wonder that I followed him at all, for in spite of the promise made by the queer voice I had faint hope of any real help from him. But I kept on, and presently we entered a cleared space where there were huts and people.

The *barrigudo* man, striding along easily in spite of his size, went straight to a hut set off at some distance from the rest. Half-blinded with sweat, humped over under the burden of my partner's hot body, I trailed at his heels.

We passed through the doorway into a dim room of shadows, where a tiny fire smoldered in the middle of the dirt floor. There the Indian pointed to a sort of legless bench or bed of woven sticks, which hung like a hammock but was straight and flat. On this I laid Pedro.

Pedro squirmed again and kicked about, and for a minute I had to hold him to keep him from rolling off. When he quieted I straightened up and turned toward the *barrigudo*. But he was gone.

Puzzled, I stared around. He could not have gone outdoors, for I was between him and the spot where he had last stood, and I should certainly have known it if he had passed me. Yet there was no other opening in the house except a small smoke-hole in the roof ten feet above me, and he surely could not have gone out there. But he was not in the place. The huge creature had vanished into air.

Peering at the walls about me, I found no sign of any door except the one where we had entered. The walls were made in basket fashion of tightly woven sticks and creepers. On them hung strange and horrid things—skins of deadly snakes and huge lizards; great black poison-spiders; skulls of ugly beasts and of fish with terrible hooked teeth; a vampire bat, and other things of the sort. But all these were dead. No living thing was in the room but ourselves.

As I gaped around I thought I heard a slight chuckle somewhere, but whence it came I could not tell—indeed, I was not sure that I really heard it. Then came a thing that made me forget it. Behind me sounded the hiss of a snake.

I whirled, looked, and saw on the farther wall the head of a big boa. Yes, *senhores*, only its head—a head as dead as the skins and skulls near it. But as I looked at it its mouth slowly opened; and out of that mouth came a hissing voice that told me to go.

The head closed again and hung silent as before. Feeling rather prickly, I stood watching it until a slight rustle near me drew me around again. There beside Pedro stood a great figure muffled in a garment of bark-cloth.

Senhores, I was now so confused and bewildered that I recoiled and leveled my gun at the thing. If it had moved toward me or touched Pedro I would have shot it. But it did not move. It only stood there, and though I could see no eyes on it, it seemed to be watching me with no fear whatever.

As I scowled back at it I thought it must be the *barrigudo* man, but then I saw that it was much taller than he had been—so much taller that it could not be he. Moreover, it seemed not even to be human. It was armless and headless.

The cloth hanging over it showed no sign of a man's head underneath. It hung as if from a pair of shoulders whence the neck and head had been sliced off. Seven feet high, shapeless and silent and still, it loomed up in that dim and smoky room like a specter born of fog and fever and nightmare—a thing which the eyes saw but which could not exist; a thing which had taken shape as silently as the *barrigudo* had vanished. And again there came to me the thought that I was crazed: that I had fever or worse, and all this was delirium.

Then the Thing spoke. Out from the folds of cloth rolled a voice, deep and powerful, unlike any voice I had yet heard here.

"The dead live. The living die. The blind see. The seer is blind. This man dies, yet shall live. You live, but you shall die. Go, but remain."

Without realizing it, I let my rifle sink. Stupidly I stared at the Thing before me and tried to make sense of its words.

"Go!" came the voice, deeper than ever. "Three suns shall set, two shall rise. When the third sun sinks low this man shall walk again. Until then, go and stay."

"I will not go," I growled. "I stay with my comrade while he lives or until he is surely dead. Whatever you are, help him if you can."

"Go!"

"*Vive Deus*, I will not!"

The Thing and I fronted each other for minutes, neither of us moving. Then it said:

"You would help your comrade? Then take from the wall that vampire, which shall draw the fever from him."

Glancing around, I saw the dead vampire, which I had hardly noticed before. I went to it and tried to take it down.

But it was fastened tight. So I pulled harder, then yanked at it. Suddenly it came away, and from behind it a quantity of dusty powder fell into my upturned face.

The dust stung my nostrils and choked my throat. I coughed and turned back toward Pedro, carrying the vampire. But I did not reach him.

A swift chill ran down my back. My muscles stiffened. The house whirled. The headless figure swelled to a huge blot. I felt myself falling. Then I was floating in some place far, far down, where all was still.

After a long time I found myself lying on a bare dirt floor. Above me was a roof, around me were walls, beyond me was an open door; but they were not those of the house where I had fallen. The walls were bare mud, and in this house was no fire, no sick comrade, no shapeless monster—not even my rifle. As I realized that my gun was gone I reached to my belt for the *machete* which usually hung there. That too was gone.

I started up. As I reached my feet I turned dizzy and nearly fell again; but soon the place stopped whirling and I became steady. At once I strode toward the doorway.

But before I reached it, it was blocked. Two men jumped into it from outside and stood with spears leveled at my stomach. I stopped and peered at them.

They were tall, well-muscled fellows with clean faces which looked good-humored but rather determined. Presently one of them smiled slightly.

But they held their weapons ready.

"What is this?" I grunted. "Drop those spears and step aside."

They stood their ground. The one who had smiled answered:

"Sit down and be still. You can not go to the House of Voices until it is time."

"I do not understand," I told him. "What house is that? And what house is this?"

"The House of Voices is the one where the other stranger lies. You will stay here while he stays there. Make no trouble, if you are wise."

I asked where my gun and *machete* were, and why I was held here. They looked at each other in a puzzled way, and one said they knew nothing of gun or knife. I was here, he added, because Pajé ordered it. I would remain here until Pajé gave the word to free me.

Now I knew that the *pajé* of a tribe is its medicine man, but never before had I heard Indians speak the word with such respect. This man had used it as if it meant God. And I saw that what this Pajé had ordered would be done. Yet I growled again, told them to get out of my way, and advanced on them.

Their faces tightened, their arms tensed, and their shoulders swayed forward a little. They were in deadly earnest. Unless I stopped they would plunge those spears into my body. So I halted, laughed as if I had only been joking, squatted, and rolled a cigaret.

They relaxed, though they still watched me closely. Studying them through my tobacco smoke, I thought the wisest plan would be to pretend friendliness and talk of other things, meanwhile watching for a chance to spring and snatch the spear from the nearer man. For I was very uneasy about Pedro, and I did not intend to wait here longer than necessary.

Giving no sign of my thought, I began to talk of our journey from the Juruá. They listened with much interest. When I told of the Spotted People both nodded quickly, and the taller one spoke.

This town too, he said, was once a place of black-spotted people. He himself had been spotted from boyhood, and the black patches had grown until he was repulsive and useless. But then Pajé came to them, and with him came demons of the air who had no bodies; and by the magic of these air-devils and strange-tasting water he had driven out the black sickness and made them strong.

I smoked up my cigaret and slowly made another while I thought about this. Their *pajé* was far more powerful than any I had met in my jungle wanderings. Those whom I had seen before now were good enough at healing wounds or setting broken bones, and some of them were wise in the ways of poison; but when they had to deal with a pain or sickness whose cause was not clear they all worked in the same way.

The medicine man would make a huge cigar, and with great ceremony he would blow the smoke from this thing on the place where the sick man's pain was worst. Then he would suck that spot for a time, and at length he would stand up and take out of his mouth a long whitish thing looking much like a worm. This evil worm, he would say, was what had caused all the trouble, and now that it was out the sufferer would get well. The truth was that the white thing was no worm at all, but a soft plant-root which he had hidden in his mouth before beginning work.

Did this Pajé of theirs draw worms from their bodies? I asked. They looked puzzled and a little offended. The taller one replied that Pajé did nothing of the sort, and that he and his people were not wormy. I asked them what sort of man Pajé was. And who was the fat, dirty man who had led me to the House of Voices? Surely he was not Pajé?

Both grunted scornfully at this. No, the fat man was only a lazy drunkard and the servant of Pajé. Yet he was valuable to them because he was the only one who knew how to call Pajé when his help was needed in time of sickness. He could talk with the air-devils, too.

So the men of the town watched over him carefully when he was drunk, and saw to it that no alligator or snake or other evil thing should destroy him while he was helpless. If they should lose him they would have no way of reaching the ear of Pajé.

For Pajé was not a man like themselves, but a demon-spirit who came there when summoned and took the shape of a great headless creature without arms. When he did appear it was always inside the House of Voices. This house once had been that of an old medicine man who had little power and who finally had died suddenly in the night, leaving the people with no medicine man at all.

Then, many moons later, a drifting canoe had brought them the fat hairy man, who at that time was not fat but almost dead from starvation. They had fed him and put him in the empty house of the dead medicine man to recover his strength if he could. And he had grown strong, and after a time he had found a way of calling the air-demons, and after that he had brought Pajé himself to cure them.

As you may suppose, I did some more thinking and puzzling about this. Then I asked how Pajé worked on wounds or hurts if he had no hands. They said they did not know—even the men whom he cured did not know.

A man would be taken to the House of Voices, they said, and the fat servant would take him inside. Somehow the hurt man would always fall into a deep sleep before anything was done to his injury, and although he might stay there for days he would remember little or nothing of what went on around him while he lay there. Only a few had ever seen Pajé himself, and those few could tell only that he was a monster with a deep voice that made them quake with fear.

In driving out the spotted sickness, they added, Pajé had not been seen. The fat man had gone about and ordered certain ones to come later to the House of Voices. When they obeyed, much afraid but not daring to remain away, they had found the house empty of life.

But the air-devils had spoken around them, saying queer things and singing as if far off, and finally commanding them to drink deep of strange water in a big gourd on the floor. The same persons had to go each day for a time to the house and drink of the same water, and at length the sickness and the spots had left them. And this kept on until all in the town were well.

They asked me what had come to me in the House of Voices, and I told them. When I asked them in turn how I had reached this place where they now guarded me, they said that while they watched the House of Voices from a safe distance—for nobody ever went near that house unless called—they saw me tumble out of the door as if thrown. Then a loud voice had come, telling them to take me away and guard me. And they intended to guard me well until further orders.

While we talked the sun sank low. It glared in at the doorway, half-blinding me. I moved aside, and instantly my guards grew tense. There was small chance for me to jump them now or later—they were too wide-awake, and probably expecting me to do that very thing. Watching the path of light lengthen across the dirt floor, I remembered the words of the headless giant:

"Three suns shall set, two shall rise. When the third sun sinks low this man shall walk again."

The first sun now was sinking. Forty-eight hours must pass before I should know whether the promise was true or false. To remain here in useless idleness was all against my will.

Yet, even if I did break out of my prison, what could I do to help Pedro? Nothing. Against his fever I was helpless as a babe.

"How far is the House of Voices from this house?" I asked.

They looked suspiciously at me. Then one replied:

"Not far. Why do you ask?"

"If Pajé should call to you from there could you hear him?"

"We could hear him."

I nodded and said no more. If the House of Voices was within easy call I too could hear any cry coming from it; and the voice for which I would listen was not that of the misshapen Pajé but of Pedro. At the first sign that he was not being well treated I would fight my way to him somehow. Otherwise I might serve him best by waiting.

So I settled myself to wait the sinking of the third sun.

Before night came, other guards arrived. One of them brought my hammock, which I slung inside my prison hut. Women also came, bringing food—a big pot of thick stew which seemed to be partly of fish and partly of sweet turtle-meat. The savory odor of it put so keen an edge on my hunger that I completely cleaned out the pot.

Lying back in my hammock to smoke after eating, I spied a little smile on the face of one of the new guards. All were watching me intently. Before my cigaret was half-smoked a heavy drowsiness came over me. And as the darkness of night fell on the jungle town, the darkness of sleep numbed my mind. The vigil of the jailers had been made easy by some drug in my food

I think, *senhores*, that I was kept drugged most of the time for the next two days. I know that I felt dull and sluggish, that sleep came very easily, and that it was hard for me to keep awake long at a time. There was no chance for me to walk outside and shake off the drowsiness, for I was not allowed to leave the hut. Always guards were there to block me with ready spears.

Suspecting that my lethargy came from something in the food, I refused to eat anything the next noon, but this did no good; for I had a great thirst, and the water I drank must also have held some sleeping-powder. Both nights I lay like a dead man, and both mornings I woke with difficulty, long after the sun was up. The time slipped away in a sort of daze, and it was not until after noon of the third day that this feeling left me.

Then, rousing myself from a *siesta*, I found that once more I was wide-awake. In the doorway squatted the same two guards whom I had first seen there. As I arose they also stood up.

"What is the word?" I demanded.

"No word has come."

"My comrade—does he live?"

They lifted their brows as if to say that was a question which no man could answer. When I insisted on a reply the tall one said:

"Only Pajé or his servant can tell. Pajé has not spoken, and the fat drunkard has not been seen. The House of Voices is closed. What lies within it we know not."

"And no sound has come from the House?"

"Yes. On the night of the day when you came a hoarse voice babbled broken words as if struggling in fever. That is all. We have heard nothing more."

I chewed my lip and looked at the sun-shadows outside. The third sun had not yet sunk low, but it was beginning to slip down the western sky. The time of which the monster had spoken would soon come. And then—what?

The next two or three hours, *senhores*, were the longest of my life. I tried to sit still and talk about other matters; but my eyes always were on the creeping shadows, and at times I had to stride around the room to keep from springing at the sentinels. When at last the light began to glare in at my doorway and crawl across the floor I could no longer hold myself back.

"The time has come," I said, stepping toward the men. "Stand aside."

But they fronted me with weapons low.

"When Pajé orders it—" the taller one began doggedly.

I growled. My toes gripped the floor. But just as I was about to leap at them there came a shout outside.

"The House opens!"

We hung there as we were—poised, watching each other, but listening. And then sounded a thundering voice.

"The closed door opens. The open door shuts. Slave of fever, thou art free. Guards of the free man, your task ends. Go forth, ye two, but go not hence."

Slowly, as if not quite certain that they understood the words, the watchmen at my door lowered their weapons and glanced out. At once I walked between them into the open. My gaze darted to the House of Voices. Outside it, staring around as if bewildered, stood Pedro.

"Pedro!" I called, running toward him.

"Ah, Lourenço!" he answered, smiling in a relieved way. "So you are here."

He walked to meet me, but his step lacked its usual lithe swing. His face was drawn, his eyes and cheeks hollow, his skin pale. But he was alive and free of fever. I nearly seized him and shook him in my joy, but restrained myself in time.

"What place is this?" he asked, glancing at the Indians who were gathering. "Who are these people? How came we here? What has happened?"

"You have been sick."

"Yes, I know I have been sick, and I must have been crazed—I thought I was dead and roasting in hell with some huge headless devil watching me. I feel now as if I had been through purgatory, at least. But what—"

He stopped, staring around him again. I saw that he swayed on his feet.

"You are safe and sound now," I said, slipping an arm around his body. "Come and rest in my hammock, and you shall hear all about it."

And I drew him on toward the hut which had been my prison.

Indians, men and women, crowded beside us and behind us as we went, muttering among themselves but smiling at us. At the doorway I halted and spoke to them.

"My sick comrade is well again but very weak. Will you, my friends, bring food to make him strong?"

Several at once answered that they would do so.

"And do not put into it the thing that makes men sleep," I added. "I have slept overmuch."

At this most of them looked blank, but two of the older men grinned in a knowing way. We passed into the house, which now was unguarded, and Pedro slumped into the hammock.

"My legs are water," he muttered wearily, "and my head is a whirlpool."

Squatting against the wall, I waited for his weakness to pass. Soon his eyes opened and he repeated his questions. I told him all I knew.

"So I was not so crazed as I thought," he mused. "There is a giant without a head. And singing voices. I heard them too. I thought they must come from heaven, and wondered why I was in the other place."

His brow wrinkled, and I saw he was puzzling over what I had told him and what he had seen and heard. Presently he added—

"Are you sure we are in our right minds?"

"No, I am not," I grinned. "But we are alive, and that is something. Tell me what you can remember."

"It is not much. I became horribly sick while paddling. My head split and my body burned. Voices came and went, some singing, some speaking.

"At last I felt that I was awaking from a frightful dream. I looked around and saw fire, awful things back in the shadows—snakes and skulls and spiders—and a demon without head or arms. I was sure I had died and gone below. But I felt no pain—the demon did not torment me. Then he was gone—"

"How did he go?" I cut in.

"I do not know. I saw no opening anywhere, no light except one small fire. The monster was there and then was not there. It must have been night, and I must have slept a long time after that, for the next thing I can remember was just before I came out and saw you.

"The place was lighter then, and there was a small hole up overhead where brightness showed—the sunshine outside. Not a living thing was in sight anywhere. Then a door slowly opened and I looked out into the daylight.

"And, Lourenço, nobody opened that door. I looked straight at it and saw both sides of it as it swung, and nothing touched it. It opened itself."

We stared at each other. I shook my head, for I could make nothing of it. "And then?"

"Then a voice came. A queer little voice that seemed to come from a jaguar skull. It told me to arise and go. And I got off a strange flat hammock—it went out from under me as I did so, and I fell on the floor.

"I crawled through the door on hands and knees, fearing it might close again before I could reach it. While I was scrambling out another voice sounded behind me—a deep voice that said—"

" 'The closed door opens—the open door shuts?' "

"Yes. So you heard it. As soon as I was outside I stood up. Then I saw you."

We were silent for a time, thinking.

"Here is another odd thing, Lourenço," he added then. "The deep voice spoke in the Tupi tongue. But the odd little voice from the skull, telling me to go, used our own language—Portuguese."

"*Deus Padre!* That is strange!" I muttered. "No man here except ourselves speaks Portuguese—"

"Here is food," announced an Indian voice at the door.

A man and two women stood there. The women held bowls. The man was the taller guard who had watched me during the day. He held no weapon now, and as I went to the door he pointed to each of the bowls in turn.

"This broth for him—this stew for you," he said.

Moving his lips close to my ear, he went on in a whisper:

"In his broth is a little of that which makes sleep. Sleep gives strength. It is the order."

"Whose order?"

"It is the order," he repeated.

"And is my meat also heavy with sleep?"

He grinned.

"No. You have slept enough. Now make your own sleep."

"Who watches us tonight?"

"There is no watch. But it is the order that you stay here until the man with you is strong. Until then your canoe is hidden."

I scowled at him, but he had spoken sense. Pedro must gain strength before we went on, even though the water was ebbing steadily away.

"Where are our guns?" I demanded.

He turned away without reply. The women put down the bowls and left us. Saying no more, I took Pedro's broth in to him. He sniffed at it, tasted it, and drained it to the last drop.

I ate my own stew more slowly. When I set down the empty vessel and glanced at Pedro I found him sleeping as peacefully as a tired child.

A woman carrying a bundle came to the door, dropped her burden, and went away. The thing she had left was Pedro's hammock, brought from our canoe.

As I picked it up I saw another figure come lurching along from the direction of the House of Voices. It was fat and hairy—the *barrigudo* man who had led us there.

With the hammock under my arm I stepped out to meet him. Frowzy and filthy he might be, but he had guided my dying partner to the spot where death's hand was warded off, and now I would say my thanks and offer him reward. Yet I did nothing of the kind. For as he came near me I saw why he staggered. He was drunk—stupidly, disgustingly drunk.

His bloodshot eyes were glazed and set, staring straight past me. His heavy mouth sagged. He breathed thickly, and he hiccoughed. He reeked of liquor as if he had spilled a quart of it down over himself. His look, his reeling gait—and his smell—were those of a man who had wallowed in drunkenness for days. Sickened, I stood back and let the sodden brute stumble past, then swung on my heel and returned to our hut.

There, as I threw another look after him, I noticed that he was being trailed by two armed men. The words of our guards came back to me—that this bleary creature was the only one who could summon the great Pajé, and so he was always protected from danger while drunk.

Perhaps, I thought, the monstrous Pajé was the devil himself, and this servant of his had bartered his hope of heaven for unlimited drink. If ever I saw a man who seemed to have sold himself, body and soul, to the king of all rottenness, the Barrigudo was that man.

But the Barrigudo's future was nothing to me, and I gave him no further attention. After slinging my hammock I curled up in it. And all that night Pedro and I slept peacefully side by side.

I awoke late, but earlier than Pedro. The morning light showed that his color was better and his face did not look quite so hollow. He had rested almost twelve hours when at length he stirred, yawned, blinked at me, and lazily demanded a cigaret.

"Do we go on today?" he asked between puffs.

I shook my head.

"Not until you can swing your paddle again."

"I can swing it now."

"For a time, yes. But not all day."

I did not tell him that our canoe had been hidden and that we were under orders to remain here. That would only have made him determined to go at once and to fight any one trying to stop us. And he was in no condition for fighting.

"So you are afraid you would have to do all the work?" he laughed. "Perhaps you have it right. I feel lazy this morning. Yet we should start onward soon. The water must have sunk while we stayed here, and we are far from the Javary."

"There will be water enough. And I like the cooking of these Indian women."

"Oho! So that is it! The broth they gave me last night was delicious, it is true. I could eat more now, and meat with it."

"You shall have it."

Calling an Indian boy near the house, I told him to get food. He went away, and soon the same women and the same guard came with the clay bowls. The man looked at Pedro, smiled in a satisfied way, and went out.

After he had gone I thickened my comrade's broth with some of my turtle-meat, and we both ate our fill. When he had smoked again he arose and stretched himself.

"I am going to walk and see the place," he said.

And he went out, lounging along languidly but with far more sureness in his step than he had shown when last he walked. I followed.

Outside we stood and looked long at the House of Voices. For the first time I noticed that it was round. The wall curved away in a circle, and its high pointed roof also was round. An odd thought came to me—that the demon's house was bigger outside than inside; for my memory, though somewhat hazy, told me that its one room was rather small. But as I thought again I could see why it might have seemed small—because of the things that were in it: the heads on the wall, the fire in the middle, the flat hammock, the body of Pedro, and that giant figure looming up in the smoke. And then I forgot it, for again the *barrigudo* man appeared.

He shambled up toward us, heading for the demon-house, followed by the same men who had trailed him last night. He looked even more sodden than when I had last seen him, but not so drunk; the look of a man who had slept off some of his liquor but was stupid from the sleep and from the drink still working in him. His guardians were heavy-eyed, and it was easy to see that they had been awake all night.

I expected him to pass as before, but this time he halted near us and stared at Pedro. And Pedro stared back with disgust plain in his face.

"Phew! What an animal!" my partner sniffed. "The rest of these people look clean. Why do they not wash this beast or throw it to the alligators? An alligator will eat anything—and the fouler the better."

"This is the noble gentleman who brought us here. The Barrigudo, of whom I told you. Embrace him and give him thanks."

"Ugh!"

Pedro gulped as if sickened by the thought.

"I would rather touch a corpse that had lain in the sun. He is worse than the Spotted People. But I can thank him, unless the wind changes and blows his scent this way."

Changing then from Portuguese to Tupi, he spoke to the man.

"You are he who brought me here and called your Pajé to heal me? I am grateful for my life. If I have anything which you or Pajé want, speak. You shall have whatever I can give."

The Barrigudo made no reply. He only stared stonily at us both. His eyes, though, held an expression I did not like—a look that seemed anger. Yet why should he be offended? Such an uncouth creature surely could not understand what we had said of him in Portuguese, and he would scarcely resent Pedro's offer to reward him.

But, as I say, he made no answer. He gave one sour grunt and plodded on.

"You said you had to put a gun in his face to make him guide you," said Pedro. "I can believe it. We owe him no gratitude."

And we forgot the drunkard as quickly as we could, not even watching to see where he went.

Strolling slowly, we walked among the little houses of the Indians, who received us with a quiet dignity which increased our liking for them. Before long we found with us the tall guard who had told me of the orders and had come each time with the women bearing food.

"Are we still under guard?" I grumbled.

Looking slightly surprised, he said no: I knew the orders and of course would heed them, and he came only because his father wished to see us. When we asked who his father was, he astonished us by replying—

"The chief."

Somehow we had not thought of a chief in this place, and still less had we thought that a chief's son was one of our guards. I did not know whether to consider this an honor or an indication that the real ruler here was Pajé. But I said nothing on this point. To make talk as we crossed the clearing I remarked that the dirty servant of Pajé was drunk again.

He nodded, as if I had said the sun was hot or water was wet. Pedro, still disgusted, asked him the same question he had asked me: why they did not make that man keep himself clean. The Indian said they could not do so without treating him roughly, and in that case he might sulk and refuse to call Pajé when needed.

"And no one else can call Pajé?" I asked.

"I have said so."

"But in time he will rot himself to death. Then how can you reach Pajé?"

"We can not. But he is strong and will live many years."

"Perhaps. Yet he might leave you at any time and go to another tribe."

The Indian's face grew grim. The fat man would not go away alive, he said. And I saw that the Barrigudo, though he did as he pleased, was not much better than a prisoner.

We found the chief to be old, thin, but clear-eyed and shrewd-brained. He asked us many questions and answered none of ours. When we left his mud house we had learned nothing new, and we felt that, so far as he was concerned, we were neither welcome nor unwelcome here. The servant of Pajé had brought us to the place, and if he and his headless master wished to amuse themselves with us it was nothing to the head of the tribe.

Outside, as we stood a moment talking with the young chief, a man came up with three fine fish. One was a splendid *surubim*, as long as my leg, beautifully spotted and striped. The others were *tucunarés*, with the big eyespots on their tails. The man laid them down respectfully before the young chief, who glanced at them, then picked up the *surubim* and started away toward the House of Voices.

"The finest fish goes to Pajé," said Pedro as we strolled back to our hut. "Let us see whether he comes out to receive it."

We saw nothing of the monster, but we soon heard something from him. At the doorway of the round house the tall young savage stopped, spoke, laid the fish down, and backed away; then stopped again, seemed to listen to a voice, backed once more, swung on his heel and came straight to us.

"At the sinking of the next sun the *gambá* drums will beat," he told us.

"What does that mean?" Pedro yawned.

"It is the night of the full moon, when demons are restless. Many voices will be round about. Demons of water and air and earth will be near. No man may stay in his house, lest a devil seize him in the dark. All must gather around the House of Voices, where the drums will beat and Pajé himself will protect us. Sleep well tonight, for tomorrow night there will be no sleep."

With that he strode off toward his father's house.

"Demons seem to rule this place, Lourenço," my partner said. "Voices in the air—a monster without a head—devils who seize men in their houses when the moon is full—I shall not be sorry to leave it all behind me."

He spoke half in jest, but he expressed my own thought. We had already been delayed too long, and I had seen more than enough of this devil-ruled village.

Since there was nothing to do, we did nothing but eat, sleep, and argue about Pajé and his fellow demons until the night of the full moon came. In that time Pedro's strength flowed steadily back into him. And when the sun dropped low and we saw men carrying the long log drums to the House of Voices, the old reckless twinkle was in his eyes as he said:

"Since we must sit up and evade the devils, let us start a *pira-purasséya* fish-dance with some of these good-looking girls while the drums beat. Ask the young chief to bring out some *cachaça*, too, and we can make a real night of it."

"Playing with girls and rum is no way to dodge the devil," I told him.

"But if you have a handsome girl and plenty of drink, why care if the devil does get you?"

I knew well that he cared little for women or liquor. But I retorted:

"Your friend the Barrigudo has plenty of rum. See what it has done for him."

"Ugh!"

He wrinkled his nose as if I had put something offensive under it.

"I hope I shall not meet him again tonight. He spoils my appetite as well as my thirst."

"Have courage. I have not seen him since yesterday, and he probably is sleeping off more drink. We are not likely to be near him."

I was wrong. We were soon to be much nearer to that Barrigudo than we expected. And before we parted from him— Well, *senhores*, you shall hear.

The sun slid down and was gone. Fires sprang up around the House of Voices. The thunder of the big *gambás* filled the jungle, each beaten by a man astride the log, pounding the skin head with his knuckles. The clatter of *caracashá* rattles broke out. And all the Indians, big and little, hurried to the round demon-house where they could be safe. Walking more slowly, we followed.

The fires surrounding the House were many but small, none being very close to the curving wall. We found that there were really two rings of these fires, with a fairly wide space between the inner and the outer circle; and in this space the people arranged themselves.

As we approached, the young chief came out to meet us and pointed to a spot where we were to squat. When we had settled ourselves we found the old chief himself beside us, staring at the ground. The young chief sank down on the other side of us.

Nobody spoke. Talk would have been useless in that booming, rattling uproar. Patiently we waited for Pajé to walk out, or for something else to occur. But we waited long and nothing happened. The drummers and rattlers kept up their work without a pause, and every one else squatted or sat motionless while the bright moonlight flooded the clearing. At length I tired of it and arose to go back to my hut.

At once the young chief sprang up and blocked me. Other men also arose and moved toward us. Shouting in the tall fellow's ear, I told him I did not want to stay here, and that I would risk being carried off by devils. I wanted to get into my hammock.

But he yelled back that the danger was not mine alone. If a demon got me, that demon would keep coming back each night and taking others. And when I still insisted on going, he added that no man could be allowed to imperil the rest in that way, and that any one trying to leave the fire-circle would be killed at once.

I sat down again.

Then came a sudden break in the drumming. The door of the House had swung open. Out from it came the Barrigudo. He lifted a hand. The racket of the *caracashás* ceased. With the end of the tumult the place seemed still as death.

"Pajé, master of demons, has come," he said in a throaty tone. "Be still."

We were still. And in the stillness we heard whisperings and squeakings in the air above and around us. The air-devils also had arrived.

Thin voices spoke from nowhere—in the grass, up overhead, at the very walls of the House. And they spoke one word only:

"*Hewŷ!* Blood!"

A singing voice answered them:

"*Ehé ahráhm! Ehé ahráhm!* Wait a while! Wait a while!"

Another singing voice, high and sweet, played around in the air over us, saying nothing—only singing without words. But then, from the smoke-hole at the peak of the House, a harsh little voice croaked:

"*Hewŷ! Hahmbuya héh!* Blood! I am hungry!"

And another voice, sharp and squeaky, cried:

"*Heyimbéh! Kunyimukú!* A heart! A young girl!"

Fear showed plain in the faces of the Indians near me as they heard the demands of the dreaded demons. All stared at the roof. I too looked up there; but, seeing nothing, dropped my gaze and glanced along the line of terrified eyes gleaming in the light of fire and moon.

For a moment all was very still. Then out rolled the sonorous tones of Pajé himself:

"Seek ye the blood and hearts of beasts, not of my people. Begone from this place!"

The command came from within the House. The Barrigudo was not in sight. The door stood partly open, and in the dimness beyond it I saw a giant figure—tall and thick and headless—standing in smoke. Others saw it too. Pedro drew in his breath sharply, and the old chief gave a startled grunt. Slowly the door swung shut.

Queer snarling noises sounded on the roof, as if the hungry demons raged at the command to go. Silence followed. When it had lasted for the space of a dozen slow breaths, Pajé spoke again.

"So ye would snatch at the lives of young girls, the mothers to be? Ye would drink the blood of the strong men? Then I, Pajé, will give my people to drink of that which will not harm them but will burn you if ye touch them. Slave, take this bowl and give to all except the two strangers."

Again the snarls sounded above, with broken cries of rage. The door opened, and out came the Barrigudo, grunting under the weight of a tall clay jar of liquid. This he set down beside the old chief.

"Three swallows," he growled. "Then pass on. Do not step outside the fire circles. You and you"—looking at Pedro and me—"stand inside the inner ring. You get none of the drink of Pajé."

Wondering, we obeyed and stood watching. The Barrigudo tilted the jar. The old chief drank three times from it, arose, and made room for his son. When the young man had taken his three swallows he also moved on. And one by one, in their turns, men and women and children stopped at the jar, drank, and passed along between the fires.

At length the old chief returned, having walked all around the house, and sank into his place facing the door. Every one in the circle except Pedro and myself had taken of the drink, and the jar was almost empty.

"Let the drums beat," muttered the Barrigudo.

The old chief cried out shrilly. The thundering of the logs broke out again. Pedro and I, not knowing what else to do, squatted where we were. When we tired of squatting we lay down on our backs and watched little clouds drift across the big white moon.

For some time the drumming went steadily on, and I became so used to it that I began to grow sleepy. If this was to last all night, I thought, I might as well take what rest I could there on the ground. So I shut my eyes, and was dozing away when I noticed that the drumming seemed to be growing weaker. The drummers were tired, I thought, and should be relieved. But I did not bother to look at them until Pedro softly gripped my shoulder.

He was wide-awake and grinning. He moved his head toward the nearest drum. I looked and found that its drummer was no longer astride it, but lying beside it. He seemed asleep. Beyond him another drummer was swaying drowsily, and soon he slipped off his log and lay still. Only two of the dozen drums now were booming, and soon there was only one. Then that one stopped.

But the place was not silent. Now that the drums were quiet we could hear a chorus of snores. All around the circle lay Indians sound asleep, and others were drooping forward and slumping down on the earth. Both the old chief and his son lay as if dead.

By ones and twos they all slipped down and remained where they dropped. We heard a short, hard chuckle from the door of the round house. In the opening, his teeth gleaming in his dirty face, stood the Barrigudo.

As we looked at him he walked away from us, around the house. Returning to the door, he went in, remained a moment, and came out with an *atura* basket on his back. In his hands he held our guns and *machetes*. Straight to us he came.

"Come," he grunted.

He was sober, or nearly so. He walked away with a sure, steady stride. We arose and trailed behind him.

"Get your hammocks," he ordered, pausing before our hut.

Swiftly we untied our beds and slung them over our shoulders. Across the moonlit clearing he swung then to the edge of the deep jungle shadows. There he halted.

"A torch. In the basket."

I dipped a hand into his *atura* and found at the top a fagot of twigs and bark. Pedro lighted it. The Barrigudo took the flaming bundle and started on. I walked along behind him, Pedro coming after me. Under the trees it was very black in places, but our leader never hesitated. Before long we reached water.

The fat Indian held his torch out, and we looked down into our own canoe. He dropped our weapons into it and motioned for us to get in. Throwing in our hammocks, we did so. As we picked up the paddles he turned away.

"Wait! What does this mean?" I demanded.

"Wait! You shall see what it means," he retorted.

His torch moved a few yards along the bank, dipped, wavered about, then stood still. In a moment it moved outward. A paddle dipped. The Barrigudo also was afloat.

Along the narrow inlet the boats moved until they entered a wider space where the moonlight shone down. Here the Barrigudo pulled the torch from its fastening at the bow, plunged it hissing into the water, dropped its charred stub into the bottom of his canoe, swerved to the right, and slid on along the wide *furo*.

For hours we worked steadily westward, saying nothing. To me, after the days of inaction, it was a joy to feel my muscles loosen and stretch, to be going somewhere, even though I knew not where or why.

Pedro too, though not so strong as before his sickness, moved with his usual swaying stroke. The Barrigudo, however, with his big belly and his weight of fat and his muscles rotted by rum, soon found his task harder and harder.

Often we heard him gasp and grunt as if driving himself beyond endurance. But he kept on doggedly, though splashing more and more, until we marveled that he could still move. Not until the sinking of the moon made the channel very dark did he quit.

Then he dropped his paddle noisily into his canoe. Wheezing and groaning, he slumped forward, clasping his huge stomach. We drew alongside and waited. After a time his distress passed and he straightened up.

Beside us opened another narrow cove. He swung his head toward it, lifted his paddle, and shoved his boat into it. When well away from the *furo* he stopped again.

"Keep awake," he said hoarsely. "I must sleep. If any one calls do not answer. Wake me at sunrise."

Exhausted, he laid himself down in his canoe, gave a long sigh, and slept.

"What do you make of this, Lourenço?" my partner asked.

"Nothing, unless he is escaping with us," said I. "Yet for us it is not really an escape—we should soon have been freed. But we shall see."

"Would soon have been freed?" Pedro puzzled. "Were we not free to go at any time after I left the House of Voices?"

"No."

And for the first time I told him of the hiding of our canoe and the orders of the young chief.

"I wish I had known that," he grumbled.

"Yes, and you would have made trouble for yourself. We are out of the place now, so forget what is past. You had better sleep a little too. I will keep watch."

He retorted that he was no child and could watch as well as I. Yet after he smoked a cigaret he did curl up on our hammocks, and soon I was the only one awake.

When the sun had burned away the morning mists, I touched Pedro and prodded the Barrigudo. Pedro sat up a little stiffly, but with a smile. The slave of Pajé and of liquor had hard work to sit up at all, but after several attempts he managed it. He scooped up some water in his hands and drank it thirstily. After blinking a minute he again took up his paddle.

"*Por Deus!* Your *barrigudo* now drinks water!" Pedro laughed. "What marvel shall we see next?"

The Barrigudo gave him an ugly look through his hair. I began to suspect that the man did know Portuguese. So I spoke to him in that tongue.

"Let us eat."

He only grunted as if he did not understand and did not want to, and shoved his dugout toward the *furo*. We did not stop to eat, but pushed out in his wake.

Again he turned westward. And all through that hot forenoon, *senhores*, he kept going. Sweating, breathing hard, groaning at times, but always pulling away at his paddle, he drove onward until noon. By that time his strokes were so weak that his boat merely crawled, and we were so hungry that we were ugly.

"Are you trying to kill yourself and us with work and hunger?" I complained. "What does all this mean? Where are you going?"

Slowly, looking us straight in the eyes, he answered:

"*Ehéh ahôh putáre heretamo kotéh.* I am going away to my country."

So that was it. Somehow it seemed strange that this creature could have any country other than the place where we had found him. Yet I did not despise him now as I had. His grim fight to keep going in spite of his clumsiness and his rum-rot made me respect him a little. I was about to ask him, in a more civil tone, where his country was, when Pedro broke in.

"So are we. But we have eaten nothing today, and I am going ashore now to eat and rest a while."

The Barrigudo watched him a minute, then stooped, drew something out of his basket, bit off a piece, and threw the rest to us. It was a flat cake of pressed leaves and bark, wet and sticky as if it had been soaked.

"Chew that," he said. "Swallow."

Seeing that he was already chewing his own, we each bit off a chunk and ground it between our teeth. It tasted both sweetish and sour, quickly filling our mouths with water. After we had swallowed a few times our hunger left us and we felt refreshed.

"What is it?" Pedro asked.

"*Petéma.* Tobacco," he replied with a slight grin. "*Yahôh uáhn.* Let us go now."

And he resumed paddling.

"It is no more tobacco than my foot," Pedro snorted in Portuguese. "But I will not let that bag-belly outpaddle me."

And his shoulders also began to sway again and we moved on.

It was sundown when we stopped at last. Up another inlet we went, around snake-like curves, and into a large, rounded pool.

"Here we are safe," panted the hairy man.

Picking a shelving spot, he drove his dugout ashore, high and hard. As the canoe struck he tumbled forward and lay wheezing. When he was able to get up he crawled out on hands and knees, looking more than ever like a huge monkey.

While we landed he sat in the soft mud by the water, his head hanging, his eyes closed; and he stayed there until we had put up our hammocks, made a fire, and prepared to eat.

"Come and eat," I called.

Wearily he lifted his head and slowly he got up. But he did not eat. He looked at the fire, then stumbled over to it and flopped down beside it.

"*Anîh hahmbuya héh.* I am not hungry," he sighed—and went to sleep sprawling on the bare ground, with the smoke creeping over him.

We let him lie. We did not feel hungry either at first, but after the first few mouthfuls we ate like starved men. When we were full we were stupid from fatigue and heavy eating. After building up the fire so that it would burn slowly and long, we tumbled into our hammocks; and I fell asleep at once.

When I opened my eyes on a new day the Barrigudo was gone.

My *machete* also was gone. The rifles were there, however, and nothing else was missing. And when I looked at the water's edge, there was his canoe, just as he had driven it up at sundown.

Of the man himself, though, there was no sign—no blood on the ground, no fresh tracks near the water. He had not been killed or carried off, and he seemed not to have walked away. He had simply vanished.

Wondering, I made breakfast and awoke Pedro. We called, but got no answer. So, after some talk and argument, we ate and smoked, intending then to search the bush. Before our cigarets were finished, however, a deep voice spoke behind us.

"Good morning!"

The words were English. The voice was not that of the Barrigudo, yet it was familiar. And the man we saw as we whirled and looked was not the Barrigudo either—not the Barrigudo we knew; but it was such a man as the Barrigudo might be if, by some miracle, he should become clean.

A broad, heavy white man stood there. Yes, *senhores*, a white man— burned to a coppery brown by the sun, black-haired of body as well as of head, but a white man for all that. His whole body glowed as if it had been scrubbed and scraped and scrubbed again. His hair was not long and greasy like that of the Barrigudo, but cut close to his broad skull; and his scalp, too, was rosy as if rubbed almost raw.

Under his black brows a pair of deep brown eyes looked straight at us without wink or waver. His mouth was not loose-lipped but set in a resolute line. His head was up and his shoulders back; and, though he was overfat, both face and body were those of a man strong and self-reliant.

Open-mouthed, we stared until he spoke again.

"Understand English?"

"Y-y-yes, *senhor*," Pedro gulped. "We both speak it. But—but are you— the Barrigudo?"

"I was. Yesterday. Today I am—somebody else."

He talked slowly, halting for words as if it had been so long since he had last used his own language that it did not come easily to his tongue.

"Now that I am fit to do so," he went on, "I will eat breakfast. Been cleaning up at a little pool back in the bush."

Calmly he advanced and handed me my *machete*. In a dazed manner I took it.

"Yours," he nodded. "I used the back to scrape myself and the edge to saw off my hair. Overdid the haircut a bit. Shall have to make a leaf hat now. What have you to eat?"

Dumbly I arose and got out more *farinha* and dried fish. With the *farinha* I tried to make some *chibeh*, but I paused to stare at him again and spilled half of the water.

"Never mind the *chibeh*," he said, gnawing off a chunk of the *pirarucu* fish. "I will make it myself. Sit down. You seem upset."

A little vexed, I put my mind on my work and made the *chibeh* as it should be. Placing the gourd on the ground, I made a new cigaret and watched him eat.

"Roll me a smoke too, if you please," he added. "Haven't had one for four years. Now that I have quit boozing I need a smoke to steady me."

"You have stopped drinking?" I repeated as I reached for my pouch.

"I have. It's gnawing at me now, but I'm through with it. ——— the stuff! It's been my curse. I'll beat it or die trying. And I'll not die."

He bit savagely into the fish again, and chewed it as if grinding up with it his craving for drink. He ate his *chibeh* in the same fierce way. When that was gone he drank heavily—of water. After that he swiftly lighted the cigaret I had made, sucked the smoke into his lungs, coughed, choked, tried again, and made better work of it.

"Got to learn to smoke all over again," he grumbled. "It makes me dizzy and it tastes rotten. But it helps some.

"Now you fellows are bursting with questions, I suppose. Shoot them quick. We've got to move."

"Anything you wish to tell us, *senhor*, we shall be glad to hear," Pedro replied. "We ask no questions about matters that do not concern us."

"Thanks. Mighty decent of you. Then I'll say this much now, for it does concern you: About another day's paddle from here we hit a rambling sort of river running northeast. Are you hunting for a way to the Amazon?"

"No. We seek the Javary, in the northwest."

"Oh. I see. Probably this *furo* continues northwest after we reach the river. Not sure about that, though. We'll see. If you go northwest I leave you at the river. I travel northeast."

"To the Amazon?"

"To the Amazon. Then to the Atlantic. Then to America—North. Three A's in a row. They spell 'home' to me. Let's go."

He heaved himself up, winced from the pain of stiff muscles, clamped his jaws, and marched to his canoe. As soon as we could gather up our hammocks, weapons, and food we entered our own craft, and again we were off.

All day we kept on his wake. All day he drove himself to keep his paddle going, eating nothing, only chewing a few mouthfuls of that "tobacco" of his which banished hunger and subdued fatigue. And as mile after mile crept past and the sweat continued to roll off him he seemed slowly to shrink— shrink to firm muscle and slough off his gross fat.

Whether or not this was only my fancy, I know that when we stopped that night on the far side of his rambling river—for we did reach it late that day—he was shaped more like a man and less like a monkey. And his face, with new lines eaten into it, was that of a map, fighting a hard but winning fight.

That night, too, he bathed himself again, though so tired that he could not stand steadily. And he ate and smoked before he lay down by the fire.

"Take my hammock," I urged.

But he would not. And when I spoke of snakes, he retorted:

"Any snake that bites me will die of delirium tremens. There's a lot of bad booze in my system yet. I'll take the chance. Good night!"

So, as before, Pedro and I slept in our hammocks and he on the ground. And, as before, he was up first in the morning.

"Now," he said after breakfast, "we have time to talk.

"You're wondering, of course, how I came into this part of the world. Briefly, then, I was a surgeon. I was a good surgeon. But I drank. More than once I operated when I was nowhere near sober. That meant trouble ahead.

"The trouble came. There was a delicate operation—a young woman— and I was shaky from the effects of a wild night. I had to quit in the middle of the job. Another doctor finished it, but the damage was done. She never recovered consciousness. It was just as well that she didn't.

"That botch broke me. I lost my grip. I drank harder—slid downhill fast. Lost my practice and about everything else, including self-respect and hope. Never committed any crime, though. I'm clean in that way if in no other.

"Drifted into Brazil as 'doctor' of a crowd of wealthy bums who came up the Amazon on a steam-yacht, calling themselves 'explorers.' Lots of money and fool ideas, but no brains. Only thing they explored was every known variety of Brazilian booze. I was the best explorer in the bunch when it came to that.

"Had a drunken row and got put ashore at some Indian town and left there. Thought I had hit the bottom then, but there was still some distance to slide. Yes, there was.

"I kept drinking. Quit everything else—even quit wearing clothes—but I kept drinking. Went from one place to another with Indians—only friends I had left, and some of them not very cordial. I was a no-good white, down and out.

"Just how I got into that place back yonder I don't remember. Drifting around, drunk whenever I could find booze—finally got lost, starved nearly to death, woke up in a place of scabby spotted folks who had fed me and then dumped me in a medicine man's hut.

"I got well, looked for more booze, and couldn't find enough. But I fixed a way to get plenty. Then I stayed with it until you fellows came."

He paused, scowling out at the river flowing past, as if he saw the last four years of his life floating by him on its surface. We said nothing. After a time he went on.

"There is more than one way of getting booze. Buy it, make it yourself, get others to make it for you. When you're lazy and broke there are objections to all these ways. Making it yourself means work and waiting. Buying it means paying for it. And folks won't make it for you unless they receive something in return.

"Of course, a man who won't make his own and has no means of buying it has two ways left—to beg it or steal it. But there are places where even these ways won't get you much. And I was in one of those places.

"There was a little booze in that town, but only a little. The reason why there wasn't more was because the people were too sick and sluggish to work and make it. What little I could get was only a teaser for a two-handed rum-hound like me. I grew desperate. And in my desperation I got a big idea.

"I had bummed many a drink—and many a drunk—among Indians who gave it to me because I could do surgical and medical work for them. I had knocked around in this country long enough to pick up a knowledge of your jungle diseases, and also of the medicinal virtues of your native roots, herbs, leaves, barks, and so on. I had seen that scabby, spotty skin disease before, and I knew how to cure it.

"But I was tired of begging drinks; I wanted to command them. And while I was in that dead medicine man's house I got the idea. I began to play God.

"I mean just that. God created men. I had to create men too. Those spotted Indians were nothing but living corpses, and I had to take those dead-alive people and turn them into healthy folks. Otherwise they wouldn't make booze for me.

"So, for the sake of rum, I became a creator and a savior of bodies. Their souls didn't interest me. My own didn't interest me either.

"Worrying along with what rum I could get and driven by my idea, I worked like a beaver inside the round house until it was ready. Then I made the air-devils talk and sing. After that I built Pajé.

"Pajé was just the boy to handle those Indians, both before and after they were cured; and I saw to it that he never botched things as I had botched that operation back home. So everybody got well, and as the servant of Pajé I lived on the fat of the land and was soused to the collar most of the time.

"And then you chaps came along and woke me up. That's all. Make me another cigaret, please."

"But *senhor*, that is not all," I protested. "What was that work which you did in the round house? How did you make air-devils and Pajé? What is Pajé? How did you—"

I broke off and glanced upward. Above our heads sounded a sweetly singing little voice. Nothing was there; the air was empty. As I dropped my gaze again to the Barrigudo I found him grinning.

"The singing voices follow us," he laughed. "And so does Pajé."

Without moving, he suddenly boomed out in resonant tones:

"You have eyes but you see not. You have ears but your brain is deaf. I am Pajé, master of demons! I am the air-devils! I am the whole —— works! Give me that cigaret!"

It was the voice of Pajé himself.

"But how—" I gasped.

"Oh, give me the makings and let me roll my own smoke," he said impatiently in his usual tone.

When his cigaret was lighted he explained.

"I built an inner wall to the house. A false wall, with space between it and the real wall for me to move. Fixed a blind doorway on a slant in a dim spot at one side. Kept the house dark and smoky all the time to conceal it. Could appear and disappear in no time that way.

"The great Pajé was hidden between the walls. He was nothing but a light framework fitting over my shoulders, with dark cloth draped over it. Had a very thin place in the cloth so that I could see through it. Trickery and a change of voices did the rest."

"*Por Deus!*" muttered Pedro. "You fooled us with our own trick. We ourselves used such frames and great false heads to terrify Indians back on the Juruá. But yours was headless and armless—"

"And you were sick, and I kept up the demon stuff, and the Indians firmly believed I was an infernal monster and told you so. As for the air-devils, I happen to be good at ventriloquism—throwing voices around, you know.

"I had a bag of tricks inside the house too—strings which would open and shut the door or the jaws of heads on the wall, and so on. You saw some of them, Lourenço. Remember the boa's head that ordered you out and the vampire that put you to sleep? That dust that fell into your face when you pulled down the vampire was a sure-fire knockout powder.

"There were other things which you didn't see because I didn't need to use them on you. I had a very complete workshop there."

"I believe you," I agreed. "But if you yourself are the air-devils, how did you throw those voices all the way from the place where we found you to the spot where I first heard them? How did you even see us through all that bush? Why, *senhor*, you were asleep!"

"No more asleep than I am now," he chuckled. "Wasn't far from you, either. I was right at the edge of the bush, squatting and grubbing around for a certain kind of root, when you hove in sight.

"Happened to have just enough rum in me to make me feel good. Kept out of sight and tossed voices around just to see what you'd do.

"Then, finding you had sickness aboard, thought I'd look it over. While you were paddling downstream and then going up that cove looking for me I took a shortcut, lay down under a tree where you couldn't miss me, and pretended sleep. After that I had to be surly and carry out my role. Anything else?"

"Yes. What ailed Pedro, and how did you cure the Indians of spotted sickness, and—"

"Not so fast. I am not going to tell you all I know. But if ever you become diseased with that spotted ailment, make strong sarsaparilla and drink it. Very strong, plenty of it.

"Pedro had malignant fever, which kills in a few hours. You brought him to me barely in time, and I had a job to pull him through. Didn't touch a drop of rum in all the time I was working on him—didn't sleep a wink either. The minute he was out of the house, though, I gulped about a gallon of jungle lightning."

I nodded, remembering his appearance when he passed me an hour after Pedro's release from the House of Voices. After being sober and sleepless for forty-eight hours, it was no wonder that he had become drunk so swiftly and completely when the tension ended.

"Now that I know what I know," Pedro said slowly, "I am sorry, *senhor*, that I said what I did when I saw you the next day."

"You needn't be. It was exactly what I needed—a look at myself through another man's eyes. It jolted me into realization of just how much of a beast I had become.

"When I had shut myself up inside the round house and knocked out my hangover with a little homemade bracer I sat down and did some real thinking. Didn't have to meditate much concerning my exact social status—your disgust showed me where I stood.

"But I had to figure out a way to get out of there quick. Knew I had to go quick or I'd lose the ambition to go. Knew the Indians would never let me go if they could stop me.

"So I fixed them so they couldn't stop me. Scared them with the air-devils and then fed them that Pajé-drink, which was doped heavily enough to knock them cold for twelve hours. So here I am."

"And now that you are here, what will you do?" I asked.

"Go home, I told you. When I reach home I'm going to atone for sacrificing that young woman's life on the altar of Bacchus. I'm going to save a good many other lives in its place.

"No, not by surgery—I doubt if I shall ever operate again. But, as I said before, I've learned a good deal down here about native medicines, and I've experimented a lot and worked out new remedies of my own. Had to do it in order to keep up my bluff. The result is that I know powerful drug combinations of which North America knows nothing. But North America is going to hear about them soon. See that basket?"

He motioned toward the *atura* which he had brought from the House of Voices on that last night, and which now lay in his canoe.

"It's full of leaves, bark, roots, twigs, pieces of vine—stuff which you'd call rubbish. But every one of them has a big value in medicine, and I know exactly what each is good for.

"In the next few years there may be good jobs here for men who will collect those things for the North American market. Want a job like that?"

We laughed.

"Thank you, *senhor*, but we are *seringueiros*," Pedro told him. "We collect nothing but rubber, mosquito bites, and danger. Those three things keep us so busy that we have no time for anything else."

"Suit yourselves," he said, and arose. "You say you go westward from here. But you haven't found the *furo* yet, so we'll travel together until you think you've hit it.

"Now let's move. My Indian jailers may be coming this way, and I'd rather make a clean getaway than have to fight them."

He planted his big body in his dugout and pushed out and downstream. Half a mile below our camping place he slowed.

"Looks like a channel there, running west," he said. "Your *furo*, perhaps. Going to chance it?"

After studying the quiet water opening out on the left bank we decided that it was what we sought. We urged him to come with us to the headquarters of our *coronel*, who would send him home as a gentleman. But he shook his head.

"I'm through with bumming," he snapped. "I'm working my way home. Glad to have met you, gentlemen. Goodbye."

"Wait!" cried Pedro. "You must take a gun. Here is one given me by an American soldier back toward the Juruá—he and his comrades had come here on a treasure-hunting journey, led by a crazy man, and when they went back toward the Amazon they gave us each a rifle. We have another, and plenty of cartridges. Take it, *senhor*, and some of our food, and my clothes— I shall not need them."

"I'll take the gun and some cartridges if you insist. Been wondering how you chaps got those Army Springfields, but didn't like to ask. Nothing else, thanks—not a thing. I can handle myself in the bush. Thanks again, and goodbye."

He held out a hand, and we grasped it in farewell. Then he slapped his paddle into the river and heaved his boat downstream. Holding our own craft steady, we watched him until he passed out of sight. Not once did he look back.

"If he holds that pace to the Amazon he will grow much thinner than he is now," said Pedro as we turned into the *furo*.

"He will be hard as *itauba* stone-wood and free from all drink-craving when he reaches the great river," I agreed.

"Do you honestly believe he will win his fight with himself? He has far to go, and he may find Indian villages on his way."

"He will win. He has something to look forward to now. I have seen such men before. At first he drank as you and I drink when we feel like it—for the fun of carousing with others. Then he drank to drown the memory of the girl he had killed. Here in the jungle he drank to forget that he was, as he said, 'a no-good white, down and out.'

"But now he has before him the thought of home and the knowledge that he can wipe out his past. With that to draw him on, the rum of Indian villages will not snare him."

"You have it right," my comrade admitted. "A man's life depends on what is in his own heart. Yet you named him rightly when you called him *barrigudo*. Do you know what happens to a *barrigudo* when he leaves his own country?"

"He dies."

"He dies. And this man, leaving his own land, died and became a beast."

"But now the *barrigudo* is dead and a new man lives in his place."

"*Si*. It is as it should be. Now let us lean on our paddles, for we have many miles to go and the water ebbs."

We shot away along the *furo*, homeward bound.

Excerpt from The Camp-Fire

Here are the results of the readers' vote on the ten most popular stories in *Adventure* during 1920. As in previous years, we give also the ten ranking next in the vote. (S) stands for "serial," (N) for complete "novel," (n) for complete novelette, those unmarked being short stories.

Of course a vote of this kind is only a partial expression, being cast by only a minority of the total number of readers, but nevertheless it is both interesting and decidedly useful in helping us in the office fill the magazine with the kinds of story our readers like best.

	Story	Author	Type	Votes
1	Wild Blood	Gordon Young	S	5,535
2	The Bushfighters	Hugh Pendexter	N	4,311
3	Storm Rovers	Gordon Young	N	4,104
4	The Curved Sword	Harold Lamb	N	3,509
5	L'Atlantide	Pierre Benoit	S	3,495
6	Kings of the Missouri	Hugh Pendexter	S	3,457
7	A Scout for Virginia	Hugh Pendexter	S	3,186
8	The Master Plotter	Edgar Young	s	3,133
9	The Law Comes to Singing River	Robert J. Horton	N	3,051
10	The Long Trail	J. Allan Dunn	N	2,981
11	The Gate Through the Mountain	Hugh Pendexter	S	2,781
12	The War-Cloth	J. Allan Dunn	N	2,487
13	Man to Man	Jackson Gregory	S	1,998
14	Hashknife—Philanthropist	W.C. Tuttle	n	1,972
15	The McIntosh	Charles Beadle	n	1,813
16	The Messenger	W.C. Robertson & H. Bedford-Jones	n	1,517
17	**The Armadilho**	**Arthur O. Friel**	**s**	**1,513**
18	The Sun-God Trail	Edgar Young	s	1,459
19	Wolves of the Air	Ranger Gull	N	1,404
20	The Masterpiece of Death	Harold Lamb	N	1,379

Of course there a good many factors that play a part in such a ranking of stories. A story read a month ago leaves on the mind a more vivid impression than does an equally good story read eleven months ago. A long story has the big advantage of size and weight over a short one. A story read next to an unusually good one is likely to suffer by comparison more than it deserves.

But, all in all, such a vote as ours furnishes an invaluable guide in helping the editors make our magazine provide the kinds of story our readers want.

As last year, we give also a list of the shorter stories by themselves. Those marked with a * are of less than ten thousand words; the others are of ten thousand to twenty thousand.

Stories Under 20,000

Story	Author	< 10,000	Votes
1 The Master Plotter	Edgar Young		3,133
2 Hashknife—Philanthropist	W.C. Tuttle		1,972
3 The McIntosh	Charles Beadle		1,813
4 The Messenger W.C. Robertson & H. Bedford-Jones			1,517
5 The Armadilho	**Arthur O. Friel**	*	**1,513**
6 The Sun-God Trail	Edgar Young	*	1,459
7 The Liar	Captain Dingle	*	1,189
8 A Teacher of Etiquette	E.S. Pladwell	*	1,168
9 El Capitan Arrrnie	Chester L. Saxby	*	1,166
10 Promoting Polecat Perkins	W.C. Tuttle	*	1,001
11 One Weak Spot	Edgar Young	*	999
12 Rich Crooks	Gordon Young		891
13 The Eighty-One	Hugh Fullerton	*	756
14 Convoys Courageous	S.A. White	*	729
15 Intrigue	Robert J. Pearsall		651
16 Blackmail	Gordon Young	*	624
17 Lobo Simms	Buck Connor		589
18 The Bowl of Alabaster	Charles Beadle		545
19 Road-Signs and a Nose-Ring	Barry Scobee		513
20 In the Dark	Lynn Montross	*	509

The annual vote by readers is both interesting and valuable. Be making your selections for the vote on our 1921 stories. It's your chance to help in editing our magazine and to make its stories a bit more to your own personal taste.

The Bouto

No, *senhor*, that loud snort which sounded from the river just now was not made by an alligator. I do not wonder that you thought so, for this upper Amazon is full of alligators big and small—*jacaré uassú, jacaré tinga, jacaré curúa*, and others not so common—and the alligator, like other beasts, has his night call. But the sound which you heard was made by a river animal far more graceful and less dangerous—a dolphin.

Look! Over there you can see its back fin glisten in the moonlight. Ah, it is gone. It has dived, and by the time it rises again this steamer will be so far downstream that we shall see it no more.

What is that? You would like to take a shot at one? If you will pardon me, I would urge you to do no such thing. You might be so unfortunate as to kill it with your heavy bullet. Have not you and your companion learned, while exploring our Amazon headwaters, that to kill a *bouto* is bad luck?

Indeed it is true, *senhores*. Every one on the river knows that. If you do not believe it, tell some Indian that you want dolphin oil to burn in your lantern and that you will pay him well to harpoon one for you. He will answer that blindness creeps on those who use the oil of the *bouto* for light, and that even worse fortune falls on him who slays the fish.

He may tell you, too, the legend of the Bouto Woman, which you perhaps have heard before. No? At our river towns the tale is told that sometimes the *bouto* turns itself into a handsome girl whose hair is so long that it sweeps on the ground behind her when she walks. Leaving the water at night, she strolls about until she meets a man. She smiles on him and coaxes him to walk down to the riverside, saying that there they will be alone. And if he goes with her he goes to death. For at the edge of the water she seizes him around the body and leaps with him into the flood, and he is gone for all time.

Yes, it is an odd tale, as you say. But, *senhores*, an odd story is not always untrue. I will not say that I believe the *bouto* itself does this, yet—well, you North Americans have a saying, have you not, that "where there is smoke there is fire"? And queer things sometimes come about on this Amazon of ours and on the jungle rivers which flow into it—happenings which the great world outside never knows. I myself, a rubber-worker of the Javary region, have seen some such things. And now that we speak of the Bouto Woman I can tell you of something which I saw not very long ago.

The great annual flood, which turns nearly one-third of our Brazil into a vast tree-choked sea, was nearly at its end. Indeed, the flood itself was long past, and in many places the wet land had risen once more above the water. To me and my comrade Pedro, urging our canoe northwestward through the jungle toward the river Tecuahy, this reappearance of the muddy earth was both welcome and unwelcome. Welcome, because it meant that the time was near when we could return to our rubber-work in the forests of old Coronel Nunes and earn more money. Unwelcome, because we had not yet reached the river we sought, and the rising of the thick bush from under the flood had made our travel slower and harder.

We had been on a long journey to the upper reaches of the river Juruá, off to the southeast—a trip with which our work for Coronel Nunes had nothing to do, for it was made in the time of high water when neither we nor any other men could labor in the flood-swept lowlands of his *seringal*. We had gone in burning rage and hate to avenge the death of another *seringueiro* captured and tortured by a tribe of beast-men—and we had avenged it well. Then, drifting down the Juruá while I recovered from a wound, we had at length turned off westward on a flood-channel through the forest, hoping by this to return to the Tecuahy and then go down that river to the Javary town of Remate de Males, whence we had started.

On this channel, which we never had seen before, we had met with delays. Most of them were due to losing our way, but a few had arisen from more serious causes. The latest of these was an attack of malignant fever which had struck my partner suddenly and nearly swept him across a river wider even than this Amazon—the river which runs between the worlds.

But he had been saved by a white medicine-man who was at once the ruler and the prisoner of an Indian tribe; and when Pedro was strong again this man had arranged our escape and himself fled with us to a wandering river running northeast, where he had left us and struck off alone toward civilization. And now, days later, we were still driving our canoe onward, guiding ourselves by the sun and holding as true a course as we could in the maze of thick bush and blind channels.

At length, late one day as we were watching ahead for a place to make camp for the night, we saw rising ground at the right. We slowed and scanned it as our dugout floated by, but found that between it and us was mud too thin to walk on but too thick to paddle through. So we continued on, curving around a bend in the channel, until a sudden brightening of the light and widening of the water drew our eyes to the left. We found ourselves just entering a river.

"*Por Deus!* Have we reached the Tecuahy at last, Lourenço?" cried Pedro, both joy and doubt in his voice.

"It is time we did," I growled, squinting in the glare of the low sun on the wide water; "but from what I can see I fear it is not. It seems to run almost east."

"True. But this may be only a turn. Let us go down it and see."

He stroked hard and the canoe jumped. But after a swift glance at the sun I dug my paddle in deep and held back.

"Not today," I disagreed. "We must get ashore soon if we are not to be caught by black night. The sun is dropping fast."

He grumbled something, but he too began looking again at the right bank. Then he nodded sidewise and edged the bow shoreward. I swung the stern, and we floated into a little natural port. Above us were firm ground, tall trees, and only a little of the low bush growth.

Landing, we threw up a small *tambo* to keep off any night rain, slung our hammocks, built a fire and ate. Night fell. The sky was clear, but we knew the moon would be late, so, though we spoke of paddling downstream a little way by moonlight, we decided against it. The river would not disappear over night, and we were tired. Before long we slept.

Bright moonlight, breaking through openings among the treetops and shining on my face, woke me. I blinked, glanced at Pedro, turned in my hammock and let my eyes droop again. But just as they were closing they flew open. Something had moved.

I had heard nothing except the usual nightly hammering chorus of frogs, seen nothing but the dark mass of jungle sprayed with moonlight. Yet something had come between me and the moon, for its light had dimmed. And as I lifted my head and peered toward it I started. Framed in the glare were a head and a pair of bare shoulders.

They did not move. They stood out against the moonshine as if they belonged to a dusky statue with a neck nearly as thick as its body. For minutes I hung there squinting at it, and it stared straight back at me. Then the moon, rising fast, rolled up past the gap at the back of the creature; the light became more evenly balanced, and the face and form of the phantom grew more distinct. And I was more astonished than before, for I saw that it was a woman.

A woman, quite young, but with the plump shoulders and full bosom of maturity. A woman whose hair hung unbound behind her to her waist, where it was looped around her body like a belt. I saw now that she was not thick-necked, for with the change in the light her face and throat glowed pinky-brown against that black cloud of hair which at first had made her look so misshapen. And as I continued to stare I found that she was far from bad-looking.

She smiled, lifted a hand, and beckoned. I dropped my feet to the ground and sat up. At my movement she turned and began to fade away into the murky bush, still beckoning. Profoundly puzzled, I arose and took a step toward her. And just then Pedro, lying back in the shadows, cried out.

He was still asleep, but struggling with a bad dream. At his smothered yell both the woman and I jumped. For an instant she poised as if startled. Then, with a swift movement, she was gone.

Pedro yelled again and awoke. Seeing me standing there, he snatched his *machete* and leaped up and at me.

"Drop it!" I snapped.

"Oh, it is you, comrade!" He laughed nervously. "I am not quite myself— I have just been fighting with some cannibals. Why are you up?"

"Because you were howling so hard that I was looking for a rope to choke you with," I grumbled.

"Sure you were not sneaking out to make love to some lady monkey?" he chuckled.

"Not to a monkey. But I might have gone walking with a handsome young woman if you had not scared her away."

He stared, then grinned.

"So you too were dreaming—a more pleasant dream than mine. Pardon me for waking you. Were you in Remate de Males, or back at your old home below Manaus?"

"Neither. I was here. And if I dreamed I am still asleep."

Again I looked out at the bush. The woman was not there. Pedro, wondering, said nothing, and I listened. As I was about to speak again I heard a slight splash. No further sound came.

"Did you hear that splash?" I muttered.

"Yes. A fish jumping."

"Perhaps. But it came from over yonder, not from the river. In the morning I shall explore this place."

With that I sat down and told him of what I had seen. He grunted in disbelief.

"Moonshine!" he scoffed. "I have heard that men with weak heads should not sleep in the moonlight. You say the moon was shining in your eyes when you awoke. Your mind is full of moonbeams and moon-dreams. Unless"—and he laughed again—"you had a visit from the Bouto Woman of the Amazon. If it was she, beware! You know what comes to men who follow her. Did her hair drag at her heels?"

"No, but it might have done so if she had let it down. It was wound around her waist and hips like a *tanga*. Laugh if you like, but this was no dolphin-woman. Besides, a dolphin turned to a woman would be black, unless it changed color as well as shape."

"But no, it would not," he disputed. "Some of our river dolphins are entirely black, but others are black-backed and pink underneath, and some are pink all over. Have you never seen flesh-colored dolphins? They are not uncommon."

He spoke truth. It had been some time since I had seen a dolphin, and still longer since I had heard any one tell the tale of the Bouto Woman. Now, thinking about them there in the dark mystery of the jungle, I half-believed that the old legend might be true. But I said no more, and soon my partner lay down again.

"If your fishy lady comes back before dawn wake me," he yawned. "I should much like to see the famous Bouto."

And with another derisive chuckle he went back to sleep.

I lay awake for some time, listening to the night noises but hearing nothing strange. Several times I sat up and stared long at the place where that moon-born woman had stood. But whatever might have been there before, nothing human was there now. So at length I too drifted off to sleep.

Pedro's hand on my shoulder roused me. The sun was up in the sky, the smell of wood-smoke and boiling coffee was in the air and excitement was in my partner's face.

"Wake up, old lady-charmer, and receive my apologies," he said. "I knew well you were a fascinator, but I never suspected that fish would turn into women for your sake. The Bouto Woman was here last night! Come and see!"

A few feet east of our *tambo* he pointed to the ground. There in a soft spot was the print of a bare foot.

We had worked barefoot in building our hut at sundown, but this track could not have been made by either of us. It was much too small. In another place a couple of yards farther off Pedro pointed out another footprint of the same size. Working back through the bush, he showed me more of them here and there. The trail brought us to water.

"This is an *enseada*," he explained. "It must run in from somewhere downstream. Your woman seems to have walked out along that fallen tree and plunged into the water. There is no track anywhere else along the shore."

As he said, the trail began and ended at the base of a tree stretching out into the quiet water. I stepped out along the floating trunk and on its rough bark I spied little dabs of earth scraped off the feet which had passed along it.

Fifty feet out from shore, at the point where the first branches jutted upward, I halted and scanned trunk and limbs. They showed no sign that a canoe had been tied there. And the *enseada* itself, as I looked along it, held no indication of life. The woman had come from the water and gone back to it, leaving nothing but a few scattered footprints.

"Before you jump in after her," Pedro called, "come back to the fire and have some breakfast."

"I am not jumping after her or any other woman," I retorted, turning toward shore.

And we hastened back to our boiling coffee.

When we had eaten and stowed our few belongings in the dugout we pushed off downstream, keeping near the right bank. The hill on which we had camped stretched along the river for perhaps a mile, rising steep from the muddy waters and seeming unbroken by any cleft. Yet we had already found one dent in it—the small port where we had spent the night—and we looked for another opening where the *enseada* began. And before long we found it.

It was so narrow and so overgrown that if we had not been hugging the shore and watching for it we should have passed it without a glance. And even when we forced our way through the half-drowned bush choking it up we were not sure that it was what we sought, for it turned to the left and seemed to end. But as we paddled on we found that it did not stop there but looped sharply back around a point. Turning the point, we held our paddles and stared.

Before us rose a wall of thin, straight palm-logs standing on end in the water. The posts stood close together, yet not too close, to let the water flow through between them. They were lashed to one another by loop after loop of tough woody vines and bush-rope, and the whole wall looked firm enough to last for a lifetime. It extended up the steep banks on either side, rising to a height a little above the topmost flood mark. In it we could see no gate, and no path showed around either end. It seemed made to let water in but keep all else out.

"*Por Deus!*" Pedro said softly. "This is a queer thing to find in uninhabited jungle. No dolphin-woman made this, nor any other woman. It is the work of a strong man."

"I do not like it," I muttered. "It looks like a trap."

He nodded. But instead of answering he held up a hand for silence. Beyond the barrier sounded splashing.

Softly, silently, we stroked our canoe up to the poles. Pedro, in the bow, leaned forward and peered through one of the narrow openings.

"*Nossa Senhora!*" I heard him whisper. Then, turning his head and shielding his mouth with one hand, he added, "The Bouto!"

Quickly but quietly I worked my end of the boat around until I too could look through. And there in the water, some distance away but unmistakable, I saw the woman who had beckoned to me in the moonlight.

In truth, she seemed a dolphin woman. She was swimming and playing about with the smooth ease of a fish, disappearing sometimes below the surface, staying under until it seemed that she must have drowned, then gliding into sight again at some place a long way from the spot where she had vanished.

After floating quietly a moment she would splash water upward with both hands and go down backward, her feet kicking a white smother as they sank.

And then we would see her pink toes peep out somewhere else, followed by her hands and then by her flushed face, above which her black hair was piled in a cone resembling a dolphin's snout.

She turned over with a gleam of sleek arms; she swam on her right side and then on her left; she even went feet first, her toes held above water. And we clung to the poles and marveled.

"She is better than the dolphin itself," Pedro murmured. "I have never seen a fish that could swim backward as she is doing."

It was not only her skill that held me quiet, however, but her fearlessness. Neither of us, though we could swim if we had to, would think of sporting about as she was doing—there are too many perils waiting for a swimmer in our waters. Alligators, huge water snakes, bloodthirsty *piranhas*, barb-tailed *araya* devil-fish, electric eels which shock and stun, and other deadly creatures too foul for me to speak of—all these lurk under the surface that looks so harmless to a stranger, and we were too old in the ways of the jungle streams to expose ourselves to them. Yet this dolphin woman seemed to give them no thought, and she suffered no harm.

At length she tired of her play and came swiftly toward us in a final dash. Swerving toward the left bank, she reached upward and caught at something we had not noticed—a little platform on poles, like the *moutás* which our Indians set up in the waters of the jungle pools when shooting turtles. One of the posts supporting this was notched to form a ladder, and up these notches she climbed to the platform.

There she sat breathing a moment. Then she arose, unbound her cone of hair, pressed the water from it, and shook it loose to dry.

Senhores, that hair was longer than she herself. It hung down below the *moutá* on which she stood, and her head tilted backward a little as if drawn down by the weight of it. Against its blackness her face and figure glowed far more clearly than when I had last seen her, back in the dark jungle under the wan light of the moon. Plump, smooth-skinned, unclothed except for a tight-drawn *tanga*, glistening with the water-drops rolling down her shapely form, she still seemed the Bouto Woman of the old tale—a dolphin such as Pedro had mentioned, black of back and fair of body.

Yet her face, as she stood with chin upward and gaze fixed on the jungle beyond, did not seem that of a woman nimble-witted enough to lure men to destruction. Somehow it looked rather blank, and the eyes seemed to stare as unwinkingly as those of a fish.

A choking sound from Pedro drew my attention away from her. He was struggling to hold his breath. His effort failed. He burst into a snorting sneeze.

Muttering a curse, he looked again through the palm wall. So did I. The woman turned sharply toward us, watched the logs a moment and probably saw our canoe through the openings. With a leap she cleared the space between her platform and the land. There she stood still again, frowning. Then, instead of running away, she calmly came toward us.

While she was balancing herself along the abrupt slope we pushed the canoe to shore and waited. Her head rose over the wall and hung there, peering down.

"*Boa dia, senhorita*," Pedro greeted her. "I hope we have not disturbed you."

She made no answer. Her steady stare rested long on his face, then passed to mine. A slow smile came on her full lips, and I knew she recognized me. But still she did not speak. Presently a hand rose over the wall and beckoned. And the invitation was not to Pedro but to me.

I sat still, for this was most astonishing. Never before had a woman ignored my handsome partner for me. As you *senhores* can see for yourselves, I am so plain that women are not likely to notice me at any time, and certainly not when I am with such a tall, graceful fellow as Pedro. Now, with this attractive woman preferring me to him, I was as much surprised as if our canoe had suddenly grown legs and. started to walk up the slope.

Watching me, she laughed quietly and continued to beckon. Pedro turned to me.

"Why do you not go?" he demanded. "Must your lady come down here and carry you? Use your legs."

I stepped out on the bank. But there I stopped, glancing again at the wall.

"Come with me," I said in an undertone. "As I said before, this place looks like a trap. Perhaps no harm is near, but we had best make sure. Here you are walled in on three sides, and the way out is not easy."

"So you think there may be a reason for trying to separate us?"

"I do not know. But I do know that two men can be killed more easily when apart than when together. And, as you have said, no woman built that barrier."

He nodded, fastened the boat to a post and followed me, rifle in hand. The woman frowned, but still said nothing. After a slippery climb up the bank we crossed the wall at the point where the last and shortest stakes joined the steep earth. By that time the woman had started away, and we trailed in her footprints, balancing ourselves with difficulty on the wet clay. When we came above the *moutá*, however, we found a path where the soil was packed into a narrow shelf, and from that point we trod more easily and could look at other things besides the ground.

The woman, I noticed, had again looped her hair around her waist. Then, as I glanced beyond her, I noticed something else. A couple of hundred yards farther along the ravine the top of another wall of poles showed above the water. Now I understood why the woman could swim here without fear.

These barriers would keep out *araya*, *piranha* and all other evil creatures except those so small that they could do no serious injury. True, a great snake or alligator might come into the place from the land, but this was hardly probable. Walled in at both sides by abrupt declivities, barred at both ends by the posts, it formed a long pool where a good swimmer could play unharmed.

The path twisted upward and began to zigzag back and forth. We dug in our toes and mounted to the top. There, under big trees, the ground was nearly level and almost free of undergrowth. Still silent, we three walked onward to the base of a great prostrate *massaranduba* tree which at some time had come smashing down and which, though lying on its side, still loomed high over our heads.

We had seen such prone giants often before, and now we only glanced at it and would have passed on. But at a spot some ten feet beyond its towering roots the woman halted, pointed and stepped straight into the tree itself.

"*Por amor de Deus!*" exclaimed Pedro. "A house cut in the virgin wood!"

It was so. We stared at the strangest house we had ever seen. Above us that huge trunk rose for nearly twenty feet, and from its lower side had been hollowed a home about eight feet high and fifteen feet long. The enormous weight of the tree had driven its underside solidly into the soil when it struck, and the space between its lower curve and the ground had been filled in with smaller logs and clay, forming a nearly straight wall at each end of the cavity. From the roof to the earth an outer wall of small palm-logs had been built, with a window and a door. The inside of the place was very dark.

"No woman made this," I mumbled. "It took more than one man and many days of chopping."

"Perhaps not," he disagreed. "See how black the bark is at the ends and up above. It was not chopped out, but made as we make our canoes—burned out and then finished with the ax. One strong man could do it easily."

"True. But let us look at the man who made it."

Then, raising my voice, I called gruffly:

"Ho there! Come out!"

No one came out. The woman appeared in the window and stood there, a question in her face. No other creature showed itself.

"Is no man here?" I asked.

With her slow smile she shook her head. Her beckoning hand appeared at the window. And, as before, she motioned to me, not to Pedro.

"The strangeness grows," said my partner. "A woman who swims better than a fish is rare. A woman who lives alone in manless jungle is unheard of. But a woman who will not talk—it is a miracle!"

Without reply I walked in at the door, rifle ready. But no man lurking in the shadows menaced me. She had told truth—no man was there. Yet, as my eyes grew accustomed to the dimness, I saw that a man had been there. Not only one man, but three.

From pins in the wood wall hung the clothing of three men. And in a corner stood rusty rifles and *machetes*.

"Where are those men?" I demanded, pointing.

With a wave of the hand she signed that they had gone away.

Peering again at the rusty weapons, I thought their owners must have been gone for some time. And they had left clothes and guns behind.

"Are they dead?" I snapped.

She nodded.

"How? What killed them?"

Her cool brown eyes did not waver—nor did she speak. Another calm movement of both hands and a shake of her head told me that she did not know how they had died.

Her unbroken silence irritated me. I asked rather sharply whether she had no tongue. Smiling again, she stuck out her tongue and wriggled it impudently at me. It looked as good as my own. I growled, seized her shoulder with my left hand and tried to scare her into speech.

"Talk, or I will thrash you!" I threatened, trying to look ugly and brutal.

It did no good whatever. She laughed in my face, lifted a hand, raised my fist with a smooth strength that astonished me—and then drew my arm down around her waist.

I twisted my hand free and stepped back hastily.

"Pedro!" I yelped. "Come in here!"

His chuckle sounded at the door.

"I have been watching," he told me. "But why call for me? She is yours without a struggle."

"Er—ah—look at those things!" I stammered, hot-faced, jabbing a thumb toward the weapons and clothes.

"Yes, I saw them. That was what brought me to the door—your question about men."

His face sobered and his eyes narrowed as he looked from the guns to the woman.

"What killed those men?" he barked.

She pouted, shook her head again and then motioned for him to go.

"Very well," I said. "We shall both go. *Adeos, senhorita.*"

But she caught my arm again and held it, and once more I was surprised by the power of her grip. As I paused she moved her mouth as if eating, then nodded to each of us in turn.

"Yes, we will eat with you if you like," I consented. "But I stay in no place where my partner is unwelcome."

She released my arm, pointed to a hammock slung against the far wall and motioned for us to rest there. Then from a stool under the window, where we had not observed them, she picked up a pair of trousers with belt and *machete*. Stepping into these, she buckled the belt around her and started out.

"A queer way to prepare a meal for visitors—to strap on a *machete* and leave them," Pedro remarked.

"This whole matter is too queer to suit me," I said. "I am going with her to watch her. Stay here and look over those guns—and anything else you see. Our tongues and ears are useless, so we must depend on our eyes."

And out I went after her.

She was walking along the trunk of the *massaranduba*. I made no attempt to sneak and spy, but followed openly. She looked back, waited until I reached her, then went on toward the head of the tree, glancing at me now and then in a way which was neither bold nor shy but very friendly. As I usually do when with women, I kept my mouth shut. And thus, wordless, we passed around the great sprawling treetop and walked on into the forest beyond.

Past other tremendous trees, towering so high that their heads were lost beyond the roof of branches above us, we went. Around a dense mass of thorny bamboos we made a circuit, and then we came among trees of medium height, corded and draped with vines, which hung from above and mingled with other vines matted on the ground. Here the woman slowed and looked searchingly at the vines. Presently she stepped to a liana, drew her *machete* and cut off a piece about a yard long. With this in her hand she turned toward the *enseada*.

Down the bank, which here was far less steep than at her swimming place, we went to the edge of the water. There, concealed in a small hollow, lay a short canoe in which was one paddle. Entering this and lifting the paddle, she motioned for me to squat in the bow. I did so, facing her.

She pushed the craft out, turned it to her left and sent it gliding down the inlet. Around a double curve we floated. Looking over one shoulder, I saw that the *enseada* now became wider and straighter; and a gunshot beyond us I spied a tree lying far out in the water, its butt on shore. Studying it, I knew it was the trunk on which I had walked out that morning, trailing this woman.

We did not reach that tree. She swung the canoe into a small cove at the left, and we got out on shore. There she held the piece of vine against a tree, pounded it with her *machete* until it was well mashed up and threw it out into the still water of the cove. After that she sat down at the base of the tree and motioned for me to sit beside her.

More puzzled than ever, I scowled at her and at the crushed vine. The vine floated almost motionless, and the dark water around it looked slightly milky, as if some whitish juice from the wood were soaking out of it. As

I looked back at her she raised a hand toward the sun, moved it a little westward, dropped it and pointed at the drifting vine, lowered it again to the place beside her. I took this to mean that in about half an hour the vine would do something, and that meanwhile I was to keep her company.

So I squatted against the tree—not so close to her as she had indicated—and made a cigaret, which I offered to her. She took it, and when I had rolled another I lit them both. She puffed at hers as if she had smoked before, but not recently. And then for a while we sat there burning tobacco.

While I sucked smoke I remembered that we had not given her any account of ourselves. Perhaps if I did so she would break her stubborn silence. So I told her my name, where we worked, and as much of our recent history as seemed best. Her eyes showed interest, but she never spoke. And when I questioned her as to who she was, whence she came, and how long she had lived here, into her face came that blank look I had noticed before, and she stared straight before her.

Then she leaned forward, looking at the water. There on the placid surface was something more than the vine—the glistening side and light belly of a small fish.

Its gills were wide-open, and it seemed dead. I was quite sure that it had not been dead long—some other creature would have devoured it. And in another few minutes I became certain of this. Without splash or struggle, three more fish came drifting up from the depths. And, one by one, others appeared here and there on the surface. And not one moved so much as a fin.

The woman rose and stood looking them over. None was large, but there were enough to make a meal—if they were fit to eat. Yet she stood quiet as if waiting. And before long the water showed its first sign of life. Wriggling weakly, a fine big *pescada* came up, gasped a few times and was still.

At sight of that creature I sprang up, thinking only of getting him before he should give a twist of his tail and disappear. Then I stopped short as the meaning of it all flashed on me. The woman was fishing with the *timbó*.

I had heard of this before, but never had seen it. The *timbó* is a poisonous liana, and if it is crushed and thrown into still water its juice will stupefy and kill the fish near it. Yet the flesh of the fish is unhurt—the creature seems to be stifled rather than poisoned—and it can be eaten without harm. And there was no need for me to hurry about capturing that *pescada*, for he never would move again. He was as dead as if his backbone had been severed.

With a motion of the head the woman stepped into the canoe, and I followed. A few strokes brought us to the *pescada*, and I lifted him in. The dugout moved around among the other fish, and I spied a couple of rather small *tucunarés*. These also I gathered up. The rest we left behind us.

Around the double twist in the winding water we returned, to the little cove and thence to the dug-out house. When we entered it Pedro was lying lazily in the hammock, seeming half-asleep.

"Our friend is a witch," I told him with a slight wink. "She dropped a vine on the water and the fish arose to feed us. It is magic."

The woman looked pleased. He winked back to me. As she picked a small knife from where it stuck in the wall and went out again to clean the fish he swiftly arose.

"The men who died had money," he whispered in my ear.

Somewhat surprised, I glanced at the clothing on the wall. It looked as poor as our own. And my surprise almost became disbelief when he added—

"Twelve thousand *milréis!*"

"*Deus meo!*" I muttered. "Are you sure?"

"Sure. It is all in one great roll, tied with busk-cord, lying there in the corner under those rifles as if it were a mere lump of dirt. The guns are Winchesters, .44, such as we use. The *machetes* are Collins, like ours. The clothes are the same as we should wear. And I believe the men were *seringueiros* like ourselves."

"But three *seringueiros*—where would they get twelve thousand *milréis?*"

"Perhaps by gambling with others. Or perhaps more than three men have died here, and the guns and clothes of the rest are lost or thrown away. And—hush! Let us go outside."

We lounged out, meeting the woman coming toward us. She entered the place, but came out almost at once with a piece of that queer stony stuff which sometimes is found floating down our streams and which our Indians believe to be hardened river-foam*. We watched her return to her fish, lift the knife and scrub rust from the blade with the foam-stone. She gave us the same slow smile as she passed, and in her gaze we saw no suspicion.

Strolling idly away, we acted as if only looking about us. I noticed that between her house and the edge of the bank no small growth stood, and that we could see for some distance up and down the opposite hilltop. Perhaps the light of our small fire had glinted through the jungle last night and caught her eye, or its drifting smoke had been borne to her on a breeze, to arouse her curiosity and send her to spy on us as soon as moonrise gave enough light. We walked on until we could continue talking.

"Twelve thousand *milréis!*" I muttered. "And this woman led us straight to her house and left you, a stranger, there with that money while she went fishing with me. She certainly is not sly—at times she looks as if her mind slept—and yet she is not simple either. She shows us everything and tells us nothing. I can make neither head nor tail of it all."

---

* Pumice stone, water-borne from the Andes. Used by Brazilians to scour rust from metal.

"Nor I," he admitted. "What do you think her to be? White, or only partly white?"

"A *mameluca*," I judged. "Like ourselves—white, with a little Indian blood. Beyond that I can not guess what she may be."

"We can only watch and wait," he said. "Asking questions is useless. Let matters shape themselves."

But as we idled back to her I thought of one question which she might answer, and which meant much to us. When we were beside her again I pointed toward the river and asked—

"Tecuahy?"

She nodded.

"Praise God!" I rejoiced. "Our fight with the bush is over. What part of the Tecuahy is this? Where does the Branco flow in—above or below here?"

At the word "Branco" she started. A sudden wild light flared into her eyes. Then she dropped her head and went on with her work.

We glanced at each other. On the Branco, a river three hundred miles long which enters the Tecuahy from the west, are a few *seringales*. Where *seringales* are, there must be *seringueiros* to work them. The clothing and weapons—and perhaps the money—in her house were those of *seringueiros*.

We began talking of the Branco and of rubber-workers from there whom we had met at Remate de Males. But it did no good. She only arose, made a fire and began cooking the fish.

We shrugged our shoulders and gave it up. As Pedro had said, talk was useless.

While we ate of the fish—which she had cooked very skillfully—and while all three of us smoked again afterward, Pedro and I were as silent as the woman herself. I was puzzling, planning one way after another to solve the mystery, and throwing away each plan when it was made. My partner too was thinking; and so also, perhaps, was she, though neither her face nor her acts gave any sign of what passed in her mind.

The sun beat down fiercely, and the day grew sweltering hot. There under the big trees we should have been fairly cool; but no breeze moved, and the hot air from the sluggish river crept over the hill and around us like unseen steam. I wished we were out of the place and on our way down the Tecuahy. The wish brought me to a decision.

"We thank you for your hospitality," I told her. "We should much like to know more of you and be your friends. But since you will not talk to us, we are only wasting time. So as soon as it grows cooler we shall go."

Her eyes opened at that. She shook her head.

"Let us go now instead of waiting," said Pedro. "It can not be hotter on the river. What is the good of delaying here?"

The woman gave him a look of sullen anger. As we arose she also stood up. Again she shook her head. Then she smiled at both of us and moved her hands as if swimming.

Now neither of us was a powerful swimmer, for, as I have said, we seldom swam because of the hidden dangers of the streams; but we could keep ourselves afloat well enough, and the thought of a cool swim in safe water struck us as pleasant. We agreed at once. She turned and led the way toward her enclosed bathing pool.

"Do you really intend to go?" Pedro asked softly.

"I intend now to swim," I returned. "Perhaps when we have soaked our heads we can think of something. If not, we had best go."

And we followed the wordless woman on through the forest and down her zigzag path to the little *moutá*.

There she coiled up her hair, loosed her belt, dropped the trousers which probably had belonged to some *seringueiro* now dead, and stood in only that close *tanga*. As we were wearing nothing but tattered shirts and breeches, we had only to lay our weapons in the path, pull off our shirts, and jump to the *moutá*. As I landed on that little platform she left it in a graceful dive.

Her spring made the thing sway under me, and I tottered and nearly fell off it. And before it grew steady I did fall.

"Have care!" came Pedro's cry as he leaped from the bank.

I had just caught my balance when his weight struck the *moutá*. It wobbled violently, we grabbed each other, and then we tumbled sousing into the water.

When we came up, snorting and coughing, the woman was floating nearby and laughing at us. We caught the posts and clung there, regaining our breath and grinning. She swam smoothly away, then went under and disappeared. While I was looking for her to come up beyond the spot where she had gone down, her head bobbed up almost in my face, startling me so that I nearly fell backward again. She had turned and come to me under the surface, and now she and Pedro both laughed at my sudden jump.

Feeling rather foolish, I let go my hold and struck out into the pool, enjoying its coolness and proving that I could swim. My strokes, I felt, were awkward compared to her easy movements, but I did not flounder. Behind me sounded a splash as Pedro also took to the water. I swam on until he caught up and passed me, when I turned back.

"Keep on!" he called. "I will race you to the other side."

But I was breathing a little hard, and as I now was nearer to the platform than he I panted:

"I will race you—to the *moutá!*"

Glancing back, I saw him swerve and knew he had accepted the challenge.

So I began swimming my hardest. I beat him to the posts, but by only about two strokes; and the effort winded me. For that matter, it winded him too.

The woman had climbed up the ladder-pole to watch us from the top of the little stage. Looking up, I found a queer expression on her face. For the first time since we had come, she looked crafty. But as she caught my eye the expression disappeared and she smiled that slow smile. Pointing to the opposite shore, she vaulted out and began swimming the instant she struck the surface.

In less time than it had taken us two clumsy men to swim halfway across and back, she reached the other side and returned to the posts where we rested. And in spite of her speed she was not gasping when she ended her trip—only breathing a little faster. She looked at me as if expecting praise; so I spoke the simple truth.

"You are a wonderful swimmer," I said. "I have never seen a woman swim so well."

"Nor any man either," added Pedro. "You are a fish—a real *bouto*."

She smiled at my compliment; but when he called her "*bouto*" she lost the smile. For a second I thought her eyes gleamed with the same wild light which had shone there when she heard the word "Branco." But it quickly died. She glanced up, then motioned for us to climb the ladder. We were quite willing to sit and breathe a while, so up we went. She followed.

While we sat and rested, Pedro and I argued jokingly as to which of us was the faster in the water. He declared he could have won if I had not kicked so much water into his face. I replied that excuses did not win races. The woman leaned forward quickly—almost as if she had expected some such argument—and began to talk in her sign language.

She pointed to the pole barrier at the farther end; then to me and to a point some twenty yards away; then to Pedro and to a place ten yards nearer; last to herself and the *moutá*. After that she moved her hands as if swimming, then swept one hand past us and again pointed to the poles.

"You will race both of us to that wall?" asked Pedro. "You will give my comrade a start of twenty yards, and me ten yards, and then beat us both?"

She nodded, teeth flashing and eyes alight.

"It is a long swim," he laughed, measuring the distance, "and I do not doubt that you can win. But you must swim to prove it. Lourenço, when she and I reach the poles I will come back to help you."

"Indeed?" I scoffed. "You will be much more than ten yards behind when I touch that wall. She may beat me, but you will not."

"You must swim to prove it," he repeated.

Without reply, I jumped off and headed for the wall.

Knowing that he would not start until I had gained my lead, I took my time. When I reached the ten-yard point I heard him splash in. I swam on, still slowly, until a second splash sounded. Then behind me came Pedro's shout:

"Swim! I am going to crawl right up your back!"

I grinned and struck out hard and fast.

The wall seemed very far away, but I knew Pedro was not much better at swimming than I, and I hoped to cover a good distance before being overtaken even by the dolphin woman. Once I looked back, finding that she already had gained on him, but that he was no nearer to me than before. Then I fixed my eyes on the wall and stroked onward without thought of anything except finishing the race as fast as possible.

Soon I was breathing hard. My legs began to feel a little tired. I wished I had done more walking lately, for many days of canoe travel had weakened me somewhat from the waist down. But the wall was growing larger, and still neither my comrade nor the woman had caught me. I began to think I might win over both of them. The thought gave me more power, and I struggled on faster than before.

Somewhere behind me sounded a gurgling gasp and a splash. I grinned again. Pedro had caught a mouthful of water, I thought, and would have to slow up. My arms were tiring now, but I still held the lead and I was determined to keep it if I could. I listened for other splashes which would show he too was tired, but none came.

Suddenly I felt that it was strangely still.

The thought drew my head around. I found myself alone. Both Pedro and the woman had gone down.

Instantly I swirled around and started back. The woman might be swimming under water, but Pedro would not; he could not hold his breath well enough. That gasp I had heard came back to me. Had Pedro drowned? Had they both drowned? Or was some monster here which had dragged them under to a death more frightful than drowning?

Madly I scooped water in my effort to reach the spot where my partner might be. I dropped my face and stared down, seeing only blackness. I lifted it again, gasped—and saw something ahead.

Something shapeless, something gone as soon as seen—a heel, an elbow, a clenched hand, perhaps—showed for an instant on the surface. I fought toward it. It disappeared before I reached the place, but I knew where it had been. Lowering my head again, I peered down as I swam. Just as my straining lungs made me raise my mouth for air I caught a glimpse of something below.

Snatching a deep breath, I put my face under the surface once more. Beneath me floated a pale shape, moving very feebly. Something else seemed to be with it. I did not waste time in watching it. With all my power I threw myself down to the dying thing.

I looked into the swollen face of Pedro, staring upward with eyes that saw nothing. And as I grabbed at a limp arm I saw another face just below his. It, too, seemed swollen, but its eyes were alive. In them was a chill glare that was horrible to see. For a second it struck me cold, that awful face under him. Then I yanked at the arm I held and started clawing my way upward.

The terrible face moved away from him. An arm fell away from around his throat. A light body darted away and swiftly rose. Pedro too rose, and, strangling from spent breath, I broke out into the sun and air.

Another head was near me on the surface, its mouth open and gasping like mine. It was that of the woman. As I got my wind and turned to support Pedro's face above water she came at us both. I looked again into the glaring eyes I had seen under water—eyes agleam with murder. A hoarse, horrid sound came from her—a sound like a killing animal of the jungle. She was Death.

Pedro's arm moved a little in my clutch. I pulled him to one side, away from the woman, and stroked hard with my free hand. She came on, reaching for him and for me. Turning again, I stabbed my open hand at her, intending to shove her away. I did not quite reach her. But my hand, striking along the surface, spurted water into her face just as she drew breath. She choked, coughed and stopped.

At once I was off again, striking for the nearest bank and towing Pedro, who was still trying to swim. Thrashing along through the ripples, nearly exhausted, I had gone several yards when something under me clutched at one ankle.

The clutch missed, but it threw me into blind panic. Pulling up my legs, I kicked backward and down with all my force. One heel struck violently against something. I kicked again, but felt nothing. And then somehow I got myself and Pedro to the land.

Just above the water's edge was a small hollow in the bank, and I managed to climb into it and haul Pedro out. Then I fell, totally exhausted. For a few minutes I lay recovering some strength, Pedro lying across me, quivering and moaning and weakly belching water. When I was able to sit up his eyes showed that consciousness was coming back to him. I got to my knees and worked on him until he could breathe without choking.

While I helped him I looked around repeatedly for the woman, but saw her nowhere. If she had swum ashore she had done it quickly and quietly. I remembered our weapons, lying back there in the path by the *moutá*, and wished they were nearer. If that deadly woman got our guns she could come along the top of the bank and shoot us like cornered rats.

So, seeing that Pedro was in no further danger of suffocation, I scrambled up the bank to the top and ran to the *moutá*. Our guns, *machetes*, and shirts lay in the path as we had left them. The footprints in the path, too, all pointed toward the platform. Nobody had come up there since we three had gone down it together. And nowhere along the *enseada* could I see any person.

Back along the path I went with our belongings until I was above Pedro. There, as I stood looking down at the pool where we had just fought for life, I thought of the clutch at my ankle, remembered the thing I had kicked so hard—and I saw something. Down there in the darkness something light showed; something which seemed only a paler shadow than the rest, but which might be—

I slid down to my comrade. He was sitting up against the clay, looking weak and wan, but alive and awake.

"Where is she?" he whispered.

"I am afraid," I answered soberly, "that she is out there. I am going to see."

You can not guess, *senhores*, how I dreaded to enter that water again. But I did enter it, swam out to where I had seen that pale shadow, and went down. And when I came up I brought the Bouto Woman with me.

Yes, she was there—very still now, and so far down that I had hard work to reach the top again. She made no movement when I towed her to shore, nor after that. I toiled long to bring back her life, but she never breathed again.

"God help me, I have killed her!" I told Pedro, who now was able to help me.

And I spoke of my kick at the thing which grasped my leg, and of what had gone before.

"You did not kill her," he said. "She drowned. She is full of water. Your kick stunned her, perhaps, or knocked out her breath; but the kick itself did not kill. And even if it had killed, she was trying to murder us. I was almost dead—I was blind and had lost my senses. Do not reproach yourself."

Then he told me what had taken place out there. She had caught up with him, as he had expected. But then, instead of passing, she had made a swooping dive, seized an arm, turned him on his back and dragged him down headfirst. She was under him, clutching him around the throat, and he could neither free himself nor even reach her. She had only to keep her grip and hold her breath while he drowned himself with his fierce struggles.

"But why?" I wondered.

"Do not ask me why any woman does anything. She did not like me, we know. Perhaps she thought that if she killed me you would stay and be her man. You were ahead, racing for the poles, and she probably thought you would not look back until you reached them. By that time she could stifle me, rise and swim after you as if nothing had happened. You would think I had exhausted myself and drowned alone after she passed me in the race."

I thought this over and disagreed.

"That may have been her plan," I said, "but I do not think that was her reason. There is something else. We must look further for the cause of this thing. Let us see what is in her house."

So up the bank we worked, bearing with us the strangely silent woman who now was silent for all time. Back to the base of the *massaranduba* we carried her, and there we laid her down in her hammock and carefully looked over everything in the house. But we found nothing to show who she was or why she should wander under the midnight moon to our camp and try to destroy us when we in turn came to her.

As Pedro had said, the house had been made by fire and ax. We found the ax—an old rusty tool which had not been used for a long time, and which bore no mark to show whence it had come. We closely examined the guns, *machetes* and clothing, and became fully convinced that they were those of rubber-workers. We counted the money again, peered into cooking pots and gourds and everything that could possibly hold a clue. And when we ceased searching the place we were none the wiser.

"Why would you kill us?" Pedro mused, looking down at her. "We have no money—we are ragged rovers of the bush; and you did not care enough about money even to hide twelve thousand *milréis*. We offered you no harm, gave you no insult. And those other men—what did you do with them? Are their bones out there below that black water where you dragged me under?"

After a moment of thought I said:

"Let us go outside and look around. We have not yet been down behind this tree. Perhaps something is there."

Something was there. A little way back towered a big *moratinga* tree beneath which stood no bush. And in this natural clearing the ground was studded with five crosses.

"Five of them!" my partner exclaimed. "So there have been more than three men."

"Perhaps not. Perhaps there were three men and three women, and all died but she."

"The same hand made all those crosses," he pointed out. "Each leans a little to the left. Each cross-arm droops a little downward at the left. And"— he bent and examined the bush-cord holding the crosspieces—"each cord is knotted in the same way."

It was true. We studied them, pondered, wondered, and searched farther. And we found nothing.

As we returned to the house the sun smote into our eyes. We squinted at each other and nodded. The day was going, and we had no mind to spend the night there. Taking the rusty ax and our *machetes*, we returned to the *moratinga* tree. After working there a while we made another trip to the house and back to the little cemetery. And when we left the tree for the last time a sixth cross stood beneath it—a cross which neither leaned nor drooped, but stood straight.

Back at the empty *massaranduba* we looked at each other.

"Twelve thousand *milréis* do nobody any good here," Pedro suggested.

"And there may be someone on the Branco who needs it," I added.

"If we pass the Branco we can go up and see. Or better still, we can go straight to Remate de Males as we intended, and question some of the Branco men waiting there for the time to go back to work. Old Jorge Faria might know."

In the glare of the dying day we tramped along the bank of the *enseada*, down the zigzag path, past the *moutá* on which still lay a dead man's breeches and *machete*, and over the pole-wall beyond which our canoe floated. Out through the twisting, bushy inlet we wormed our way to the sullen river, whose dirty waters now looked like a golden path in the long sun-rays. Then, with a long breath of relief, we shoved our paddles in deep and jumped the dugout away toward the next bend, bound for Remate de Males. With us went the twelve thousand *milréis*.

Days later, gaunt and tattered, out of food and cartridges, we reached the town. When we had left it the street was several feet under water; now it was bare ground. When we had gone men had shaken their heads and said we went to death; now they stared as if we were ghosts. But at the store of our old friend Joaquim the trader we soon proved that we were not too dead to attack a jug of *cachaça*, and as the news spread that we had returned, our fellow *seringueiros* came in from all around the town to help us drink and hear the tale of our wanderings.

Among them came Jorge Faria, a veteran rubber-worker of the Branco, always smoking and seldom speaking. We were watching for him, and as soon as he had had a drink we got him into a small room behind the store, where we could talk undisturbed. And to him we told the whole tale of the wordless woman who swam like a dolphin and was deadly as a *jacaré*.

His eyes widened as we talked, but he said no word. When we told of the leaning crosses he spat excitedly and put his pipe back in his mouth upside down. And when from under our waistbands we produced the money, which we had divided into two packets and fastened to our belts with strips torn from our shirts, he dropped the pipe.

"The Bouto!" he croaked.

"Oh, no," Pedro said wearily. "She swam like a *bouto*, but she was no fish turned woman. She was—"

"The Bouto," Jorge insisted. "Not the Bouto, of the Amazon story, but the mad daughter of Lino Cardozo—she who was called the Bouto because she had a madness for drowning. Have you not heard of her?"

We had not.

"She was mad from birth. Three months before she was born her father, Lino, a rubber-worker on the Branco *seringal* of Senhor Fontoura da Gama, stumbled and fell off the river-bank. Before he could get out of the water a *jacaré* rose and seized him. Lino grabbed a root in the bank and hung to it, screaming for help while the beast dragged at him. But before aid could reach him his hold broke and he was pulled down.

"Lino's wife saw it all, and the shock nearly turned her mind. And when the girl-child was born she had a twist in her brain. Yes, and a twist in her eye, for she never saw a thing exactly straight: anything which stood straight seemed to her to lean to the right, and if she stuck a stick in the ground she always slanted it a little to the left. This oddity soon became known, but of the kink in her mind nobody knew for years.

"It is true, she was not quite the same as the other children on the *seringal*, even when small. There was her habit of slanting things to the left, and besides that she was slow of speech—"

"She could talk, then?" I cut in.

"Yes, if she would. But once when she was about ten years old she said something that angered her mother, who beat her soundly. And from that day she held her tongue. Not one word did she ever speak after that. Queer, yes; but she was a queer girl. As I said, she was slow of speech before that day, and often she would stare in a vacant way as if her mind had flown for a moment. But she was a strong, plump child, and nobody suspected she was mad. 'Only a little odd,' was what the da Gama people thought of her.

"Perhaps her new habit of remaining dumb made her madness worse—I do not know. But before that time she had learned to swim, in a little *igarape* where the men built a wall of poles to keep out dangerous creatures, and had become a much better swimmer than any of the other children; and now the kink in her brain began to work. You might think her father's death and her mother's horror would make her fear the water, but it was not so. Instead, her twisted mind told her to drag things under the water, as the *jacaré* had dragged her father to death.

"At first she pulled down only sticks and pieces of log which she threw into the *igarape*. Then she began swimming below the other children and catching them by the feet or around the body, scaring them and often making them choke. And one day she pulled down a boy and almost drowned him before he could fight free.

"That made the rest fear her. They named her 'Bouto,' and they would not swim with her more. They drove her from the *igarape* when they swam there, and she had to do her swimming when they were not at the place. But every day she was there, seizing her logs and fighting to keep them under the surface. And I have heard—for I was not on the Branco in those days—that when a log escaped her she would pursue it with a glare in her eyes that chilled those who watched.

"Yet it was only in the water that she was dangerous. On land she was only a harmless, slow-smiling girl who slanted sticks to the left."

Jorge stopped, found his pipe, filled and lit it. When he went on, his eyes were on Pedro.

"She was fifteen when I first went to the Branco. And in that year a tall, slim young fellow who had newly come to work on the da Gama estate made love to her. She had become quite handsome, and he—well, he did not intend to marry her. But she thought he did, and she liked him well until a *batelão* arrived from down the Javary, bringing a police officer who arrested the man for murdering his wife at Fonte Boa.

"The killer had a revolver, and so did the policeman. After the smoke cleared away the da Gama men had to bury them both.

"From that time on she hated men who were tall and slender—like you, Pedro. But men like Lourenço, shorter and more broad—she still liked them well enough."

I nodded, feeling that now her preference for me and her dislike for Pedro were explained.

"It was two years more," Jorge continued, "before another man really interested her. He was Bento Batalha, a heavy-muscled, cold-eyed man who was almost as silent and nearly as good a swimmer as she. Where he came from, and why, he never told, and we never asked. One does not ask too many questions on the Branco.

"Whether Bento and the Bouto ever talked to each other I do not know; nobody ever heard them. But whenever Bento went to headquarters he and she swam together in the walled *igarape*. There her madness broke out as before, and several times she tried to drown him. But he was too strong for her and always broke away. And instead of fearing these life-and-death struggles in the water he seemed to enjoy them, for he always had a grim smile when he came out. A queer man. A queer couple.

"Now the girl, being well-grown, helped her mother work around the house of Senhor da Gama, who, after the death of Lino, had taken the mother as his cook. She knew the house as well as Senhor da Gama himself—perhaps better. And when she and Bento disappeared together, as they did before long, something else disappeared also. Ten thousand *milréis*."

"Aha!" we cried, glancing at the money.

"Ten thousand *milréis*," Jorge repeated. "That and a canoe, Bento Batalha, the Bouto of the Branco—all gone between dark and dawn. And none has ever been found." We rolled cigarets. Then I said:

"There were five crosses under the tree. There are twelve thousand *milréis* here—two thousand more than da Gama lost."

"Yes. And it is six years since the Bouto vanished. In that time quite a number of men have left the Branco and have not returned. Most of them have gone out to the Solimões, but some were not seen after leaving the Branco. One of the crosses under that *mandiroba* may be that of Bento. The other four—who knows?"

"Four men could easily have had two thousand *milréis* among them," Pedro agreed. "Batalha, the thief, probably had more than one reason not to hurry out to the big river. He made that house, built those pole-walls, and perhaps lured a few *seringueiros* in there to visit him—and to go swimming with his woman. Then he himself swam with her once too often."

"Who knows?" Jorge said again.

We smoked on, looking at the money. We knew Jorge was honest and would soon return to the Branco. And I said—

"The mother of the Bouto—does she still live?"

"She lives," Jorge answered, reading my thought. "And the two thousand *milréis* which do not belong to Senhor da Gama would be a fortune to her. She grows old, and she has nothing."

We passed the packets to him.

"See that she gets it," I said. "Nobody knows of this but us three, and nobody shall know of it until you have returned to the Branco. And now I am thirsty again."

And when Jorge had tied the money under his waistband we went back to the outer room, where the crowd waited to buy us more *cachaça* and hear more about us.

So ends the tale, *senhores*, of the Bouto—the killer who was born in madness, mated in turn with a murderer and a robber, and died at last under the heel of a man fighting to save his comrade. Tonight this big moon, which showed us that dolphin back yonder in the river, shines down also on the ruins of the *tambo* where she first came to me, the huge *massaranduba* in whose butt yawns a black and empty home, and the tall *mandiroba* beneath which stand six crosses—five leaning and one straight.

Under that straight cross lies a tale that is told. But under the slanting sticks rest five more stories which none of us shall ever hear. They are locked for all time in the jungle—which is forever dumb.

July 18, 1921

Excerpt from The Camp-Fire

Something from Arthur O. Friel in connection with his story in this issue:

> I have taken the liberty of making Lourenço call the dolphin a fish, which is not quite correct. The dolphin is, of course, a cetacean mammal—sort of a little brother of the whale—and not a fish at all. But the Brazilian rubber-worker would hardly be likely to know that, and he certainly would call it a fish. For that matter, there are plenty of well-educated Americans who don't know the difference either.
>
> —ARTHUR O. FRIEL.

Glossary

(*Italicized* terms are believed to be Portuguese, unless otherwise noted.)

açai: palm

aguardente: fire-water

amanhã: tomorrow

apuyáh (Indian): man

araya: sting-ray

bárbaro: barbarian

barracão: house; shack

barriga: belly

barrigudo: potbellied

batelão: barge

bicho: animal

bouto: river dolphin

caboclo: acculturated Brazilian Indian; copper-colored mulatto

cachaça: white rum

cachoeira: waterfall; rapids

cachorro: dog

camarâh (Indian): friend

campo: field

capitão: captain

capybara: world's largest rodent

caracashá (Indian): tubular rattle

carrapato: tick, found in dry brush

casa: house

cauim: traditional beer of South America

chibeh: a cereal

coaita: four-fingered monkey

coronel: colonel

cucuju: extremely bright South American firefly

demônio: demon; devil

enchente: seasonal flood

enseada: cove

erekuâhn (Indian): husband

farinha: meal from ground tubers

festa: party

furo: puncture; water channel

gambá (Indian): log drum

igapó: seasonally flooded forest

igarape: narrow waterway; creek; canoe path

igarité: long canoe

itauba: stone-wood

jabuti: red-footed tortoise

jacaré: alligator; caiman

lago: lake

lingoa geral: standardized form of Tupi languages

machadinha: small iron hatchet

machete: double-edged saber

maloca: communal Indian hut

mandioca: cassava; shrub with edible root

massaranduba: cow-tree

mato: weeds

matupá: grass

milréis: former monetary unit of Brazil

montaña (Spanish): mountain

montaria: flatboat

mortál: delicate

motuca: biting fly

moutá (Indian): platform on poles

museu: museum

mutum: curassow; long-tailed game bird

pajé (Indian): medicine man

pajémarióba (Indian): a bitter medicinal herb

patrão: master; business owner; landlord

peccary: wild tusked mammal, similar to a boar, which roams in groups of ten or more

petéma (Indian): tobacco

piranha: carnivorous freshwater fish

pira-purasséya (Indian): fish-dance

pirarucu: large freshwater fish

pium: tormenting fly, found near rivers

praia: beach

Quichua (Spanish): language spoken in Ecuador and Columbia

realejo (Indian): organ-bird

restinga: tongue of land between waters

seringal: rubber estate

seringueira: Brazilian rubber tree

seringueiro: rubber gatherer

Solimões: the Amazon River, from the Brazil-Peru border to the confluence of the Rio Negro

surubim: catfish

surucucú: bushmaster snake, venemous

tambo (Spanish): lodging; a place to store provisions

tanga: thong, g-string

tatu: armadillo

tempo da friagem: cold spell

terras cahidas: fallen river banks

timbó: poisonous liana

trompetero: trumpet-bird

tucandeira: large black ant with a poisonous bite

Tupi: language family of South America

uirá-mimbéu (Indian): fife-bird

urubu: black vulture

vargem: land inundated by extraordinarily high floods

vasante: seasonal ebb

zarabatana (Indian): blow-gun

OFF-TRAIL PUBLICATIONS
Specializing in the era of American pulp fiction

THE WEIRD DETECTIVE ADVENTURES OF WADE HAMMOND
By Paul Chadwick
Volume 1: 10 stories, 180 pages, $18
Volume 2: 10 stories, 172 pages, $18
Volume 3: 10 stories, 202 pages, $18
Volume 4: 9 stories, 232 pages, $18

> *The Wade Hammond stories complete in four volumes. In these chilling adventures, all from the classic 1930's pulps,* Detective-Dragnet *and* Ten Detective Aces, *freelance investigator Wade Hammond battles a series of weird enemies. Some of the best of 1930's pulp fiction.*

DOCTOR COFFIN: THE LIVING DEAD MAN
By Perley Poore Sheehan • Introduction by John Wooley
8 novelettes, 178 pages, $16

> *Weird stories from* Thrilling Detective, *1932-33. A former character actor who faked his own death, Doctor Coffin runs a string of mortuaries by night and fights crime at night. One of the strangest detective series.*

SUPER-DETECTIVE FLIP BOOK: TWO COMPLETE NOVELS
From the pulp *Super-Detective*:
"Legion of Robots" (November 1940) by Victor Rousseau • Introduction by John McMahan •• "Murder's Migrants" (March 1943) by Robert Leslie Bellem and W.T. Ballard • Introduction by John Wooley
2 short novels, 174 pages, $18

> Super-Detective *started as a Doc Savage-like adventure pulp, then changed format to hardboiled detective. The* Flip Book *features a novel from each of the two phases with intros exploring the historical background. Exciting!*

PULPWOOD DAYS: VOL 1: EDITORS YOU WANT TO KNOW
Edited by John Locke • 180 pages, $16

Numerous articles from the writers' magazines by and about pulp editors, with ample biographical profiles. Editors include: Frank E. Blackwell (Detective Story, Western Story), Ray Palmer (Amazing Stories, Fantastic Adventures), Robert A.W. Lowndes (Columbia Publications), Edwin Baird (Weird Tales, Detective Tales), and many more.

GANG PULP
Edited by John Locke • 19 stories, 294 pages, $24

Hardboiled stories of the criminal underworld from the first year (1929-30) of the gang pulps: Gangster Stories, Racketeer Stories, etc. These violent tales came under immediate censorship pressure; the history is explored in an in-depth essay. "A remarkable work of popular-culture scholarship"—Mystery Scene, Fall 2008.

THE GANGLAND SAGAS OF BIG NOSE SERRANO
Volume 1: DAMES, DICE AND THE DEVIL
Volume 2: HORSES, HOBOES AND HEROES
By Anatole Feldman • Introductions by Will Murray
Each: 4 novels, 266 pages, $20

The first two volumes (of three) of the Big Nose Serrano novels from Gangster Stories, 1930-32. Feldman was the best of the gang pulp authors, and Big Nose was his most inspired creation, the berserking king of Chicago gangsters.

THE CITY OF BAAL
By Charles Beadle • Introduction by John Locke
7 stories, 240 pages, $20

Authentic stories of African adventure from an author who had traveled the lands he wrote about. Lost cities, strange tribes, jungle magic. Six stories from Adventure *(1918-22) and one from* The Frontier *(1925).*

AMAZON STORIES: VOLUME 1: PEDRO & LOURENÇO
By Arthur O. Friel • Introduction by John Locke
10 stories, 222 pages, $18

Friel's first ten stories from Adventure *(1919-20), following the strange experiences of two Amazon Basin rubber workers as they explore the jungle. The best of pulp adventure fiction.*

THE OCEAN: 100TH ANNIVERSARY COLLECTION
Edited by John Locke
20 stories, 234 pages, $18

Munsey's The Ocean *(1907-08) was one of the first specialized pulps, a sea-story magazine. The best adventure stories are included here, along with 30+ pages of nonfiction material, a history of the pulp, and extensive author profiles.*

FROM GHOULS TO GANGSTERS:
THE CAREER OF ARTHUR B. REEVE
Edited by John Locke
Vol 1 (fiction): 21 stories, 264 pages, $20 • **Vol 2 (nonfic)**: 260 pages, $20

Reeve was the leading American detective-story writer of the early 20th Century, with his scientific detective, Craig Kennedy. The astonishing breadth of his career is explored for the first time here. Vol 1 includes a cross-sction of fiction from all phases of career, including many never-before-reprinted pulp stories. Vol 2 provides a 40-page biography; an extensive Art Gallery of cover repros, interior illos, ads, etc; a 75-page guide to Reeve's work in all media; and more. An "excellent piece of scholarship"—Mystery Scene, *Spring 2008.*

CULT OF THE CORPSES
By Maxwell Hawkins • Introduction by John Locke
2 novelettes, 150 pages, $13.95

Two weird detective stories from Detective-Dragnet *(1931) by a forgotten master.* "Cult of the Corpses" *puts a detective on the trail of a murderous voodoo cult in Manhattan.* "Dealers in Death" *features the insidious Mr. Letherius, a specialist in undetectable murder. Introduction discusses the weird-detective trend of the early '30s, and the career of Maxwell Hawkins.*

Shipping: $3.00 media mail; $6.00 priority
Check or MO to:
Off-Trail Publications
2036 Elkhorn Road, Castroville, CA 95012
Paypal: offtrail@redshift.com

www.ingramcontent.com/pod-product-compliance
Lightning Source LLC
Chambersburg PA
CBHW030352020726
47493CB00003B/791